30108

Pontypridd
CF37 2DY
Telephone 01443 486850

L140.823 RAB

Dylid dychwelyd neu adnewyddu'r llyfr erbyn neu cyn y dyddiad a nodir uchod. Oni wneir hyn codir dirwy.
This book is to be returned or renewed on or before the last date stamped above, otherwise a charge will be made.

Rhondda-Cynon-Taff County Borough Libraries
Llyfrgelloedd Bwrdeistref Sirol Rhondda-Cynon-Tâf

Grosvenor House
Publishing Limited

All rights reserved
Copyright © Roberto Rabaiotti, 2013

Roberto Rabaiotti is hereby identified as author of this
work in accordance with Section 77 of the Copyright, Designs
and Patents Act 1988

The book cover picture is copyright to Roberto Rabaiotti

This book is published by
Grosvenor House Publishing Ltd
28-30 High Street, Guildford, Surrey, GU1 3EL.
www.grosvenorhousepublishing.co.uk

This book is sold subject to the conditions that it shall not, by way of
trade or otherwise, be lent, resold, hired out or otherwise circulated
without the author's or publisher's prior consent in any form of binding or
cover other than that in which it is published and
without a similar condition including this condition being imposed
on the subsequent purchaser.

A CIP record for this book
is available from the British Library

ISBN 978-1-78148-594-1

Chapter 1

'Wow! Who's she over there?'
'Wow! Who's he over there?'
The two questions were asked simultaneously from opposite ends of the living room, which throbbed to the beat of *Sugar, Sugar*. The eyes of the two questioners met fleetingly before the connection was broken by an impenetrable barrier of bouncing bodies and bobbing heads. The room was a splash of rainbow colours as the vibrant shades of clothing mixed with the swirling ribbons and balloons that were tied to light fittings and various items of furniture. The temperature bordered on boiling point and the window panes streamed water that formed tiny pools on their sills. The brows of the happy-faced dancers glistened brightly under the ceiling lights and moisture beads soon turned into rivulets which flowed through whatever groove or furrow they could find on their faces. The whiff of damp clothing added to the already heady concoction of odours that included beer, wine, cigarette smoke and, most obviously of all, marijuana. The excitement was building; in less than two hours it would be 1970. No one knew what the decade would bring, but optimism was high following the breaking down of social barriers and explosion of youth culture in the 1960s. People hoped it would be more like the love of Woodstock than the war of Altamont.

'I've no idea. I've never seen her before.'
'I've no idea. I've never seen him before.'
'She's pretty gorgeous, you've got to admit.'
'He's pretty gorgeous, you've got to admit.'
'Let's go and chat 'em up. Her friend's pretty tidy as well so I'll move in on her and leave you to blondie, though if she gives me the eye I hope you'll let me have a crack.'

'In your dreams. She looks far too nice a girl to want to mix with a pillock like you.'

The two friends laughed and followed up with large swigs from their cans of lager for courage before threading their way through the throng of dancers, both of them burping quietly to settle their stomachs.

'Look, I think he's coming over.' Blondie saw the two figures approach and instinctively pushed back her long, corkscrew-curled hair that flowed down to her shoulders like a Pre-Raphaelite angel. She felt as though someone had taken a blowtorch to her cheeks and hoped they hadn't turned as red as the glass of plonk in her hand.

'Hello. Hope you don't mind if we join you. I'm Ian and this is Rhys.' Ian did not extend his hand but just straightened his back to impose his height and, hopefully, his command.

'Hi, it's nice to meet you. I'm Karen and this is Vicki.'

'Not seen you round these parts before. Do you know Don?'

'Not very well, but I know his girlfriend, Jen, 'cos we work together at the hospital, East Glam. She invited us along. I never really come up this way to Pontypridd.'

'You enjoying the party?'

'You bet. It's a gas. Don's got a great groove going and there's plenty to drink, which always helps. Not long to go now and it'll be the New Year. I can't believe another one has gone so quickly. It's frightening.'

'You don't need to tell me that,' Ian replied with a slight shake of the head, puffing out his cheeks, a little taken aback by the hip language he was not used to hearing. 'It's a big year for me coming up as I'll be twenty-one, though why that's such an important birthday I'll never know. It's not as if you can suddenly do something legal, like.'

'Yeah, you're right there,' Karen replied with a smile.

The conversation faltered and they both took sips from their drinks, their lips suddenly dry. Karen rocked her head gently from side to side and mouthed the words *'Honey, honey ...'* in time to the music, not looking Ian in the eye. The pause unnerved him and he took another sip from his can. He glanced at his friend, hoping he would utter his first words to help him out. But Rhys just stood transfixed, staring at Vicki, who held his stare in turn easily without blinking. They were beaming like the Bisto Kids and, despite their not having said a single word to each other, the feeling between them was anything but oppressive. They had both been in relationships before but neither of them had ever experienced the sensations that were flowing through their bodies at this particular moment. They felt warm, comfortable, slightly tingly and very excited. Cupid had most certainly struck, his arrow hitting home like a thunderbolt.

'He does have a tongue, you know, girls, but when faced by such beauty, he's been known to go a bit schtum.' Ian was trying to charm his way out of the awkward silence.

They all smiled and Ian did not fail to notice the quick glance Karen gave him before shyly turning her head away. This encouraged him and he moved more closely towards her with his back half-turned to Rhys and Vicki. The two couples had been formed and Ian thought that Rhys had better say something quickly before Vicki thought him a moron. Nothing much I can do for him now, he concluded, before giving Karen the widest smile he could muster. She reciprocated and his confidence rose.

'It's very nice to meet you, Vicki.' These were the first words Rhys ever said to her.

'It's very nice to meet you, Rhys.' These were the first words Vicki ever said to him.

One of the dancers trying to impress his partner stumbled and fell into Rhys, pushing him into Vicki.

'Sorry, butt.'

'No probs, Dai.'

Instinctively, Rhys and Vicki held onto each other's arms to maintain their balance, but, as they parted, Vicki ran her left hand lightly down Rhys's right forearm at exactly the same moment that Rhys did the same to hers. They stood only a few inches apart, breathing in the intoxicating aromas of their bodies.

'Sorry 'bout that, Vicki.'

'No need.'

Sugar, Sugar ended and the mood changed as *Michelle* started to play. Most of the dancers left the living room, either to cool down, or, more likely, to raid the kitchen for drinks. One couple remained in a close embrace, moving slowly to the music. Rhys and Vicki walked over and joined them. They both smiled when the smooching couple began to snog without a care in the world. A surprised Ian wondered where Rhys had discovered his magic touch. He could not believe he'd made such quick progress after barely saying a word, while, to his disconsolation, Karen had excused herself to go into the hallway to talk to another friend. And this after all my best lines, too, he mused. There's no justice in the world. Ah, well, may as well go to the kitchen and get pissed, I suppose. As Rhys and Vicki began their slow dance, holding each other with the delicacy of a first-day butterfly, Vicki sang along quietly to her favourite song of the Beatles. '*Michelle, ma belle, sont les mots qui vont très bien ensemble, très bien ensemble ...*'

As a way to break the ice, Rhys dipped his toe in the water to start up the first conversation they would ever have together. 'So, you speak French then?'

'Well, hardly. I'm just singing along to the words. I do speak a bit, though, because most winters I go off to my father's chalet in Val d'Isère.'

Rhys was nonplussed. 'Val dizzy, did you say?'

'No. Val diz eh. It's a ski resort in the French Alps. I love it there.'

'And your dad's got a place?'

'Yeah. He's had it for years.'

'Never been skiing myself. The school ran a trip a few years back but my mum and dad couldn't afford it so I didn't go. Not sure I fancy it anyway; sounds a bit too cold for my liking.'

'Oh, it's wonderful. You really must try it sometime.'

The conversation ended, mainly because Rhys had run out of things to say. He knew nothing about skiing and was keen to change the subject. As he was about to do so, Don rushed into the room. 'Enough of the slushy stuff; let's get something on a bit louder.'

Ignoring the dancing couples, he removed *Michelle* from the record player and replaced it with *My Generation*. This gave Rhys the excuse to disengage from Vicki and they walked over to the corner of the room where they had left their drinks. Rhys took a slow sip, followed by another, and then another, before nervously commenting on how pretty Vicki looked. She just about made out his words above the pulsating electric guitar and smiled in delight. The compliment was totally justified for Vicki looked amazing. Her hair framed two oval-shaped, pale blue eyes, so bright and welcoming that it was almost impossible for Rhys to take his own brown eyes off them. Her skin was a golden-brown that radiated health with just a few faint freckles on her cheeks to tease him. Her smile only served to show off her perfect, sparkling, white teeth, so white and perfect in fact that Rhys even wondered whether they were real. He instinctively closed his mouth, knowing that the yellow tinge to his own were poor by comparison.

Rhys also admired Vicki's figure. She was of average height but there was no mistaking her lean, athletic build. He was convinced she was not carrying an ounce of fat on her, well, perhaps a little on her behind, which curved slightly and enticingly from the base of her back. She wore knee-length, fawn-coloured boots with long, cream laces tied from bottom to top. Black tights, or were they stockings, Rhys thought dreamily, were visible below the hem of her chocolate-brown, corduroy miniskirt. Over her lime-green shirt, Vicki wore a spruce-green, woollen waistcoat with a kaleidoscope of cotton flowers sewn haphazardly around. Her shirt was buttoned low enough to reveal an ample, upright bosom. Rhys tried to glimpse for any sign of a lacy bra but Vicki's erect nipples soon alerted him to the fact that she was not wearing one at all, which only served to pump a gallon of lust through every vein of his body. A stainless-steel chain supporting the CND symbol was hanging around her slender neck, though his eye was more instantly attracted to the numerous chains of beads of every shape and colour imaginable that complemented it. For a split second, he saw a resemblance to Jane Fonda and immediately imagined Vicki in the same catsuit with her bare breast showing that the fabulous film star wore in *Barbarella*. But it was her hair that drew his next comment.

'I must say, the way you've done your hair really suits you. I love that corkscrew style.' Rhys virtually had to shout to make himself heard as Pete Townsend thrashed at his guitar in the background.

'Thanks. I'm glad you like it. It's so hard to look after, though. I copied the idea from a man, actually, Marc Bolan.'

'Who's he?'

'Marc Bolan? He's the lead singer of Tyrannosaurus Rex.'

'Never heard of them.'

'They've had a couple of records out recently and I reckon they could be the next big thing. They're a sort of folksy-electric band. I think they're great.'

'So a bit like Dylan then, now he's gone electric?'

'Yeah, I suppose so, though Bolan is much better looking. He's like sex on legs, just gorgeous.'

'Perhaps I should do my hair like him as well then?'

Vicki lowered her head before raising it again to look back up at him. 'You don't need to. You're very good looking as you are.' She blushed slightly.

Rhys was momentarily lost for words. He could not remember anyone saying that to him before. He knew his previous girlfriends must have thought the same or they would never have gone out with him in the first place. It was sort of assumed rather than explicitly said.

'Well, thanks,' he finally returned, his face lighting up. He was so taken aback, he took another sip from his can to recover his composure. 'This Mark Bolland bloke. Tell him to change the name of his band or shorten it at least 'cos it's a real mouthful.'

'I will if I ever meet him.'

They laughed.

'I don't know whether it's because the music's so loud or because I've had too much to drink but do I detect an English accent there? You're not from around these parts, are you?'

'You're right. I'm from Surrey, born and bred.'

'Really?' Rhys replied, unsure where Surrey was, but knowing, or so he thought, that it was somewhere in England.

'Yeah, Godalming.'

'Where? Gobbledygook, did you say?' Rhys answered with a grin.

'Ha, ha. Godalming. You know, it's near Guildford.'

Rhys had heard of Guildford, though he wasn't sure where it was exactly. 'That's near London, innit?'

'Sort of. It's about thirty miles away.'

'I've only ever been to England once before. In fact, it's the only time I've ever been out of Wales. We went on a school trip to Bristol Zoo. I'll never forget it. A hippo pissed on Dai Griffiths. Hilarious, it was.' A slight chuckle followed his words. Vicki smiled, flashing those wondrous teeth of hers. 'We didn't half get into trouble afterwards though, 'cos we left a load of empty cans on the bus and, because we were underage, the bus company went mental with the school. All school trips were stopped for a year. It meant me missing out on another trip to England as we were supposed to be going to see some boring old bridge in a place called Colindale. Can't say I was sorry.'

'I think you mean Coalbrookdale, where the first iron bridge was built.'

'Yeah, Colindale, just like I said.' A cheeky grin followed which almost made Vicki melt with desire. 'How come you ended up at a party in Ponty then?'

'It's through Karen. She was my pen pal for years before we met up. She lives in Cardiff and I've been to stay with her a few times now. She's been up to my house as well and come down to see me in university, in Exeter. This is my first time in Pont ... ee ... prid.'

Rhys smiled at her pronunciation. 'Pont ... ee ... preethe, it is, not Pont ... ee ... prid.'

'Oh, sorry. Pont ... ee ... preethe.'

'That's better,' he replied kindly. 'Are you at university now?'

'Yeah, it's my final year. I'll be leaving in the summer.'

'Exeter. At least I know where that is. It's in Cornwall, innit?'

'You're close. It's in Devon, actually.'

'You sure?'

'I'm positive.'

'Mmm. Shame that. I was hoping you might have brought a pasty or two with you. I'm starving.'

Vicki chuckled and smiled back, their eyes meeting and fixing without any sense of unease. Rhys was about to continue when the door burst open and Ian entered.

'Sorry to butt in, Rhys, but you're needed next door.'

'Why, what's happening?'

'Right ...' But before Don could continue, Howell interrupted him once again, living up to his name of Chief Sneak.

'Mr Chairman, it is with great displeasure and utter disbelief that I have to raise yet another point of order with you. You see, Rhys's offence is minor when compared to the information I have just received, information so startling it can scarcely be believed.' Howell looked at Rhys with an expression of total dismay which led the others to do the same.

'Wha'? Wha've I done now?' Rhys was baffled.

Mark sensed what was coming and filled Rhys's glass up to the brim, drawing a look of sheer horror from Rhys's face. After a theatrical pause, the Chief Sneak carried on. 'Not only was Rhys fornicating with this young lady but I've discovered that this young lady is ...' Another theatrical pause followed, but this time much longer than the first, as Howell looked each of the participants in the eye, before revealing, '... from ENGLAND!'

Howls of disgust rang out around the room accompanied by a flinging back of arms and shaking of heads in utter contempt.

'ENGLAND! Is this true, Rhys? Are our girls not good enough for you anymore?' The chairman could hardly believe his ears and sought a denial. But none was forthcoming.

'Well, she could possibly be, like, you know, from England,' Rhys blustered.

The chairman had heard enough. 'The whole pint down in one,' he proclaimed dismissively with a flick of his hand.

This time, Rhys did not bother to plead mitigation, took another deep breath and sank his pint as quickly as he could. It took twice as long as the one before and, when finished, he was convinced he needed to spew. To further muted applause and comments of 'nice one', he decided to remain seated and allow his stomach to settle. He kept quiet, fearing that opening his mouth would render less-appealing emissions than words. He knew that at this rate, he might well be paralytic by midnight, and the game had not even started yet! He was determined to try and stay as sober as possible, as he wished to be in a reasonable state for when he met up with Vicki later. She had never left his mind for one single second and he craved to see her again.

Chapter 2

'HAPPY NEW YEAR!'

The bellowing voice was unmistakable to Rhys's ears though muffled in sound; it was unmistakable because it was the voice of his mother and muffled because a pillow lay across his head, clasped tightly in place by his hands.

'HAPPY NEW YEAR!' his mother repeated in a second attempt to elicit a response from her son. But, as before, Rhys did not move a muscle and his mother smiled in a resigned manner before gently patting him on the back of the shoulder. She decided to let him sleep a little longer and was secretly grateful to leave the bedroom that stunk of booze and farts.

Happy New Year? Rhys's brain finally cranked into a smidgen of life. He was sure this was the first time he'd heard anyone say it. But hadn't he been at a party the night before? He was certain he had. Hadn't he seen in the New Year then? He must have done. How come he was in his bed? How did he get home? He couldn't remember a thing. His throat was parched and his tongue licked incessantly at his lips, the distinct taste of whisky making him shudder. Why was the taste so evident? What had he got up to? He tried hard to think back to the night before. Thankfully, the fog in his head gradually began to disperse as brightly coloured pictures filtered their way through.

'That's right; I was at Don's party with the boys.' He paused before straining to remember more. It crossed his mind that the words he had just croaked were his first of the decade. Or were they? 'What time did I get home? I can't remember a thing.'

His head was throbbing and he continued to lick at his lips. He was desperate for a drink of water but dared not budge an inch from his comfortable position in bed for fear of bringing on some searing pain. 'Why this taste of whisky?' he whispered to himself. He screwed up his face and concentrated as hard as he could to recollect what had happened at the party. 'That's right; we were playing *Buzz*.' He recalled Ian bursting away from the table, hand over mouth, in need of a chunder. This drew a smile from his lips, his first of the decade. Or was it? He strained further to remember whether Ian had made it to the toilet in time but his brain was a blank. The whisky, he pondered once more. Oh, that's right, I remember now. Don got us all to toast the New Year with it at the end of the game just before midnight and then another to toast the new decade. Rhys grimaced at the memory of the fiery taste hitting the back of his throat. And then Ian, the pisshead, got us to toast the year just gone. He must have had a good spew earlier 'cos there's no way he would have done that otherwise. Rhys grinned and wished that he'd gone for a puke himself beforehand. Oh, and Howell then got us to toast the decade just gone and another for Brian Jones. The memory of the recently deceased Rolling Stone saddened Rhys and he shook his head at the waste of such a great talent.

After a few silent seconds, Rhys blew out his cheeks. Unfortunately, this only served to make his stomach heave and he urged himself to remain as still as possible to settle it down. At the same time, he tried to stop thinking about the night before as the effort only accentuated the pounding in his head like a jackhammer on Tarmac. How he wished to relax and fall asleep, but this desire eluded him. Instead, he felt hot, clammy and irritable, finding it impossible to stay still for more than a few minutes at a time. Eventually, he turned round in his bed and cast off the pillow with a flourish. The bright sunlight that streamed through the gap in the curtains lasered in on his eyes and made him groan.

'Why do I do it?' he asked himself with a sigh for the first time in the decade, in the definite knowledge it would not be the last. He fidgeted uneasily, trying to rediscover his most comfortable position, and ventured another tentative opening of his eyes. He resisted the pain and, through narrow, flinty slits, gazed to his right to check the time. Ten-forty, displayed the tinny, round-faced alarm clock with two small bells on top. Thank God he hadn't set it to wake him up. The bells were so loud that in his present state his head would have exploded. Ten-forty, he mused. Is that early or late? Usually it was the latter but, on days off, perhaps it was the former. It's sort of in-between, he mulled, sitting on the fence, which only added to his state of unease as he was unsure whether he should be getting up or not. He kept his eyes open and observed the black patch in a corner angle where two of the walls met the ceiling. The aqua-green wallpaper had started to peel away quite markedly and the ugly black and yellow stain lower down suggested that more would soon be following. The black patch was definitely getting bigger, he thought, like a cancer spreading.

'I must do something about it,' he muttered decisively. 'One of my New Year resolutions,' he added as an afterthought. 'My only New Year resolution,' he followed up with a raised eyebrow, Roger Moore-like. But almost as quickly as he had said it, he let out a deep sigh in resignation, knowing that this resolution would probably fall by the wayside like all the others in previous years, and one in particular. 'I must get out of Ponty and find myself a better job.' He had said this every New Year's Day for the past five years since leaving school. 'Look where I am, still stuck here with no prospect of getting out.' He sighed again, feeling trapped, and he fidgeted once more in his bed. He continued to stare at the damp patch in the corner and realised that there was an additional incentive for him to do something about it for, at this rate, his poster of the exquisite Raquel Welch wearing only a fur bikini was likely to come down at the same time as the rest of the wallpaper. The thought brought the biggest smile to his face that decade. Or was it?

'VICKI!' From nowhere, Rhys shouted out her name. Her radiant smile suddenly appeared to him like the sun after an aeroplane exits the clouds at take-off. 'Vicki,' he repeated, this time more quietly. He was now wide awake, his head seemingly no longer throbbing and his throat not quite so dry. 'Vicki,' he repeated once more as if his brain no longer had the capacity to say any other word. He slumped back deeper into his bed. What happened? Where is she? I was meant to see in the New Year with her. A queue of questions hit his brain, one after the other. What have I done? His state of excitement quickly turned to one of distress. 'I've fucked up again,' he admonished himself angrily. 'Fucking drink has ruined everything. Am I ever gonna learn? She was absolutely gorgeous and I messed up.' So intense were his feelings that he didn't realise he was thinking aloud. 'Fuck knows what happened, but even if she did see me after *Buzz,* I was so out of it she would have probably buggered off with someone else anyway. And who can blame her? What a start to the year? Just typical!'

He turned his head to the side and pulled up the sheet and blankets to cover his shoulders. The shiny pale orange bed cover, full of stains, had already fallen to the floor in his agitation. He noticed that one of the doors of the second-hand wardrobe he had recently bought was hanging loose. Everything seemed to be falling apart in his life, he thought, feeling sorry for himself.

'Vicki,' he whispered one more time, shaking his head. He lay still, deflated and disappointed, but then his spirits surged as he remembered the way she had said how good looking he was and how she had so obviously liked to be in his company. He recalled how she never recoiled once from the slight touches he gave her. But then his optimism drained away as he wondered whether this was just a consequence of her kind nature and if she did the same with everyone she met. Who knows? Anyway, I'm never likely to find out now, he concluded with a heavy heart and a fierce ache in his stomach. So agitated did he feel, he turned round once more in his bed, but then he suddenly became energised by some powerful flows of determination coursing through his veins. 'Come on, let's not give up. With a bit of luck I can still get hold of her number from Jen via her friend, Karen, I think she said her name was.' Saying the words emboldened him and it quickly crossed his mind whether he had in fact already obtained her number. He tore from his bed, flinging the sheet and blankets to all corners, and shot over to his Levi's which were lying neatly over the back of a scuffed and sagging leather armchair. It never failed to amaze him how, even when steaming drunk, he always managed to undress himself and put his things away tidily. He dug deep into each of the five pockets, but, other than a scrunched-up betting slip with another loser scribbled on it, there were no other bits of paper to be found. Decidedly flustered, he tossed his jeans back onto the armchair and grabbed his wallet from the bedside table. It was empty, not even a pound note or two to gladden his heart, which drew a rueful expression from him. He took two paces to the fawn-coloured duffel coat that was hanging from the back of the door. Like his jeans, the pockets were empty. 'Shit,' he muttered sotto voce, sitting down on the edge of the bed, the picture of dejection. 'I suppose Jen's my only hope,' he said without conviction. But his inherent dejection only served to release a sense of realism within him. 'Come on, who am I kidding? She's obviously clever, going to uni and all that, and her family sounds pretty rich to me. Where did she say she lived? Some place near Guildford and her uni's in Exeter if I remember right?' Guildford and Exeter sounded so far away that she may as well have said Timbuktu as far as he was concerned. He shook his head, resigned to the fact that he would never see her again. 'And let's be honest, why would someone like her be interested in someone like me? What can I offer her? Nothing.'

Rhys's dejection turned to depression as he considered his plight. To make matters worse, the headache returned as did the taste of whisky. 'Where am I going with my life?' He had no answer. A moment later, the door of the bedroom creaked open and his mother shuffled in with a wide smile on her face. She was wearing an ancient, nylon dressing gown that had once been a deep shade of red but which was now a faded pink. So see-through were the dressing gown and thin cotton nightdress underneath that they barely covered up her private parts and Rhys quickly had to avert his eyes out of embarrassment. She was holding a cigarette, unsurprisingly, for Rhys never saw her without one, and the fingers of her right hand were stained nicotine yellow. She was barefoot, her toes arrowing in on each other and her bunions crusty. But her smile was kind, warm and loving.

'Happy New Year,' she pronounced as she sat down next to him, putting an arm around his back. She kissed him on the cheek.

'Thanks, Mum,' Rhys returned with a sorry grin. 'Happy New Year to you too.' He placed an affectionate kiss on her cheek and held her hand, squeezing it lightly. 'Let's all hope for a good one.' His mother smiled back and leaned her head into his.

'How was the party? You didn't half make a racket when you came in last night. You woke us up.'

'Sorry about that. I didn't mean it. Was Dad okay?'

'Oh, God, yes. Don't worry about him. He loves you dearly, you know that?'

'Course I do. And I love you both too.'

Rhys's mother squeezed his hand and looked down at the floor, red-cheeked, before taking another drag on her cigarette. 'Must have been a good party; you didn't come in until three.'

'Really!' Rhys went quiet for a moment, wondering what he had got up to in all that time. 'It was great. Don always puts on a good do and everyone was in a happy mood as you can imagine. I must admit, I was a bit out of it, though, and I'm ashamed to say I can't remember midnight or much after.'

'You do surprise me!' Rhys smiled ruefully and patted his mother's hand. 'Any nice girls there?'

'Oh, come on, Mum, you're still not trying to marry me off, are you? I'm not twenty-one yet!'

'Me and your father were already married two years by your age.'

'Funny how I was born only two months later then,' Rhys declared with a beaming smile. His mother playfully thumped him on the thigh and they both burst out laughing. Rhys placed his arm around her shoulder and clasped her tightly. 'No, sorry to disappoint you, Mum, but there weren't any nice girls around last night. Such would be my luck.'

'Oh, that's odd, because a very sweet one with a strange accent rang for you about an hour ago.'

Chapter 3

'Hello Vicki, it's Rhys.'

'Oh, hi Rhys, it's Karen, actually. I'll go and fetch her. Happy New Year, by the way.'

'And to you, too, Karen,' Rhys replied breathlessly.

He had bolted down the stairs from his bedroom in two seconds flat and, as he waited for Vicki to come on the line, he heard his heart pounding hard and fast as if Charlie Watts was hammering away on it with his drumsticks. He picked at some loose hessian threads in the worn carpet with his big toe, trying to stay calm at the same time. His mother plodded slowly down the stairs after him, winked and went into the kitchen. She fussed around nonchalantly, pretending not to listen in on the conversation.

'Hi Rhys.'

'Vicki!' he exclaimed loudly.

'No, it's still me. Vicki's just coming.' Karen smiled on hearing the excitement in Rhys's voice.

'Hello Rhys.' Finally, an English accent came on the line. 'And how are you feeling this morning?' The question was followed by a knowing chuckle.

'Hi Vicki. Thanks for calling earlier and, to answer your question, pretty rough if I'm honest.'

'I'm not surprised! You certainly had a lot to drink.'

'Don't remind me. My head feels like it's got the whole percussion section of the London Philharmonic

Orchestra inside.' Rhys heard a throaty laugh on the other end of the line. 'Oh, Happy New Year, by the way.'

'You wished me that last night.'

'Did I? God, I was so out of it. Sorry for being such a pisshead and I apologise now for anything stupid I might have said or done.'

'Don't worry, there's no need. You were really sweet and funny, actually.'

'Was I? Well, thank God for that.' Rhys's tone exuded massive relief. 'How did you get hold of my number, by the way?'

Vicki burst out laughing and Rhys wondered what was so hilarious.

'You gave it to me, don't you remember? Actually, you stuffed it in the pocket of my skirt. You couldn't get your hand out and nearly pulled it down!'

'You're joking! Did I? I don't remember a thing. I'm really sorry.' Vicki was about to reply when Rhys interrupted her. 'I'm glad I did.'

There was a tangible pause on the other end of the line before Vicki replied in a low voice. 'I'm glad you did, too.'

A few seconds of silence followed but they were anything but awkward, the two of them experiencing a delectable tingling inside their bodies.

'So you're in Cardiff at the moment?'

'Yeah, but if you're around, I'd love to meet up. I'm back off to Godalming tomorrow and then uni straight after.'

'You took the words right out of my mouth. I'd love to see you today.' Rhys was also conscious that the cost of the call was racking up and money was tight in his family. 'Let me think where?'

'How about I come back up to Pont ... ee ... prid?'
'Pont ... ee ... preethe, please!'
'Oh, I am sorry. Pont ... ee ... preethe.'
'That's better.'

They both laughed before Vicki resumed. 'I've got my car with me so I could be with you in half an hour. Shall I pick you up?'

'No, don't come to the house, we can meet in town.' Vicki picked up the slight hint of embarrassment. 'We can get a nice coffee and sandwich in the Royale. Oh, shit, I just remembered, it's New Year's Day, isn't it? All the caffs will be closed. It's going to have to be a pub then, though I'm going to be on the orange squash, don't you worry.' Rhys heard a chuckle on the other end of the line. 'Tell you what, let's meet in the White Hart. It'll be easy for you to find. Coming into Ponty, just follow the station sign and you'll see the pub opposite. You can't miss it. In fact, you can park in the station car park. It'll be alright today.'

'Great. Shouldn't be too difficult to find. See you, what, in half an hour?'

'Make it forty-five minutes. I've just got up and, believe me, I need as much time as I can get to look half decent.'

'Forty-five mins it is then. See you later.'
'Can't wait.'
'Nor me.'

As they put the receivers down, they both lingered a few moments and smiled. In the kitchen, Rhys's mother smiled too.

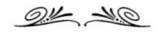

The White Hart was busier than Rhys was expecting and, as he sipped nervously at his shandy, he stretched his neck to keep an eye out for Vicki's arrival. The pub's customers were in high spirits, constantly passing in front of his eye line, and requiring him to make head movements both up and down and left and right. He had only been in the pub five minutes but his pint was already two-thirds empty. The background music, swirling smoke and smell of booze began to rival that of Don's party, though, thankfully, the temperature was more agreeable. Christmas trimmings still hung forlornly above the bar and across the back wall and, to his irritation, a huge red and silver star was stuck to the glass of the front door, blocking his view of who was arriving.

'Alright, Rhys? Happy New Year, butt.'

'Yeah, same to you, Steve.'

'Gonna watch Ponty on Saturday? Maesteg, innit, they're playing?'

'Yeah, I'll be there. Should be a good match, and Bob's fit again, I hear.'

'That's good news. Our lineout's been rubbish without him. See you then.'

'Yeah, Steve.'

As Steve walked away, the door opened and a rush of freezing air accompanied Vicki's entrance. Her facial expression was inquisitive, like a new-born foal experiencing its surrounds for the very first time, as she sought out Rhys. She had deliberately arrived five minutes late so as not to enter the pub before him. She was still struggling to find him when she heard a voice calling out her name excitedly.

'Vicki, Vicki, over here!'

Vicki looked towards the direction of the deep, bass voice that had made her tremble the first time she heard it the night before and saw Rhys waving his arm furiously. He was smiling broadly and Vicki went tingly on seeing him. He was so handsome, even more so than she remembered the previous night. She approached his table where Rhys stood up to greet her. They hugged each other and kissed quickly on the lips. It seemed as if they had known each other for years already. An audience of admiring and approving eyes looked Vicki's way, more than one or two of them lecherously. She was, after all, the only female in the pub.

'Here, take this seat. I've been keeping it for you. What would you like?'

'I'm definitely off the alcohol. I might not have been as bad as you last night but I wasn't feeling so clever myself this morning. And now with these bags they've brought out you blow into, I don't want to be stopped for drunk-driving. Tell you what, I'll have a bitter lemon, no ice, thanks.'

'Give us a sec then.' Rhys had taken a couple of paces when he turned back round to face Vicki. 'By the way, you look absolutely lovely.' And with that, he threaded his way through the drinkers to the bar.

Vicki sat down feeling as though she was the most beautiful woman in the world. She, in turn, could not take her eyes off Rhys as she looked him up and down. At over six feet tall, though the Cuban heels of his boots accounted for more than an inch of that, she thought he looked wonderful. His perfect, round bum was squeezed so tightly into his drainpipe jeans that she thought the denim would rip open at any moment. His hips and waist were narrow and lean in contrast to his chest and shoulders, which were so broad she thought he must be a builder or a disciple of Charles Atlas at the very least. He was not quite as broad as Mr Universe, the incomparable Arnold Schwarzenegger, but she didn't think he was far off. His face, however, softened the muscularity with his brown, angelic, doe-like eyes and wavy black hair not dissimilar to those of Paul McCartney. Vicki doubted that even the newly-wed Linda Eastman would be able to tell any facial difference between her Beatle and Rhys.

Rhys returned to a beaming Vicki and placed the bitter lemon on the table. He sat down opposite her, another pint of shandy in hand. 'I hope the pub's alright? I'm sure it's not as smart as the pubs you get in Gobbledygook ...'

'Godalming!'

' ... but it's nice and cosy.'

With bare, hard, wooden tables and chairs and a total lack of furnishings, Vicki thought the White Hart anything but cosy. She didn't admit to this. She didn't care.

'I thought you were off the beer today?'

'I thought so as well but the walk here livened me up a bit so I thought I'd try a shandy. Glad I did, though I'll have an orange juice next time, I think. Might've been better if I'd stuck to the shandy last night by the sounds of it.'

'You can say that again!' Vicki exclaimed with raised eyebrows and a grin.

'Sorry I didn't see in the New Year with you.'

'But you did! You really can't remember a thing, can you?'

'I'm ashamed to say the last thing I can remember is playing *Buzz* with the boys well before midnight.'

'That's right. I came looking for you and you were all upstanding toasting this, that and the other.'

'Don't remind me, I can still taste the whisky.' Rhys screwed up his face and licked at his lips instinctively.

'You all came into the living room then and someone put on the telly. When Big Ben struck twelve, you grabbed me and swung me around, planting kisses all over my face. In fact, Karen's got a massive bruise on her leg from where my heel caught her.'

'Oh, no. Tell her sorry for me, will you?'

'Oh, she's fine. Don't worry. She had more problems fighting off your friend, Ian. He wouldn't let go of her. It didn't help him that his breath stunk of sick!'

Rhys put his head in his hands and started to laugh and Vicki joined him.

'I can't wait to see him next. He'll be squirming with embarrassment.'

'It'll be interesting when you see Don next as well,' Vicki threw in, teasing him.

'Why's that?' Rhys replied, his eyes wide with expectation.

'Well, there was a bit of a commotion soon after midnight 'cos Jen couldn't find Don anywhere but then saw him out the back having a snog with his ex, apparently. She went mad, calling him every name under the sun and flailing away at him with her fists before they went upstairs. You could still hear them arguing from there. A few minutes later, she stormed off, slamming the front door so hard it splintered the frame. Karen shot off after her but she was gone. She was in a right state.'

Rhys sat with his mouth open, cradling his shandy while Vicki recounted the sorry tale.

'What an idiot! I knew he still had the hots for Megan but that's really unsubtle. He's gonna lose Jen if he's not careful, and she's a lovely girl.'

'Going to? I think it's gone beyond that!'

'Oh, fuck, I hope not. What a way to start 1970.' Rhys shook his head with dismay and concern, which Vicki returned with a rueful grin and the slightest of nods. 'And where was I then when this bit of drama was taking place?' Rhys continued with trepidation, looking Vicki straight in the eye and taking a swig of his drink.

'Oh, you were singing and dancing away as happy as Larry. We had a few together, actually. It was great fun, though you did nearly break my back once or twice.'

'I am sorry.'

'No need. I enjoyed myself a lot ... more than a lot.'

Rhys smiled and touched her hand in recognition of the kind words, drawing a smile from Vicki, too, when replying, 'I may not be able to remember anything but I'm sure I did as well.'

'Oh, there's no doubt about that. I lost you after a while and wondered where you'd got to. Eventually, I found you in the kitchen, slumped in a chair, fast asleep, but with the ends of your mouth turned upwards, a bit like the Joker in *Batman*. You looked really peaceful and happy.'

'How embarrassing!' Rhys cringed and covered his face in mock shame.

'Not at all. You looked lovely. I gave you a quick kiss on the forehead and left you to it. Ian assured me he'd get you home alright. We left shortly afterwards. I had a great night.'

'Well, the New Year is always special.'

'You're right, but the real reason I was so happy was that I had your phone number.'

Rhys did not know how to respond but then offered, 'And I'm glad you rung it.'

Vicki looked at him and stroked the back of his hand. All she wanted to do was jump on him and make love. Rhys stared back, thinking the same. After a few seconds, they both grabbed their glasses and took a few slow sips of their drinks, which succeeded in lowering the level of sexual voltage that crackled between them. Neither of them said a word as the electricity turned down.

The pub was almost full now and one or two of the drinkers bumped into the back of Vicki's chair. The build-up of smoke was becoming suffocating and the chatter louder and louder. Rhys knew it would only get worse so, after finishing his pint, he suggested to Vicki that they go for a walk in the park. Although the temperature was barely above freezing, the sky was a sparkling blue and the day was bathed in sunlight. 'Last night's catching up on me a bit so some fresh air will do me good.'

'Me, too.'

'You'll like the park. It's beautiful.'

'You're the tour guide.'

Rhys smiled and rose from his seat. But before Vicki could follow, he stretched out his arm and made a stop sign with his hand. 'Before we go, I think we should toast the New Year properly.'

He made his way to the bar and returned a few minutes later with a small bottle of Babycham and two half-pint glasses. He sat down again and poured the drink. Each glass was barely a quarter full.

'I'm sorry I couldn't get proper champagne and glasses, like, but this is Ponty, after all, come on!'

Vicki laughed.

'Happy New Year, Vicki.'

'Happy New Year to you, too, Rhys.' They clinked their glasses and took a sip before Vicki added, 'And decade.'

'Absolutely.'

After finishing their drinks, they were putting on their coats when a friend of Rhys drew his attention for a moment. With his eyes averted, Vicki picked up the empty Babycham bottle and peeled off the label. She gave it the lightest of kisses before folding it and placing it in her purse.

Turning right as they left the White Hart, Vicki and Rhys walked slowly down the main street leading to the town centre before turning right once more and over a bridge which served as the entrance to the public park. The cold, crisp air compelled them both to button their coats right up to their necks, the frills of Vicki's fawn-coloured Afghan seemingly extensions of her hair which glittered like gold in the brilliant sunshine. The shabby street, with newspaper wrapped around lampposts from the night's wind, was further littered with New Year debris and was a total contrast to the beautifully maintained park. Even in the depths of winter, with trees void of leaves, borders void of flowers and lawns hard and bare, it still looked welcoming, with the sunlight bringing life to the yellows, browns and blacks of the remaining flora, and the tree branches, seemingly sprinkled with the finest hint of icing sugar, casting a crazy-paving of shadows across the ground.

With ghostly white whispers of breath accompanying their every step, Vicki and Rhys strolled straight ahead from the bridge and along a Tarmac road with tennis courts to their right behind a high wire fence. They held hands; Vicki's feeling warm and snug as its bare skin nestled in his reassuring grasp. It felt like the most natural thing in the world to do. Their hands had come together the second they had left the pub and neither of them thought it necessary to make any comment about it. In fact, before they reached the park, they did not even realise they were doing so. As Rhys looked around him and breathed in the freshest of air that reddened his nostrils, the scene reminded him of one of his favourite films, *Barefoot In The Park,* though he was glad to keep his boots on. In a quiet moment, he wondered whether he would ever be in a position to take Vicki to New York and recreate the magic of Robert Redford and the delicious Miss Fonda. The reality drew a resigned look from his features but he locked the idea away in his head. At least he could dream.

'What a fabulous park,' Vicki proclaimed as they entered the cricket field. Its outfield was in such good condition that, despite the time of year, they would not have been surprised if a line of players strolled on behind them.

'I thought you'd like it. It would have been criminal not to have gone for a walk on a day like this.'

'You're right.'

'It's the only good thing the town's got going for it as far as I'm concerned,' Rhys replied harshly.

'Oh, I don't know. From what I've seen of it so far, it's got a sort of grittiness and edge to it I like. And the people are really friendly.'

'Yeah, you're right, I suppose, but there's a lot of poverty here as well, certainly when compared to where you come from. Other than mining, there's not that many jobs around and you'll never catch me going down the pit. I couldn't bear it.'

'I don't blame you. It sounds terrifying to me.'

'My dad's a miner, or he was, anyway. He's got a bad back and coughs all the time 'cos his lungs are full of dust. He's been on the sick for two years and I can't see him ever working again. Mind you, if he gave up the fags, his chest would improve, I'm sure. He's always banging on about money being as tight as a Scotsman on Burns Night, but, between him and my mum, they must smoke half of it away.' Vicki gave a little chuckle but went quiet again as they circled the boundary, interested to learn more about Rhys's family. 'I'm being a bit unfair if I'm honest. They're always putting themselves out for me. I love them more than anything and I know they feel the same way about me.' Vicki squeezed Rhys's hand and looked up at him with a loving smile. 'Saying that, I think Dad's a bit disappointed with me 'cos we've always been a family of miners and, as I'm an only child, there's a good chance that'll end with me. If I ever have children, I'll never let them go down the pit.'

'You'd like children then?'

'Oh, yeah, one day, definitely. I'd love a son. He'd be the new Barry John, running out for Wales with number ten on his back. I'd die happy there and then if that ever happened.'

'Who's Barry John?' Vicki asked mischievously.

Rhys stopped abruptly in his tracks and virtually pulled Vicki's arm from its socket as she continued to stroll along without letting go of his hand.

'Who's Barry John?' Rhys repeated Vicki's question with incredulity. 'You're pulling my leg, aren't you? He's only the best rugby player who ever lived.'

'I'm only winding you up! Even I've heard of Barry John. He's not bad, I suppose.'

'NOT BAD! You really are taking the piss now.

Vicki began to laugh and Rhys joined her, though somewhat half-heartedly. They resumed their walk around the boundary until Rhys changed direction for the rugby field where the Pontypridd team played their matches.

Vicki picked up the conversation. 'My dad loves rugby and always goes to the internationals at Twickenham. He's a member of Esher and goes most Saturdays.'

'Funny you should mention Esher. I've no idea who they are but whenever they show the rugby results on *Grandstand,* I notice they always lose.'

'You don't have to tell me that! I can't remember the last time I saw my dad happy after a match.' After a short pause, Vicki carried on. 'His favourite player is Bob Hiller, who plays for the Harlequins, I think.'

'I know Bob Hiller; he's the England full-back. He's the one who digs up half the pitch to rest the ball on before kicking for goal.'

Vicki thought she'd wind Rhys up further. 'Do you think he's better than Barry John?'

'I'm not even going to dignify that question with a response,' Rhys replied haughtily before they burst out laughing.

On entering the rugby field, they wandered up to the rusty and scarred single-bar barrier that ran the length of the touchline on their chipped and gouged concrete pillars. They both rested their elbows on it, gazing out onto the field. The whole of the middle section, running from one set of posts to the other, was full of brown and black rutted sods with a hint of green dotted around.

Only closer to the touchlines did the green of the grass predominate. Vicki looked up at the small ramshackle of a grandstand, wondering if it was bomb damaged from the war, with its broken and splintered seats and holes in the corrugated iron roof. She wondered why any spectators would ever want to sit in it let alone pay a premium to do so.

'So you like rugby then?' Rhys asked, edging along the barrier towards her until their shoulders were touching.

'Yeah. I don't follow it that closely but I do like it. It strikes me as being a real man's game. Don't ask me about any of the players, though, 'cos I only look out for their bums and legs! If anything, I prefer football, mainly because I can understand it better.'

'Yeah? Who do you support? I like football as well. Cardiff City's my team.'

'I support Chelsea.'

'What! Those fancy dans down the King's Road in London? You're kidding?'

'It's the Fulham Road, actually. What's wrong with Chelsea? They're a good side, what with Ossie, Chopper Harris and Charlie Cook playing for them. I went to see them once. An old boyfriend of mine took me. I enjoyed the game but I've never been so frightened in all my life. We were standing in the Shed. It's a part of their ground; you've probably heard of it. Well, I may as well have been in a zoo. Chelsea fans are just animals, shouting abuse and threatening violence all the time. And as for racist chanting, the less said the better. Never again.'

Rhys laughed as he pictured Vicki standing among the skinheads, cowering with fear. Her reference to an old boyfriend did not bother him in the slightest. He felt so at ease in her company that he already considered her his own girlfriend, believing that she thought the same of him as well. He was not mistaken.

'Brrr ..., it's a bit cold here in the shadow,' Vicki blurted out a with a sudden shiver. 'Let's keep walking.'

Rhys slipped his hand into Vicki's and led her out of the rugby field, past the orchard field and towards the bandstand right in the centre of the park. The path they followed was bathed in sunshine, which soon warmed them up. A number of couples passed them in the opposite direction, one or two of them acknowledging Rhys and wishing them a happy New Year. Vicki returned the compliments of the season but was surprised to observe how young some of the girls were who were pushing prams. Copying some of the passing couples, Rhys let go of Vicki's hand and put his arm around her back. Vicki reciprocated and, as she turned her face up towards him, he kissed her lightly on the lips. He was rewarded with a tighter hug from Vicki. They proceeded past the bandstand until they arrived at the large circular paddling pool, drained of water and littered with mud, leaves, discarded paper and crumpled cans. In addition, the pool's light-blue paint was badly eroded in parts. Someone's going to have a big job doing that up before the summer starts, Vicki thought, casting her eye over it. Alongside the pool were some swings, see-saws and slides which also required some care and attention before the onset of warmer times. Finding a spot in the sun, Rhys led Vicki to the pool's low rim where they sat down. Instinctively, they raised their faces and closed their eyes, loving the warmth.

'This is so nice,' Vicki sighed.

'Absolutely.' After a brief pause, Rhys added, 'The sun's not bad, either.'

Vicki beamed and rested her head on his shoulder, her eyes still closed. Rhys placed his arm around her and kissed the top of her head, the fine strands of her hair sticking momentarily to his lips.

'I could stay here forever.'

'Me, too.'

They remained sitting on the rim of the pool for a full fifteen minutes, barely saying a word to each other. Occasionally, they caught the eye of passers-by and exchanged contented smiles.

'I can't remember a January day as beautiful as this. Usually, it's tipping down.' Rhys's words were uttered with a sleepy air, his cheeks tingling from the sun's rays. 'I bet tomorrow will be the complete opposite, grim and miserable as usual. It'll be back to work, too, for some of us, to compound the misery.'

'What do you do?'

'I work in a cash & carry, lugging boxes around.'

'Cash & carry?' Vicki queried. 'What's that?'

'You don't half live in a sheltered world,' Rhys teased. 'It's basically a wholesaler that sells stuff to the trade, not to individuals for their own use. You know, pubs, restaurants, shops generally. They buy in bulk so the produce costs less.'

'Mmm, I understand now. And you lug boxes around?'

'Yeah, pretty much. The warehouse is enormous and I put incoming produce onto the shelves or help take it to a customer's car or van. Every now and then they let me on the forklifts. They're lethal, I tell you. The first time I drove one, I nearly took one of the boys' heads off.' Vicki chuckled aloud beside him. 'I've been working there since I left school and, 'cos they know me well, they trust me on the till now. It doesn't pay much but at least it's a job.'

'You don't fancy doing something else then?'

'Come on, let's walk. I'll be sunburnt at this rate and my arse is starting to ache. We're not designed to sit on concrete.'

Vicki chuckled once more and stood up at the same time as Rhys. They placed their arms around each other's backs and ambled slowly in the direction of the pitch and putt, Vicki leaning her head into his shoulder.

'You're not hungry, are you, by the way?' Rhys asked politely.

'No, thanks. I had a good breakfast.'

'That's good because, thinking about it, I don't think there's anything open today, not even a chippy for some scrumps. There's always the new chinky, I suppose. They never seem to be closed. I tell you what, I'll buy you a nice stale pork pie or sweaty, three-day-old cheese and onion sandwich wrapped in cellophane, if you prefer, from the pub when we leave the park later.'

'You certainly know how to treat a lady.'

'Lady? Where?'

The comment earned Rhys an elbow in the ribs. They stopped at the high wire fence to watch some golfers hack their way around the pitch and putt, a wayward ball landing in a ditch only a few feet from where they were standing. As it was unplayable, they both heard the distant exclamation of 'Bollocks' as the golfer discovered where his ball had ended up, and laughed.

'Didn't know it was open today.'

'Do you play?' Vicki enquired.

'Yeah, I've been round a few times. My best is seventy-seven.'

'Is that good?'

'Well, the par's fifty-four so I don't think Tony Jacklin's gonna lose any sleep if they let me play in The Open this year.' Vicki smiled. 'Going back to your last question, I'm desperate to do something else, something different, but it's not easy when you've only got one 'O' level and three CSEs. One of those is a grade one, though, so that means I've got the equivalent of two 'O' levels in reality,' Rhys added proudly. 'I want to get away from here, you know, find a job in Cardiff or Swansea, with a place of my own, or even further afield. I've been saving up, but, after paying keep to my mum, I never seem to have much left at the end of the week. I'm trying, though, and I've got a bit in the bank.'

Vicki squeezed his hand. 'Don't give up. I'm sure you'll find what you're looking for eventually. God loves a trier.'

Rhys looked down at her. 'That's a nice expression.'

'An Irish girlfriend of mine told me it in uni.'

'If that's the case, perhaps I should go to church more often. God may appreciate that and I wouldn't have to try so hard then.' They both laughed, drawing a serious look from the hacker who was trying to defy the laws of physics and logic by attempting an impossible shot. 'What about you? What are you studying at uni?'

'I'm reading English.'

'I can read English as well. In fact, that's what I got my 'O' level in.' Vicki nudged him in the arm. 'That's what all the contestants say on *University Challenge*, "Reading". It always sounds a bit funny to me.'

'Yeah, it does. So you watch *University Challenge* then?'

'God, you've got to be joking. I can't understand the questions let alone know the answers. That Bamber

Gascoigne has got to be the cleverest bloke in the country. I prefer *Mr and Mrs* myself now that *Take Your Pick* has finished.' They looked at each other and smiled before breaking out into a chuckle. 'Let's go this way.' Rhys led Vicki in the direction of the swimming baths, hidden behind an imposing brick wall with only the narrowest of entrances. Unsurprisingly, the scarred and slightly rotten, faded green wooden door was bolted shut. On top of the wall, broken shards of glass were embedded in the concrete layer, leaving no doubt in anyone's mind that entrance by this means was strictly forbidden. 'We used to have some laughs in there in the summer but I haven't been for a couple of years. It's mainly for kids now.'

'What kind of laughs?'

'Well, mainly doing dives and bombs and stuff like that, though the attendant always went mad at us and threw us out once. Later on, we were more interested in seeing the girls we were in school with in their bikinis. We were a right bunch of lechers, I tell you. Ian used to hold his stomach in all the time, even if he always denied it. It was so obvious, though, 'cos when he thought the girls weren't looking, his gut used to hang out over his Speedos.' Vicki smiled at the image as they strolled back towards the tennis courts. A wooden bench became free as the occupants wandered off and, as the sun was shining invitingly on it, Vicki and Rhys took their places. 'Ah, this is nice,' Rhys declared, turning his face to the sun once more, his eyes closed.

'So you'd be quite happy to move away from Pont ... ee ... preethe then?' Vicki's question was a non sequitur but she was eager to hear affirmation of Rhys's earlier statement for her mind was already thinking ahead.

'Oh, yeah. There's no doubt about that.' There was no follow-up from Vicki so Rhys carried on. 'What about yourself? What are you going to do after uni? Have you got a job lined up?'

'Nothing definite. I might go into marketing or something like that. My father knows one or two people so hopefully he'll be able to pull a string or two for me.'

'What's marketing?'

'Well, it's like advertising and promotions, stuff like that.'

'Mmm, sounds interesting,' Rhys replied insincerely. 'Will you stay in Exeter then?'

'God, no. It's too quiet and isolated for my liking. My father works in London so he'll probably help me find something there.'

'London, the Big Smoke. It must be brilliant there. I'd love to go one day, you know, see Carnaby Street and all that. I think I'd really like city life. Small places like this and the countryside do my head in.'

'Yeah?' Vicki's response was enthusiastic and she turned to look him in the eye, only to see them still shut, his head tilted back, enjoying the sun's rays, a contented grin etched across his face.

'I'd have loved to have been in Grosvenor Square when that big demonstration took place,' Rhys continued as more images of London flashed through his head.

'I was there!' Vicki shrieked.

'Yeah!' Rhys opened his eyes and looked at her.

'Yeah, right outside the American Embassy we were. It got a bit mad so we headed off before the trouble started. I'm glad I went, though, 'cos the US has got no right being in Vietnam, bombing all those people to smithereens. It's a disgrace.'

'I agree with you. They should be fucking ashamed of themselves.' Rhys followed up apologetically in a more measured tone. 'Sorry about the language, it's just I feel very strongly about it.'

Vicki laughed. 'Don't worry, I do, too, and I've heard and used worse!'

'What! A nice, young English girl like you? Never!' Rhys laughed with her. 'I'd have given my right arm to be there. Those Yanks think they're so high and mighty.'

'I had an inkling last night that you might have supported those demonstrations in London and Paris a couple of years back.'

'Oh, and why's that then?'

Unexpectedly, Vicki broke into song. '"*Everywhere I hear the sound of marching, charging feet, boy, 'cos summer's here and the time is right for fighting in the street, boy ...*" Do you recognise that?'

'Course I do. It's the Stones, *Street Fighting Man*. Why d'you ask?'

''Cos you were singing it at the top of your voice last night when Don put *Beggars Banquet* on.'

'Oh, no, was I? I can't remember a thing.' Rhys slapped his hand against his forehead which drew a chuckle from Vicki. 'I shouldn't be surprised, it's a great song. I love the Stones. Going back to the Yanks, it's disgusting the way they've treated Muhammad Ali, you know, Cassius Clay.'

'I agree,' Vicki concurred.

'Taking away his boxing licence the way they did just because he's got some principles and refused to go to Vietnam. Shameful, it is.' Rhys followed up with an impersonation of the great World Heavyweight Boxing

Champion. '"*I ain't got no quarrel with them Vietcong ... No Vietcong ever called me nigger.*"'

'I didn't know Ali came from Pakistan?' Vicki's remark earned her a playful elbow in the ribs.

'He's superb, a real hero of mine, so talented, funny, good-looking, and a brilliant fighter.'

'You can say that again. He's sex on legs, I tell you.'

'You like that expression?'

'Yeah. It sums up gorgeous men perfectly.' Vicki stared deeply into Rhys's eyes, making it obvious that he was included. Rhys smiled back, holding her stare with ease and squeezing her hand.

'I think we've got quite a bit in common, you and me. Like you, I'm against Vietnam and I'm against nuclear weapons as well. I noticed the CND chain you were wearing last night. They should be scrapped.'

'So you do remember something then?'

'More than you realise,' Rhys replied with a wink.

'Yeah, nuclear weapons are horrific. I can't believe civilised people would ever consider using them. They frighten me to death. Do you remember that stand-off over Cuba a few years back? I was only a kid at the time but I remember my mother and father looking really worried whenever the news came on. They really thought a nuclear war might break out.'

'Yeah, I remember it well. Horrible it was. I could feel the tension in my house, too. I think that's when my parents started to smoke. They haven't stopped since!'

'He did well, Kennedy, to get us out of that. Terrible what happened to him later on, though. I'll never forget it. I was having my supper when the news came on that he'd been shot. My mother shrieked and dropped a plate. She cried all night afterwards.'

'Yeah, that was awful,' Rhys agreed with a slow, resigned shake of his head.

'They say everyone can remember what they were doing when they heard the news.'

'Yeah, that's right.'

'What were you doing then?'

Rhys thought for a moment. 'I can't remember, if I'm honest.' And, after a slight hesitation, they burst out laughing.

'Tragic, it was, for that to happen to someone so young and good-looking,' Vicki concluded.

'Sex on legs,' Rhys threw in mischievously, which earned him a payback nudge in the ribs.

The afternoon was moving on and the sun lowering in the sky. They had been sitting in shadow for ages but so enjoyed each other's company that neither of them noticed the sharp fall in temperature or increasing gloom. Eventually, Vicki looked at her watch and raised her eyebrows in surprise. 'God, is that the time? I told Karen I'd be back by four and it's gone that already.' She emitted a long sigh, not wanting to leave Rhys but knowing that she had to.

'I suppose you'd better get a move on then.' There was no mistaking the disappointment in his voice.

Rhys had been dreading this moment and, as they rose from the bench, hand in hand, they proceeded quietly back over the bridge and out of the park in the direction of Vicki's car. They were both deep in thought. What now? Rhys asked himself. She'll soon be back off to Surrey and Exeter. That'll be it. The next time she comes to Wales, that's if she ever does come back to Wales, will be God knows when. This knowledge depressed him and he lowered his head. His spirits lifted higher than the sky, however, when Vicki finally spoke, even if slightly hesitantly.

'I don't know what you think or what your work commitments are but I'd love it if you came to visit me in Exeter. A friend of mine is having a party on Saturday week and it'd be great if you could make it that weekend.' Her heartbeat doubled its rate as she waited nervously for his response. To her ecstasy, her state of trepidation was as fleeting as the shadow of a passing bird.

'I'd love it. In fact I can't wait.'

The grip of their hands tightened and they turned their heads to face each other, their expressions as sunny as the afternoon had been. They soon arrived beside Vicki's white MG Roadster with black, detachable vinyl roof.

'What a fantastic car. Did you come up with eight score draws or something on the pools? It's beautiful.'

'No, it was a present from my parents for my twenty-first a couple of months back,' Vicki replied, slightly embarrassed.

'You're very lucky,' Rhys returned, patting the bonnet, but with no hint of envy, ridicule or sarcasm. He was genuinely happy for her.

Vicki opened the driver's door and retrieved a scrap of paper and pen from the glove compartment. 'This is my number in Godalming and this one is for my house in uni. And this is the address, by the way,' Vicki advised as she scribbled away with Rhys peering over her shoulder. 'I've got yours.' She handed it to him. He looked at it briefly before stuffing it in his back pocket. 'Don't lose it now!' Vicki sounded almost desperate.

'Don't worry. There's no chance of that.'

Having returned the pen to the glove compartment, Vicki turned round, stood full square to Rhys and grasped both his hands. 'I've had a fantastic day, a fantastic New Year. I'll never forget it,' she declared, looking him full in the eye.

'The same here. It feels like a dream almost, just perfect. I can't wait to see you next weekend.'

'Nor me. Make sure you ring before, though. I just love listening to that voice of yours and we'll have to tie down the arrangements.'

'Don't worry, I will.' A few seconds later, Rhys ran his hands up Vicki's arms and placed them on her shoulders, easing her towards him. He gave her a protective, loving cuddle before kissing her fully on the mouth for more than a minute, uncaring of what any passers-by might think. After a final hug and slow release of hands, they parted, Vicki taking her place in the driver's seat. 'Drive carefully now.'

After a short pause, during which Vicki started the engine, Rhys found a question to ask. 'Does this house of yours in Exeter have a spare room? If not, I'll be quite happy to crash out in the living room. I'll bring a sleeping bag with me.'

Vicki glanced up at him with eyes overflowing with mischief. 'We don't have any spare rooms and the living room's chock-a-block. Oh, and there'll be no need for the sleeping bag.'

Rhys had smiled a lot during the afternoon but he gave his widest one of all at this moment. 'I was hoping you'd say that!'

CHAPTER 4

Vicki shifted nervously on her feet on the concourse of St David's railway station in Exeter. The train from Cardiff Central was running four minutes late. Those four minutes seemed like a lifetime to her. The past week had been a living hell waiting for this moment to arrive, dragging on so slowly she thought the sand in the timer was defying gravity. She never believed a week could last so long and concluded that God must have been dawdling when creating the heavens and earth. And now those damned infernal demons were teasing her for a few minutes longer.

The concourse was a hustle and bustle of activity, as it always was at five-thirty on a Friday evening, as travellers arrived and departed for the weekend. Long gangly-haired students in scruffy clothes mingled with soberly-dressed business people who invariably looked suspiciously and often snobbishly at them. Vicki's Afghan coat gave her away as a student, but, beneath it, she wore impeccably pressed Wrangler's which showed off her pert round behind and long straight legs perfectly. They were tucked into high-heeled, pointy-toed, black and white cowboy boots. The extra height, she knew, would show off her legs even more. The whole afternoon had been a period of bother and fluster as she contemplated what to wear, flinging virtually her whole wardrobe onto the bed before finally deciding. Her choice of top was also intended to show off her figure to the maximum. The tight, black, lambswool roll-neck sweater succeeded in this objective and, when posing in front of the mirror back in her bedroom, she had expressed a quiet 'Thank you' to Diana Rigg, who, as Emma Peel in *The Avengers*, had given her the inspiration for it. She wore, as ever, no make-up. She did not need to and her only accessory was the CND chain. The majority of the men and more than one or two women who passed close to her eyed her with sexual intent. Vicki was aware of this though she gave nothing away in her facial expression. She was used to it, after all. At last, the Cardiff train pulled in.

'Where is he?' Vicki muttered impatiently, straining to look over and around the heads and backs of the other waiting people blocking her view. A steady flow of passengers from the train walked past her but there was no sign of Rhys. Vicki fretted, wondering if he had missed it for some reason, but, finally, after an anxious couple of minutes, she saw him at the back of a mass of travellers in the distance walking in her direction. She shivered with excitement and nerves at this first sighting and broke out into a broad smile. She was tempted to shout out his name, like one of the paparazzi might to a distant celebrity, but he was too far back. A few moments later and yards closer, Rhys's scanning eyes homed in on a wildly flailing arm and his smile, Vicki swore, lit up the whole railway station. Her body tingled when she realised he had seen her. She thought he looked wonderful and noticed some similarities in the way they were dressed, for he, too, was wearing a black roll-neck sweater, though more loosely fitting than hers, and it was only the brand that distinguished their jeans, Rhys wearing his favourite Levi's. Their coats and footwear differed, however, Rhys wearing a heavy, leather biker's jacket and shiny, black winkle-pickers. In his right hand he was carrying a holdall.

'It's great to see you again, Vicki,' Rhys declared, his eyes open wide with delight. He let go of the holdall and gave her such a big hug that he lifted her off her feet.

'And you,' Vicki replied before kissing him on the lips, her arms wrapped around his neck and shoulders and feet still dangling in the air.

'You look fantastic,' Rhys commented, finally lowering her to the ground.

'You, too. My God, we must be telepathic or something. You'd think we were twins,' she added, eyeing his clothes and her own up and down.

'Yeah, you're right,' Rhys chuckled without knowing what 'telepathic' meant.

'The car's outside. It's only a short drive to the house; we'll be home in a tick.'

Rhys picked up his holdall with one hand and, clasping Vicki's hand with his other, they walked out of the station into the misty, freezing night air that hung around them like spectres.

'Sophie and Jill are dying to meet you. I've been boring them all week about you coming.'

'Well, I hope I come up to expectations then. If I remember right, you said you shared with just the two of them?'

'That's right. They're lovely girls, a bit mad and scatty, but really good friends. I think they're out at the moment but we'll all set off together for the Cowley Bridge later. There's a good crowd meeting up at the pub tonight. You'll like them.'

'Sounds good,' Rhys replied nervously, hoping he'd fit in well with the gang. Of more immediate concern was whether he would fit into the passenger seat of the MG Roadster as he bent his legs almost right up to his chest. Vicki roared up the engine and pulled sharply out of the car park. She could not wait to get home quickly enough.

'Like I mentioned on the phone, there's a party tomorrow night at Bill and Mike's place. It's a real tip but they know how to throw a good party. It should be great.'

'I'm up for it. Can't beat a good party.' Vicki turned her head towards him and smiled. 'Keep your eyes on the road! I haven't come all this way just to see the inside of Exeter A&E.'

A few minutes later, Vicki pulled up outside her house. It was in total darkness, confirming, as she thought, that her friends were not yet at home. They crossed the threshold and she flicked a switch, bathing the hallway, which had deep primrose walls, in a dirty-yellow hue.

'This way.'

Vicki led Rhys up the stairs onto a landing. They walked past a bedroom and then entered another, the next one along, opposite which was a bathroom, the freshly painted white door of which included a large pane of frosted glass. Rhys's immediate impression was that the house was in excellent condition. He had been expecting something more in keeping with the dreary housing that accommodated students of the Polytechnic of Wales in Pontypridd. There was a mirror-bright parquet floor in the hallway at the base of an imposing staircase, which possessed such a heavy brown varnished banister that Rhys wondered whether it had been constructed from reclaimed railway sleepers. It was glistening, just like the parquet floor, and so much so that both their sheens could only have come about through years of thorough polishing. The steps and landing were adorned with a thick, green and white patterned carpet, which looked virtually new to his eyes, with no threadbare areas as far as he could see, and all the brass fixtures and fittings shimmered when the light from the mock Victorian glass globes beamed down on them from the ceiling.

'Make yourself comfortable, I'm just going to the bathroom a sec.'

Vicki's bedroom was much the same. The walls were all newly painted in an ivory cream while the matching pine double wardrobe, chest of drawers, desk and chair all looked in top condition even if the furniture appeared too modern for the Victorian dwelling. The carpet was the same as that of the landing and stairs. The only piece of furniture that appeared remotely in keeping with the age of the house was a beaten-up old leather armchair, not dissimilar to the one in his own bedroom, which was festooned with soft toys and one large burgundy and white cushion. Unsurprisingly for such a house, the ceiling was high and the room spacious. On the walls, Vicki had taped a number of posters. Two of them depicted colourful Parisian nightclub scenes. Rhys was only familiar with the can-can dancers, flaunting their knickers as they kicked their legs high up in the air on stage at the Moulin Rouge. Two other posters were more recognisable. Rhys marvelled at the one of the incomparable Jimi Hendrix plucking at his guitar with his teeth before fixing his eyes on the laughing Warren Beatty and Faye Dunaway, who, as Bonnie and Clyde, were speeding away in their getaway car. The only item of furniture that raised his eyebrows was the bed. It, and the bedside table, matched the other pine furniture exactly but was only a single. 'Well, at least it'll be cosy,' he muttered under his breath with a grin.

While waiting for Vicki, Rhys took off his jacket as the room was boiling hot, the heat emanating from two large, charcoal-grey cast-iron radiators. He placed the jacket over the back of the armchair, just avoiding the head of the green egg-shaped Humpty from *Play School,* and rolled up the sleeves of his sweater. At the same time, he heard a distant hiss from the bathroom and the door unlocking. Vicki soon reappeared in the bedroom, considerably shorter than before, as she was holding her boots in her left hand with the socks stuffed inside. She pushed the door behind her and it shut with a reassuring thud. She tossed the boots onto the floor and walked over to Rhys. On tiptoe, she placed her arms around his neck, pressed her crotch into his and sought out his mouth with hers. They kissed passionately, both of them conscious that Rhys was becoming aroused.

After a moment, Rhys took half a step back and removed the CND chain from around Vicki's neck and put it on the bedside table. He then gripped the bottom of Vicki's sweater and carefully lifted it over her head, flinging it onto the armchair behind him. He unfastened her bra and eased her arms through the straps, letting it drop to the floor. The sight of her naked body took his breath away. Staring at her breasts with a delicious grin, he cupped them in his hands and ran his thumbs across her nipples. Vicki, too, looked down at her breasts and then back up at Rhys, smiling, as if to convey that they were all his to play with. She looked down towards the front of Rhys's jeans and began to unfasten his belt and unbutton his fly. The fourth button gave her difficulties and Rhys helped her with the task, drawing chuckles from them both at their impatience. Once unbuttoned, Rhys sat down on the edge of the bed and removed his boots and socks. He then stood up and pulled both his jeans and underpants down simultaneously, stepping out of both inelegantly and nearly toppling over. Vicki eagerly grabbed the bottom of his sweater and pulled it over his head. Rhys helped her and removed his T-shirt with the same movement. She marvelled at his body, his chest so broad and shoulders so strong that Adonis himself would have been proud of them. His stomach rippled with rock-solid muscles and his skin had the sheen of a Derby winner.

Rhys stood naked, his erection at its maximum, angling upwards and prodding firmly into Vicki's stomach. He gently clasped Vicki's arms and guided her to the foot of the bed, sitting her down and directing her to lie back. He undid a top button and pulled down the zip of her jeans. As he grabbed them by the waistband, Vicki raised her hips to allow him to pull them off more easily; he removed her skimpy white panties in the same movement and dropped them both onto the carpet. Vicki's head was slightly raised, looking down the full length of her body, her stomach flat and taut. She could see Rhys gazing at the tightly curled light brown hair between her legs.

'You look amazing, Vicki, just amazing.'

'You don't look so bad yourself.'

With a smile on his face, Rhys knelt down, parted her legs further, and moved his face towards her crotch. Instinctively, Vicki laid her head back and closed her eyes in anticipation of what was to come next. She felt the tip of his tongue and Vicki came almost immediately, so turned on had she been, her head pulling forward before thudding back onto the pillow. Rhys heard Vicki sigh and felt the tension in her body as he ran his hands over her stomach and waist. Holding her firmly, he tasted the gorgeous moisture and Vicki came again. This time the sigh morphed into a groan before she raised her legs so that her feet rested across his back. She lowered her left leg and slid the front of her foot up and down his right buttock. Rhys felt a toenail digging into his flesh, arousing him even further, before Vicki moved both her feet round to his front. He had to edge back to allow them to pass.

Vicki's feet found Rhys's erection and, placing them either side, she ran them gently along the shaft. He closed his eyes, held her feet, and increased the tempo. He began to pant and became worried that he might come too quickly so he stopped and moved her feet apart. Leaning down, he ran his tongue teasingly along the insides of her legs and, when he arrived at her feet, he slowly sucked at her toes, starting with the little one of her left foot and working his way along until he ended with the little toe of her right. At the same time, he placed two fingers inside her and lightly rubbed her with his thumb. Vicki came again, loudly. Rhys then told her to turn over; she responded without hesitation. He knelt over and gently kissed her buttocks; their whiteness contrasted vividly against the golden skin of her back and legs. He began to nibble at them, bringing a smile to Vicki's face and a number of red marks formed.

Parting her cheeks, he ran his tongue up and down and in-between them before he moved his face away and stood up. His tongue was aching so much he thought it was going to break off. He placed his hands onto Vicki's hips and beckoned her to raise them higher still. She did so, supporting herself on her hands and knees. Rhys penetrated her at once and thrust as hard as he could, slapping noisily into her buttocks. Vicki thought that her eyes were going to pop out of their sockets, and this time the sighs gave way to high-pitched cries. The louder she cried, the harder Rhys thrust until she emitted an extended shriek that Rhys was worried would disturb the whole neighbourhood. He, too, was on the point of coming, but not just yet, he thought. He pulled himself out of Vicki and lay down on his back next to her. Droplets of sweat dripped from the end of her nose onto his chest as she leaned over him.

'It's my turn now,' she whispered with a dirty grin. 'There's still plenty of life down there, I see,' she added before pushing back her hair and lowering her head. Very slowly, she slid her mouth up and down the shaft, every so often pushing down on it so hard that it hit the back of her throat. She heard Rhys moan and pant softly, which turned her on immensely. Rhys tilted his head forward to observe Vicki's actions. Her breasts were hanging freely and he cupped his left hand around her right one and fondled it with the lightest of touches, massaging the nipple between his forefinger and thumb. To reciprocate, Vicki massaged his balls. Rhys allowed his head to fall back onto the pillow; the pleasure was overwhelming. While continuing to slide her mouth up and down the shaft, Vicki occasionally looked up at Rhys out of the corner of her eye to see whether he was enjoying the experience. She need not have worried. A short time later, Rhys tugged at Vicki's arm and beckoned her to straddle him.

'I'd better put a johnny on first,' Rhys panted. 'I'm not sure how much longer I can hang on; you've got me going so much. I brought some with me.'

'I've got some as well. Hold on.' Vicki quickly leaned over and opened the drawer of the bedside table. She removed a newly purchased packet containing twelve condoms, hurriedly ripped off the transparent paper, opened it and pulled one out. She tore off the top of the wrapper with her teeth and removed the condom, the smell of rubber and spermicide hitting their nostrils simultaneously.

'That's exactly the same brand and size packet I bought,' Rhys said inanely, as if it was somehow interesting.

Vicki did not reply, her attention fixed firmly on putting the condom on Rhys as quickly as she could. The second she had done this, she raised her hips and manoeuvred him inside her. She leaned forward, resting on her hands and moved her hips up and down. Her eyes closed and she began to sigh before pushing ever harder and faster and her sighs once more turned into loud cries. Rhys observed her face crumple with the effort as the sensation permeated her body. Her concentration was total. He raised his head and found her nipples with his lips, sucking and licking at them avidly. Immediately, Vicki emitted her highest-pitched cry yet and her head fell forward, her sweat-soaked hair lashing against Rhys's face and chest. A few moments later, she raised her head, her mouth open, her eyes closed. Sweat dripped from her nose and chin. She finally opened her eyes to observe Rhys gazing at her. 'I'm not finished with you yet,' he whispered with a glint in his eye.

'You're unreal,' Vicki replied, panting.

With Vicki still straddling him, Rhys placed his hands on her hips to help ease himself forward and upright into a sitting position. At the same time, she manoeuvred her legs around his back. He placed his hands under her buttocks and, with a great heave, lifted both Vicki and himself off the bed. He shuffled over to the wall opposite until Vicki's back slapped hard against it, her feet hanging loosely either side of him. Rhys then thrust as hard and as fast as he could with his hips. The muscles in his thighs were straining to their limit under the weight and sheer physical effort of it all; moisture beads formed on his brow and shoulders and down the centre of his back. Vicki hung onto his shoulders tightly, her nails digging deeply into his flesh, and cried out loudly in time to each thrust from his hips. Sweat was soon cascading down both of their faces. Rhys, too, emitted loud grunts as he pushed harder and faster. Finally, he could hold back no longer and he came with an extended groan. On feeling Rhys's body shudder, Vicki came too, her head riding up high before slumping forward and over Rhys's shoulder. For a few minutes, they neither moved nor spoke as they allowed their panting to return to steadier breaths and they remained in the same position against the wall. It was Rhys who was the first to speak.

'What a ridiculous sight this must be. Now that's what I call "sex on legs"!'

Vicki burst out laughing. 'You're right there!'

When her laughter had subsided, Rhys took a step back to allow Vicki to place her feet onto the carpet. The relief in his thighs almost matched the sensation of his orgasm. He took her hand and led her back to the bed where they lay down next to each other, Vicki on her side with her right arm and leg over him. She removed the condom and dropped it onto the floor. He noticed a speck of blood on her shoulder. A ridge in the wall had pierced her skin.

'You've got a small cut here. I hope it doesn't hurt or sting, like.'

'I can't feel a thing. I don't remember doing it; I must have had other things on my mind,' Vicki replied with a grin. She moved her arm and leg off him and lay flat on her back, pushing Rhys right over to the edge of the bed until he almost fell off. A small pool of sweat formed between her breasts and in her navel. Rhys flicked at them with his forefinger and droplets splashed everywhere. 'Stop it!' Vicki commanded in a jocular tone, grabbing his hand.

'Hellllloooooo, Vicki, how are you doing in there?' The faint but clearly audible question thrown at her in a "I know exactly what you're doing" voice startled them and, instinctively, they both looked towards the door. Without their knowing, Sophie and Jill had arrived home and were standing outside the bedroom, their hands over their mouths to stop them giggling. 'We'll be off to the pub in a min. Are you *coming*?' Sophie's pun touched Jill's funny bone and made her splutter with laughter. They clasped their hands over their mouths even more tightly to drown out the noise and their cheeks reddened like beetroot, Jill having to wipe away the tears from her eyes. Inside the bedroom, Vicki and Rhys could hear them and smiled.

'Not now, Sophie, we'll be coming later.' This triggered Rhys and he began to laugh. Jill and Sophie were now corpsing in hysterics and gave up even trying to hide it. Vicki wondered what was so funny until it finally clicked and she, too, broke out into a giggle.

'We'll see you later then. Don't do anything we wouldn't do now. Have fun. Byeeee.'

Sophie and Jill finally left them, their faces beaming and desperate to tell their friends all about it.

Vicki snuggled up more tightly to Rhys and ran her finger over his washboard stomach, noticing that he was starting to become aroused again. 'We'll have to get up in a minute. At this rate, by the time we get ready and down to the pub, the evening will be over.' Rhys did not reply for his eyes were staring at the poster of the Moulin Rouge. 'Penny for your thoughts?' Vicki said as she continued to run her finger up and down his stomach.

'Nothing really. I'm just looking at the poster. Paris must be a fantastic city. I wonder if all the girls are like those dancers over there flashing their knickers,' he added with a lecherous Sid James-like chuckle. 'I wish I could read French; I can't make out any of the words. You speak French, don't you?'

'I don't think knowing the words to *Michelle* constitutes speaking French, somehow.'

Rhys turned to face her. 'Actually, come to think of it, I do know some French,' he declared proudly but with a hint of mischief. 'Soixante-neuf.'

Vicki smiled before allowing herself to be turned round by him into the relevant position.

༺ ༺ ༺

Vicki and Rhys never did get up in a minute. In fact, the only time they got up that weekend was to go to the bathroom or to fetch some snacks and drinks from the kitchen, which they invariably included in their sex games. They found it impossible to keep their hands off each other. By Saturday evening, even Sophie and Jill had given up asking Vicki when they were likely to make an appearance. At least Vicki always replied back through the bedroom door, so assuring them that they were still alive. That's not to say that Sophie did not get to see Rhys, even if only a blurred outline of him, as she peered through the frosted glass of the bathroom door on Saturday morning. What he was doing to Vicki in the bath, with water splashing everywhere, got her juices flowing and her own boyfriend wondered with immense satisfaction what had got into her that evening.

But now, as the sun started to dip on a lazy Sunday afternoon, Rhys knew that it was finally time to get up and prepare to leave as his train would not wait for anyone. Vicki knew it too, and resigned herself to the fact, a tear forming in her eye.

'I can't leave it any longer, Vick, I've got to get up.' His tone conveyed his reluctance and sadness. Vicki did not reply, fearing that she would burst into tears if she did. The room stank of sex; a mix of rubber, sweat and sperm. It also stank of wine, beer, stale bread, crusty cheese and pickles but no longer of chocolate, however; Vicki and Rhys having earlier re-enacted the legend of the Mars bar made famous by Marianne Faithful and Mick Jagger.

Rhys finally stirred and swung his legs round, planting his feet on the carpet. He tried to stand up but his legs felt as jelly-like as those of a boxer on the receiving end of a Joe Frazier left hook. The rest of his body felt as if it had been rucked over by the ferocious All Blacks pack of forwards. His thigh muscles and shoulders were aching and his body was marked and lined with scratches and bruises. He looked down to where he was experiencing a throbbing sensation, but this time it was through pain rather than desire. It was the same for Vicki as she slid her feet off the bed and onto the carpet. Her body was marked and her cheeks flushed. Her mouth and chin were red raw as a consequence of Rhys's bristle scraping her face. The same redness was evident on the inside of her thighs and she was almost unbearably sore. They sat next to each other, Vicki's head resting on his shoulder, naked, tired and sad. Three used condoms lay at their feet, soon to join all the others and empty packets in the wastepaper bin. Despite her soreness, Vicki nudged Rhys hard in the ribs as she reminded him of how she had missed out on one further fuck due to the fact that, in a moment of merriment, he had shown her his party trick of blowing up a condom over his head until it burst. It had been funny, she had to admit, so she let him off.

'First thing tomorrow I'll be down the laundrette with these sheets. They're disgusting.'

'You might be better off burning them. I can't believe any washing powder will get these clean.'

Vicki smiled but there was an inherent sadness to it and she stroked his thigh with affection. Rhys finally stood up and shuffled over to the armchair. He unravelled his clothing and began to dress. Vicki remained sitting on the edge of the bed, casting her eyes over him, before accepting defeat by dressing herself. They did so in silence, both of them recalling the vivid and exhilarating events of the past couple of days. But, other than the sex, what struck Vicki about Rhys was how kind and considerate, caring and funny he was and how he encouraged her to realise her ambitions. He wanted her to do well, to succeed, to be confident and to push hard to fulfil her dreams. She shivered with excitement when he told her that he would help her all the way as best he could. She knew Rhys lacked her education, broader experiences of life and connections, and that his background had acted as an anchor to his ambitions while hers had acted as a sail, but he showed not one iota of resentment or jealousy. What had he said? It's the way the cards have fallen. You make do with the hand you are dealt with. Don't complain, just get on with it and do the best you can.

For his part, Rhys wondered when he would wake up from this blissful dream. Had he really just spent the weekend with the most beautiful girl he had ever set eyes on? And not only beautiful but warm, loving and caring. During the journey down to Exeter, he had been worried that, in the cold light of day, Vicki would realise that someone from his background was not for her and that the weekend would turn out to be an unmitigated disaster. But not a bit of it. She was genuinely interested in his life back in Pontypridd and even keen to meet his parents. She encouraged him not to give up on his ambitions, not that he had many, other than to get a better job and move to a larger town or city. She even made him believe that London was not out of the question. London, he always believed, was just an impossible dream. Vicki had dispelled that totally. They had conversed for hours, easily, and on all manner of subjects, which led to their laughing, crying, arguing, discussing, getting angry and getting sad, depending on which. Vicki had opened his eyes to so many new possibilities. When she told him that he possessed the kindest heart she had ever known, he was forced to hide his face from her as he could feel his eyes welling up with tears. No one had ever said such a beautiful thing to him before in all his life.

The house was deathly quiet as they left the bedroom and walked down the stairs. Vicki thought that she might start to cry at any moment. Jill and Sophie were both out, the latter no doubt round Giles's house, her chauvinist pig of a boyfriend. Vicki loved Sophie, she was her best friend, but, for someone who claimed to be a liberal feminist, it amazed her that she would go out with someone like Giles. It was like Germaine Greer cosying up to Hugh Hefner.

They were soon on their way to the station, Rhys's hand on Vicki's thigh as she drove in silence. Rhys, too, was quiet. They were sad to be parting but ecstatic at the same time. They both knew they were in love. They would not admit it to each other just yet, but they knew that that time would not be far off.

'I can't wait to come down again next weekend,' Rhys finally declared. 'The next few days are gonna be really hard.'

'The same here.' After a short pause, Vicki carried on, her voice brighter and her eyes shedding their sadness. 'Saying that, I'm going to need the week to recover!'

Rhys grinned. 'I know what you mean! Must get down to Boots to stock up.'

'Me, too,' Vicki replied with a smile.

'Hey, if we wanna make a few quid, why don't we buy some shares in Durex first? Their price will go through the roof.'

Vicki chuckled. 'Yeah, that's not a bad idea. Might be easier if I go on the Pill, though?'

'Let me know when you do. We'll sell the shares before then.'

They burst out laughing which did not stop until they arrived at St David's. They were on time but had only a few minutes to spare. On the concourse, they hugged each other, neither of them wishing to be the first to break off. Vicki's eyes were moist and Rhys felt a lump in his throat.

'Only a few days to wait. I'll call you tomorrow.'

'Tonight, please,' Vicki choked.

'Okay, tonight.'

Rhys finally let go of Vicki, picked up his holdall and turned to catch his train. After only a couple of paces, he turned back with a broad grin on his face. 'Oh, by the way, it was nice meeting your friends and the party was great.'

Vicki giggled and blew him a kiss, the happiest she had ever been in her life.

June 1970

Chapter 5

'Now where is it? It's got to be around here somewhere.'

The impatience in Rhys's voice reflected how hot and bothered he felt for he had been sweltering away for nearly five hours in his father's mustard-coloured Mini despite having the windows open wide.

It was scorching hot outside, being Midsummer's Day, and he was running late, not helped by the fact that at one stage the car had over-heated and broken down. While waiting for it to cool, with nothing better to do than gaze at the rusty wheel arch from the side of the road, he was worried that he would never make it to his destination in time ... if at all. But now, as it loomed closer, he knew he would soon be arriving and this came as a massive relief to him.

The day was an important one for Vicki had invited him to a party to celebrate her parents' wedding anniversary which coincided with the longest day of the year. It would be the first time Rhys had met them and he was on edge, keen to make a good impression.

With Vicki having received a first-class honours degree, the party would be a double celebration. She had been shocked but ecstatic when she heard the news, never imagining it possible. It had been Rhys who had made her believe that she was capable of it. Right up to the day of the first exam, he had continually urged her to believe in herself, to believe that she was bright, intelligent and diligent. His final words before she entered the Great Hall on campus for that first exam were 'show them what you've got', his fist clenched in front of him to inspire her, like a rugby captain rallying his team before entering the field of play. Vicki went in emboldened and confident and it paid dividends for she had succeeded like he said she would.

'Here's the lane,' he muttered, glancing at the scribble on the piece of paper on the passenger seat, the words corresponding with those on the name plate at the entrance to a narrow road on his right. 'She said it's just along here.' He indicated and turned in, the Mini almost at walking pace as he drove along the lane which was lined either side by neatly trimmed hedges and passing numerous cars parked bumper to bumper to his left. He was intrigued why there were so many and blew out his cheeks at the quality and expense of them. There were even two E-Type Jaguars, his favourite car of all.

He slowed down to barely a crawl as he passed the end of the line of cars and arrived at two imposing, black wrought-iron gates. To their side was a pedestrian gate which was open. He stopped in front and saw the beautiful, double-fronted stone house at the end of a short gravel drive. Next to the house was a triple garage, outside of which he recognised a white MG Roadster.

'Fuck me, I didn't think she lived in a house like this!'

He drove on, wondering where to park the Mini, as another long line of cars stretched far down the lane the other side of the gate.

'They must all be going to the party,' Rhys concluded. 'She said it was only a small affair with a handful of close friends. They must have a hell of a lot of close friends!'

Eventually, a quarter of a mile further on, the line of cars came to an end and Rhys pulled in. To his astonishment, for he had never seen one before in real life, he was parked next to a Rolls-Royce. When Rhys stood back to admire it, flexing his shoulders at the same time to relieve their stiffness, it seemed as if its massive grille would open up and devour the tiny Mini.

He wandered back down the lane, becoming more nervous with each step he took. This is a much grander party than Vicki had let on, he realised with a frown, admiring the cars. He wondered whether the four warm cans of lager in the Tesco carrier bag he was holding were appropriate for such an occasion. He was even more worried, however, at his choice of clothes. 'It's very casual, wear what you like.' He recalled and spoke Vicki's nonchalant advice word for word, then scolded himself for not asking her to be more specific. At least his Levi's 501 Shrink-To-Fit jeans, which covered his shiny tan Chelsea Boots, were new, though they felt a little tight, as if he had sat in the bath for too long in them. Well, either that or he had put on a bit of weight. He held in his stomach as he strolled up the lane, trying to relieve the strain around his waist, but then cursed when he noticed a couple of specks of oily dirt from the Mini's engine on his thighs. His blue and white gingham Ben Sherman shirt showed off his muscular torso to the maximum but he was conscious of the whiff of perspiration, which was impossible to hide, and regretted not spraying on his Old Spice deodorant that morning, not wanting it to clash with his Hai Karate aftershave. Rhys was also worried whether the Levi's waistcoat was a bit over the top. With all the denim he was wearing, he felt like a cowboy.

Finally, a moment later, with butterflies fluttering alarmingly in his stomach, he arrived at the pedestrian gate, passed through, and walked up the gravel drive, each crunch beneath his feet sounding like a step closer to the hangman's noose. He sucked in some enormous deep breaths, gulping down as much air as he could to try and calm his nerves. This was not what he had been expecting at all. In fact, it was worse, for when he pulled down on the handle of the butler bell, a tall, straight-backed, impeccably dressed man answered. He was wearing beige linen trousers and brown suede loafers. His sparkling white cotton shirt bore not a single crease and was as fresh as newly mown grass at the start of the cricket season. The two open buttons revealed wisps of grey-brown hair on a Mediterranean-tanned chest. Despite the heat, he was wearing a lightweight navy-blue blazer with a white silk handkerchief protruding with a flourish from the breast pocket. On his wrist, Rhys noticed a chunky gold watch. It was a Rolex.

'Yes?' Vicki's father enquired, looking Rhys up and down as if he were a workman arriving to carry out some job in the house.

'Oh, hello. Is Vicki around? I'm Rhys.'

'Ah, Rhys. Could you just wait a minute?' and with that Vicki's father turned away, leaving him on the doorstep without even the courtesy of a smile, handshake or invitation to come in.

Rhys stood stock still, feeling extremely self-conscious, an outsider looking in, as across the threshold hordes of elegantly dressed guests mingled in small groups with glasses of champagne and wine in hand. He witnessed two young girls dressed in black dresses and white pinnies refilling glasses. A third girl was offering canapés from a silver tray with the friendliest and politest of smiles. Some of the guests looked at him with intrigue before turning back to their conversations, wondering why he had not used the tradesman's entrance.

Thankfully, after what felt like the longest minute of his life, Rhys heard a familiar voice and saw Vicki rushing towards him. He opened his eyes wide. She looked beautiful beyond belief. She was wearing the finest of silk dresses that fell just above the knee with the thinnest shoulder straps imaginable. The dress carried a print of tiny red, yellow and pink flowers and was shaped perfectly around her waist, hips and behind. Her bronzed legs were bare and she wore oyster-white high-heeled shoes, with her rosy-red painted big toes protruding from the open fronts, matching the colour of her fingernails. A thin gold chain hung around her neck while a thick gold bangle was pushed high up one of her wrists. Her honey-blonde corkscrew hair was as luxuriant as ever and, to Rhys's surprise, she wore the faintest hint of mascara and pale blue shadow on her eyes.

'Rhys!' Vicky virtually jumped into his arms and gave him a smacker of a kiss on his lips. The closest guests raised their eyebrows in surprise. 'Where have you been? I thought you'd be here earlier.'

'I had a bit of trouble with the car and it took me longer to get here than I thought. But anyway, here I am.'

Vicki clutched his hand and led him into the hallway and then into the enormous living room which Rhys thought even larger than a tennis court, and for a doubles match at that. He was in awe as he surveyed the room's splendour, magnified by the blazing sun casting thick beams of yellow-white light through the leaded panes of the striking windows. Even he had to crane his neck right back to gauge the height of the ceiling which held a glistening chandelier at its centre. His two-up, two-down back in Pontypridd would easily fit in here, he thought incredulously. All the furnishings were of the highest quality and the furniture gleamed in the sunlight. The fawn carpet was so new and plush that Rhys was afraid to walk on it, nervous as to what piece of detritus might be sticking to the bottom of his shoes from the well of the Mini. The guests matched the splendour of the living room. He felt like a tramp.

'I've got a bone to pick with you. You didn't tell me there'd be so many people here and you could've warned me about the dress code,' Rhys whispered as Vicki asked one of the girls to fetch Rhys a glass of champagne.

'Oh, you look fine. Don't worry about it,' Vicki replied with a dismissive flick of her hand. 'In fact you look wonderful,' and she squeezed his hand in affection.

'You do, too, just stunning.'

Vicki looked up at him with a smile so sunny the room lit up twice as brightly.

'I must introduce you to my parents; they've been dying to meet you.' She tugged at his hand and directed him to the back of the living room where her parents were talking to some other guests. Rhys realised as they approached that her father was the man who had answered the door. 'Sorry to interrupt. Mum, Dad, this is Rhys,' Vicki declared proudly. The guests her parents were talking to said they would catch up with them later and moved away.

'Oh, Rhys, it's nice to meet you at last,' Vicki's mother replied, in an accent so perfectly English it seemed she had slid the apostrophe into the correct place herself. She looked him up and down with a lopsided smile before extending her hand. Her tone was not the most enthusiastic and Rhys understood immediately that she was not too impressed.

'It's a pleasure to meet you, too, Mrs Mitchell, and you, Mr Mitchell.' Rhys's words sounded over-rehearsed and he shook their hands rather too formally. Vicki's father, who stood grim-faced, could barely bring himself to say hello.

Facially, Vicki's mother was the spitting image of her daughter, with only a couple of lines across her brow and crow's feet around her eyes to reflect the difference in age. Figure-wise, however, there was no comparison. Her hips had clearly seen leaner days and her behind was so big, Rhys childishly thought, that she would most certainly pack one hell of a fart. On the underside of her bare arms, wrinkly flesh hung loose and wobbled about unattractively. Her large-patterned dress was rather frumpy and a size or two too small for her, accentuating a wide undulation of fat across her stomach. What was more, her feet were jammed so tightly into her black patent shoes, Rhys thought they would burst like balloons at any moment. The colour of her shoulder-length, straight hair with centre-parting matched her daughter's but was limp and straw-like due to overuse of peroxide.

'Vicki's told us so much about you?' Mrs Mitchell continued.

'Not everything, I hope!'

Rhys regretted saying it the second the words tumbled out of his mouth and Mrs Mitchell's smile dissolved in front of him. Her husband looked away. Vicki gave him a nudge which only made matters worse and the ensuing silence inched into awkwardness. 'Shall I get rid of that carrier bag for you?' Mrs Mitchell eventually asked, stiffly, looking down at his hand.

'Yeah, if you wouldn't mind. I brought a few cans of lager with me. Sorry they're a bit warm but they've been in the car all day.'

Mrs Mitchell beckoned one of the girls to take the bag from Rhys and instructed her to put the cans in the fridge. She did not reveal that this was to keep them out of view rather than to cool them. Mr Mitchell sighed in an obvious manner and looked around the room with heavy-lidded detachment to see whom he might speak to instead of this hillbilly. He was even more determined to do so after Rhys's next comment.

'Wow, is that a colour telly over there?' Rhys's eyes were open wide in wonderment as he gazed at the television set in the corner. 'I've never seen one before. I hear all the newsreaders and presenters are wearing multi-coloured ties these days to show off.'

Mr Mitchell finally spoke, his tone belittling and sarcastic, though Rhys did not pick up on it. 'Yes, it is, and we'll put it on for you later if you can stand the excitement.'

'Really! That would be great,' Rhys replied as if he would soon experience the most incredible event of his life.

Vicki had remained quiet during these initial exchanges but could see that her parents thought little of her boyfriend and, inwardly, she was glum, for she had so wanted them to like him. It's early days, she tried to convince herself despondently.

'So you've come all the way from Wales?' Mrs Mitchell enquired, though she knew that he had.

'Yeah, that's right. It took longer than I thought 'cos the Mini broke down. I keep telling my dad to change it.

It's seven years old now and done over sixty thousand miles, but, you know, money's tight so he can't afford it.'

'And what does your father do?'

'He's a miner. Well, he was, anyway, before he did his back in. He's on the sick now and probably won't work again.'

'I'm sorry to hear that,' Mrs Mitchell replied insincerely. Her husband stood next to her, stony-faced, saying nothing.

'Oh, before I forget, congratulations on your wedding anniversary and could I just say that your house is absolutely beautiful.' Mrs Mitchell smiled and thanked him as did her husband. This example of his charm and politeness was the only reason they could fathom, so far, why their daughter liked him so much. Mrs Mitchell acknowledged grudgingly that he was quite good-looking, in an obvious sort of way, to her eye, but, deep down, she was appalled at her daughter's choice of boyfriend. She didn't even need to ask her husband what he thought.

Things only got worse, however, when Rhys resumed. 'You must be so proud of Vicki getting a first-class honours degree. I certainly am.' He looked down at Vicki who smiled back. 'I'm sure she'll do really well in the job she's starting. We found a nice flat together in Battersea the other day and we can't wait to move in.'

Mrs Mitchell almost spilt her drink at the news for this was the first she had heard of it, likewise her husband, who gave his daughter a murderous look that would have made Charles Manson proud. Vicki went bright red and looked down at the carpet, shifting her feet uneasily. Rhys stood there bemused. He thought Vicki had already told them.

'Victoria, this is news to us. When were you planning on saying anything?'

The tone of her mother's voice was calm as she did not want to create a scene in front of her guests but her husband had to take two deep breaths to stop himself from breaking out into a rage. They were aware that Vicki had found a flat to rent but knew nothing about Rhys moving in with her.

'I was going to tell you later,' Vicki replied weakly, her chin seemingly stapled to her chest and eyes still fixed firmly on the carpet.

The silence that ensued threatened to suffocate them as Vicki's parents tried to make sense of the news. Rhys shifted on his feet, knowing he had put one of them well and truly in his mouth. It came as a relief to them all when Mrs Mitchell eventually addressed him.

'So you've found a job in London as well?'

'Yeah. I'm really excited about it. I'm gonna be a post boy at Marks and Spencer's head office in Baker Street. My mum's already onto me about getting her some discount and wants me to find out why they don't accept Green Shield Stamps,' Rhys replied, laughing, though no one else did. 'It's the first time I've ever had to wear a suit. Vicki had me traipsing round Oxford Street all day to find one.'

'A post boy? You must be pleased?'

Once again, Rhys failed to recognise Mr Mitchell's sarcasm.

'Yeah. I can't wait,' he replied proudly.

Mrs Mitchell was about to speak but her husband interrupted her and took control. 'Victoria, we'll talk about this later; we've got to go and mingle with our guests. Come on, Penny.' He beckoned his wife to join him. 'It's been nice meeting you, Rhys.' The way he said it suggested he would not be unhappy if he never saw him again.

Vicki's parents walked off with angry stares directed at their daughter. They didn't even bother to look at Rhys. Vicki's face was a picture of gloom and she sipped nervously from her glass of wine. Rhys took a larger sip from his glass of champagne. He needed it.

'Sorry for putting you in it, Vick. I thought you'd told them?'

'I was going to. I just wanted to find the right moment.'

'Well, they know now. Don't worry, Vick, they'll come round to the idea. It can't be easy knowing your kids are growing up and going their own way.'

'Yeah, I suppose you're right,' Vicki replied uncertainly. It quickly became apparent to her that Rhys had not understood that the problem was him and not necessarily her leaving home. She knew her parents would be delighted if she found a suitable boyfriend and would have no qualms about her moving in with him if she did. She bit her tongue, not wishing to upset Rhys, but she was determined to fight it out with her parents when the time came. 'I'm sorry about my parents' attitude, Rhys. They can be so pompous sometimes.'

'There's no need to say sorry. Like I said, I'm sure they'll come round to the idea. Your mum and dad are really nice.'

Vicki looked up at Rhys and smiled for she knew he meant it despite her parents' best attempts not to be. That's why she loved him so much. He was honest and genuine and only ever saw the good in anyone, unlike her younger sister Fiona's boyfriend, Jeremy, whom you couldn't trust an inch, but whom her parents adored because he was a bond trader in the City of London. Talking of the devil, Vicki saw them approach, accompanied by Sophie and Giles.

'So, Vicki, this must be Rhys?' Fiona began, her eyes dancing in fascination as she stared at him a little too long for Rhys's comfort.

'Rhys, this is my little sister, Fiona,' Vicki advised, emphasising the word 'little'.

'Nice to meet you, Fiona,' Rhys replied, extending his hand. 'Hi, Sophie, Giles, hope you're both okay?'

'Nice to meet you, too,' Fiona returned, shaking his hand and holding onto it longer than was necessary, her eyes burning into him. Vicki had told Rhys that her sister was a bit of a man-eater and already he could understand why. No doubt she had to take the initiative herself, however, for, in complete contrast to her sister, Fiona was no oil painting. She was short and dumpy with thick calves and a moon face. Her chestnut-brown, Vidal Sassoon-inspired urchin hairstyle, which she modelled on Mia Farrow, didn't suit her at all and only accentuated the chubbiness of her cheeks. It crossed Rhys's mind whether Mrs Mitchell had been a bit naughty with the milkman, or whether they had collected the wrong baby from the maternity ward, so little did she resemble Vicki.

'I'd like to introduce you to Jeremy.'

'Nice to meet you, Jeremy.'

'Nice to meet you, too, Taffy,' Jeremy replied with a cheese-grater grin. He tried to sound friendly but the reference to 'Taffy' came out in a very condescending manner. Fiona, Sophie and Giles all laughed along, though Vicki's and Rhys's half-smiles were forced. Rhys took an instant dislike to him and thought he had even less of a chin than Giles. He had met Giles a few times in Exeter and couldn't stand him. The way he belittled Sophie in front of everyone was appalling and embarrassing, and he was more right-wing than Hitler and Mussolini combined. He couldn't understand why Sophie put up with it and knew the first time he had met her that her liberal feminism was false and an excuse to appear modern. She loved nothing better than to run around for Giles and do whatever he wanted. She had a good heart, though, and Rhys could see why Vicki liked her so much. They, too, were moving to London, as Giles was taking up a position as a trainee with the international division of Barclays Bank. Sophie never spoke about work, but, then again, Giles was loaded. His parents had bought him a penthouse flat overlooking Lord's Cricket Ground and Rhys and Vicki suspected that Giles wanted Sophie to stay at home all day to maintain it in all its splendour, a role she appeared quite happy to play.

'So, Rhys, what happened to you socialists on Thursday? You took a right drubbing.' Giles could not disguise his unbridled glee at the Tories being returned to power in the General Election.

'I'm still in shock if you want to know. I can't believe it. It was a real surprise and the country'll suffer for it now, you watch. I blame the World Cup, myself, you know, England losing to West Germany last week. Everyone was miserable after that and took it out on Harold and the government.'

'Never thought we'd be so grateful to the Huns,' Jeremy chipped in with a smirk. Fiona laughed along sycophantically. 'Wilson was absolutely useless,' he went on, flicking away a loose thread from the lapel of his royal-blue, pinstripe seersucker jacket as if the ex-Prime

Minister had been responsible for putting it there in the first place. 'Mind you, Heath's a bit too European for my liking, what with him wanting to join the Common Market. I say we should stay out. We are British, after all. We don't want anything to do with those scummy foreigners.'

'Here, here,' Giles hollered.

'Here, here,' Sophie and Fiona repeated like parrots.

Rhys and Vicki said nothing. They despaired at the arrogance and small-mindedness of these male representatives of Little England and their toadying partners.

'Sophie, darling, would you mind tootling off to fetch me a glass of champers from one of the girls?'

'Of course not, Giles.' And with that, Sophie hurried off to satisfy her boyfriend's command without batting an eyelid.

Rhys glanced at Vicki who was furious at her friend's pathetic submission. Her fury only intensified when she heard Giles's next whispered comment. 'She might have got a two-one but she knows her place.' He guffawed throatily, as did Jeremy and Fiona, before nudging Rhys on the shoulder. 'You keep a tight rein on Vicki now. Don't let that first of hers go to her head. Mustn't let these fillies rise above their stations, you know.'

Giles, Jeremy and Fiona guffawed even louder, drawing the attention of some of the other guests. Rhys and Vicki remained stern-faced, Vicki biting her lip with all her might to stop herself from answering back angrily. Rhys was perplexed at Giles's attitude. 'I'm really proud of Vicki and you should be of Sophie, too. Vicki can do whatever she wants in her life and I'll always be there to support her. I'll never treat her like a doormat. All this women's libbers stuff is great as far as I'm concerned. Why shouldn't women get on?' Vicki stroked Rhys's back as a sign of her love and agreement and their three companions stopped laughing. Rhys locked his stare on Giles with eyes as cold as a winter's dawn and as hard as a dictator's heart until the latter was forced to look away. Everyone went quiet and the atmosphere was thick enough to chew.

'Jeremy pulled off a trade worth squillions the other day, didn't you, honey?' Fiona suddenly threw into the conversation, changing the subject and eager to show off the worth of her boyfriend. 'He's probably the best bond trader in the City,' she added fawningly.

'Is that right, Jeremy?' Giles was all ears waiting for the response as nothing got him more animated than the subject of money.

'Yes. A very satisfying trade it was, too,' Jeremy replied with a whinnying laugh, as Fiona clutched his arm proudly, looking like a girl who believed the greatest man on earth was all hers. With a frown, Jeremy yanked his arm away sharply as he did not want her creasing his Pierre Cardin jacket and Herbie Frogg shirt.

No doubt he's spending it on his other girlfriends, Vicki thought. It was common knowledge that Jeremy was carrying on behind her sister's back while she was away at university in Bristol. Fiona utterly refused to believe it.

Rhys was totally flummoxed as he listened to Jeremy and Giles discuss high finance in the City. He had no idea what a bond trader was or did and, frankly, he couldn't care less. He just wanted to extricate himself from this group of God's chosen few and talk to someone who spoke a language he understood. Outside of Vicki, he despaired that such a person was in attendance. But then, to his heart's delight, through the French windows that opened up onto the garden at the back of the house, he caught sight of Karen standing alone. He had forgotten Vicki telling him that she would be coming and staying over just like him and couldn't wait to listen to the familiar lilt of a Welsh accent. 'Excuse me everyone. I can see Karen in the garden all by herself. I'll just go and say hello.'

'Catch up with you later,' Giles replied, looking over his shoulder and wondering impatiently where his doormat had got to with his drink. He was just being polite and did not mean what he said. He thought Rhys was just an unsophisticated, uneducated nonentity and, like his friends in Exeter University who had met Rhys, wondered what Vicki could possibly see in him once you stripped away the good looks. Fiona and Jeremy were also inclined to that way of thinking, judging by their initial impressions, though Fiona imagined a roll in the hay with him would probably be a fabulous experience. In a moment of pomposity, she thought herself as Lady Chatterley and Rhys as her gamekeeper lover. Fiona certainly had a high opinion of herself.

Thankfully, Vicki also found a reason to escape the obnoxious pigs and her stupid sister. 'I just need to talk to those friends of my parents over there a min, Rhys. I'll join you in the garden later.' She touched his thigh lightly before walking over to a group of people standing by the window. Rhys left at the same time and made his way into the garden.

'Hi, Kar.'

'Oh, hi Rhys. How you doing?'

'Good, thanks. Always nice to see a friendly Welsh face.'

'Same here. It's a bit intimidating in there if I'm honest. I can't really understand what they're all on about.'

Rhys nodded and grinned. 'You can say that again. I just had to get away from Giles and that Jeremy bloke. God, they're so dull.'

'Yeah, you're right. That Giles is a right wanker.'

'Karen! Wash your mouth out with soap and water. I never knew nice Cardiff girls used language like that.'

'We don't usually but blokes like him bring out the worst in us.'

They both chuckled and gazed out over the secluded tree-lined garden with the lawn so immaculate it would not have looked out of place on the Centre Court at Wimbledon, though it extended so far and wide that Rhys thought it at least the size of a football pitch. With the sun still high in the sky, they both had to admit that the scene was idyllic. Other guests were mingling on the patio, enjoying the warmth, and when a couple left the swing seat Rhys tapped Karen on the shoulder and pointed it out to her. He walked over to it and Karen followed. They sat down on the soft cushions and gently rocked themselves back and forth, Karen holding her face up to the sun.

'This is very pleasant, you have to say.'

'Yeah, Rhys. Beats my backyard in Cardiff with the coal shed.'

'It's a different world here, innit? Vicki's very lucky.'

'Yeah, she is, but she's so lovely you'd never think she came from such a privileged background. She's so down to earth and caring. That's why I like her so much.'

'And that's why I love her so much, too,' Rhys declared.

Karen turned her face away from the sun and looked at him. 'She loves you as well. You know that, don't you? She'd do anything for you.'

'And I would for her. She's everything to me.'

Karen smiled before adding, half playfully, 'I know she is, but if you ever hurt her, I'll cut your balls off, and with a blunt knife at that, alright!'

Rhys laughed. 'I'll never hurt her, never, you can rest assured of that.'

'Good.'

There was a lull in the conversation and they gazed around the garden at some of the other guests. Karen sighed in awe of some of the beautiful outfits worn by the young women. Rhys decided that the next time he needed some trousers, he would open up his mind and look for something other than denim jeans.

'Her mum and dad seem nice,' Rhys suddenly threw in.

'Yeah, they are. They're always really friendly towards me.'

Rhys wanted to agree the same towards him but hesitated. 'I wish Vicki had warned me about the dress code. I could have worn the suit I bought at C&A the other day. When her father answered the door I could tell he wasn't too impressed. He must have thought I was a right country bumpkin.'

'Oh, I'm sure he was alright about it. He's a real gentleman who's done very well for himself. He started off with nothing, apparently, though Vicki's mum comes from a wealthy family. He's a top knob in the City now.'

'We had a bit of a chat and I put my foot right in it, though I blame Vicki if I'm honest.'

'Oh, what happened?'

'Well, I mentioned the flat we're getting together 'cos I thought they already knew but Vicki hadn't said a word to them.'

'You didn't, did you?' Karen looked at him wide-eyed, her mouth slightly open in surprise.

'Yeah. Like I said, I thought they knew. They became decidedly frosty after that and I think Vicki's in for it.'

'God, I know Vicki was really worried about telling them. That must have been excruciating.'

'Yeah, it was. I don't know why Vicki hadn't told them, though. Strange that.'

'Well, it is a serious move, isn't it? I think she knew she might have some trouble.'

'Why's that?'

'Well, I think they probably thought she'd find a nice young man from around these parts, preferably with a few quid in his pocket, like her sister has.'

'I could never imagine Vicki going out with a prick like Jeremy.'

'You're right there, Rhys, no chance.'

'So, you believe her parents might think I'm not good enough for her then? I thought they were only offy towards me 'cos they didn't know anything about us moving in together and that it must have come as a bit of a shock to them to know that their little girl is finally leaving home to live with someone.'

Karen didn't reply straight away because she knew she was treading on sensitive ground. She'd had many chats with Vicki about Rhys and her parents and knew exactly what they thought. When Vicki had spoken to them about him, his background, his education, his prospects, they had become very concerned. They were ambitious for their daughter and thought Rhys might hold her back. Karen was truthful but diplomatic in her reply to Rhys, knowing that the issue was more serious than she could reveal. 'Umm, there is a bit about them not thinking you're good enough for their daughter, I have to admit, but then again I think most parents believe that of their kids, so I wouldn't worry about it too much. Vicki's crazy for you and you know how single-minded she is. When she puts her mind to something, she always gets what she wants. Once they get to know you better, they'll be fine.'

Rhys went quiet, thinking about Karen's reply. Deep down, he had feared that her parents might disapprove of him, but, now that it had been confirmed, it hurt. 'I was hoping her parents wouldn't be such snobs ...,' but, before he could finish the sentence, Karen shot him down.

'They're not snobs, I tell you. Well, perhaps her mother is a bit. Her dad started at the bottom, slogging his guts out as a fish packer in Billingsgate Market in the East End of London. At the same time he was doing that, he put himself through night school to improve his education and eventually found an office job in the City. He's running a top brokerage firm now. You've got to hand it to him. They just want the best for their daughter, that's all.'

'Oh, thanks, Karen.'

'Sorry, but you know what I mean. It's like what I said, once they get to know you better, they'll be fine.'

Rhys wasn't convinced but he wasn't short of fighting spirit, either. 'I suppose her dad's story's a bit like what I've got in mind. Now that I've got my foot in the door at Marks and Sparks, I'm gonna work my way up. It's what I told Vicki. Being a post boy is just a start. You watch, Karen, I'll make 'em all proud of me.'

Karen smiled and touched his arm. 'Good for you,' she replied. But she did not reveal her doubts and was unable to look him in the eye.

As midnight approached, only Vicki, her family, Karen and Rhys remained outside on the patio, relaxing after what had been an enjoyable but exhausting day. The temperature was still in the low twenties and they were sipping glasses of champagne under a pitch-black sky pincushioned with stars. The bulb in the glass globe that sat on top of an ornate mock Georgian lamppost shone brightly and mixed with the light spilling through the windows behind them. Two floodlights fixed on the wall above their heads cast a carpet of white across the lawn as if searching for escapees from a prisoner of war camp, printing jagged black shapes in the areas where the shadows stood out sharp. Mrs Mitchell had finally kicked off her shoes, her feet sore and swollen. She was sitting on a white wrought-iron chair next to her husband, her head resting on his shoulder, her eyelids flickering every so often as she struggled to stay awake. Fiona and Karen were sitting with them around the garden table, chatting animatedly about the merits, or not, of David Bowie or, more cattily, surmising what on earth John Lennon could possibly see in Yoko Ono.

Unlike his wife, Mr Mitchell's senses remained alert and he glanced over occasionally at his elder daughter sitting next to Rhys on the swing seat. Neither he nor his wife had allowed meeting Rhys, and the news he had relayed, to ruin their enjoyment of the party, resolving to put the matter aside until the next day. As the evening progressed, they had barely come into contact with him and deliberately moved out of his way if a coming together appeared likely. Now, as Mr Mitchell caught sight of him putting his hand on his daughter's thigh, he just wished that Rhys would go up to bed, get up early in the morning and leave, and, most importantly of all, never darken his or Vicki's doorstep again.

For her part, Vicki knew that she would be facing a difficult confrontation with her parents the following day. She was up for the fight, though, and made repeated loving gestures towards Rhys, such as grabbing his knee, kissing his neck and stroking his thigh, to demonstrate to her parents where her loyalties lay. It was fortunate that her mother was feeling sleepy for she would not have taken too kindly to seeing her daughter deliberately run her hand over his crotch. That even made Rhys jump.

'I think it's time we went up, darling,' Mrs Mitchell suddenly said, stifling a yawn, as she moved her head from her husband's shoulder.

'You're right. I'm whacked,' he replied, sitting up straight and extending his arms high above his head.

Karen and Fiona were still babbling away as if the night was young, full of energy. Fiona had not even noticed her parents stir.

'I think I'm ready for bed, too,' Rhys whispered wearily to Vicki. 'I'm knackered and all this champagne has gone to my head. It's been a long day and I could do with a good night's sleep.'

Vicki sat up straight and released him, extending her arms out in front of her like a cat stretching its legs after a long sleep. 'Yeah, same here.'

'I'll go and get my bag from the car.' Rhys stood up and walked back into the house and out the front door.

'What time will Rhys be leaving in the morning?' Vicki's father asked.

'About ten, I think, because he needs to get the car back to his father by mid-afternoon.'

Mr Mitchell noted the time and gave the slightest of nods.

'That's right. Rhys is giving me a lift to the station,' Karen cut in, though Fiona wittered on as if she still had Karen's full attention.

'Oh, you mentioned you were meeting your mother in London. I remember now. You will pass on my regards to her, won't you?' Mrs Mitchell interjected.

'I will do, thanks. We're meeting at Paddington Station and then going on to Harrods.'

'Oh, wonderful. You must visit the food halls. They're stupendous.'

'I'm sure we will. We might take in a show later on as well.'

'You're just a bit too early for *Oh! Calcutta!,*' Vicki threw in with a laugh. 'That doesn't premier until next month.'

'Judging by all the fuss, I think my mum would have a heart attack if she saw all that naked flesh cavorting on stage. She was brought up a good Baptist girl, you know.'

Everyone began to laugh, including Fiona, who made a mental note to see it at the earliest opportunity.

When the laughter subsided, Mr Mitchell took his wife's hand and they stood up together. They wished the three girls a good night's sleep and kissed them lightly on the cheek. After moving his face away from Vicki, her father looked at her sternly before saying in a low voice, 'And we'll have a chat tomorrow; you, your mother and me.' Both Karen and Fiona heard the comment and looked away, knowing the reason why. Vicki just stood grim-faced and said nothing. Her parents departed, her father's arm around his wife's shoulders as they walked back into the house. They didn't bother asking Vicki to wish Rhys a good night on their behalf.

A couple of minutes later, Rhys returned, bag in hand. 'I missed your parents then?'

'Yeah, they've gone up,' Vicki replied a little unhappily. 'I'll show you to your room.'

Rhys picked up on Vicki's air of discontent and put his arm around her, kissing her lightly on the head. Vicki smiled and her spirits lifted. Fiona noted that, though Rhys was a bit of a blithering idiot in her mind, he did at least possess good manners and charm.

'Here you are,' Vicki declared as she opened the door to one of the spare bedrooms upstairs. She switched on the light and they walked in. Rhys briefly took in the spacious surrounds before dropping his bag to the floor. Vicki half-closed the door behind her and, instinctively, they nestled in each other's arms, kissing longingly and voraciously. 'Sorry you can't stay in my room tonight but my parents would never allow it, you know, under their own roof and all that.'

'Oh, God, don't worry. My parents would be the same.'

Vicki released Rhys and took a couple of paces back to the door. Before exiting, she turned round with a beaming smile and wished Rhys a good night before whispering, 'Don't lock it. I'll see you later.'

Rhys's smile mirrored Vicki's. It had been a tiring and trying day but at least it was going to finish on the highest of notes.

Chapter 6

'I'll see you in London next Saturday then. Can you believe it? Our own place! I can't wait.'

Rhys was as excited as a small boy meeting Father Christmas for the very first time. He was also feeling mightily relieved as he stood next to the lonely Mini, holding Vicki in his arms, for breakfast with her family had been purgatory, full of stilted conversation and unhappy faces. He had never felt so uncomfortable in all his life, gobbling down his cornflakes and toast more quickly than the time taken by Mrs Mitchell to butter a croissant. He couldn't leave the house fast enough. But with everyone else slowly savouring their breakfast, all Rhys could do was wait and sit there like a dummy, staring at his empty plate and dish, uncertain what to do with his hands, and observing the faces of Vicki's parents which expressed 'uncouth' loud and clear. It had not helped matters, either, that he had forgotten to pack another shirt, compelling him to wear the same one as the day before. Not even scrounging some deodorant from Vicki to spray on the shirt's armpits could mask the unmistakeable stench of stale sweat, in total contrast to Mr Mitchell's fresh, immaculately pressed Turnbull & Asser.

The doorstep farewells were equally uncomfortable but mercifully shorter. There were cursory handshakes but not for one second did Rhys witness a smile. And Vicki's parents couldn't even bring themselves to lie by saying that they hoped to see him again sometime. At least Fiona had been friendly, even managing a hug, pressing her crotch rather hard into his.

'Yeah, I can't wait, either. It's like we're starting new lives, just so exciting,' Vicki replied, clutching Rhys tightly.

'Come on, you two, or we'll be here all day,' Karen cut in impatiently, gooseberry-like. She had stood aside as the two love birds cooed at each other with nothing better to do than wonder whether Rhys's Mini would get her to the station on time or, judging by the rust, at all.

'Right, Kar, let's get going,' Rhys finally commanded, releasing Vicki and sliding into the driver's seat. Karen jumped in next to him after giving Vicki a quick hug.

'I'll call you in the week to tie up times for Saturday,' Vicki advised, looking through the open driver's window. Rhys gazed deeply into her eyes, smiled and acknowledged her with a nod.

The car started first time, much to Karen's relief. Rhys made a three-point turn and, with a final flashing smile and wave, drove off down the lane, the exhaust smoking worryingly. Vicki stood and stared, wiping a tear from her eye. She loved him so much. The pain of his being away for only a week was enough to crush her.

When the car disappeared from view, she turned her mind to her parents. They had been so rude to Rhys, acting as if he didn't even exist, she spat, no longer able to prevent her coiled anger from spiralling to the surface. Vicki knew that when she got back to the house, her confrontation with them would be immediate. Steeling herself, she took two deep breaths in an effort to summon up whatever reserves of strength she possessed for the battle ahead. She strode purposefully back down the lane and crossed the threshold of the front door with a skip for she was determined to be on the front foot attacking the bowling. She stomped into the kitchen, her face in a rage, and, with a furious tone to her voice, tore into her parents who were sitting with Fiona at the long, fashionably distressed, shabby chic table. 'Well, I hope you're proud of yourselves!' she rasped viciously.

'How dare you raise your voice at us like that, Victoria,' Mrs Mitchell shot back, standing for no nonsense. 'Remember who you are and who you're speaking to, Madam, and what's brought this on, anyway?' she continued assertively, feigning surprise.

'Oh, don't give me that,' Vicki volleyed back, moderating her tone. 'You both know exactly what I mean, treating Rhys as if he were something the dog brought in. I've never been so embarrassed in all my life.'

'That's not true,' Mrs Mitchell replied unconvincingly, avoiding her daughter's eye.

'Oh, yeah,' Vicki returned, rolling hers in incredulity.

'Victoria, please sit down, will you?' her father interrupted in a measured voice, 'and calm down.'

'Why should I?' Vicki replied a touch childishly.

'Sit down and shut up!' her father barked authoritatively, his look severe. Fiona lowered her eyes but failed to hide the hint of a smirk while doing so.

Vicki was seething but her father's command took the wind out of her sails and, after a moment's hesitation, she pulled back a chair and joined her family at the table. Her father deliberately waited another minute before beginning to speak, pouring himself a coffee in the meantime. He hoped that a period of silence might calm his daughter down. 'Now, that's better. Let's all talk about this sensibly.'

'What do you mean by *this*? He has got a name, you know. It's Rhys, if you haven't forgotten.'

Mr Mitchell trod carefully, like a day-old lamb. 'What we mean by *this* is your relationship with Rhys. As you can imagine, your mother and I were somewhat taken aback when we found out you were moving in together. You could have told us first.'

'Well, I was just waiting to find the right time, that's all,' Vicki replied unconvincingly.

'Why the need to wait? You could have told us as soon as you'd decided. We're not old fashioned, you know that. We understand these things,' Mrs Mitchell butted in.

But before Vicki could reply, her father did so for her. 'It's because you knew we might not approve of him. That's it, isn't it?' Vicki's silence and fixed stare at the table top confirmed her father's opinion. The silence stretched out, so much so that Fiona began to fidget uncomfortably in her chair, but at least an air of serenity had descended on proceedings. But this did not last for long for Mr Mitchell was determined to air all his views, however brutal. He had not risen to his position in life by being a shrinking violet. 'And to be frank, we don't approve.' Vicki's guts churned, and even Fiona trembled, for they were now getting to the heart of the matter.

'And why's that?' Vicki retorted stiffly. 'Is it because you disapprove of people who are kind, generous and understanding?'

'Don't be silly, Victoria. I'm sure Rhys is all of those things but if you want to get on in life and make something of yourself, you need … more.'

'Oh, you can be such a snob sometimes, Mum,' Vicki exploded, flinging a hand dismissively in front of her. 'It's all about background and money with you at the end of the day, isn't it?'

'That's not true, Victoria, and I resent that! How can you say such a thing? Look at your father; he started from nothing. It's not about background, or money, it's about ambition and wanting to get on in life. Your father worked twelve hours a day in Billingsgate but still got his qualifications from night school. Look at him now.'

'Jeremy's got lots of qualifications,' Fiona threw in smugly and unhelpfully. She earned herself a tirade of abuse from Vicki.

'Oh, why don't you shut up, you fat cow?' Vicki screamed, her face twisted in fury, resembling a Turneresque storm. 'And why won't you accept he's fucking every girl he can get his hands on, you stupid old bag?'

'VICTORIA! That's enough. Apologise to your sister,' Mrs Mitchell broke in angrily. Her father looked daggers at her.

'Why should I? She knows I'm right.'

Fiona possessed the hide of a rhinoceros, however. She remained seated and appeared the most composed person in the room. She replied measuredly but cuttingly at the same time. 'You're just jealous, that's all. Only because Jeremy earns oodles of money and owns a big house in Kensington while Rhys is some country bumpkin who barely knows how to hold a knife and fork properly. You're the one who won't accept the truth.'

An enraged Vicki stood up, lips pursed, to aim a slap at her sister, who cowered away in anticipation, but then thought the better of it. She sat down, but her stare towards Fiona remained murderous.

'Let's all calm down,' Mrs Mitchell broke in, 'and let's leave Jeremy out of this.'

The kitchen returned to silence but the atmosphere was sulphuric.

'Good morning, Mrs Mitchell, Mr Mitchell, Victoria, Fiona.'

The greeting expressed from the door by their long-standing cleaning lady startled everyone. She had let herself into the house a few minutes earlier without anyone noticing and, on hearing all the raised voices in the kitchen, decided to start work in the living room first. She needed access to the Pledge and duster in the kitchen, however, so took advantage of the temporary lull to gingerly make her approach.

'Oh, good morning, Maria. I didn't hear you come in,' Mrs Mitchell replied. 'If you need to grab anything, just go ahead.'

Maria busied herself in a couple of cupboards as quickly as possible and hurried out, closing the door behind her. She knew all about tension in the air, for her own Italian family was always in such a state.

Mr Mitchell tried to bring some decorum back to proceedings. 'Let's keep our voices down and talk sensibly about this. Victoria, before you say another word, just listen to what I have to say. Your mother and I have only got your best interests at heart. You're a very bright girl and we're extremely proud of you. When I heard you'd got a first, it was one of the happiest days of my life.' Vicki lowered her eyes, a touch embarrassed, but warmed on hearing her father's kind words. Fiona looked glum. She didn't like praise being lavished on her sister and knew that she was unlikely to match her academic achievements. 'You're starting a new life in

London in an excellent company and the world's your oyster, but we worry that your involvement with Rhys will only hold you back.'

'Why, what do you mean? You think you know him but you don't.'

Vicki's reply was as sharp as a paper cut and the brief ceasefire was on the point of breaking down. Mr Mitchell was determined to remain composed and to sound as wise and persuasive as possible, like when gently requesting his staff to reconsider their over-optimistic sales forecasts. But before he could carry on, his wife interrupted him, tossing a hand grenade into the battlefield and making matters worse. 'It's important to have a good man at your side, Victoria.'

'But Rhys *is* a good man! How can you say such a thing?' Vicki fired back with the force of a cannonball, her cheeks crimson.

Mr Mitchell rolled his eyes at his wife's crassness and experienced the damp, seeping unease of despair like rain in a leaking shoe as the vitriol returned. The voices became raised once more and no one cared whether Maria could hear them or not. Fiona looked down, smirking. It was at moments like these when being the only male in the household made Vicki's father feel impotent as reason flew out of the window to be replaced by high emotion.

'You just won't listen, will you, Victoria? Go on then, throw your life away and get involved with that blithering idiot of yours for all I'm concerned. I don't care, it's your life.' Mrs Mitchell had snapped and brushed her husband's hand away as he tried to calm her down. Vicki just stared incredulously at her, open-mouthed. Even Fiona was shocked. 'What's he got going for him? Nothing!' Mrs Mitchell yelled. 'Three 'O' Levels, that's all.' Vicki averted her look, remembering the lie she had told her mother a few weeks earlier. 'And what does he do? He packs boxes in a warehouse. Wow! You must be proud of him. Of course, he is moving up in the world. He's going to be a post boy at Marks and Spencer,' she continued sarcastically. 'And no doubt when you give up work to start a family one day, he'll really be in a position to support you, won't he? Use your head, Victoria, for God's sake.'

'Dad started at the bottom. Why can't Rhys?'

'Your father's one in a million. Can't you see that? And, by the way, what's wrong with Jeremy? He's hard working, intelligent and ambitious, just the type you should be looking for.'

Fiona looked up with a contented grin like the fattest of cats who'd just found the creamiest of creams poured over the tastiest of mice.

'And you're the one who said to leave Jeremy out of this! You make me sick sometimes.'

'How dare you speak to your mother like that!' Mrs Mitchell screamed back. Her husband was convinced he could see steam pouring out of her ears. 'And don't think we didn't notice you running your hand up his crotch last night like some cheap whore. Your father told me all about it this morning.'

Maria dusted away diligently in the living room, shocked at the shouting in the kitchen. And she thought *her* family was mad.

'How dare you? How dare you say something like that to me? You should be ashamed of yourself!' Vicki was beside herself with anger and stood up abruptly, tipping over a glass of orange juice as she pushed hard at the table. Fiona had to jump smartly out of the way to avoid it. Her father attempted to put his hand on Vicki's arm to sit her down but she punched it away with all her might and ran to the door. Before exiting, she turned round, screaming. 'Well, there's nothing you can do about it! I love him and we're moving in together next week and that's that. You can all go and fuck yourselves for all I care.' And with that, Vicki burst out of the kitchen, slamming the door behind her, and ran up the stairs to her bedroom.

'VICTORIA! How dare you use language like that to your mother and father! Go on then, run off with that Midnight Cowboy of yours,' Mrs Mitchell snorted, like a horse after a gallop, recalling the unsophisticated hunk from the recent film of the same name, 'and see what I care!' She was fuming and shouting so loudly that the noise would have sent a family of howler monkeys whimpering for cover. Incandescent, she did not even react to the orange juice dripping onto the glazed Sicilian tiles she had so painstakingly imported from Italy to grace her kitchen floor. Her husband turned the glass up and dabbed at the dripping with some kitchen roll before putting his hand on his wife's shoulder. No one moved a muscle, like Renaissance statues. Fiona stared downwards in complete shock at what she had just heard. She couldn't wait to tell Jeremy. This was an experience she had to share with someone.

Vicki threw herself onto her bed, having slammed yet another door behind her. She lay on her back, seething, and locked her eyes on the ceiling. Tears quickly formed and she fingered them away. How could they be so nasty? she asked herself. She had never seen her mother in such a state. And Fiona, the stupid cow! She hoped Jeremy would break her heart and teach her a lesson.

As the minutes ticked by, Vicki's heartbeat returned to something closer to normal and she regained her composure. Worryingly, however, for it had never crossed her mind for one nanosecond before, she wondered whether what her parents had said contained more than a degree of truth.

Chapter 7

'Wait!' Rhys's sharp command stopped Vicki in her tracks. She had just turned the latch key in the Yale and half-opened the door. The wood of its frame was markedly rotten and the British Racing Green paint of the door itself peeling badly. When Rhys had first seen the flat, he wondered whether it had been a job lot flogged off by Lotus. They had just collected the key from the letting agent, handed over their deposit and first month's rent, and were in a high state of excitement. Even the climb up three flights of stairs to the top floor of the once grand Victorian town house, carrying two heavy suitcases each, failed to dampen their mood.

'Why, what's up?'

'Nothing, but I think we should do this properly,' and, before Vicki could say another word, Rhys scooped her up into his arms. 'Isn't this the way it's done, crossing the threshold for the first time, like?'

'Usually after you get married,' Vicki replied with a wide smile.

'Is that a hint?' Rhys returned curiously. Vicki did not answer but the lingering smile told Rhys everything he needed to know and it was certainly not discouraging. He smiled back and gave her a quick kiss on the lips. 'Here goes,' and with that, he stepped over the threshold and into the gloomy narrow hallway, so narrow in fact that Vicki, still lying across Rhys's arms, had to tuck her head and legs in to avoid scraping them against the walls.

After only a few strides, they arrived in the living room. Besides the bedroom and bathroom, it was the only other room in the flat. In one of the corners, the landlord had fixed a cupboard above a free-standing gas cooker with grill. Alongside it was a flimsy wooden table, beneath which sat a pedal bin. Next to this was a sink unit with Ascot boiler above. The corner of the living room was the kitchen.

In the centre of the room, a two-seater sofa in a blotchy, burgundy velour fabric was positioned next to an armchair which was covered in a worn, faded cotton fabric printed with large white water lilies. When she first saw it, Vicki had jokingly referred to it as their Monet armchair. Rhys had not had a clue what she was on about, and still didn't. The fabric down its back was badly shredded, no doubt caused by the claws of a previous occupant's cat. Vicki and Rhys had been explicitly told by the agent that pets were strictly forbidden. Perhaps this was why the previous occupant left, Rhys mused, as, after setting Vicki down, he pushed the sofa and armchair against a wall to create more space, leaving faint meandering lines across the original stripped floorboards which had been stained amber gold.

Vicki loved the floor and it was the main reason why she had reluctantly gone along with Rhys's view that they should take the flat. Sensing this reluctance at the time, Rhys had agreed to Vicki's request that they should stay for a short period only, perhaps a year or so, during which time they would build their savings and find a better place. Rhys was happy to accommodate her, though he personally loved the flat.

While Rhys was pushing back the sofa, Vicki had taken two steps to the room's only window and looked down onto Latchmere Road. A steady stream of cars, vans and buses flowed up and down the hill, for their flat was positioned on the gradient of the road close to where it joined Lavender Hill. Rhys had been excited beyond words to know that he was going to be living near the road which carried the name of one of his favourite films, *The Lavender Hill Mob,* and it was the first thing he told his mother when he rang her that afternoon to confirm their accepting the flat. She, too, had been excited, joking with Rhys whether he was able to see Alec Guinness and Stanley Holloway walking along the road from his window. Vicki had joined in the merriment but soon put a dampener on it when reminding them that they had probably never set foot in the area in the first place as the film had been made in Ealing.

The view from the grimy window was hardly compelling and neither were the pillar-box red walls Vicki saw when she turned round, which only made the flat look gloomier in her eyes. Rhys had promised to paint over them as soon as they moved in, a condition the landlord had agreed to, so long as they paid for the materials themselves. The landlord isn't Peter Rachman, I hope, Rhys had said to Vicki at the time and, to be fair, the flat could not be classed as a slum like those owned by the notorious Notting Hill property tycoon, but it wasn't far off. Like Lotus, Rhys had wondered whether the Post Office, too, had ventured into selling paint and he joked with Vicki that he would contact the Royal Navy next to see whether they had any cheap battleship grey on offer.

'Just get white, please,' Vicki replied and then repeated, worried that Rhys might actually look into it.

But none of this mattered to Vicki as she followed Rhys out of the living room into the hallway and back outside onto the landing to fetch the suitcases. She was simply beside herself with joy at moving into a property of her own with the man she loved. Ever since she had been a young girl, she had dreamt of such a moment. Yes, the flat was minuscule, a kaleidoscope of ugly colours and clash of different styles, but most of that could be changed easily enough, she reasoned, and they wouldn't be there for long, anyway. What was more durable was her love for Rhys, her love of London and the promise of an exciting new job.

They re-entered the flat, dumped the suitcases and shut the door behind them. As Rhys pushed at the bedroom door, it banged into a hard object on the other side before it was even half open. So small was the bedroom that the double bed dwarfed it, and, once they were both inside, the gaps between the outer frame of the bed and the wardrobe and chest of drawers were so narrow that they had to shuffle sideways to get round to the opposite end. Fortunately, an original built-in cupboard gave them additional space for their belongings.

'I don't know about not being able to swing a cat in here, I think you'd struggle with a mouse,' Rhys joked with a smile which turned into a grimace when he noticed a patch of black in the corner nearest the window.

Vicki was more concerned at the mattress which was sagging, threadbare and included a number of stains. 'That's going straight away!' she exclaimed, crinkling her nose. Rhys agreed, though it didn't look too bad to his eye. After another cursory glance around, he stood full square to Vicki and took her in his arms, hugging her with all the love and affection he could muster. She reciprocated, leaning her head into his chest.

'Well, this is it, the start of a wonderful new life together,' Vicki declared.

'Absolutely. I'm just so excited,' Rhys concurred, stroking the palm of his hand lightly up and down her back.

'Me, too,' Vicki replied and, though Rhys could not see her face, he felt her smile against his chest. He smiled, too, before indulging in a bit of mischief.

'You know, Vick, we've talked so much about loads of stuff these past few months but I don't think I ever asked you whether you were religious or not.'

Vicki moved her head back and looked up at him with a befuddled expression. 'What do you mean?'

'Well, as this is our first day, we're gonna have to christen the flat, aren't we?' Rhys explained with that glint in his eye which Vicki knew meant only one thing. The feel of his erection against her confirmed it.

'I can't say I am but I'm not averse to getting down on my knees.'

Having done so, what she did next was not something you would see in any church.

December 1973

Chapter 8

But their new life together had not turned out to be so wonderful.

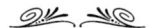

༒

Rhys was lounging barefooted on the sofa, wearing his stripy pyjama bottoms and Led Zeppelin T-shirt, with one leg on, one leg off. He was watching the small black and white television set and laughing along to *Are You Being Served?*. An empty plate with knife and fork lay on the floor next to him, a smear of deep orange providing the clue that he'd eaten baked beans on toast for his tea. The new sitcom was turning out to be one of his favourite programmes though Vicki thought it was average. The two loops of wire aerial were fixed in their optimum position for reception on top of the set. The slightest adjustment would result in a screen of fuzzy dots and, on more than one occasion, Rhys had had to be sharp with Vicki to be careful not to knock it.

Vicki was sitting in the armchair, which still retained its shredded printed covers. Her legs were curled up beneath her and a blanket was keeping her warm. This was her usual position now, her own private nest, though, for the first eighteen months, they had always snuggled up together on the sofa. She stared blankly at the screen, wondering what Rhys found so funny in the ridiculous Mrs Slocombe and the unoriginal double-entendre of her 'pussy'. Her spirits were low despite it being only a couple of weeks away from Christmas, a time of year she usually adored. Rhys had bought a miserable-looking fake Christmas tree, with shimmering silver foil for pine needles instead of the real ones that Vicki preferred. To her, the angel on top and assortment of dangling baubles looked as old and worn out as she was feeling and she wondered from where on earth he could possibly have bought them. Probably from Steptoe and Son, she mused, breaking out into the thinnest of smiles for the first time that evening.

The dreary tinsel stuck to the walls was not that much better, but then again, she couldn't complain, for she had asked him to arrange the Christmas decorations in the first place. After all, he had been out of work since the summer, and had time on his hands, while she was bringing in the bacon building her career as a marketing manager in the London office of an American company that manufactured clothing fabrics. She loved the job and, although the company was quite happy to take its pound of flesh, she never complained. After only a few months, her boss had left and Rhys pushed her day and night for a week to apply for the open position. Vicki thought it a waste of time for she was certain that they would be seeking a more experienced person. Eventually, she agreed, calculating that even if she failed, the company would recognise her ambition. Incredibly, she had succeeded and now controlled a department of ten with only her new boss, the sales and marketing director, standing between her and the company's top UK position itself, which carried the American corporate title of president. President Victoria Mitchell, Rhys would tease her in bed, bowing in reverence. He told her she'd make it before her thirtieth birthday. Once again she thought it nonsense but Rhys had the happy knack of proving her wrong time and time again. He truly believed in her ability, which only made her believe more confidently about herself, and she loved him for it.

As her mind wandered, she looked around herself. Not much had changed since their moving in together. The useless landlord and even more useless letting agent had still not resolved the mystery of the Ascot boiler, which burned one day and not the next, but at least it was going through one of its less erratic phases for the time being. The walls were now white, well, a pinky white, if Vicki was honest with herself, for even three coats of emulsion had not been sufficient to completely hide the pillar-box red beneath them. The window panes were as grimy as ever, more so in truth, for it was impossible to gain access to the outside to give them a good wipe. Boxes of clothes and books and lines of shoes ran the length of the bottoms of the walls as there was no other space for them. The same was true along both sides of the hallway which was now only passable in single file. In the bedroom, the black patch next to the window refused to disappear despite their best efforts and they had given up even trying. The old mattress had gone, thank God, and the new one was standing up well to their vigorous love-making - though, recently, it had not had much to stand up to at all. Vicki had taped a new poster of the now-famous Marc Bolan onto one of the walls and Rhys had joked whether this was because she secretly wished to lust over him when they were making love. Vicki had laughed uproariously at this but admitted to herself that it was not so far away from reality.

She only felt reasonably happy in the bathroom, which was modern at least, with an avocado-green bath tub and sink and white porcelain toilet. The canary-yellow tiles were acceptably clean, though, as there was no outside window or extractor fan, they had to wipe away some mould every now and again as the condensation settled in the grouting between the tiles and around the rim of the bath and sink. Rhys could be a bit tidier and cleaner in a perfect world, Vicki thought, but she had quickly come to realise that she was not living in a perfect world and, more disconcertingly, believed that she never might.

Thinking about the flat depressed her, so, for the umpteenth time, she closed her eyes and tried to shut it out. A loud cackle of laughter from Rhys drew her attention and, on re-opening them, she gazed down at him lying back on the sofa. Physically, he had changed little over the years though she had detected some flecks of grey in his hair by his temples which was now so long it covered his shoulders. He, too, had adopted a corkscrew hairstyle, in keeping with his idol, Robert Plant. Perhaps his stomach was not as washer board hard as when they had first met but then neither was hers in truth. She had put on weight recently though she still managed to fit into her work skirts easily enough. In reality, she knew they had stretched and expanded to accommodate her. Had she lost the incentive to stay trim? Was it a reflection of her relationship that she didn't care anymore? Vicki recognised these as worrying signs.

But her greatest worry was that they had not made the slightest upward progression in their relationship. As an individual she had, but, as a couple, they had in fact regressed. They were still stuck in this shit hole of a flat with no prospect of leaving. How Vicki laughed at the initial suggestion that they would be gone within a year. The main reason for this, in fact the only reason, was Rhys. He had totally underestimated the cost of living in London and his meagre savings had been eaten up faster than a bowl of food in front of a well-walked dog. But, fundamentally, the main problem had been his inability to hold down a job. He had lasted three months at Marks and Spencer before being told he had failed his probationary period. He was diligent but often lackadaisical and too trusting in the punctuality of the London Underground system. When the Sieff family themselves had begun to complain about the tardiness of their mail, Rhys was deemed responsible and his departure became inevitable. This had come as a terrible blow to him and it was two weeks before he plucked up the courage to tell his mother, who was nonetheless understanding. They had even both raised a chuckle when Rhys told her to forget about any discounted knickers for now and roared in laughter when she replied that she would have to go without as a consequence. He was determined to find a similar job and registered with a number of agencies, and every day, without fail, he would scour the appointments pages of the *Evening Standard*. Interviews came and went with no success and, as time passed by, Rhys became increasingly despondent. Vicki was his rock, however, constantly encouraging him and telling him not to give up, which raised his spirits. But weeks without work turned into months, during which Rhys had been able to contribute barely one new penny to their financial commitments which rested heavily upon

Vicki's shoulders. Her promotion had helped, but, at the end of each month, she found she had little left to build any savings.

Eventually, Rhys accepted that it was time to hang up his suit and put on his overalls again. He had desperately wanted to avoid going back to a job in a warehouse but he couldn't live with himself being a burden on Vicki. Accordingly, he returned to what he knew best, however badly paid, but even this was not without difficulty as tough economic times led to his being laid off on three separate occasions, joining the scarcely believable one million unemployed which the country registered for the first time in its history. Rhys blamed Heath and the uncaring Tories for this and longed for Labour to return to power. His last job had been at a timber merchant's in Putney which he had held down for almost a year. But since being let go, there had been nothing. He had tried hard to find work, for he was no slacker, but, for now, Lady Luck was deserting him.

The suit had made another airing, nonetheless, when Vicki and Rhys had attended the wedding of Giles and Sophie in the summer, just two weeks after Rhys had lost his job in Putney. It had been held in the delightful St Nicholas Parish Church in Arundel, followed by a reception in Arundel Castle itself. It had been an exquisite affair with the great and the good of Sussex and London society in attendance. Vicki had felt completely at home mixing with her old friends, but, for Rhys, the whole day had been worse than torture. At the reception, he found himself sitting next to Jeremy and some other chinless wonders and contributed little to nothing in the way of conversation, not understanding anything they were talking about. Their attempts to include him, by asking about his work, led him into telling a number of tongue-tied, far-fetched lies about a managerial position in a multi-national timber merchant's, with a head office in Sweden, from where they sourced the wood. Vicki cringed in embarrassment, her cheeks suffusing with blood, when she observed the sceptical looks on the faces around her. The closest the owner of the timber merchant's in Putney had ever been to Sweden was when he watched his favourite seedy films in a dingy cinema in Soho.

There had been one conversation at the reception, however, to which Rhys had contributed, but, after which, he experienced real unease. His table had been discussing the militant miners who, if not out on strike, were constantly threatening. Everyone at the table had been appalled at their behaviour, believing them to be holding the country to ransom for unreasonable demands in pay and working conditions. When Jeremy had commented that he would like nothing more than to line them all up and shoot them down, everyone had laughed, with the exception of Rhys, but, to his horror, including Vicki. He noted how she nodded when another criticism of the miners was opined around the table while at home she was always more sympathetic. Vicki had always supported the need to improve the lives and conditions of the working class and had always voted Labour in general elections. It was the goodness of her heart that was one of her main attractions to Rhys and vice versa. They both cared about people, particularly vulnerable ones. But now she was agreeing with the almost fascist opinions of the likes of Jeremy. Rhys looked at her with an expression as hard as drill bits, but she ignored him. When Rhys entered the conversation with insightful comments in support of the miners, everyone listened, firstly in shock that he actually possessed a tongue, and, secondly, because his arguments carried merit. But, ultimately, no one could agree or support his views, not even Vicki. When the conversation moved onto another subject, he looked daggers at her once again, but, as before, she ignored him. Rhys was so inwardly annoyed that he even ungraciously thought that Vicki's sober suit and absurd wide-brimmed hat only served to age her and make her look as frumpy as her mother. The episode played restlessly on their minds for the rest of the day but neither of them ever mentioned it again.

How Rhys hated Jeremy and Giles and their cronies. When he and Vicki had first moved to London, they had met up on occasion when Fiona was in town or at the invitation of Sophie. Giles's penthouse was stupendous with a direct view of the wonderful Lord's pavilion while Jeremy's house off Kensington High Street was equally impressive, if not more so. It would have been churlish to believe otherwise and both Vicki and Rhys had complimented them warmly and genuinely, wishing them well in their new homes. It hadn't mattered to them in the slightest that their flat bore no comparison; they were deliriously happy. But, as time went on, and further opportunities arose to meet up with Sophie and Giles and Jeremy and Fiona or even Vicki's other old housemate, Jill, when she was in town with her equally affluent boyfriend, Rhys would more often than not make an excuse and leave Vicki to go off by herself. Eventually, it came to the point when she didn't even ask him anymore.

Latterly, this arrangement suited Vicki more and more as she took the opportunity to discuss Rhys with her best friends. Sophie, Jill and Brenda from the office could not fail to notice how increasingly unhappy Vicki was becoming, but, in equal measure, she could not hide the obvious love and affection she still held for him. But her circumstances depressed her: the shitty flat with no prospect of leaving; the financial pressures; Rhys's depressions, though he tried desperately to hide them from her; the feeling that they were doing less and less as a couple together; their diminishing sex life. Vicki confided in her friends how she would love to get married and start a family, but how could she? Most upsettingly, she wondered whether she and Rhys would ever be in a position to do so. And yet, he was so caring and loving and strong, and in possession of a heart that held more gold than Fort Knox. He never interfered in anything she wanted to do. She could do what she liked, when she liked. He never told her what she could or could not wear or when she could or could not go out. He was not possessive in the slightest and she felt free, without any shackles, which was wonderful. Her friends often shifted in their chairs when Vicki said these things for she knew their boyfriends were not so accommodating.

Pleasingly, Vicki had made up with her family as, ultimately, the love between them was too strong. Her parents had concluded that there was nothing they could do about her relationship with Rhys. It was up to Vicki now. She was a big girl and she would have to live and learn through her own mistakes. They had given vent to their feelings and, despite her protestations, knew that deep down she would reflect upon them. They had never visited her flat for Vicki had never invited them. They suspected the reasons why and never pushed it. In fact,

Mrs Mitchell was inwardly relieved, for it would have depressed her no end to witness her daughter living in what she would regard as a hovel.

They had encountered Rhys on just two other occasions since their first meeting, both times being on Christmas Day, in 1971 and 1972. To their surprise, they had actually warmed to him a little for, despite all his faults, he was invariably kind and well-mannered, and often funny. They could also see how much their daughter loved him. Nonetheless, it never changed their opinion that he was wrong for her and that he would hold her back, as events were proving to show. As time moved on, Mrs Mitchell's maternal antennae were picking up on Vicki's unease and doubts, and she suspected that it would only be a matter of time before Vicki came to her senses. When she learnt that Vicki would be coming for Christmas by herself this year, as Rhys had decided to spend it in Wales, she knew that that time was not so far away.

'Hey, Vick, I know you don't like the programme but you've got to admit this John Inman bloke is really funny. That poofy walk of his is hilarious.'

'Yeah, he's quite funny, I suppose,' Vicki replied in a disconsolate tone.

'It's gonna be really weird in January when the telly goes off at half ten. Well, that's what you get if you vote Tory. Bring back Harold, I say.'

Vicki didn't reply. Politics was the last thing on her mind. The previous evening, the Prime Minister, Edward Heath, had announced that due to the continuing industrial action on the part of the miners, Britain would go onto a three-day working week from the start of the New Year. One of the measures introduced to reduce energy consumption was the early closing down of television programmes each evening. Rhys's comment only served to depress her further for it was a reminder that the New Year was lining up to be a miserable time of austerity everywhere. Britain is as shitty as this flat ... and this relationship, she mused. She was determined to do something about it and decided to think long and hard over Christmas.

But then, all of a sudden, Vicki perked up as she remembered the party she was going to the following evening. A customer of her company had invited her and a few colleagues to a Christmas bash at his apartment in the newly built high-rise tower of the Barbican Estate, a prestigious development in the City of London. Initially, Vicki had not been in the mood, but Brenda had badgered her for days on end about it and, eventually, she gave in and reluctantly agreed to go. It was a clear sign of her worsening relationship that she had not asked Rhys to accompany her even though partners were invited. As ever, Rhys was happy for Vicki to do as she pleased and hoped that she would have a good time. It was also a clear sign of her worsening relationship that the deciding argument for her agreeing to go was when Brenda threw into the conversation with a saucy grin, "And, who knows, you might even get to meet someone nice". Brenda knew that Vicki was ready to move on, that the dew was running off the rose.

And Vicki did meet someone nice. He was one of the most famous men in the country.

CHAPTER 9

Tommy Slater was lying on his back in his king-size bed, his hands behind his head, moving his neck and eyes only a fraction to observe the spacious and comfortable surrounds of his newly acquired apartment in the Cromwell Tower of the Barbican Estate. He approved of what he saw and was pleased that he bought it. In the background, *Tubular Bells* was playing on low volume, a record he adored and never failed to play at least once a day like seemingly everyone else in the country.

The modern apartment was bright and airy, and so new that the smell of paint and plaster still lingered. There were plans for two additional towers on the estate and he was certain that their apartments would sell like hot cakes just like the ones in his. It even crossed his mind whether property development was something he could pursue after he hung up his football boots, for the current captain of West Ham United and England was savvy enough to know that that day was not so many years ahead and, were he to pick up a bad injury, considerably sooner. He didn't fancy buying and running a pub like the vast majority of retired professional footballers. Yes, property development was definitely something to think about for the future, he mused, for it seemed an easy way to make a shedload of money very quickly indeed.

On the other hand, his new friend and neighbour, Solly Bernstein, was trying hard to convince him to invest his money in the rag trade and, in particular, his own garment-making business in the East End. Tommy grinned at the image of the exasperated open-armed Solly shaking his head and telling him he was making a mistake when he politely declined.

'I'm only looking after your best interests, Tommy, my boy.'

'Yeah, Solly, I'm sure you are.'

He liked Solly, nevertheless, for he was amusing and gregarious and he was looking forward to his party in the evening.

The warmth and softness of his bed and the quiet of the early morning instilled a reflective mood in him. He was twenty-seven years old and at the peak of his stellar career. He was a superb centre-half and considered by many to be the best defender in the world after displays which included stopping the peerless Brazilian genius, Pelé, and superlative Dutch wizard, Johan Cruyff, from performing their particular brands of magic. He was revered in England and around the world, with the looks and public image that made mothers dream that their daughters would bring him home one day as their boyfriend. Only George Best was more famous among footballers in England but he was definitely the last person any mother would want their daughter to meet.

Tommy smiled as he lapsed into recollections of his footballing battles at Wembley, Old Trafford, the Maracanã and San Siro, and also of his wonderful East End parents and home in Hackney. But where did his incredible ability come from? This was always a mystery to him for his father could barely kick a ball while his brother never progressed further than the football pitches of the famous Marshes nearby. He knew where his six feet in height and fair good looks came from, however, for he was the spitting image of his father, with both of them possessing short, tight, blonde curly hair and piercing sky-blue eyes. He grinned with relief at the knowledge that his father still maintained a good barnet, and hoped that his own would last equally as long.

Another way in which he resembled his father was in the manner he held his head up high and back ramrod straight. Together with his height and shoulders as square as a tailor's model, they added to his charisma and air of command. He did not know whether these characteristics were genetic or not, or whether they resulted from his observing his father as a young child, for he had been in the army and always seemed to march rather than walk around the house. But where he differed from his family, and especially his brother, was in his ruthless, steel-eyed determination to succeed in whatever he did; this innate competitiveness ran through him like lettering through Brighton rock.

When it became obvious as a young boy that he was overflowing with God-given footballing talent, he made a promise to his family that he would play for his beloved West Ham United and England one day. On witnessing their dubious frowns, he added that he would not only play for these teams but also captain them. While his brother laughed his head off, his parents noticed instead the obsessive, almost demonic look in his eyes which convinced them that he had a chance. They knew he would pursue his dream like a hound would a hare. His father, in particular, swelled with pride at seeing such confidence in his son. And he hadn't let them down.

But if truth be told, his clean-cut, good-boy public image was highly exaggerated. He had broken many girls' hearts following countless one night stands, caring little to nothing for their feelings and often brutally telling them where to go in the morning. Indeed, if he had cut a notch in the bed he was lying in on all the occasions he had shared it with a different girl, it would have collapsed a very long time ago.

He had treated his childhood sweetheart, Cheryl, dreadfully, over many years, turning her into a nervous wreck over his infidelities. The unknowing public at large loved them as a couple and was somewhat in shock when Tommy revealed in the *News of the World* during the summer that, with huge regret, they had decided to split up. In reality, it was more a massive relief than a huge regret, for the fights and arguments and tension between them had nearly driven them both insane, though none of this was ever publicly circulated. The overriding reason for this was because Tommy cultivated excellent relationships with all the sports' editors of the national newspapers. In return for interviews and tips about West Ham and England, they all agreed not to publish any information which could undermine his image. Accordingly, all approaches from the kiss-and-tells were dismissed out of hand. When Cheryl had given an interview to *Woman's Own,* tearfully revealing the truth about their relationship, Fleet Street had gone into overdrive, opining that Cheryl's comments were those of a demented, bitter girl unable to come to terms with rejection. This public view took hold and Cheryl was driven to medication, so ill did she become. Tommy also knew what the newspaper reporters got up to on the long trips away from home when England were playing and there was always an implicit threat that their better halves might just get to know should anything negative be written about him.

In addition, Tommy made it clear that nothing should ever be written about his relationship with those old school friends of his who had gone off the straight and narrow. He was fiercely loyal to and held great affection for the friends he had grown up with and would turn a blind eye to any knowledge he might have acquired concerning their thievery, thuggery or worse ... and there had been worse. This loyalty was returned and any bad-mouthing of Tommy often resulted in a good beating or slash across the cheek with a knife. Tommy did not necessarily approve of their actions but he would never condemn them, either.

For its part, Fleet Street was invariably happy with these arrangements for Tommy's tips, which he would share around evenly, were often headline-making and any interview he gave was thought-provoking and contained gems of information. Circulation figures soared whenever an interview with Tommy Slater was published. And, in any case, why would Fleet Street want to cultivate another bad boy image when they had enough material on the likes of George Best, Frank Worthington and Stan Bowles to cut down the whole Amazon rain forest for paper? Yes, Fleet Street was happy with Tommy and Tommy was happy with Fleet Street. The arrangement suited them both. Tommy was in control, and he liked nothing better than to be in control.

Tommy's recollections of his childhood and, more specifically, of his growing up in the loving bosom of his close-knit family, which were so vivid this particular morning, only re-stirred those deep-rooted pangs of desire of his to have such a family himself. These pangs had been growing more strongly in each passing day and he knew that the time had come to find a wonderful girl with whom he could share the rest of his life. He had always imagined that girl to be Cheryl but he now accepted that it was never meant to be. He was fed up of all the one night stands and stupid flirtations. He wasn't a teenager anymore and his parents had been five years younger than he was now when they had got married. He felt ancient by comparison. And his younger brother's wife had already borne him two beautiful children, Alfie and Daisy, on whom Tommy doted. Yes, it was definitely time to settle down. It was not as if he had missed out on the joys of youth, after all. Far from it!

'Morning, big boy. And how are you today?'

Tommy turned his face away from the girl who was sharing his bed and sighed when she tried to snuggle up more closely. He didn't budge an inch, hoping that she would quickly get the message that he wasn't interested.

'Okay, Debs, I suppose,' Tommy responded without any warmth. In fact, he tried to make it sound as cold as possible.

'It's Donna, not Debs,' came the grumpy reply.

Tommy couldn't even be bothered to apologise. Debs, Donna, they were all the same to him. God, there were more groupies hanging around the England football team than the Rolling Stones, he reflected, remembering how he had met Donna after the match against Poland in October. He had taken down her number that evening but only rang it a couple of days earlier. How he regretted it, and particularly so now, when he glanced down at her puffy face, with half her slap wiped away, and tits so big and saggy that they spread and flopped across her chest like two wobbling jellies topped with cherries. And no ordinary cherries, either, but two giant ugly ones, so giant in fact that if she stood up straight, he was sure he could hang his coat up on them, and his heavy sheepskin one at that.

'I have to get up in a minute and get over to the ground for training.'

'What, at seven-thirty in the morning?'

'Yeah, we're meeting up early. With all these Christmas and New Year games coming up one after the other, we need to get ourselves properly prepared.'

'Still seems a bit early to me,' Donna replied grumpily, snuggling up tighter and running her hand up between his legs.

Gordon Bennett! Can't she take a hint? Tommy thought in despair. He began to feel irritated though she was slowly bringing a part of him back to life. This was always the worst moment, he knew, trying to get rid of the girl in the morning. It never ceased to be crucifyingly awkward when they lingered expectantly for him to arrange another date, and the ultimate feeling of relief when they finally departed was enormous. It had to stop, though. He had to settle down. Once he had got rid of Debs, sorry, Donna, it would be all over; no more one night stands.

Tommy was on the verge of spelling it out as plainly as possible that she should sling her hook when, looking up at him with a filthy grin, she increased the tempo of her hand movement. Tommy considered, well, perhaps just this one last time. But there was no way he was going to gaze at that rough, lipstick- and mascara-smeared boat race of hers, and so, without feeling, he put his hand on the back of her head and pushed it firmly down towards his crotch.

CHAPTER 10

'Victoria. Brenda. How lovely to see you! Thank you for coming, and may I say how delectable you both look?' Solly Bernstein, in his customary open-armed pose and oozing charm, was as effusive in his greetings as ever when answering his doorbell for the umpteenth time that evening. The two young women smiled back a touch nervously but their confidence rose on hearing the compliment and they quickly relaxed for Solly possessed that warmth of personality that put everyone at ease. And he was correct; they did look delectable.

Vicki had ummed and ahhed for ages at home earlier, trying to decide what she would wear for the party, and it had taken Rhys's intervention to finally make up her mind. When he saw her gazing in the mirror, her face a picture of doubt, wearing her white flared dress that fell just above the knee and told her she looked amazing and even more beautiful than Jaqueline Bisset, that was good enough for Vicki. Despite their problems, Rhys still possessed that touch of magic that made her feel like the most beautiful woman in the world. The dress was in reality more suitable for the summer and left her arms bare, so she wore a fine, navy-blue cashmere cardigan over it. On her feet, she fastened her strappy, navy-blue sandals, which, like her dress, were more appropriate for the summer, but, which, nevertheless, were her favourites. She decided not to wear any tights for she felt sexier without them despite the weather being cold and sleety outside. Having booked a minicab, which would collect Brenda on the way, she knew she would barely have to face up to the elements in any case and, even when she did, she would be covered up in her royal-blue overcoat for protection. As ever, when dressing up for a special occasion, she wore only the slightest hint of any make-up. It was only when she was en route to Brenda's, however, that she became concerned about how nautical she looked, how she might look like a sailor with all the blue and white she was wearing, and how too underdressed she seemed for the season. Was she making her intentions too obvious? Without thinking it at the time, she now realised that, subconsciously, she probably was and her earlier confidence quickly sank. In truth, her worries were misplaced as Solly's compliment was on the money. She looked stupendous.

The same was true for Brenda, though in a different way. She was wearing a fashionable inky-black corduroy maxi skirt which covered her knee-length tan boots. Vicki disliked the new maxi style and thought there was enough material in Brenda's skirt to upholster her sofa. On top, she wore a crisp bright-white blouse, unbuttoned low enough to reveal the edge of a white bra which held in her ample bosom. Over the shirt, she wore a tightly fastened burgundy and grey striped waistcoat which served to accentuate her cleavage and athletic figure. She was taller than Vicki, with long wavy brown hair framing a rather serious-looking face that appeared older than her thirty-one years. Brenda always looked serious, or was it just a permanently resigned expression formed over years of waiting for her boyfriend to propose marriage? They were going through one of their bad patches at the moment so she had not invited him along, not that he would have gone anyway. But while Brenda knew Vicki was ready to move on from Rhys, she still harboured hopes that everything would work out well in the end with her Trevor.

'Come in, come in,' Solly carried on enthusiastically, kissing them both twice on the cheek and thanking them profusely yet again for coming. 'Let me take your coats and, tell me, what would you like to drink?'

Before receiving a reply, Solly beckoned Vicki and Brenda to follow him and, after putting their coats on top of a number of others in a bedroom, they proceeded into the spacious oblong kitchen, all gleaming stainless-steel units and glistening white tiles, the table and work counter overflowing with bottles of booze and platters of nibbles. A few guests were milling around, chatting away, glasses in hand, the male ones eyeing Vicki and Brenda in an obvious manner. Solly asked each and every one of them, hand on shoulder, if they were enjoying the party and reminded them to feel free to grab a drink at any time and to dip into the food. Vicki and Brenda smiled at each other. You had to hand it to Solly, he knew how to make everyone feel at home. 'Now, tell me again, what's your poison?' Solly asked.

'I'll have a gin and tonic if you don't mind,' Brenda replied, looking at Vicki as if to seek her approval.

'And the same for me, thanks,' Vicki concurred with a grateful smile.

'Roger and John are in the living room with their delectable wives,' Solly continued as he mixed the drinks.

'Ah, they've arrived, have they?' Brenda replied in reference to their work colleagues and wondering whether Solly thought every woman he met was 'delectable'.

After placing a slice of lemon into each of their drinks, he handed the two glasses over and invited them to follow him into the living room where the inimitable voice of Frank Sinatra, Solly's hero, could be heard singing *The Lady is a Tramp* in the background.

'Hello, Vicki, Brenda. Long time no see,' Roger began in an attempt at a joke as they had in fact all been together earlier in the day. 'I think you know Betty,' he carried on, introducing his wife, 'and Phyllis,' introducing John's.

The doorbell rang and Solly excused himself.

'Yes, we met once before,' Vicki replied, shaking the hands of the two wives, who in turn shook Brenda's.

Betty and Phyllis smiled, if somewhat forced and wary as they eyed Vicki and Brenda, wondering what the true relationship was between them and their husbands, for they were both young and very attractive. Vicki was about to resume speaking when John cut in, looking over her shoulder, his eyes agog.

'Crumbs, look who's just walked in?' Vicki and Brenda turned their heads round. 'It's Tommy Slater,' John continued, not that he needed to spell it out.

They all locked their eyes on him as he proceeded to the other side of the room, accompanied by Solly, who introduced him to his business partner in yet another attempt to convince him to invest in his company. When it came to business, Solly didn't like to hang around.

Vicki's group all looked away, not wishing to appear rude by staring, and Roger took up the conversation. But Vicki wasn't listening and in fact couldn't care less whether she appeared rude or not as she continued to fix her gaze on Tommy. As a non sequitur to Roger's hushed history of their company's involvement with Solly's, Vicki eventually turned and interrupted him. 'My God, I knew he was good looking but he's even better in the flesh. He's absolutely gorgeous.' Roger stopped in his tracks and they all looked at Vicki, the dumpy middle-aged wives thinking her somewhat childish.

'Calm down now, Vicki, let's not get all excited,' John replied with a grin.

But Vicki was getting all excited. She was possessed by the same trembling feeling she had experienced when first meeting Rhys and which she subsequently convinced herself she would never experience again. How wrong she was. As Roger re-started the conversation, Vicki occasionally glanced over at Tommy out of the corner of her eye, totally oblivious to what Roger was saying. He was so handsome, she acknowledged, with that straight back deportment of his, as he towered over the short and portly Solly and his even shorter and more portly business partner, Isaac. She also noted that he was unaccompanied.

Tommy was wearing black, flared crimplene trousers without a hint of a crease or wrinkle in them anywhere. His tan, slightly platformed high-heel slip-ons made him appear taller still and only added to his air of command. Like his trousers, his sage-green shirt was impeccable as was his wide, bright-orange Windsor-knotted tie. His spruce-green, double-breasted worsted jacket, with fine herringbone weave, contoured his body so perfectly and showed off his broad shoulders and narrow waist so flatteringly that Vicki believed it must have been cut and sewn in Savile Row. Vicki could also see how Tommy was becoming slightly exasperated during the course of his conversation with Solly and Isaac, who was sombrely dressed and particularly distinctive due to his two braids and black wide-brimmed hat.

'Hey, Solly, why don't we talk about this some other time?' Tommy finally interjected with a sigh. 'I don't even have a drink in my hand, you cheapskate,' he added with a smile, showing an empty palm and placing his other hand on Solly's shoulder.

'You're right, Tommy, my boy. Tonight is for fun. Business can wait another day,' Solly responded, looking at his partner who nodded his agreement. It was enough that Tommy had not rejected them out of hand and was willing to discuss their proposal another time. 'And my manners are appalling,' Solly carried on, slapping his hand hard against his forehead. 'What would you like to drink? I'll go and fetch you one.'

'I could murder a cold beer.'

'And a cold beer it will be then,' Solly replied, touching him on the forearm before heading out to the kitchen.

Tommy followed his tread and then gazed around the room, feeling decidedly uncomfortable standing next to Solly's uncommunicative and miserable-looking business partner. His eyes fell immediately upon an attractive girl wearing a white dress and navy-blue cardigan, with long, blonde corkscrew hair. 'Wow, I wonder who she is?' he said to himself, loud enough to stir Isaac into looking up at him.

Tommy continued to stare at Vicki, who was side on to him, and noted that her group did not include a man of similar age amongst them. Vicki was unaware that Tommy was looking at her until, turning her head a touch, she glanced at him out of the corner of her eye. Unexpectedly, their eyes met and Tommy gave her the broadest and brightest smile she had ever seen, which even lit up the gloomy Isaac next to him. Instinctively, she turned her head away, but she could not hide the widening of her mouth or blushing of her cheeks from Tommy.

'Here you are, Tommy, my boy. A nice cold glass of Löwenbräu for you.'

'Cheers, Solly,' Tommy replied, taking a large gulp. It was so cold and strong that it watered his eyes and made him shiver. 'Tell me, who's that girl over there in the white dress and blue cardigan?'

'Where? Over there? Oh, that's Victoria Mitchell,' Solly returned, straining his neck to look around some of the other guests in the living room. 'She's the marketing manager of an American company that supplies me with cloth for my schmutter.'

'She's a very pretty girl.'

At this moment, Isaac made his excuses and walked away. He could see in which direction the conversation was heading and it was not one in which he had any interest.

'She is that, and a very sweet girl as well, I must say. Hard as nails, though, Tommy, my boy. Can never get any money out of her for my marketing campaigns,' Solly continued, shaking his head and pursing his lips. 'Would you like an introduction?'

'Sure, at a suitable moment.'

And with that, Solly left Tommy's side and sidestepped his way around the other guests to Vicki's group. Tommy threw his head back in exasperation, cursing Solly for being as subtle as a medieval mace fight, as he watched him whisper something into Vicki's ear right in front of her friends. They all looked in his direction, which made him feel extremely uncomfortable, and the best he could do was to grin back cheesily. But you had to hand it to Solly for, a few seconds later, he turned back towards him with Vicki in tow. Tommy observed the expressions of surprise on the faces of the others in Vicki's group and particularly on that of the other young woman, who looked as if the on-the-run Great Train Robber, Ronnie Biggs, had just entered the room.

'Victoria, my darling, I'd like to introduce you to Tommy Slater,' Solly pronounced with his arm around her shoulders like a caring father and as if she might never have heard of him before. 'You probably know that Tommy is the esteemed captain of the England football team,' he continued unnecessarily. Tommy held out his hand for Vicki to shake. His grip was firm though the skin was soft. They beamed the broadest of smiles to each other. 'Well, let me leave you two together now, but please do grab yourselves a drink and tuck into the food whenever you want. I wouldn't want any of it to go to waste.'

'Thanks, Solly, I'm sure we will,' Tommy replied and Vicki concurred. Solly finally left them and made a beeline for the record player where he placed another Frank Sinatra LP on the turntable.

'Well, Victoria, it's very nice to meet you.'

'Please call me Vicki. Only Solly and my parents call me Victoria.'

'Well, Vicki, it's very nice to meet you, too,' Tommy returned, trying to be funny and raising the smidgen of a smile on her face. 'Sorry for the way Solly broke into your group over there. I only mentioned what an attractive girl you are and how I wouldn't mind an introduction and the next thing I know he's off like a dog chasing a stick.'

'Oh, that's okay,' Vicki replied, her confidence boosted by Tommy's compliment. 'We all know what Solly's like. If he's anything, he's a bundle of energy and certainly not shy in going forward.' Vicki hesitated a moment before adding, looking Tommy straight in the eye, 'I'm glad he did.'

'Yeah, I'm glad he did, too.' They both lowered their eyes for the fleetest of moments, not saying a word, and took the opportunity to take a sip of their drinks. The attraction they held for each other was obvious and they both knew it. 'So, Vicki, Solly tells me your company supplies him with cloth?'

'Yeah, that's right. He's a good customer of ours, though, between you and me, it would help if he paid his bills on time more often. He's always pleading poverty and asking for lower prices, but, judging by this flat and the Jag he drives, I think he's doing alright.'

'I'm sure he is,' Tommy replied with a nod.

'How do you know him, may I ask?'

'I've only just met him to be honest. He's my new neighbour as I've just moved into number forty-two along the corridor. We've had a few chats and he's good company, even if he is a Spurs supporter. He'd like me to invest in his business as some security for when I finish playing football, but I'm not all that keen.'

'You've still got a few years ahead of you, surely?'

'Oh, yeah, at least six or seven before I hang up my boots. But, you never know, an injury could end it all tomorrow, so Solly's not wrong in getting me to think about my future. I'm more interested in property development, you know, buying and doing up old wrecks and selling them on afterwards. There's a handy profit to be made in that.'

'You'd need to be David Nixon and Merlin the Magician all wrapped up in one to make a profit out of my dump of a place in Battersea,' Vicki responded, arching her eyes to the heavens, but immediately regretting it. She had opened the door to questions about her living arrangements which she didn't think was such a good idea in the circumstances. Tommy was about to say something when, fortunately for her, another guest came over and shook him by the hand, telling him what a great admirer of his he was. Tommy had a quick word with him before turning back to Vicki. Luckily, he resumed on a different subject.

'Sorry about that. Where were we now? Yeah, getting back to Solly, where I might get involved with him is by modelling some of his new clobber, you know, his new collection of suits in particular. I think it could be quite lucrative for both of us and it's something I know I'd enjoy. I've always liked nice whistles and it'd make a change from endorsing some of the products I've done recently like frozen pies. It'd certainly be a lot more glamorous!' Tommy chuckled.

'That's right, I remember now the one you did for Fray Bentos on the telly around your kitchen table with Cheryl.' Vicki had deliberately thrown in Cheryl's name to gauge his reaction. She had read that the relationship had come to an end but she never knew whether what she read in the press was always correct.

'Yeah, disgusting they were, those pies,' Tommy replied, pinching his nose, 'but please don't tell them,' he whispered conspiratorially into her ear, 'because it was a nice little earner and I wouldn't mind them asking me again.' The sensation of his breath on her skin was like a puff of warm air on a long summer's evening and made her tingle with desire, a feeling Tommy was all too aware of.

Simultaneously, they burst out laughing, drawing the attention of Vicki's work colleagues across the room. They all looked at each other in amazement and revelled in the gossip that would go around their company at this turn of events. With Brenda, the biggest gossiper of the lot in their midst, this was guaranteed. Vicki was fully conscious that her spending time in the company of Tommy Slater would inevitably lead to this but she couldn't care less. She was suddenly eager for more ... a lot more.

Tommy could tell that Vicki was digging for information on Cheryl, putting a few ferrets down a hole and seeing if any rabbits would pop out. He had nothing to hide and welcomed telling her the truth for he had already fallen for her and wished nothing better than to deconstruct any imaginary barriers that might exist between them. 'Saying that, I'd have to do the ad by myself next time as I'm not with Cheryl anymore, as you're probably aware.'

'Yeah, I had read that. I'm sorry,' Vicki replied, not meaning it.

'It was a real shame but we just grew apart the older we got. When we first met we never thought it would ever end, but, you know, things change.' Vicki nodded. 'It got a bit messy and she was badly advised with that interview she gave to *Woman's Own*, talking all that nonsense, but, hey, that's life, I suppose, as Esther Rantzen might say.'

Vicki smiled at the clever reference to the new and increasingly popular magazine-style television programme but her head had clocked that Cheryl was definitely off the scene and she felt a warm glow inside. The conversation died as Vicki was more interested in absorbing and understanding what Tommy had just said rather than responding to it and they both took the opportunity to sip from their drinks once again.

'I need a fresh one,' Tommy finally proclaimed, showing Vicki an empty glass. He looked at hers which also needed a refill. 'Let's go into the kitchen and get ourselves a drink. Don't know about you but I'm feeling a bit peckish so I think I'll take Solly up on his offer and grab something to eat.'

'Good idea.'

Tommy led the way, stopping briefly to have a quick word with and accept the handshakes from some of the overawed guests. Vicki waited beside him and glanced over to her work colleagues, who all projected their most knowing smiles at her. She blushed back at them. Frank Sinatra was imploring his love to *"Come fly with me, let's fly, let's fly away ..."*, which Vicki mimed along to, wishing madly it was Tommy singing it to her with the same intent. At last, Tommy freed himself from a final well-wisher and set off for the kitchen, Vicki following close behind.

'What do you fancy, Vicki?'

'I think I'll have another gin and tonic.'

'Tell you what, I'll mix that for you while you grab me a beer.'

As Vicki opened the top compartment of the stainless-steel Smeg fridge which rose high above her head, thinking that this compartment alone was twice the size of her fridge at home, she ventured a jocular quip at Tommy, who, before grabbing the Gordon's bottle, munched down a tiny smoked salmon sandwich. 'So, this new collection of Solly's you might model, will the colour scheme be claret and blue?'

'Ha ha, who's the funny one? I'll always be proud to wear the Hammers' colours on the pitch but they might look a bit odd in a whistle, though you never know these days 'cos any colour seems to go. Would you mind grabbing the tonic from the fridge while you're there?' As Vicki reached for a small bottle of Schweppes, Tommy resumed light-heartedly, pouring a measure of gin into a tall glass. 'Anyway, I'm not sure I should be talking to a Chelsea supporter, as you're one of our biggest rivals.'

Vicki was taken aback as she closed the fridge, holding the necks of the bottles of Löwenbräu and tonic water in the fingers of one hand. 'How did you know I was a Chelsea supporter?'

'Oh, come on, Vicki, it's obvious,' Tommy replied, turning round momentarily to face her, a piece of lemon in one hand and small knife in the other. He was smiling broadly. Vicki looked nonplussed. 'Firstly, you live in Battersea, where a lot of their supporters come from and, secondly, you're wearing their colours.'

Instinctively, Vicki looked down at her dress and cardigan. She shook her head, slightly embarrassed. 'When I put this on, I can assure you Chelsea's colours were the last thing on my mind.'

Taking the bottle of tonic from her hand, Tommy grinned. 'I'll tell you something, you look a lot better in those colours than that madman 'Chopper' Harris does,' as he recalled a particularly vicious kick on the ankle from the Chelsea hard man. He stopped for a second and then gazed lovingly into Vicki's eyes before adding with the faintest of nods, 'In fact, you look absolutely stunning.'

Vicki thought her knees were going to buckle at such a lovely compliment and she had to look away, so discombobulated did she feel. She was lost for words and, in a daze, she sought the bottle-opener to take the top off his beer.

'I think this is what you're looking for.' Tommy had already picked it up to remove the top from the Schweppes bottle. As he held it out, their fingers touched and their eyes met. Vicki made no effort to take the opener and Tommy made no effort to release it.

Eventually, after a few delicious seconds, Tommy slackened his grip and Vicki removed the top of the Löwenbräu. She poured it into a glass and handed it to Tommy, who, in turn, handed her the gin and tonic. Not a word passed their lips for almost a minute and, with her head in a whirl, Vicki considered the platters of food on the sideboard. She spent an age choosing between the cheese and pineapple on a stick, sausage on a stick, wide array of vol-au-vents and sandwich triangles. She couldn't concentrate and may as well have been considering a selection of lipsticks for all she knew, so tizzy had her mind become. She just needed to gather her thoughts a second. Finally, she selected a vol-au-vent overflowing with prawn cocktail sauce, grabbing a bright-red serviette at the same time.

For his part, Tommy was experiencing the same shivers of excitement as Vicki and took a large gulp from his glass to compose himself. He absolutely adored her. A handsome couple entered the kitchen at that moment, momentarily breaking the spell that bewitched the two love birds, but so obvious was the love in the air that the woman asked apologetically whether they were disturbing them.

'Not at all,' Tommy replied with his most charming smile. 'In fact, we were just leaving.' This was news to Vicki but she followed Tommy out of the kitchen and into the living room, tugging at his arm to indicate a space in the opposite corner to where her work colleagues were standing.

'Cheers.' Tommy raised his glass in salute and took a sip of his drink. Vicki did the same. Feeling more relaxed, they then started to speak simultaneously, each interrupting the flow of the other.

'Sorry, Vicki, you go first.'

'No, you go first.'

'Beauty before the beast.'

Vicki grinned and was about to say something when Tommy began to speak with a cheeky smile. Vicki thumped him playfully on the arm, pursing her lips, and they both laughed. Finally, after taking another sip of her drink, Vicki took up the conversation. 'So, West Ham United? You must come from the East End then?'

'I'm sure my accent's a bit of a giveaway as well but, yeah, you're right. In fact, I'm a true Cockney. My family's originally from Bow and I'm proud to say I was born within the sound of the bells before we moved to Hackney. How about you? Please don't tell me you're from Chelsea?'

'No. I was born in Guildford, actually, near to where my parents live now, but I can honestly say I've got some East End blood in me 'cos my father was born in Plaistow.'

'Really?'

'Yeah. In fact, his first job was in Billingsgate Market.'

'You're kidding! That's where my old man used to work.'

'God, what a coincidence. I wonder if they ever knew each other. Mine was there just after the war for a year before he met my mum. My parents were only eighteen when they got married and he moved to Guildford where my mum's family was living.'

'My dad was working there during the war when he got called up. He got demobbed in 1947 and returned to Billingsgate. They probably missed each other then.'

'Probably. That's the year my parents got married and I know he was working as a clerk in the City by then, though he did do his eighteen months' National Service soon after. Yours truly came along the following year,' Vicki added, opening up her arms as if receiving the applause of an audience.

'I was born in 1946 as a result of my old man coming home on leave the year before. Well, I suppose they had to make the most of it.' They both laughed. 'In fact, my dad was in Egypt when I was born and celebrated hearing the news by diving into the Red Sea.'

Vicki smiled and could see in Tommy's eyes how much he loved and admired his father. 'Did you always want to be a footballer?'

'Good question. I loved the game as a kid and was always kicking a ball about in the streets with my mates and my brother but I can't honestly say I wanted to be one at the time. In fact, all I really wanted was a good office job, a bit like your dad, I suppose, and for my parents to be proud of me. For a working class family to have a son in a suit and tie behind a desk was high ambition. But it transpired I was pretty good at football and got scouted by West Ham, so I signed on as an apprentice and the rest, as they say, is history.'

'Your family must be very proud of you?'

'Oh, yeah, no doubt. But not when I first signed.'

'Oh, why's that then?'

'Because they're all Orient supporters.'

Vicki laughed, triggering Tommy to do the same. When it subsided, they gazed into each other's eyes, both holding the look with ease. A moment later, Solly was at their side, as if appearing from nowhere, and he put his arms around their shoulders. 'Victoria, Tommy, I hope you're both enjoying the party. Grab yourselves another drink whenever you're ready and please tuck into the grub.'

'Thanks, Solly. The party's great,' Vicki replied with warmth in her voice.

'Yeah, just superb, Solly,' Tommy agreed. He turned his head back round to face Vicki and added, 'Memorable, in fact.' With his arms still around their shoulders, Solly looked at them and expressed gratitude at their kind words. It was at this moment that Vicki felt like she was in a relationship with Tommy and she wanted to scream out her happiness. She had not failed to notice the many prying eyes looking their way during the evening and she loved the feeling of being one of a couple with Tommy Slater. When Solly moved away, Tommy resumed the conversation.

'Now, where were we? Oh, yeah. When I signed for West Ham, I never thought I'd go on to have the career I've had. That day, I was just happy to know I'd been given the chance to better myself, to earn a decent wage. Ultimately, that was always my motivation as a kid. All I ever wanted was a nice drum, a nice car, a loving wife and kids and a few quid in the bank for them to live a good life.'

Instinctively, Vicki's hand shot out and touched his arm; she didn't even realise she had done it. So close had they become that Tommy didn't even think it unusual. But then, Vicki's expression took on a puzzled look. 'Drum? Did you want to be a drummer in a band then?'

Tommy burst out laughing. 'You might have some East End blood in you, Vicki, but you've never lived round these parts, have you? A drum is Cockney rhyming slang for a house or flat or, more literally, a place where you live. Drum and bass ... place!'

Vicki raised her hand to her mouth and her cheeks reddened. 'Oops! I must have a go at my father next time for not teaching me that one.'

Tommy grinned and stroked her upper arm in affection, which Vicki loved. She did not budge an inch and allowed him to do it a second time. Looking her longingly in the eye, Tommy resumed. 'In my wildest dreams, I never thought my career would turn out the way it has done. I've been very lucky, though I have worked my guts out as well. The impression everyone has is that football comes easily to me, but it's not like that at all, trust me. You never read about the times in training when I take two hundred shots with my weaker foot to try and improve it and make one hundred headers to strengthen the muscles in my neck. In fact, that's what I did yesterday morning when it was minus five and bucketing down with snow. No, if you prepare well, you can control everything that goes on in a game and control is what it's all about.'

As he expressed himself, Vicki could see in his determined stare the necessary commitment of a professional athlete, and not just any professional athlete, but a winning one. She admired the way he had wanted to better himself as a boy, to make his family proud of him, to make something of himself. And how he had succeeded! Fame, admiration, wealth, he had earned it all, in addition to the love of an adoring public. And he possessed the foresight to know that he needed to look after his future as well, for the future would not look after itself. In truth, Vicki reflected, he was everything Rhys wasn't. Her feelings for Tommy were not those of a celebrity-mad fanatic but came as a result of her being with him, talking to him and understanding him. She found Tommy irresistible. But Vicki's perfect evening was about to be shattered by one seemingly innocuous question.

'Anyway, enough about me. This so-called dump of a flat of yours in Battersea, do you live there by yourself?'

Tommy registered Vicki's ill-at-ease straight away. She shifted on her feet and stared down at Solly's plush Axminster carpet, her cheeks burning. She couldn't look Tommy in the eye and her brain was a jumble of conflicting responses. Her face was strained and she didn't reply for what seemed like an eternity. What should I say? Vicki asked herself. I can't tell him about Rhys, can I? He won't be interested anymore. But Vicki knew she was a terrible liar so decided to tell him the truth. After all, her relationship was on the rocks and she'd make that clear to him. Her prevarication, however, only served to provide Tommy with the answer. If she was incapable of replying, he'd do it for her. 'You're living with someone, aren't you? A boyfriend?'

The tone of Tommy's voice was abrupt and his expression severe. The fact Vicki gave no immediate response yet again and shifted even more uneasily on her feet confirmed what he said. Tommy experienced a hollow feeling in the pit of his stomach, which quickly turned to anger in the belief he'd been led on, and the fact that he had fallen for her in such a big way only made this anger more intense. Vicki finally raised her eyes. 'Yes, I am.'

Hearing Vicki say these words was like a kick in the balls and he had to take a deep breath to maintain his calm. Vicki could see that she had hurt him even if he tried to hide it. The moment was crushing Tommy for he really did believe that Vicki could be the person to fill the only void in his life. Her stretching out of her hand in search of his only served to make matters worse and he retracted his sharply, forcing Vicki to put hers by her side and look down at the carpet awkwardly. Outwardly, he remained relatively composed, but, inside, his guts were churning. Vicki noticed him look away to survey the room, a clear sign that he was on the point of saying his goodbyes, so, in a desperate and clumsy manner, she tried to regain the initiative. 'It's not what you think, though.'

Tommy turned his head to face her. 'Oh, and how's that then?' he replied bitterly.

'Tommy, don't be like that. Please let me explain. We're living together for the moment but it's all going to end soon. Believe me.'

But Tommy wasn't convinced. 'Yeah, sure,' he replied in an offhand manner, scanning the room once more. He turned back round to look her in the eye. 'How long have you been living together?'

'About three, three and a half years.'

Tommy threw his head back dramatically. 'Huh! Sounds pretty serious to me.'

'It's not, please believe me. It was once but isn't now and hasn't been for ages,' Vicki flustered, stretching out her hand once more in search of his. Tommy prevented her from holding it but didn't stop her from stroking his forearm instead which provided Vicki with a glimmer of encouragement. But this was a mirage for, just as Vicki was about to explain her relationship with Rhys in greater detail, Tommy pulled his arm away aggressively and stared down at her. Although his tone was polite and the look on his face kind, the words he spoke, while in themselves relatively banal, hit Vicki like a bullet in the heart.

'Well, Vicki, it's been nice meeting you and I hope you enjoy the rest of the party. Have a lovely Christmas.' And with that, he walked away. In the hallway, Tommy caught sight of Solly laughing and joking in a group of three and decided to join them.

Vicki stood stock still, her head bowed, the picture of misery. She was afraid to move her legs, fearing that they might cave in under her if she did. So upset did she feel that she thought she might burst into tears at any second. Her stomach ached fiercely and she struggled to keep a lid on her emotions. She looked round to see whether Tommy was still in the room, but he was gone. Her work colleagues were still in their little group in the opposite corner, oblivious to what had happened to her. Seeing them chatting away animatedly, she went to join them. She had no other option.

'Oh, hi, Vicki. I thought you'd forgotten about us,' Brenda commented, turning round after feeling Vicki's tap on her shoulder. 'You seem to be getting on well with Tommy Slater over there,' she added with a nudge nudge, wink wink. Like her, Roger, John and their wives all stared at Vicki, expectant expressions on their faces, eager to hear whether she had anything juicy to say about her dalliance with the England football captain. Brenda could barely contain herself, so desperate was she to hear how Vicki had got on. She was already thinking ahead to Monday and that first coffee with the girls in the office kitchen, in the certain knowledge that they would not get much work done that morning.

'Yeah, he's very nice,' Vicki replied in a sorrowful tone, her expression downcast. She left it at that, much to the disappointment of her colleagues.

After a few seconds of silence, during which their stares had become a little disconcerting, Vicki asked them whether they were enjoying the party. The change of subject was obvious and a clear sign that any questions about Tommy Slater were off limits. Brenda thought that Vicki might not want to say too much in front of Roger and John and so didn't push her any further, believing that Vicki was likely to be more forthcoming in the minicab on the way home.

They chatted for another hour or so but Vicki's mind was in turmoil and she contributed little. It was clear she had a lot on her mind and the minicab could not come soon enough for Brenda. Occasionally, Vicki looked around to look for Tommy. He appeared every now and again, here and there, talking to various guests, but he never came close to where Vicki's group was standing and their eyes never met. He was smiling and laughing a lot which only upset her further. He had probably forgotten about her already, she thought. And yet, Vicki had witnessed first-hand how hurt he had been when she told him about her boyfriend and the sexual chemistry between them was explosive, like mixing nitric acid with glycerol. She knew he liked her … and probably a lot.

But then, to her horror, she saw Tommy in the hallway shaking Solly's hand. He had his other hand on Solly's shoulder and was sharing a joke with him as they edged closer to the front door. Tommy was leaving. Vicki stared worriedly at Tommy's back, mouth agape, hoping desperately that he would at least turn round to seek her out. But instead, Tommy opened the door and, after receiving a final pat on the back from Solly, walked out. There wasn't even the tiniest hint of his turning round. When Solly closed the door after him, it was as if the final curtain had descended, only more brutally, like a guillotine. The show was over.

Vicki looked down at the carpet, her eyes welling up. Brenda could feel her shiver beside her though the room was warm. Without hesitation and as rattled as a railway carriage window, Vicki excused herself and bolted off to the bathroom. Her five companions all looked at each other in bemusement. It crossed Brenda's mind whether she should go and see if Vicki was alright, but she decided against it for the moment.

In the bathroom, Vicki burst into tears. How could she feel so much for someone she had known for only half an evening? It was crazy. But the floods of tears, in reality, were the consequence of the release of pent-up emotions relating to her relationship with Rhys. These emotions were all-consuming and remorseless, always agonisingly at the forefront of her mind and in the pit of her stomach. She had held them all in, all those worries and concerns for the future, a toxic mixture that had stirred around inside her for so long. But they all poured out now, the dam finally breaching. Knowing that she could feel so much for someone else so easily only confirmed to her that she and Rhys were finished and this knowledge overwhelmed her.

Moments later, she took a couple of deep breaths to regain some composure and looked at herself in the mirror. Her eyes were red raw but at least she had stopped crying. She broke off some toilet paper and blew her nose. She started to feel calmer and knew that she had to get back as everyone would be wondering where she had got to. She was also concerned that a queue might be forming outside the door. She looked at herself one more time in the mirror. It was obvious she had been crying. 'Fuck it,' she said defiantly before leaving the bathroom to re-join the party.

As she approached her colleagues, she saw them with their heads close together, whispering like plotting co-conspirators. On seeing her, they raised their heads and smiled sheepishly. It was evident to Vicki that they had been talking about her but she couldn't care less. Phyllis and Betty were exchanging sly comments, their eyes trained on her. Noticing this, Vicki thought 'fuck 'em' once more and then pondered incongruously whether John and Roger were in fact doing so anymore. Probably not, she decided ungraciously.

'Are you okay, Vicki?' Brenda asked in a low voice, as she gently touched her arm.

'Yeah, Bren. Don't worry.'

John and Roger said nothing. They were not at their best when it came to women's feelings.

'We're going to have to make a move, Vicki. The minicab'll be here in ten minutes.'

Vicki looked at her watch and arched her eyes. It was nearly midnight already. 'God, is that the time?'

'Perhaps we should grab our coats and say goodbye to Solly,' Brenda suggested. 'We're so high up here, it'll take us ten minutes to get down to the bottom.'

'Yeah, you're right. We should make a move now.'

'Our minicab's coming in half an hour,' Roger threw in, 'so we'll be leaving shortly as well.'

Vicki and Brenda nodded and gave their two colleagues and wives a warm embrace and kiss before moving off to the bedroom. A number of people had already left and there were now fewer coats lying on the bed than when they had first arrived.

'You two girls are not leaving, are you? The party will be poorer for it,' Solly asked when he saw them in the hallway adjusting their collars.

'We have to, Solly. It's getting late and we both need our beauty sleep,' Brenda replied.

Solly threw his head back in incredulity. 'Beauty sleep! For two such delectable creatures as you. Never!'

Brenda and Vicki smiled, the latter desperately wanting to ask him for Tommy's number. But she held back.

'You're such a charmer, Solly,' Brenda returned with a girlish giggle. 'Thanks for your hospitality; it's been a lovely evening,' she continued and Vicki nodded her agreement.

'I'm so glad you enjoyed yourselves. Make sure you get home safely now.'

The three of them took a couple of paces to the front door which Solly opened. He gave them both pecks on the cheek before Vicki and Brenda finally left. As they waited for the lift to arrive along the corridor, Solly remained by the door, one foot in, one foot out, making sure everything was in order. Vicki so wished that he would come over and stuff Tommy's number into her hand. But the lift arrived with a soft ping and, with a final wave, they stepped inside, Vicki feeling wretched and on the point of bursting into tears once again. When Solly saw the floor numbers counting down, he re-entered his apartment, singing along happily to *Who Wants to be a Millionaire?* in the background.

Tommy Slater was not yet a millionaire though he felt confident that one day he would be. But the way he was feeling at this particular moment, no amount of money would ever be able to buy off the gut-wrenching pain inside his stomach. He was sitting in a low, black leather armchair, cradling a tumbler of whisky in his right hand, thinking. It was the third he had poured himself since arriving back in his apartment. On entering, he had taken off his shoes and calmly placed his jacket over the back of a chair. But when he undid his tie, he threw it violently onto the floor, as if it were infectious, and it ended up lying under his glass-topped dining room table like a cobra that had slithered through a vat of orange paint. He just couldn't get Vicki out of his mind.

As he crossed his feet on the black leather footstool, he wondered whether he had been presumptuous in casting her aside, for he hadn't allowed her to explain the state of her relationship with her boyfriend. And now, sitting back in the quiet of his apartment, he was desperate to find out. He had put two and two together but perhaps he had come up with five as the answer. But then, as he swilled the whisky round in its glass, his doubts kicked in. Deep down, he just wanted to believe something he knew wasn't true. To live with someone for three and a half years was pretty serious and, however much she may have gushed in his presence earlier, he would never be able to replace what she felt for her lover. This realisation stirred an inner anger inside him and it even crossed his mind whether he should ask his best friend Freddie Butcher, or Freddie the Flick, as he was better known because of the flick-knife he always carried round with him, to pay Vicki's boyfriend a visit and cut him up a bit. He might not look so handsome after that.

And yet, there was definitely something special between them. He couldn't just sit back and do nothing. Vicki might well be the girl of his dreams, the one with whom he would finally settle. That prize was too much to give up. He could easily get hold of her number from Solly and give her a call at work. Yes, that's what he would do.

But the doubts soon returned. Who are you kidding? Don't get het up and involved with a girl you can't have. You'll only end up getting hurt. Tommy even tried to convince himself that Vicki was no better, in reality, than all the slags who hung around the England football team. But the second he thought it, he admonished himself, for he knew it not to be true.

Finishing his whisky, he looked at his watch. Twenty past twelve. He had been sitting in the armchair for over an hour. He finally decided to turn in, knowing that he might have a different perspective on things in the morning. But, as he was about to get up, there was a faint knock on the door, so faint, in fact, it was barely audible. He hesitated a minute before he heard it again, this time a little louder. Whoever it was at this time of night was either very puny or extremely nervous. When Tommy opened the door, he could see immediately it was the latter.

'Hello, Tommy. Remember me? Can I come in?'

'Of course you can.'

And with that, Tommy took Vicki's hand and led her inside.

CHAPTER 11

The early morning sunshine was trying hard to penetrate the vertical barrier of blinds shielding the two floor-to-ceiling windows in Tommy's cavernous bedroom. Because of its size and oriental-style black-lacquer furniture, the room was not particularly cosy or welcoming. In fact, to Vicki's eye, it was rather cold and distinctly lacking in taste. But none of this bothered her as she snuggled up ever more tightly against Tommy's warm, lean body, as relaxed as a fat tabby cat curled up in front of an open fire. His skin was unblemished and pale, white even, as if it had never been subjected to the sun's rays in its time, and his torso possessed not one strand of hair. With her head on his chest and left arm wrapped around him, she smiled as she felt Tommy tug gently at her corkscrew hair, as if a coiled spring, trying to extract some bounce. It confirmed her belief that men would always be young boys at heart.

They were both wide awake but neither of them said a word. They were just enjoying the warmth of each other's bodies. After all, between their love-making during the night, they had talked and joked and laughed, and talked and joked and laughed even more until there was nothing left to say. In fact, they had barely had an hour's sleep in all that time. Now, it was just a moment to relax and enjoy the still of the early morning.

The gradual brightening of the room, however, was a sure sign to Vicki that the storm in which she would find herself after this particularly beautiful lull was very soon in coming. Her confrontation with Rhys could be tempestuous. She knew he would be worried sick where she was, but, cruelly, for the moment, she couldn't care less. Nor could she care less what gossip would be flying around the office on Monday, particularly after telling Brenda that she would not be getting into the minicab with her as it pulled up outside Tommy's building. She had left her there startled before running back inside to catch the lift back up to his apartment.

Unsurprisingly, Tommy had been eager to find out more about her relationship with Rhys, and Vicki had told him everything. He was pleased to hear it would be ending but became angry when she said she was planning on telling Rhys after Christmas, and most probably in the New Year. Tommy told her in no uncertain terms that she was to tell him immediately, the next day, and that Rhys was to move out of the flat straight away. Vicki relented, thinking logically that there was no real reason to wait. Reluctantly, Tommy had to accept, however, that Vicki could not just throw Rhys out onto the street and that there would be a short period of time when he continued to live in the flat until he made other arrangements. But she promised never to share the same bed with him again. Tommy was not convinced of this but there was little he could do about it. He would have to take her word for it and ensure she spent as many evenings as possible round his place.

As Vicki lay next to Tommy, she told herself that she was going to be open and honest with Rhys about everything that had happened. It was the right thing to do.

But it was easy to believe that in the calm and quiet of a warm bedroom away from the storm. Now, as Vicki stood outside her front door, key in hand, her confidence drained away and she took a deep breath to steady her nerves. She looked at her wristwatch for no particular reason other than to waste another few seconds before her confrontation with Rhys. Twelve noon, it showed, and soon it would be High Noon between them. After one more deep breath, she placed the key in the lock.

Sitting in the living room, Rhys heard it immediately. He jumped up from the sofa and bolted down the hallway like an Olympic sprinter. When Vicki pushed open the door, he was already standing there in front of her.

'Vicki! Where've you been? I've been beside myself. Have you been in an accident or something?'

Vicki couldn't look him in the eye as she stepped across the threshold and shut the door behind her. Her guts were churning and her throat constricted as if a ligature was being tied tightly around it. She didn't reply and brushed past Rhys into the bedroom. Rhys followed a pace behind, somewhat baffled at her brusqueness. With her back to him, for she did not want him to see her face, she took off her coat and threw it onto the bed. Rhys did not notice her take another deep breath before she finally turned round to face him.

'I'm gasping for a cup of tea.' Vicki brushed past Rhys again and walked into the living room. She crossed over to the sink and filled the kettle with water. In the background, the theme music to *Grandstand* was sounding from the television. As Rhys followed her in, he turned down the volume and eased up behind her. He placed his hands on her waist, tentatively. On feeling them, Vicki turned around, her eyes awash with tears and grasped him tightly.

'Hey, Vick, what's wrong? What's happened?'

'Let's sit down,' Vicki replied and she led him by the hand to the sofa. 'Can you switch off the telly?'

Before sitting down, Rhys stretched out his hand and turned the knob. He then joined Vicki on the sofa.

'Vicki, why are you so upset? What's happened?' he repeated softly and with concern, taking hold of her hand and lightly stroking the back of it. Vicki was about to reply when he threw in, 'Where were you last night? I was so worried.'

By the sink, the kettle came to boil but they ignored it.

Vicki couldn't bring herself to admit that she had been with Tommy. 'I stayed round Brenda's in Vauxhall,' she lied, looking down at the carpet. 'She's going through a bad patch with her boyfriend and got really upset at the party. In the minicab home she burst into tears and I couldn't just leave her when we arrived at her place. I was going to ring you but her phone wasn't working. I'm so sorry.' Vicki seemed to shrink further in her seat with every lie and she continued to stare at the carpet. She felt wretched and consumed with guilt.

'Hey, Vick, don't worry about it? I understand,' Rhys replied in a reassuring tone, lowering his head to try and get underneath hers to look her in the eye. 'You did what any good friend would have done and phones are always going on the blink these days.' However, his next words dug hard into her heart, which only added to her agony. 'That's why I love you so much.'

Vicki screwed up her face and wondered how she could bear to hurt him. But she knew that she had to. She summoned up some courage from the very depths of her stomach and was on the point of telling him it was all over when Rhys changed the subject for he had some news of his own he had been dying to impart. 'Anyway, I'm glad you're finally here, Vicki, 'cos I've had a bit of good luck. I've got a job. Can you believe it after all this time?'

Vicki looked up at him, thrown by this, and furiously mulled over in her mind what it might mean for their situation. Instinctively, she thought it might complicate matters.

'A couple of hours ago, the buzzer went, and I thought it had to be you and that you'd lost your key or something. But in fact it was Christos from the Supreme around the corner. Do you remember when I told you I was sitting in his place a few weeks back and him and his wife were running around like blue-arsed flies because their chef and waitress hadn't turned up and, being friendly with him, like, I helped them out?'

'Yeah, vaguely.'

'Well, he got fed up with them 'cos they were always sick or something and letting him down. Anyway, to cut a long story short, he's fired them. What he wants to do is more of the cooking himself with his wife, which means he needs someone up front serving and looking after customers. Well, he's asked me to do it. Apparently he was quite impressed when I helped out. So I said yeah. The pay's not brilliant, but it's not bad, either. I can certainly contribute a bit now to the rent and food, like.'

An excited Rhys stared expectantly at Vicki, waiting for a happy reaction, but none was forthcoming. To his disappointment, her face was as inscrutable as a poker-player. His excitement waned and, because the atmosphere was a touch oppressive, he added in a low voice, 'He wants me to start in the New Year when he comes back from a couple of weeks in Cyprus,' as if this knowledge might somehow be the key to unlock Vicki's happy box.

Vicki's expression remained inscrutable, however, and the smile on Rhys's face all but disappeared. After a few tortuous seconds, Vicki replied in a manner that was as cold and hard as steel for this little story only reinforced her conviction that Rhys was definitely not the right person for her. To work in the local Greek-Cypriot café seemed the height of his ambition. Compared to Tommy, he was nothing. 'I'm very pleased for you, Rhys. I hope it works out well.'

It was Rhys's turn to look down at the carpet as Vicki was clearly underwhelmed with his new job. He went quiet momentarily, feeling both inadequate and embarrassed, before mouthing weakly, 'It's the best I can do, Vicki, I'm sorry.' His sense of despair, however, was nothing compared to how he was about to feel for Vicki had finally hardened herself to break the devastating news.

'Rhys, I've been meaning to have a talk with you for some time now.' Vicki hesitated before continuing because, despite her outward air of confidence, the butterflies were fluttering alarmingly inside her stomach and she was finding it difficult to conjure up the right words. She held Rhys's expectant, almost frightened gaze despite every instinct in her body telling her to look away. The hesitation unsettled Rhys even further for he sensed what was coming next and he felt like a condemned man waiting for the firing squad to pull the trigger. 'It's not been working out, you know, you and me, for a long time now, and I don't think we're ever gonna make it. I think it'll be for the best if we split up and go our own ways.'

Having pulled the trigger, Vicki looked back down at the carpet for she found it impossible to bear witness to the destruction she had caused. Rhys did not say a word or bat an eyelid, but a rush of nausea swept over his body as powerful as a tsunami and his throat became as parched as that of a man lost in the Sahara Desert. All of a sudden, the atmosphere in the room was heavy and suffocating. As the seconds ticked by, Vicki hoped that Rhys might say something so she glanced up at him but all she saw was the man she once loved looking as ashen and vacant as a cadaver. Without knowing it, Rhys licked at his lips a couple of times, the only suggestion to Vicki that he was still alive until she detected the shaking and shuddering of his body. He lowered his eyes and began to lick at his lips more frequently and more aggressively. He also tried hard to swallow some imaginary item in his throat. Vicki had said the words he had never wanted to hear and his body was shutting down in reaction.

The silence was unbearable and Rhys's demeanour made Vicki feel dreadful. She was tempted to hold his hand, but she resisted, clasping her hands so tightly together that the veins stood out proud. Saying the fateful words had been difficult enough but disclosing the practicalities was even harder.

'I'm very sorry, Rhys, but I've been thinking about it for a long time and I know it's the best thing to do.' With a cough to clear her throat, she carried on. 'I'm going to have to ask you to move out as soon as you can. I know you'll need a bit of time to find yourself another place but I'd appreciate it if you could do it as quickly as possible. I can sleep in here, on the sofa, in the meantime.'

Rhys remained zombie-like beside her, hearing the words but not registering their meaning. He suddenly looked up at her and asked in barely a whisper, 'Why, Vicki? You're everything to me. I'd do anything for you, you know that.' Tears welled up in his eyes, which turned a dungeon dark, and he tried hard but failed to stifle a sniffle.

'It's not working out, Rhys; you must know that. We're growing apart. I'm spending more of my time alone with my friends and we seem to have less in common as each day goes by. I need to move on. I can't go on living in this crumby flat forever and I don't want to keep missing out on all the nice things in life everyone else is experiencing like great holidays and restaurants and shows. We can't afford to do any of these things. And the way we are, how could we ever hope to start a family? You know I'd love to but I'm the only one earning and we'd never be able to get by if I had to give up work.'

'But I've got a job now,' Rhys replied croakily, the words stumbling one into the other, but with a sense of optimism that he had the answer to their problems.

'You said it yourself it doesn't pay much, Rhys. It won't make any difference.'

'Things will get better, trust me.'

Vicki just shook her head and sighed. 'They won't, Rhys, they won't.'

Rhys looked away and pursed his lips tightly in an effort to stop himself from crying. He wiped at his eyes with the bottom of his T-shirt. His stomach was churning and he took a deep breath but he found it impossible to maintain his composure and the well of tears in his eyes overflowed and trickled down his cheeks. He wiped at them with his T-shirt again, blowing his nose into it at the same time. He knew it was disgusting but he was beyond caring. Vicki stared down at the floor, evaluating whether she had said everything that needed to be said so that she could walk away.

'My dream was always to get married and start a family with you, Vicki, and now you're saying it's all over.'

Vicki sighed for she knew that anything she said now would only be a repeat of what she had already told him. Accordingly, she said nothing, but Rhys's next comment discomfited her. 'It means you'll want to find someone else, won't you?'

Vicki shifted her feet and remained silent. This response confirmed to Rhys that she did. He knew that it could hardly be unexpected but to receive confirmation made him shake uncontrollably and he had to hug himself to stop. The image of Tommy flashed into Vicki's mind and she was tempted to tell Rhys about him. This was the opportunity to reveal everything, to get it all out into the open, like she had promised herself she would do. But she couldn't face it. She justified her volte-face by reasoning that her breaking up with Rhys had nothing to do with Tommy. It would have happened anyway, and soon enough, so in many respects he was irrelevant. She was also conscious of the fact that she had only just met him and that it was too early to know how things might progress. In time, Rhys would find out, but she didn't have the heart, or guts, in truth, to tell him now. It was obvious that Rhys had not considered for one second the possibility that she had stayed with another man the night before.

Stifling a sniffle and wiping his nose with the back of his hand, Rhys steadied his emotions and looked Vicki directly in the eye. His face was sad, but kind at the same time, not at all aggressive. Nevertheless, he remained desperate, evident in the pleading in his voice.

'You'll never meet anyone, Vicki, who'll love you as much as I do. You must know that. Please think again, please, I beg you.' Rhys looked away, ashamed of himself. But when desperation takes over, even the most pathetic of cards has to be played.

Vicki couldn't stand it any longer and stood up abruptly. 'I'm sorry, Rhys, it's all over. There's nothing more to say.' She had wanted to sound firm and decisive but there was an inherent softness in the way she expressed herself. But Vicki had a final sting. 'You might want to think about going back to Wales permanently, Rhys. There's no future for you here in London, you know that. It's probably for the best.' And with that, Vicki left the living room and went into the bedroom, shutting the door quietly behind her.

Rhys returned to his zombie-like state, registering that not only did Vicki want to finish with him but that she also wanted him out of her life completely. This knowledge shook him to the core and he burst into tears, sobbing uncontrollably.

In the bedroom, Vicki sat down on the edge of the bed and held her head in her hands. She could hear Rhys crying and felt downcast. She had expected it to be hard telling him but was surprised at how awful she felt. Her feelings for Rhys were clearly much stronger than she thought, or were they just a reflection of the sadness of the occasion? She couldn't be certain, only time would tell. But there was one thing Rhys had said that she did agree with. No man would ever love her as much as he did.

Rhys finally stirred after yet another night of intermittent sleep. As always, Vicki was the first thing that came into his head, to be immediately accompanied by a dull ache in his stomach. He turned over onto his back, thinking yet again about her and their relationship. He was so desperate that he liked to believe that they still had a relationship of sorts and, for the umpteenth time, he tried to work out what she would be thinking of at this very moment. In order not to sink into the deepest pit of misery, with no prospect of ever climbing back out, he had convinced himself that she would be feeling equally as wretched, and missing him madly, and that after a few days apart, the enormity of what she had done would hit her hard. Surely she would want to get back in touch and express a desire to try again?

Despite the finality of Vicki's words, the reason Rhys continued to cling onto this sense of optimism was the deep-rooted belief that she still possessed strong feelings for him. She couldn't just erase what they had been through together like some tin-pot dictator in a distant country re-writing its history. Such optimism was particularly powerful this morning and it made him feel a little better. Yes, it would all work itself out, calm heads would prevail, and things would return to the way they had been before. Perhaps this optimism was given fresh legs by the fact that it was New Year's Day and that he would be travelling back to London later that afternoon. He was starting work the following day in the Supreme and was eternally grateful to Christos for he had provided him with a valid reason to return. Without the job, he might well have stayed in Wales, as Vicki had suggested to such devastating effect, and then there would have been no hope of their getting back together again. Yes, 1974 might well turn out to be a lot better than he imagined.

As Rhys contemplated the black patch in the corner which had grown considerably larger since the last time he was back in Wales, his thoughts returned to that horrible afternoon back in the flat before Christmas. He tried desperately to expunge it from his mind but it kept springing back up as if the Devil himself had chosen Rhys to be his sole target of sufferance from now until evermore.

After Vicki had retired to the bedroom, Rhys had sat on the sofa for the rest of the afternoon, after which, and while still in a highly emotional state, he had packed a bag and shot off to Paddington Station to catch the train to Pontypridd so as to be in the arms of his loving parents. Vicki had deliberately kept out of his way and was relieved to hear him say that he would be going to Wales that evening. Selfishly, she believed it would be less stressful for her to be with Tommy, knowing that Rhys was not back at the flat wondering where she was and what she was getting up to. She didn't know whether he would take up her suggestion to remain in Wales permanently but the fact Christos had offered him a job made that possibility less likely. She frowned and shook her head at the unfortunate timing.

Back in Pontypridd, Rhys had spent the most miserable Christmas and New Year of his life. He barely saw his friends and passed most of the time staring at the television for hours on end. Not even the hilarious

Morecambe and Wise could raise a smile. His mother and father consoled him as best they could and urged him to return to Wales. His father had even had a word with the manager of the cash & carry and been assured that his old job would be waiting for him if he wanted it.

Rhys's mother had loved Vicki almost as much as Rhys himself and was saddened to hear that they had broken up. She could see in his expression how much her son was hurting and it was killing her to witness him in such a state. But her instinct told her that Vicki was serious and that the relationship was over even if Rhys found it impossible to accept. She just wanted to be close to him, to keep an eye on him and help him through his depression. Rhys had been excited when telling her about the job at the Supreme and she broke into a smile when glimpsing this fleeting moment of happiness on his face. But he couldn't fool her. The main reason he was excited was that it acted as an excuse to return to London and, as a consequence, to be closer to Vicki. His mother was worried that if he didn't come to terms with the situation, it could destroy him.

In similar vein, it was not just Rhys's parents who worried about him for his close friends had also become increasingly concerned. Initially, Ian and Don had tried to cheer him up with clichéd talk of how there were more fish in the sea and how, over the festive season, the many single girls of Pontypridd would be on the hunt for eligible young bachelors like him. Rhys had even hinted at a smile when Ian had reconsidered whether the word 'eligible' was appropriate in his case. And they joshed him along with stories of how Megan, Cerys, Siân and Helen had 'smartened up' since he saw them last. But they despaired when they could see that his heart was not in it and how he appeared to have aged considerably since the relatively short time they had seen him last. In fact, on two occasions when they had arranged to meet for a drink, Rhys had not turned up as he moped about the house, not even bothering to ring to say that he would not be coming. And this even extended to the traditional New Year's party at Don's. The memory of four years ago when he had first met Vicki would have overwhelmed him.

Now, lying on his back staring at the ceiling, the first time he could ever remember not having a hangover on New Year's Day, he convinced himself he could sort everything out with Vicki back in London. He would squirrel away his wages, after contributing to the rent, so that they could go on a wonderful holiday together in the summer, abroad even, to Torremolinos, the place to be seen, and he vowed to take her out more often and tolerate her friends. His parents had even volunteered to dip into their savings to help him along. He was determined not to take them up on their offer, but he knew that if it was the make or break to pay for a show or a nice meal, he would probably relent, so eager was he to provide Vicki with whatever she wanted. And he was determined to get out of the flat. With him earning, they could probably afford something a little better, or if they moved to somewhere a little less central, they could find a nicer flat for the same money. He resolved to spend all his spare time exploring such a possibility. Yes, these would be his New Year resolutions. He summarised them quickly in his head: new flat, summer holiday, shows, meals, Vicki's friends, more time together. And the biggest resolution of all: get back with Vicki. In fact, if things went as he planned, he resolved to ask her to marry him during the summer on a beautiful beach on the Costa del Sol. He had it all worked out and, with a happy heart, he jumped out of bed full of hope for a golden sun after a particularly horrible storm.

'Happy New Year, Mum, Dad,' Rhys exclaimed as he bounded into the kitchen where he saw his parents sitting at the table through the customary fog of smoke. He took a pace to his mother and kissed her on the cheek. The *Daily Mirror* was open in front of them.

'Happy New Year,' his parents returned in unison. But there was an inherent sadness and trepidation in their voices that reflected the looks on their faces and which Rhys picked up on immediately. In fact, they seemed to be in a state of shock.

'Why the sad faces? Has someone died?' Rhys asked, his brow creased.

Neither of his parents replied but Rhys noticed the fleeting glance they traded with each other. He then followed his father's eyes which were arrowing in on the newspaper on the table. Rhys looked down and picked it up. What he saw made his head feel faint and almost tore his heart free of his chest in shock. His legs turning to rubber, he was forced to sit down, his face taking on a sheet-white pallor. The crushing nausea he had experienced back at the flat and hoped never to experience again overwhelmed him and he put his hand to his mouth to prevent himself from throwing up. What he saw was a picture of Tommy Slater leaving a nightclub with the familiar faces of some of his West Ham teammates behind him. But his arm was around the shoulders of another familiar face who happened to have a gorgeous smile and long, blonde corkscrew hair. And when she was described as Slater's new girlfriend, Rhys could not hold the vomit in any longer.

ID: 4
April 1975

Chapter 12

With great effort, Rhys finally crabbed out of bed. He sat on its edge, stooped over, cradling his throbbing head in his hands. He wished he could just crawl under the sheets again for the rest of the day, as he did virtually every Sunday, his only day off work, but today was different. He had a lunch date in The Falcon pub on Clapham Junction and, despite his lack of energy, he knew he had to be there. He was dying to see her again.

The bed was now a single with a mattress so saggy his back ached every morning. Every possession he owned was in the room for he was now living in a bedsit off Northcote Road, not too far away from his and Vicki's old flat in Latchmere Road. That flat was now a distant memory as Vicki was happily ensconced in Tommy's apartment in the Barbican. Rhys's bedsit made his old flat look like Buckingham Palace for it was barely habitable, but at least it was cheap, or affordable more like, just, to his meagre income.

He had found the bedsit and moved in within three days of his coming back from Wales fifteen months earlier. He had been on tenterhooks during those three days, thinking he was bound to come into contact with Vicki at some stage. The tension would have been unbearable and he would not have known what to say. But, fortunately, their paths never crossed. What he did know was that he would not have been angry with her. Indeed, he would have wished her well and the best of luck despite his pain and anguish for Rhys had always believed that bearing grudges was pathetic and self-destroying. He quickly realised, however, that the reason why their paths never crossed was because Vicki was staying over at Tommy's. This realisation had ripped his guts to shreds at the time, particularly at night when he reached out to the cold space beside him in the bed, and it was almost merciful when he finally departed.

For her part, it had been well into the New Year before Vicki returned to the flat. She had been beside herself with apprehension when she turned the key in the lock because, for all she knew, Rhys might well have been at home, but, on entering, it was clear straight away that not only was he not there but neither were his possessions. The knowledge that he had moved out had come as a great relief, but despite her happiness at being with Tommy, a Hawaiian-size wave of sadness had swept over her. This really was the end and, in theory, they would never have reason to speak to or see each other again. Her stomach had ached when she observed the empty line of wire clothes-hangers in the cupboard and, to her surprise, a tear had run down her cheek.

As she pottered around the flat for the rest of that day, somewhat in a daze, Vicki at least knew that she was entering a new, exciting phase of her life without complications. Tommy was as keen as the hottest of English mustards and had already invited her to move in with him. Vicki was thrilled to be asked and wary only because things were moving at such a fast pace. After all, they had barely known each other a month. But despite that, they had become close and, on a practical level, she asked herself why she would want to stay in her dump of a flat alone when she could be living in luxury with Tommy? She was spending most of her time there anyway, so moving in made sense. Accordingly, she gave notice to the agent and a few weeks later the flat was off her hands.

The day she left, Tommy was at her side, helping with her bags and boxes. It was the first and last time he ever saw the flat. He shook his head in disgust at its decrepit state, commenting smugly what a loser Rhys must have been. Vicki grinned sheepishly on hearing the remark, not particularly liking it, but said nothing. After pulling the front door shut behind her for the last time, she followed Tommy down the stairs but couldn't resist turning round for one final look. A lump seemingly the size of an orange caught in her throat and she had to swallow many times before she could dislodge it.

Moving his hands from his head to the small of his back, Rhys arched himself in an effort to ease some of the ache before standing up and fiddling with his balls. He yawned and stretched his arms up high above his head. His lips were dry and he took a stride to the sink where he poured himself a glass of water. His face screwed up at the taste. If there was one thing he would never get used to in London, it was the hard water compared to that in Wales. Fortunately, the weather was mild though he still put on a sweat shirt. Winter had passed, which was a relief, for the heating in his bedsit was constantly on the blink, not that the landlord ever cared. For months, Rhys had worn a thick white Aran jumper over the sweat shirt and even a bobble hat at times. It was only during the course of the previous week that he had removed the black sticky tape from around the rim of the solitary window, so much freezing air did the gaps leave through. On a number of occasions when it was particularly cold he had even checked whether the air was passing through some invisible holes in the panes themselves. Not even an ancient castle in the highlands of Scotland on the windiest of winter nights could be as draughty and perishing as his bedsit, he thought.

He sat back down on the edge of the bed, for he did not possess a chair, and waited for the bathroom on the landing to become free. He had become accustomed to the sound of the bolting of the bathroom door outside to signify that another tenant in an adjacent bedsit had gone in. He had learnt that it was better to wait for him or her to exit rather than to involve himself in something around the bedsit, for it was often a race to be the next one in.

While sitting there, rubbing his toes against the rough wood of the gouged and splintered floorboards, with gaps between them so wide cockroaches the size of mice regularly surfaced, he looked around his dwelling. 'Home sweet home,' he muttered.

He lowered his eyes as he could barely bring himself to contemplate the surrounds. Mouldy black and green patches of damp spread in abundance on every wall and whole chunks of plaster had broken off in various places to reveal the bare brick underneath. The day he moved in, he had it in mind to paper the walls to cover up the unsightly blemishes, but when he placed his palm against them, his hand was so wringing wet that he knew it would be impossible to do so. His wardrobe was, in effect, an old battered and bent metal rail where he hung some clothes and his chests of drawers were the Fyffes banana boxes he had taken from the Supreme and used to transport his things over in the first place.

The landlord's assertion that the room was furnished amounted to the rotten rancid bed and three-legged bedside table. The fourth leg was a high pile of books. When Rhys had examined them out of curiosity, he saw that they were the property of the local library and so many years past their due date that they would almost certainly carry fines totalling hundreds of pounds if they were ever returned. He was as excited as a new-born puppy, however, when he came across a red-brown ten bob note inside one of them and grabbed it eagerly before realising that, with decimalisation, it was no longer legal tender. He wasn't sure if a bank would exchange it for him, but then calculated that even if one did, the country's roaring inflation rate that dominated the news programmes on his tiny black and white television set had probably rendered it worthless in any event. In fact, the economic news was so consistently bad that Rhys was not too unhappy that the picture and sound on the telly were even more fuzzy and inaudible than on the one he had shared with Vicki in the flat. A clearer picture of the economic scene would have only added to his depression. How this useless television set had not packed in yet was a modern-day miracle, he mused.

Whoever was in the bathroom was taking a heck of a long time, Rhys pondered, blowing out his cheeks in frustration. He wondered if it was the Bob Marley lookalike, who was constantly spaced-out, smoking his ganja while taking a crap. It wouldn't be the first time.

He looked up at the sink and thought it might be easier to wash himself there. Only the Ascot boiler above it made him think twice for it was so similarly erratic to the one in the old flat that Rhys was convinced they must have come off a very dodgy production line together. He stood up and walked over to it. Just his luck, no burn, and so no hot water. He wanted so much to appear his best today that, impatiently, he resigned himself once more to wait for the bathroom to become free. However, he could not control his bladder any longer and so had no option but to piss in the sink like he had done many times before. He hated doing it, for he did have standards, but needs must. Fortunately, there was never any problem with the cold water to rinse it away, but the tap was so ancient that it constantly emitted a drip which, during the night, often drove him to madness. He could now understand why the Chinese had developed it as a means of torture.

He returned to the side of the bed. 'For fuck's sake, hurry up, will you?' Rhys hollered, more to vent his frustration than in any belief he would be heard. It did not help that he now needed to take a crap. Pissing in the sink was one thing, doing the other something completely different.

Unsurprisingly, Rhys did not hear any sound of the bolt being slid across or angry hissing of the flush so he resumed his impatient wait. He looked at the minuscule white fridge in the corner, full of grubby-grey smudge marks, and wondered whether he needed to get in some supplies. He thought not and, even if he did, there would be no room inside as it was already crammed full of cans of lager. The flat top of the fridge acted as his cupboard for it supported five tins of Campbell's soup, three tins of Heinz baked beans, a bottle of Gordon's gin, a bottle of Bell's whisky and a bottle of Smirnoff vodka. As Rhys contemplated them, he thought they made the only attractive splash of colour in the room and that there might actually be something in this Andy Warhol Pop Art malarkey he had read about. Yes, the top of his fridge did brighten the room up and raise his spirits as did his Jimmy Page poster showing the maestro on stage in the coolest pose imaginable with fingers creating seemingly impossible shapes on the guitar frets. Only one other item raised his spirits more, the framed picture of him and Vicki on the bedside table, smiling in utter joy with their arms around each other. Gazing at it, Rhys picked it up and kissed it lightly before setting it back down again.

Mercifully, the throbbing in his head was becoming less intense with every passing minute, as he knew it would, for, over the past fifteen months, this was a daily experience. His splitting up with Vicki had driven him to such despair that booze had become his only crutch and there had not been a single night when he had not demolished a few lagers and glasses of the harder stuff. It was costing him a fortune, but, then again, he never went out anymore to spend money on anything else. But he valued his job and was never late for work and always carried out his tasks effectively. He had come to enjoy working for Christos and his wife, Eleni, who both valued Rhys in turn.

The drink had aged him, nonetheless, of that there was no doubt, and he often slumped in disgust over the sink in the bathroom when he saw the bags under his eyes and lines across his forehead each morning in the mirror. His hair was lank and greying more extensively by the temples and the sparkle had been extinguished from his eyes. And while he always turned out appropriately dressed for work, when he returned to his bedsit he would invariably sling on his old Led Zeppelin T-shirt or sweat shirt and faded tracksuit bottoms.

For a short period, he had taken his clothes and bed linen to the nearby laundrette on a regular basis, but, to his shame, he had not washed any of them now for almost a year. He chided himself to make the effort but he never did. His only concession to personal hygiene was the occasional wash and bath and rinsing of his work trousers, shirts and underwear in the sink. With Vicki gone, he concluded, what was the point anymore?

His life without her was a living hell. He couldn't stop thinking about her and recalling all the wonderful times they'd had together. The thought of Tommy Slater escorting her to fabulous places and having fun, making her laugh, kissing her and making love to her was enough to drive him to suicide, which he had contemplated on more than one occasion. He would invariably shed tears while clutching a glass of booze in his stinking bedsit, unable to comprehend how it had all come to this. Without fail, he would grasp the picture frame and take it to bed with him each night, gripping it tightly against his heart. It was the only way he could be with her. And yet, surely she still had feelings for him? How couldn't she? It was impossible not to, wasn't it? It was only this belief that kept him alive.

Eventually, and thankfully, Rhys heard the bolt of the bathroom lock slide back. He glanced quickly at his watch. He still had forty-five minutes and The Falcon was only down the road. Plenty of time, he told himself. He jumped from the bed like a cheetah on the chase and shot out of his room, towel in hand. He observed a pale and heavily freckled back and shock of red hair walking away from him down the corridor. It was Paddy then who had been in the bathroom. For an Irishman, Rhys found him very reserved and furtive. He wondered whether he had anything to do with the IRA who were presently very active in their terrorist campaign around London. Rhys often reflected whether Paddy was hoarding guns or making bombs in his bedsit and whether one would ever go off by mistake. The way Rhys felt about Vicki, it would have been an act of mercy if one ever did and brought all his pain and suffering to an end.

Rhys entered the bathroom and bolted the door before dropping his tracksuit bottoms and sitting on the toilet. He was excited to be seeing her again after such a long time and keen to know how things were going. Paddy had knocked on his door a few days earlier to say there was a girl asking for him on the pay phone in the hallway downstairs. Other than his mother, this was the first time anyone else had ever called him. When leaving his old flat, in a moment of desperation, he had left the phone number of the bedsits on the sofa in the living room, hoping Vicki might keep it though fearing she would more likely throw it in the bin. When Paddy knocked and relayed the news, his heart leapt higher than Dick Fosbury and he froze on the spot in disbelief. Quickly gathering himself together, he rushed down the stairs and grabbed the dangling receiver.

'Hello,' Rhys mumbled nervously and expectantly, his voice barely audible.

'Hi, Rhys. It's Karen.'

'Hi, Rhys. Long time no see.'

On hearing Karen's voice behind him, Rhys turned round and stood up from the bar stool. With a beaming smile, he gave her a big hug and a peck on the cheek. Karen's face was pink and brow sweaty. She looked a little flustered.

'Sorry I'm late but I still can't get my head around this transport system. I thought I could get a direct train from London Bridge but I had to go to Waterloo instead,' Karen declared, putting a holdall down by her feet and unwrapping her scarf. 'Don't know why I'm wearing this, it's so warm today.'

'Jesus, you've grown since I saw you last,' Rhys commented, his eyes twinkling, as he looked down at Karen's knee-length bright-white boots with six-inch platforms.

Karen followed his eyes and laughed. 'The things we do for fashion. These are an absolute nightmare; I've nearly broken my ankle God knows how many times as it is. I tell you, Gary Glitter's got a lot to answer for.'

'They might be a nightmare but they look great on you, I must say,' Rhys replied with charm, leaning back a little to get an even better look at them, 'and you're right about the transport system. That's a nightmare, too. If you're in town, the best stations for Clapham Junction are Waterloo and Victoria,' Rhys advised like a true Londoner. 'Anyway, you're here now. What would you like?'

'Just a coke, thanks. I've drunk far too much this weekend already,' Karen replied, pulling up another bar stool. 'You weren't waiting long, I hope?' she continued, noticing that Rhys's pint was almost empty.

'Ten minutes, that's all. I was just flicking through the *News of the World* on the counter here.'

'Anything interesting?'

'Nah, not really. There's a grainy picture of Keith Moon stoned out of his head in some club somewhere and Woody from the Bay City Rollers has got a new bit of stuff, apparently. Oh, and Cardiff City lost again.'

'Some things never change then.'

They both laughed.

'He should be careful, Keith Moon. The way he's going, they'll find him dead one day,' Rhys opined with concern. 'So, how are things with you then?' he carried on, attracting the barman's attention and requesting a coke and pint of Young's.

'Oh, same as usual. Nothing changes much in Wales. I'm still working in East Glam; I like it there. The other nurses are really friendly and now Labour is back in power they're spending a bit of money around the place.'

'Good old Harold,' Rhys approved with a nod, handing a pound note to the barman and taking two glasses in return.

'Don't know if you've heard but Jen's packed Don in?'

'Really. I didn't know. I haven't been in touch much with the boys this past year.'

'Well, he was always messing her about and seeing his ex behind her back.'

'Is Jen alright about it?'

'God, yeah. She's already got a new man; some bodybuilder from Merthyr. I've not met him yet but he's a real hunk, apparently.'

'That'll piss Don off for sure,' Rhys replied with a snigger. 'He might be a lot of things, Don, but a bodybuilder he ain't. Anyone special in your life then, Karen?'

Karen lowered her eyes and her cheeks blushed, making Rhys regret asking the question. It was a bit personal after all.

'Nah. Haven't got time for men,' Karen lied. 'Too busy at work, I am,' she added weakly with a hint of embarrassment. 'They're all a bunch of shysters, the lot of them, if you ask me. Can't trust them an inch, any of them, present company excepted, of course.'

Rhys smiled. 'I'm glad you added that last bit. I'd like to think I'm not like that.'

'No, you're not, actually. Vicki still speaks fondly of you.'

There it was. Her name had been mentioned. Rhys's body juddered as if he was sitting in an electric chair. He went quiet and sipped nervously from his pint, unable to look Karen in the eye, before putting it back down on the counter and staring into it like a fortune-teller might a crystal ball. Karen observed the effect Vicki's name had on him and took a couple of swigs of her coke.

Rhys was eager to learn more about Vicki and here was his chance, the comment that she was still fond of him increasing his confidence. But his innate lack of selfishness surged to the surface and he knew it wouldn't be right to bang on about Vicki all afternoon. It was rude, more than anything. Karen had gone out of her way to come and see him and would be leaving afterwards to catch the train to Cardiff. He had to know what was going on in Vicki's life, that was for certain, and Karen had just spent the weekend with her, but he would ask her later. The spectre of Vicki disorientated him, however, and he struggled to pick up the thread of the conversation. It took Karen to break the silence.

'So, Rhys, how you been doing?'

The area by the bar counter was filling up with lunchtime drinkers and they began to feel crowded out.

When one such drinker accidentally nudged Rhys's arm, spilling a little of his beer, he suggested to Karen that they move to the only free table available, which happened to have a view of Arding and Hobbs, the imposing department store, which stood opposite The Falcon on the corner across the road.

It was a beautiful April day and the sun was shining brilliantly and warmly through the windows. It was a day to lift the spirits. Karen readily agreed to Rhys's suggestion and, grabbing her holdall, she tottered behind Rhys, who, having pocketed his change, walked over to the square brown table, which was covered in enough beer stains, scratches and ink marks to have intrigued a connoisseur of abstract art. They sat down on the hard, round wooden chairs, the same colour as the table, and shifted their bums to make themselves comfortable. The customers sitting either side of them were enjoying a smoke as well as a drink and a whirly mist of grey-whiteness floated up to the ceiling, mixing with the millions of dust particles made visible by the streaming sunlight.

'That's better,' Rhys commented. Before finally answering Karen's question, he took a swig of his beer. 'I'm doing okay, thanks,' though his instinctive look down at the table suggested otherwise. Sitting directly opposite him, Karen could see more clearly the haggard features of his face and inherent sadness in his eyes. 'I'm living just up the road in a bedsit, which is alright, I suppose, if you don't mind putting up with an out-of-his-head Rasta and shifty Irishman, cockroaches and soaking wet walls,' he chuckled ironically, 'and no hot water.' Karen smiled sadly. 'But my work is going really well,' he continued, his face brightening.

Karen was uncertain whether he was being ironic again and so asked in a neutral tone, 'You still at that Greek-Cypriot café then?'

'Yeah, the Supreme, just up the hill there, close to the last flat. What, I've been there fifteen months or so now and I think the owners, Christos and his wife, are happy with me. I do pretty much everything for them, you know. I serve the customers, clear up, sort out the stock, run errands, sweep and wash the floors, anything they want me to do in fact. Not so long ago, when Eleni, that's Christos's wife, wasn't too well, I even ended up in the kitchen and did the cooking.'

'Yeah?'

'Yeah. I'm a real dab hand, you know. They don't serve anything fancy so all I had to do was grill a few sausages and chops and fry some potatoes and eggs. I even made moussaka, the only Greek dish they actually offer.'

'Yeah? How d'you make that? Sounds a bit exotic to me.'

'Oh, it's easy. You just pull the tin foil off and stick it in the microwave.'

They both laughed and Karen could see that he clearly did enjoy his work.

'Microwave? Aren't they these new cooking contraptions or something I've heard about recently?' Karen asked unsurely.

'Yeah. They're amazing. God knows how they work but all you have to do is put some food inside and it's cooked in like two seconds flat. Christos swears blind by it but I think the food comes out a bit soggy for my liking, you know, pies and sausage rolls, stuff like that.'

'You've turned out to be a right old gourmet then?'

'Oh, I wouldn't say that. It's not like I'm Fanny Craddock or anything, but I do enjoy it, and Christos hasn't ruled me out doing even more if I have to. With me being in the kitchen and running round for him as well, I'm gonna be even more knackered at the end of the day.'

Karen grinned. 'Well, if not Fanny Craddock, then more like that Galloping Gourmet bloke who was on the telly it sounds like to me?'

Rhys laughed. 'You're not wrong there! I really like Christos and, although the pay's not fantastic, he's very fair. With the way inflation is, he keeps raising my money without me even asking and throws in a free meal for me every day as well. When I come to think of it, my cooking's pretty good because of all the meals I used to make when I was with Vicki. With her working, I'd always have her tea ready when she came home in the evenings and she never left much on her plate.'

The mention of Vicki served to soften his voice and, with his eyes misting over, he stared down at his pint in deep reflection of the best days of his life. Karen observed him and smiled sadly. She felt drawn to stroke his hand to signal she understood his pain but held back, thinking it probably unwise.

'Yeah, she survived, so your cooking couldn't have been all that bad,' Karen replied after a short delay. 'In fact, she put on a few pounds when she was living with you, though I didn't dare mention it to her,' Karen added with a whisper as if Vicki was standing behind her.

Rhys dabbed at his eyes with a tissue. 'Great days they were. Happy days ... the best.'

Karen thought Rhys might burst into tears at any moment but he soon regained his composure and, taking a huge gulp, finished his beer in one long swallow. With his eyes still pouring misery, Rhys stood up sharply and asked a little croakily, 'Same again?'

'I'll get them. It's my turn.'

'Thanks for offering, Karen, but I haven't seen you in ages and you've put yourself out to come and see me, so I don't mind.'

'Well, that's kind of you. I'll have a bottle of champagne then.'

They both chuckled.

'I'm a bit peckish so I'm gonna get myself a cheese and pickle roll as well. Fancy something to eat? Besides that, I think they've got cheese and onion, ham and cheese and ham and tomato. Or you might prefer a pork pie or scotch egg?'

'A ham and cheese roll would be great, thanks.'

Rhys went up to the bar and stood with his back to Karen. As he tried to attract the barman's attention, he ran his hand through his hair a number of times which only made it stand up on end in an unruly mess.

Resting her elbows on the table, with her hands supporting her face, Karen looked him carefully up and down and noted the rather tatty clothes he was wearing. His jeans, in particular, were so bald in patches that it was not difficult to work out the colour of his underpants underneath. What was more, Rhys's jeans were drainpipe in style though the fashion of the day was for huge bell-bottoms, only confirming to Karen that they had to be many years old. On his back, the maroon Harrington jacket was washed out with seams abraded white and his pale yellow shirt beneath it was badly creased with a markedly frayed collar.

Despite his evident enjoyment at work, Karen could not fail to conclude that Rhys was on a downward spiral. He had aged noticeably and was plainly not looking after himself and, as he was already on his third pint, it was impossible not to miss the tell-tale signs that he was drinking too heavily. It was also clear that he was missing Vicki madly and Karen felt wretched for him. He might not have a lot going for him materially, she thought, but he was kind, considerate, gentle and warm-hearted. At the end of the day, she mused, weren't these the most important qualities of all?

'Here you are; one coke and one ham and cheese roll.' Rhys turned back to the counter to retrieve his pint and roll before sitting down. 'Just like being back at the Supreme, this, you know, serving food and drink, like,' he commented as they unwrapped the cellophane.

As Rhys bit into his roll, some tiny shiny-brown chunks of pickle dribbling out over his hand, he looked around the pub which was now heaving. Sucking on his hand, he compared it to the Supreme. 'Busy in here, innit, Kar? Just like the caff. I tell you, Christos must be doing a bomb for it's always full.' Rhys acknowledged someone at the counter who was a regular in the Supreme. 'But, then again, they do get good grub and great service there, don't they?' he added with a grin.

'Oh, when's that? On your day off?'

'Very funny.'

They both smiled and bit into their rolls. As Rhys wiped his mouth with a white paper serviette which seemed to smear the pickle rather than absorb it, he could resist it no longer and so asked the question he had wanted to ask for over a year. He felt on edge and the words came out in such a low trembling voice that Karen could barely hear him. 'So, you've been to see Vicki then. How's she doing?'

Karen knew the question would be coming at some stage and so, before answering, she wiped her mouth and sipped her coke to gather her thoughts. 'Oh, she's fine.'

Karen took another bite from her roll and chewed slowly. Rhys wondered whether this was all she was going to say for she seemed to take an age doing so and swallowing, and when she had finished that, she took a slow sip of her coke. Rhys was so impatient to know more, he even tried to evaluate the tone of Karen's voice. Was it enthusiastic or was there a sense of resignation, boredom, even, in the way Vicki was feeling? Mercifully for Rhys, Karen had not swallowed her tongue along with the roll and picked up the conversation, though going slightly off the point. 'I stayed over on Friday and yesterday with her. Last night, we met up with her sister and Jeremy, and Giles and Sophie.'

'Was Tommy Slater with you?'

'No, he wasn't. He was playing away at Arsenal, apparently, so couldn't join us.' Rhys took another bite from his roll, wondering why Slater had not been able to join them as Arsenal was a London club. 'We went to this ultra-posh restaurant on the Strand. Simpson's, it's called. I nearly died when we turned up; it was so plush. I knew I'd be in trouble when Vicki dressed herself up to the nines, just like Fiona, and I saw the two boys all suited up. I only brought a scruffy denim skirt and blouse with me and was really worried they wouldn't let me in. They must have thought I was some cowgirl from *The High Chaparral* or something. Anyway, when I looked at the menu, I thought I was going to have a heart attack. The prices were astronomical but, luckily, Giles volunteered to pick up the whole tab. Apparently, he and Jeremy take turns to pay.'

'So Giles must be doing well? Wasn't he in some international bank or other?'

'No! He got the sack, so Vicki told me, though Sophie maintains he left of his own accord because they weren't ambitious enough for him. She's such a pillock, is Sophie. She just sits there fawning, not saying a word. She's become so dull 'cos she doesn't do anything. She just hangs around their penthouse, apparently, waiting to get pregnant, but they've had no luck there so far. I reckon it's because of all the drugs Giles is taking.'

'Drugs!' Rhys exclaimed, his features creasing in astonishment.

'Oh, yeah. Giles has got it bad. He was constantly shooting off to the toilets last night and his nose was as red as a robin's breast each time he returned. It was so embarrassing. Cocaine, he was taking. His eyes were all glassy and he was saying stupid things that made no sense at all, though Sophie laughed along, the stupid cow. That's why he lost his job, so Vicki told me. Apparently, he's putting so much coke up his nose it's a wonder his head doesn't explode.'

'He's loaded, anyway; he doesn't need to work. Perhaps it suits him to stay at home trying to get Sophie preggers?'

'I tell you, Rhys, he's got it so bad, he either can't get it up or the drugs have messed up his sperm count. They've got problems those two.'

'Wow. That's a turn-up for the books.' Rhys took another gulp of his beer. 'And how's Fiona?'

'There's another one for you!'

'What do you mean?'

'Well, she's living with Jeremy now and working as a trainee in some poncy estate agency. Vicki tells me she's screwing some guy at work to get her own back on Jeremy, who's still putting it about big time, apparently. I think Fiona's finally coming round and realising that what everyone's been saying is true. The tension between them was terrible last night; they could barely bring themselves to look at each other. But she's driven by money and thinks everything will work out well in the end. She'll learn the hard way one day, that one.'

'What does Vicki think about it? And her parents?'

'Vicki's washed her hands of her. She's fed up of telling Fiona to leave him. It's the same with their parents. They can see that Fiona's making a fool of herself and that she's going to get badly hurt at some stage. They'd prefer it if she met someone loving and caring rather than some rich shyster.'

'Huh! That makes a change.'

'Why do you say that?' Karen replied defensively.

'Well, they're only interested in rich blokes for their girls.'

Karen sighed. 'You really have got Vicki's parents all wrong, you know. They just want their daughters to be happy, to be with boyfriends who'll look after them and treat them well. Money doesn't come into it. Sure, it helps if their boyfriends have got a few quid but it's not their biggest concern.'

'Mmm.' Rhys was clearly not convinced and took a gulp of his beer while Karen took a swig of her coke. He looked over the rim of the glass at her and took another large gulp. He had nearly finished his pint already. The conversation had gone off on a tangent and Rhys was keen to bring it back onto the subject of Vicki, which Karen had cleverly side-stepped, Rhys thought, like one of his favourite rugby players, the brilliant, twinkle-toed

Welsh wing, Gerald Davies. The extra gulp of beer was for courage. 'So, what do Vicki's parents think of Tommy Slater then? It must have come as a hell of a shock when they found out Vicki was seeing him?'

'I think it was at first, as you can imagine, but they've got used to it by now. I think they find it stranger seeing Vicki's name and photograph in the newspapers every so often. I haven't seen much of them lately so I don't know what they really think. At the end of the day, it's up to Vicki what she does and who she goes out with.'

Rhys took Karen's comment as Vicki's parents not being overly enthusiastic about Tommy Slater, but, then again, he thought he might be reading too much into it. Ultimately, he was just looking for the finest of threads to hang onto.

'And how is Vicki?' As before, Rhys could barely get the words out and he looked down at the table top like a schoolboy waiting to hear the teacher's report opposite him.

'She's okay,' Karen replied in a neutral voice. 'She seems happy enough and has got used to living in Tommy's flat, just about.'

'What do you mean?'

'Well, the flat, or apartment, as Tommy insists you call it, is very big and in a nice part of London, but his taste is pretty naff and Vicki found it hard at first to feel at home in it.'

'I'm sure Vicki would have added her own touches by now. She's got a great eye.'

'That's the thing, though. Tommy won't let her. He has the flat the way he wants it and Vicki doesn't get a look in. He can be very selfish.'

'Oh.'

'Yeah. I suppose that's how he's become a top footballer. He's very single-minded and obsessed at getting his own way.' Karen took another swig of her coke before continuing. 'I could tell he didn't really want me around this weekend; I was afraid to touch anything, to put anything out of place. He seemed to keep his eye on me all the time whenever I went to do something. It was hard work. I could tell Vicki was a bit embarrassed.'

'Mmm. Knowing Vicki as I do, I wouldn't have thought she'd like that very much?'

'Yeah, you're right. She's mentioned it to me a couple of times now, this selfish streak of his. She finds it a bit disconcerting sometimes.'

'Really!' Rhys's tone was higher pitched than he planned it to be but it reflected his excitement at knowing that perhaps Tommy Slater wasn't Mr Perfect after all. Karen's next words excited him even more.

'Oh, by the way, before I forget, Vicki knows I'm seeing you today. She gave me your number in fact. She asked me to pass on her love and she hopes everything is going well with you.'

Rhys couldn't reply. It was as though someone had superglued his lips together. This was the first piece of communication he had received from Vicki since the day they parted and he struggled to find the right words to answer Karen back. He was in a tizz and feeling the best he had felt by a million miles since that fateful day. Without thinking or knowing it, he finished his beer, stood up and went to the bar to order another. It was only when he was there that he turned round and asked Karen whether she wanted another coke herself. But, as he waited for his pint to be pulled, he regained a semblance of rational thought and realised that Vicki was only being polite, but so miserable had he been for so long, he was desperate to read the most positive intentions into even Vicki's most mundane, friendly words.

'Here you are.' Rhys placed the two glasses on the table and rammed the change into his back pocket.

'Thanks.' Karen took a sip and, looking over the rim of her glass, saw Rhys sink half his pint in one go.

'So, is it President Mitchell yet?' Rhys resumed in a happy mood.

'Sorry?'

'Sorry, I should have explained. It's a private thing between me and Vick. If she gets to become the managing director of her company in London, she'll be called president. It's something to do with the fact it's an American company and that's what they call the top boss over there, apparently. It's got nothing to do with her becoming the US president or anything like that. By the way, what a crook that Nixon turned out to be! Good riddance to him, I say.'

'Yeah. All that Watergate stuff was incredible. I couldn't take my eyes off the telly last year. I agree with you. Good riddance to Nixon, another shyster.'

'You certainly know your shysters?'

Karen laughed. 'I like to think so. I think I've got good intuition when it comes to men.'

Rhys couldn't resist it, the alcohol loosening his tongue and unlocking the chest containing his private thoughts which began to spill out. 'And Tommy Slater? Is he a shyster?'

Karen looked at Rhys and their unblinking eyes met. She half-smiled and took an age over a sip of her drink. She appeared to be deep in thought and prolonged his agony by taking another sip. Finally, she put the glass down and sat on the fence. 'The jury's out.' Rhys grinned and took a swig of his beer. That was good enough for him. 'I don't know anything about this president thing but Vicki's doing really well in her job. She's the sales and marketing director now.'

'What! At her age? That's incredible. Do tell her I'm really chuffed for her when you speak to her next ... and tell her I think about her all the time.' Rhys lowered his head in slight embarrassment for admitting this last sentiment. Karen smiled back sweetly but said nothing. 'I told Vicki she'd be president before she was thirty. She thought I was mad but I believed in her. She's only one step away now. By the sounds of it, I think I was too pessimistic. She'll get there way before then.'

'She could, 'cos, how old is she now? Twenty-six?'

'Yeah, twenty-six,' Rhys took another swig before adding poignantly, 'six months and seventeen days.'

Karen smiled sadly at Rhys and if she didn't know it already, she knew it now. He was still hopelessly in love with Vicki. 'Let's hope she makes it then, as she loves that job, and they must think the world of her.'

'Definitely. She'd make a brilliant president.' They both laughed for the title sounded so un-British and they couldn't get their heads round to the idea that their friend would be a 'president'. 'Another drink?'

'No, thanks, Rhys,' Karen replied, looking at her watch. 'I'm going to have to make a move in a minute. I don't want to be late for my train and I'd better leave now 'cos I'm bound to get lost on the Underground.'

'Paddington's quite easy from here. Get the train round the corner to Victoria and then the Circle Line to Paddington.'

'You're right. I've got it scribbled down here somewhere,' Karen replied, looking at a scrap of paper which she had removed from her holdall.

'Let's hope they're not working on the lines like they often do on Sundays.'

Karen threw him her most worried look. 'I'd better get a move on then, just in case,' she declared, stuffing her scarf into the holdall. She stood up straight and looked at Rhys, who had risen from his chair at the same time, thinking he might have another pint for the road when Karen left. 'It's been lovely seeing you again and thanks for the drinks and roll.'

'Yeah, it's been great. Keep in touch and, you know, whenever you're down this way, give me a call.'

'I will. Same when you're in Wales. Here's my number.' Karen grabbed a beer mat, rummaged in her bag for a pen, and scribbled down her telephone number. She passed it to Rhys, who looked at it quickly, before folding it in half and stuffing it into the front right-hand pocket of his jeans. Looking sheepish, but emboldened by the beer, Rhys had one final request to make of Karen.

'Umm, I don't know how to say this, but if you're speaking to Vicki, tell her that it'd be nice if she got in touch and, you know, we could even meet up for some lunch or a drink sometime, for old time's sake, like. Nothing heavy, you know. I do miss her.'

Karen put her holdall back down on the floor and her expression turned sorrowful. She could see how much Rhys was hurting. 'I don't know, Rhys,' she answered after a palpable hesitation, unable to look him in the eye.

Rhys was uncertain whether Karen meant she could not pass on the message or whether Vicki was unlikely to take him up on the offer. He didn't reply as he didn't know what to say. But then, what Karen said to him next only served to confirm that she had waited until the very end to impart the worst of the news. She had wanted to tell him earlier, but, witnessing his misery, she had bottled out. It wasn't any of her business after all, but now it didn't seem fair. Rhys had to be told, however much it would hurt him; he would find out soon enough, anyway. Plucking up every ounce of courage she possessed, she looked at him with a resigned look and sighed. This time, she did reach out for his hand and held it.

'I'm really sorry, Rhys, but it's probably not a good idea because Vicki and Tommy are getting married in the summer.'

Rhys's whole body shook as if the Americans and Soviet Union had finally unleashed their nuclear war.

July 1975

CHAPTER 13

'Phew! Thank God for that. Home sweet home.' A perspiring Vicki dumped the heavy suitcase and shoulder bag onto the hallway floor. Tommy followed close behind but walked straight into their bedroom before depositing his two suitcases onto the floor. He, too, was perspiring for it was thirty-two degrees outside with high humidity thrown in to further discomfort them.

Tommy tore off his Hawaiian short-sleeve shirt, patterned with cavorting yellow, red and blue dolphins, and flung it on top of the luggage. He kicked off his tassel loafers and jumped onto the bed where he stretched himself out on the jet-black, gold-trimmed satin spread with multi-coloured dragons breathing red and yellow forked fire embroidered full-length. He turned his head to the side to look at himself in the mirrored sliding doors of the fitted wardrobe that ran the full length of the wall. Vicki hated the bedspread and black satin sheets underneath and couldn't bear to look at herself in the mirrors. The room was like a brothel, she thought, but when she had suggested replacing the doors one day, Tommy had been sharp with her, saying that he liked them the way they were. He made up with her afterwards with a loving cuddle and kiss, but he got his way as he always did.

Vicki closed the front door behind her, picked up the suitcase and shoulder bag and joined Tommy in the bedroom. She put the case back down and blew on her hand, the palm of which was lined, red and sore. She slung off the shoulder bag and, observing Tommy out of the corner of her eye, sensed that he was in the mood for sex. She wasn't. Perhaps she could just toss him off quickly to reduce his ardour and leave her alone, she pondered.

They had just returned from their honeymoon on the French Riviera where they had stayed in the wonderful Carlton Hotel on the seafront in Cannes for two weeks, with fabulous views overlooking the Mediterranean. The hotel was the epitome of chic, luxurious splendour and Vicki adored it, but Tommy thought it 'old' and overrated. He was often surly with the staff despite their being highly courteous and professional. Vicki noticed how Tommy liked to throw his weight around, being a well-known personality, much more than he ever did when she had first met him. It had led to an angry confrontation with the hotel's manager one day when, unusually, the staff had forgotten to leave the customary bowl of fresh fruit in their room. It was the most minor of mistakes, which was rectified immediately, but, to Tommy, it was as if the end of the world had arrived. Vicki had been embarrassed beyond words at his foul-mouthed rage at the manager. It had to be perfect for Tommy, and he had to have his way.

'I'm just going to run myself a bath,' Vicki advised, stepping smartly into their en suite and locking the door behind her before Tommy had the chance to suggest she joined him in bed. She normally took a shower but a bath would take longer and, with a bit of luck, Tommy might have a wank in the meantime.

She kicked off her wedges and stripped out of her long linen trousers and cheesecloth shirt. Her bra and knickers followed quickly. Taking one pace to the bath tub, she turned on the two taps. They were painted gold and the water gushed out of the open mouth of a similarly-coloured fish. Vicki hated a lot of the things in the apartment and these bathroom fittings were at the top of her list. The fish's eyes were so unattractively bulbous, they reminded her of Marty Feldman and, with its mouth open wide, the fish looked as if it had just been caught and was struggling for breath on the river bank. When sitting in the bath, it seemed to just stare at her, which was extremely off-putting, and gave Vicki the creeps.

After sprinkling a few Lux flakes into the rushing water, Vicki turned round and looked at herself in the mirror. She sighed and shook her head in disappointment. What she saw was the svelte body of a beautiful young woman but while her face, arms and legs glowed a healthy golden brown, her torso was a pasty white. When they had decided on their honeymoon destination a few weeks earlier, Vicki was excited at the prospect of lapping up the glorious Mediterranean sunshine. She had purchased the most minuscule of bikinis and was eager at some stage to sample the beaches of St Tropez further along the coast where topless bathing was all the rage. But when she and Tommy crossed over the promenade in front of the Carlton for the first time and sought out their private loungers and umbrella on the beach opposite, he became angry when she slipped off her towelling robe to reveal the bikini.

'No man is going to see you wearing that. Take it off and put on your one-piece.'

'But I don't have a one-piece.'

'Well, go and buy one, now!'

Vicki recalled this conversation as she stared at herself in the mirror. Thankfully, her patchwork body began to fade from view as the glass steamed over but not before it reflected the bath tub filling up rapidly behind her. She angled her body round and turned off the taps. She was about to step in when she glanced down at her linen trousers. She kicked at them hard and they flew across the room, landing at the foot of the bidet. She couldn't stand the sight of them anymore for she had worn them on far too many occasions during the honeymoon. She had so looked forward to wearing the three pairs of hot pants she had taken with her to show off her hot legs, but, once again, Tommy had been aghast when she had put on one of the pairs for the first time the evening they had decided to spend in Nice, ordering her to take them off as if he was bellowing a command at a dopey full-back. Observing the slim young women parading down the Promenade des Anglais in their hot pants, brimming with confidence, made Vicki feel like a frumpy middle-aged woman.

Stepping into the bath tub, Vicki sat down, slid her bum forward and leaned back so that only her head, breasts and knees were visible above the water line. However hard she tried to relax, she still felt on edge, not helped by the fact that she struggled to avoid the stupid, gormless stare of the fish nozzle in front of her. She lapped some soapy water over her porcelain-white breasts and then repeated the action a couple more times.

'St Tropez? What a laugh!' she exclaimed quietly. 'My tits look like a couple of iced buns.'

No, it had not been the honeymoon of her dreams and indeed she craved returning to work on Monday, to the job she found so challenging and rewarding and which she loved so much.

Her thoughts quickly turned back to Tommy, however. He had changed, of that she was certain. At the beginning, he had been so much fun to be with. They had attended numerous functions together and she had met many interesting people including, during one jaw-dropping occasion, the ravishing Marc Bolan. Incredibly, when sharing a word with him, the equally gorgeous David Essex had joined them. At that particular moment, Vicki looked around her and truly thought she was in Heaven.

Tommy seemed to know everyone and meeting so many people of achievement was a million miles away from the life she had led with Rhys. Vicki also enjoyed the trappings of success. Even if she did not share the same tastes as Tommy, the apartment was spacious and immaculate, with Rosa, their cleaning lady, carrying out all the chores she used to hate doing herself. There was always a table available at whichever restaurant they fancied going to at a moment's notice and theatre tickets for the most popular of shows were never a problem. Tommy gave her his attention and showered her with clothing and jewellery, though she often wished he hadn't for, at times, it just seemed wasteful. But at least he cared for her. And she did love him ... or thought she did.

But, bit by bit, and without Vicki truly understanding why, Tommy appeared increasingly insecure around her, which, for the captain of West Ham and England, with the plaudits of the whole country ringing in his ears, seemed incredible to Vicki. If anything, it should have been the other way round, for Vicki never failed to notice the female attention around Tommy whenever they were out together socially. And who knew what he and his teammates got up to when they were staying away in hotels? But none of this bothered Vicki. She knew what

Tommy felt for her and she trusted him implicitly. No, for whatever reason, the insecurities were the other way round.

Vicki lapped some more water over her breasts as she contemplated this. It was a pleasant feeling to be alone even if only for a few minutes. Tommy could be so stifling at times, she thought, recalling how he barely let her out of his sight on their honeymoon and how he gave off his air of disapproval whenever she went out with her friends in London. Vicki had wanted Karen to come and stay again when Tommy went off on West Ham's pre-season tour, but he had flatly refused, as if he was worried they would go out and rip up the town and fuck every man in sight.

Why was he so possessive? Vicki knew Tommy was madly in love with her and cherished a family, as she did. Was he afraid of losing her? Vicki believed this to be unquestionably part of the reason. The closer they had become, the more he seemed to fear that she might leave him, for she represented everything he wanted in a wife. As a result, his controlling instinct took over. How she longed to have more freedom ... just like when she was with Rhys.

The water was cooling down and goose bumps rose on her shoulders when she raised herself up momentarily. She leaned forward and pulled out the plug. When a third of the water had drained away, she put the plug back in and leaned back once more. With the big toe of her right foot, the nail painted a pale pink shade, she pushed at the hot water tap and the water rushed through the fish's mouth once more as though it was vomiting. When the water covered her shoulders, she pulled at the tap with her toe and the fish stopped spewing. A few tiny beads of perspiration formed on her brow. With her mind turning to Tommy once again, she chastised herself for her critical reflections. She did love him after all, she convinced herself, just about, and she had been thrilled when he had asked her to marry him. She would not have accepted if she did not love him, surely? Didn't they both want to start a family? Of course they did. Having a baby was their dream and soon they would make it happen. As Vicki lapped more water over her breasts, making the nipples stand out proud, she started to worry why she was suddenly so questioning of him. She put it down to her grumpy mood and was certain it would pass quickly. Well, she hoped it would, anyway.

Vicki thought back to their wedding day just a couple of weeks earlier. Unbelievably, the weather had been terrible as rain cascaded from the skies, the only day in June it had rained all month. Was this a sign? Was the Almighty telling her something? She shook her head at such ridiculous questions.

The day had passed off well enough, though the church in Whitechapel was modern and rather scruffy. Tommy was adamant about having the ceremony there and, as ever, he got his way. Vicki had finally relented after a serious argument for she had so longed to marry in her local parish church, St Peter & St Paul's, in Godalming, a perfect setting, and where a church had stood for over a thousand years. Wasn't it her prerogative as the bride to decide where she would get married? Not in Tommy's book.

The guest list was dominated by Tommy's friends and family and included a scattering of well-known figures in the fields of sport and entertainment. The whole day was too brash for Vicki's taste and, while her parents said nothing about it, she knew they thought the same. Everyone was friendly, nevertheless, and many of Tommy's friends made her laugh on numerous occasions. There were plenty of rough diamonds among them but they were warm, genuine and welcoming people even if one or two of them had seriously troubled the magistrates in their time. Ironically, the one person she did not care for was Tommy's best man, Freddie Butcher. Vicki had met him a few times before and, in her eyes, he was a nasty piece of work, though Tommy would have been furious with her if she ever admitted such a thing. It was only at the wedding that she learnt that his nickname was The Flick, and the reason why. The knowledge made her stomach churn.

But one overriding memory of the wedding day stood out for her and it was a memory she would never be able to share with anyone else. When her father escorted her down the aisle to the sound of *Here Comes The Bride,* her mouth stretched from ear to ear in apparent joy, she could not stop herself from wishing that the man who awaited her was Rhys.

And it was Rhys who came to mind now as she lapped more water over her breasts. She missed him ... more than she could ever have imagined. They had lost touch, to her profound regret, and it was only when Karen had told her about their get-together that she discovered what was happening in his life. Things were clearly not going well for him at all, which consumed Vicki with guilt, for, rightly or wrongly, she felt responsible for a lot of his pain and anguish. When Karen told her he was missing her terribly, Vicki's disconsolation mirrored that of Rhys's and it took a big effort not to burst into tears.

Initially, she had been so infatuated with Tommy that, cruelly, she hadn't given Rhys a moment's thought, but, as her relationship settled down and she came to know Tommy better, the contrast in the way he treated her and how Rhys had treated her became more apparent and her mind frequently wandered back to the wonderful memories of their time together. Nevertheless, it was the correct decision to leave him, she tried to convince herself for the thousandth time, as she stretched out her legs, her feet rising and appearing either side of the gormless fish. Observing them, she twiddled her toes, remembering fondly how Rhys so liked to play with them. The memory turned her on and she brushed the fingers of her right hand across a nipple before lightly rubbing it between her forefinger and thumb. But, thinking rationally, what Karen had revealed only confirmed what she had believed all along, that they would never have had a bright future together if they had remained a couple.

Periodically, Tommy would ask her about Rhys, increasingly so as time went on. He wanted to know more about his character, what they had done together, where they had gone together and, most distastefully, which angered Vicki no end, what they had done together in bed ... or elsewhere. Tommy's jealousy grew more intense and, while at the beginning it was understandable, lately, he had barely been able to contain his fury at the mention of his name. Ironically, and to Vicki's exasperation, it was Tommy who did the mentioning, not her. But as Vicki wiped some perspiration off her brow, she wondered yet again why? Was she projecting positive vibes about Rhys without her knowing it? Was it obvious to Tommy when he observed her faraway expression that she was thinking about Rhys? This was not the first time she'd had these reflections, but now she was more readily willing to believe that her feelings for Rhys were being picked up by Tommy.

And why had Tommy lied to the press? Why? It was obvious. He had wanted to make a point; that he was a winner; that he had succeeded; that he was number one; and that Rhys was a loser and a bum. That whole episode made Vicki shiver with anger, despite the warm water, as it always did whenever she thought about it.

On the morning of their wedding, an interview that Tommy and Vicki had given to the *Daily Mail* a few days earlier had appeared with great fanfare. In it, they expressed their happiness and excitement and talked openly about the love they felt for each other and how they wished passionately to start a family. It was a much sought-after interview for interest in the marriage of the England football captain was immense. They had both been delighted at the way it had gone and afterwards posed for some typical 'happy couple' photographs, some of which appeared alongside the interview.

As Fiona tended to her sister in her hotel room that morning, their mother brought in a copy of the newspaper. They were eager to read the double-page centre spread and opened it flat across the bed. The pictures were excellent and the interview informative, light-hearted and well written. But right at the end, some quotes were attributed to Vicki which she knew she never said. They stated how lucky she was to be marrying such a person of distinction and how she shuddered at the memory of her former boyfriend who had turned out to be a drunk and a waster, and how Tommy had rescued her from a potential life of drudgery.

She concluded by saying that when she was younger, she had made a number of foolish decisions, the most regrettable of which being her entering into a nightmare relationship she wished most emphatically to forget.

Vicki was furious when she read these quotes and this episode only served to put her on an edge she could have done without for the rest of the most important day of her life. She knew Tommy was behind it, in cahoots no doubt with that crony of an interviewer. It was only when they were boarding the flight to Nice the following day that she confronted him about it. Tommy angrily denied telling lies and even had the front to tell Vicki that he swore he heard her saying what had been attributed to her and that she could not simply backtrack now. When they stopped arguing, Tommy sat back in his seat to await the take-off and closed his eyes, but Vicki couldn't help noticing a satisfied grin on his face as if he were the Duke of Wellington leaving the fields of Waterloo victorious in battle. Neither of them said a word to each other the whole flight. The honeymoon had got off to a bad start and, in Vicki's opinion, it never got better.

'Get a grip of yourself,' Vicki suddenly blurted out in the bath, in an attempt to rid her mind of these depressing recollections. She even turned her head round to the door, fearing that Tommy might have heard her. But, thankfully, no looming shadow approached the frosted glass. Vicki turned her head back round and made herself comfortable once more. 'You've got to move on,' she scolded herself in a whisper. 'What happened in the past is over. You're married to a wonderful person now. Forget Rhys.' Her words were forthright and decisive. But as she lapped yet more water over her breasts, she knew she was kidding herself and her forefinger and thumb played gently once more with her nipple. She couldn't get the picture of Rhys doing the same to her out of her mind and, on this occasion, she didn't try to. Closing her eyes and feeling aroused, she moved her left hand down between her legs and lightly rubbed herself with the end of her forefinger, imagining that it was Rhys's tongue. Soon, the rubbing became swifter and, with a low sigh, she brought herself to orgasm.

'You've been in there long?'

'Yeah, it was just nice to relax and have a good soak,' Vicki replied contentedly, wrapping a towel around her hair. 'I needed that.'

'Fancy a coffee?'

'That'd be great, thanks.'

Fortunately for Vicki, Tommy had moved from the bedroom into the kitchen where he was perched on a stool by the counter. He stood up and poured some water into the kettle before flicking down the switch to let it boil. He grabbed a claret and blue West Ham United mug from the cupboard and tipped a teaspoon of brown Nescafé granules inside. He added a splash of milk and a sweetener which he knew Vicki always took. Vicki sat down on another stool and rubbed at her hair. She was wearing a white fluffy dressing gown and her skin glowed a healthy shade of pink.

'Now that you're here, Vicki, I wanted to talk to you about something. I was going to mention it in Cannes but I thought I'd leave it till we got back.' Vicki continued to rub at her hair, wondering what Tommy had on his mind. But before Tommy said another word he turned round and enveloped her in his arms. Vicki stood up and they kissed quickly on the lips. 'I'm so happy, Vicki. I can't believe I'm married to such a gorgeous girl and to think we might even have a little toddler running around before long. Having a beautiful family at home is the most important thing in the world to me.'

'Yeah, same here,' Vicki replied a little less enthusiastically.

'I can be a bit old fashioned at times, you know that, but sometimes the old ways are the best. Going out to work and coming back home to a loving wife in an immaculate house, just like my old man did, is something I've always wanted.' Vicki didn't say a word, fearing what Tommy was building up to. Her smiling face changed to one of curiosity. In the background, the kettle came to boil and steam blasted out of its nozzle. Knowing that whatever Tommy wanted, he got, his next words stunned her. But, with resignation, she knew she couldn't beat him in a fight and her eyes began to moisten. 'That's why I want you to resign and give up your job on Monday.'

August 1976

CHAPTER 14

'Thanks, Rhys, that was great.'

'Pleasure,' Rhys replied with a contented grin as he removed the empty plates from the table where two regular customers were sitting. He took them straight into the kitchen and placed them on top of a high pile of dirty dishes. Eleni was at the sink in her red and white striped apron trying hard to keep up with the conveyor-belt of crockery and cutlery coming her way.

'This is like painting the Forth Bridge,' she blurted out as she scrubbed away.

Rhys laughed as he picked up two plates of sausage, mash and onion gravy from the table beside Christos who was standing in front of the cooker wearing his fat-splattered, grey-white chef's jacket. The three of them were perspiring, as not only was the kitchen like a furnace, but also because they were in the midst of the hottest summer in years. It was thirty-five degrees outside. *Test Match Special* was on the radio, high up on a shelf next to an ineffectual, anthracite-black grease-smeared fan, and the heat was certainly on the England cricket team as Brian Johnson relayed the fall of yet another wicket at the hands of the scorching-hot West Indian fast bowler, Michael Holding.

'What a great team they are, these West Indians,' the cricket-mad Christos commented. Rhys lingered a moment before serving the customers, turning his ear to the radio, eager to hear the latest score. He loved cricket almost as much as rugby and was endlessly fascinated that a Greek-Cypriot did so as well, seeing as there was no history of the game in his part of the world. 'Viv scored two ninety and that must be Holding's tenth or eleventh wicket in the match so far. It'll be all over soon.'

'Yeah, and let that be a lesson to Tony Greig. All he's managed to do is fire them up. What the heck does he expect if he goes round saying how much he wants to make them grovel? The West Indies are hardly likely to take a white South African-born captain of England saying that lying down.'

Christos chuckled as he placed a pork chop into a frying pan which instantly burst into a sizzle. 'You're right there, Rhys.'

Rhys returned to the dining area and placed the plates in front of two burly workmen who were wearing baggy shorts and vests, though their feet were shod in sturdy thick-soled boots. They, too, were perspiring and had already gulped down their pints of orange squash in two seconds flat. As Rhys brought them some ketchup and mustard from another table, he caught sight of a customer who had finished his plate of bacon, eggs and fried bread and, moving towards him, asked whether he would like a dessert.

'I think I'll have a nice bowl of vanilla ice cream, Rhys. It's so bloody hot,' he answered, wiping his brow with a napkin.

'Ice cream coming up,' Rhys replied with a grin, picking up the empty plate and cutlery, wiping away some crumbs and sponging down the table before striding back into the kitchen. Once there, the extended applause from the radio indicated that the West Indies had taken another wicket. 'What's happened, Christos?'

'Selvey's out, first ball. Clean bowled Holding. That's his fourteenth wicket they just said, amazing. One more to go and the match will be all over.' Eleni puffed out her cheeks as Rhys placed the dirty plate on top of the never-ending pile and sought a dessert bowl for the ice cream. 'It's been a brilliant summer for the West Indians around here, thrashing England the way they have,' Christos carried on, moving the pork chop around the frying pan with a fork. 'You can tell by the look on their faces how happy they are whenever they come in. Good luck to them, I say, they're really nice people.'

'Yeah, I agree with you, Christos. Showing Greig up like that is one in the eye for apartheid. They're disgusting, those racist supremacists back in South Africa. Who do they think they are?'

Christos and Eleni nodded in agreement but said nothing, busying themselves in their work. Rhys found a clean dessert bowl and walked over to the fridge. The mention of apartheid brought back yet more memories of Vicki. It had only been five minutes since he had thought of her last. He was finding it impossible to get her out of his mind. Like him, she was so against what was happening in South Africa. Rhys wondered whether this was still the case, recalling how she had seemingly changed her tune over the miners. He hoped not and believed deep down that she wouldn't have changed her views. She had a good heart, he reflected, just like he did. As he opened the large, round ice cream tub, a relieving flow of cold air was released and he lowered his head to feel it on his face. He dug into the rock-hard block, struggling to produce two good-sized scoops for a customer he particularly liked. He finally managed it and replaced the lid. When he turned round, ready to deliver it to the customer, Christos was standing in front of him, wiping his hands on a tea towel, his expression serious.

'Are you planning on shooting off tonight, Rhys?'

'No, not really. I've got nothing arranged.'

'Ah, good, because Eleni and I would like to have a chat with you when we close.'

Rhys felt his stomach churn for Christos sounded very matter-of-fact rather than his usual happy-go-lucky self. He was certain he had bad news for him. 'Yeah, fine,' he answered, trying, but failing, to hide the concern in his voice.

'Maybe after we lock up you can stay behind a few minutes. It shouldn't take too long.'

'Sure, Christos. No problem.'

'Good.' And with that, Christos turned round, read Rhys's scribble on a small piece of paper, and sought the ingredients.

Rhys walked past him and out of the kitchen, ice cream in hand. His mind was in a spin. He couldn't afford to lose this job. It was the only good thing that had happened to him since he and Vicki had split up, the only bit of stability he had in his life, the only reason he got out of bed every morning. Without it, he feared he'd just rot away in his hovel of a bedsit, drinking himself to an early death, with only Vicki's picture to keep him sane. After serving the ice cream in a daze, he failed to acknowledge the customer's gratitude for the first time ever.

Only two customers remained, sitting opposite each other at a table near the door. The girls had been gossiping for ages, their knickerbocker glories having been consumed at least an hour ago. But now, as the conversation finally died, one of them looked at her wristwatch and then at the clock on the wall at the back of the café, opening her eyes wide in disbelief at the time. It was nearly six o'clock. Rhys was sweeping under some tables but caught her eye and, leaning his broom against a chair and wiping his hands in his apron, went over to the counter to fetch their bill. Finding it and placing it on a stainless-steel salver, he took it over to them.

The girls were attractive and wearing skirts so short that Rhys wondered whether his stare at their bronzed legs was all too obvious. If it was, they appeared not to be put out by it as they smiled at him warmly. The second he placed their bill on the table, one of the girls put a pound note on top and Rhys took it away to the till. He pondered whether these would be the last customers he would ever serve in the Supreme. He sought the correct keys, pressed down on them hard and, with a loud ring, sixty-four pence showed in the display. He tucked the pound note away and counted out the change before returning to their table. The girls were already standing and, leaving ten pence on the salver, exited the café. Shutting the door behind them, Rhys locked it and turned the open sign to closed. He stood rooted to the ground for a second and lowered his head, his heart rate quickening. This was it; the end. Turning back round, he returned to their table, pocketed the ten pence and, picking up the tall ice cream glasses, took them into the kitchen.

'Last ones, Eleni.'

'Thank God for that,' she replied with some relief as she considered her red and wrinkled hands.

Christos did not say a word as he wiped down the cooker. Rhys took this as a bad sign and returned to the dining area. He ran a cloth across the table the girls had been sitting at, placed the chairs neatly underneath and resumed his sweeping. Another ten minutes and he would be finished for the day. Judging by what he had observed in the kitchen, so would Christos and Eleni. Rhys desperately hoped it would be just for the day and not forever.

As he moved some chairs away to gain easier access beneath the tables for his broom, a knot formed in his stomach. He was at a loss to understand why Christos would want to let him go for he was now convinced that this was the reason why he had been asked to stay behind after work. He had been a good, reliable hard worker, and versatile as well. He served, he cleaned, he swept, he cooked, he fetched and he delivered. There was nothing he had not been prepared to do and both Christos and Eleni had complimented him many times on his work. He wondered if it had anything to do with his more recent appearance for he knew he had become increasingly bleary-eyed and dishevelled. The drink was also taking its toll on his energy levels and, by mid-afternoon, he had regularly begun to feel more tired. He did not think that this had affected his performance adversely but perhaps Christos thought otherwise. The knot in his stomach tightened further at the knowledge that it would soon be all over and so tense and upset did he feel about it that he fought hard to stop the tears welling up in his eyes. Failing to do so, he wiped them away with the cuff of his shirt.

Without warning, Christos and Eleni suddenly appeared together in the dining area. Rhys carried on sweeping, pretending not to notice. Eleni went to sit by herself at a table. Christos went over to the till and, after pressing down on some keys, took note of the day's takings. He stuffed some notes into his back pocket and the remainder into a hessian bag which he would count up properly later before depositing it in the bank the next day. Placing the sweeping brush down, Rhys picked up a hand brush and swept the detritus into a pan. He tried to look upon things more positively and, if Christos did want to be critical of him, he would promise to improve his performance and plead for another chance ... beg even.

'Doesn't matter if you haven't finished yet, Rhys. Come and sit down with us,' Christos finally commanded as he walked over to join his wife.

'Just a tick, Christos. Let me deposit this in the bin,' Rhys replied tentatively, his purpose to show his diligence, but, in truth, more to extend his stay of execution another few seconds. But once he had done this, Rhys found no further excuse not to join them, and so, after wiping his hands on a cloth, he sat himself down at their table, his eyes unable to meet theirs directly.

'Right. Thanks for staying on, Rhys,' Christos finally began. 'Eleni and I have been thinking a lot these past few months about this business and what we want to do with it.' Rhys averted their looks, his hands clenched together underneath the table to stop them from shaking. 'The reason for this is because we've been considering our own future.'

Rhys looked up and could only mutter, 'Oh.'

'Yeah. In our heart of hearts, we want to go back to Cyprus, back to Paphos, where our families are. After talking it through, we've decided to go back home.'

Rhys's eyes darted between Christos and Eleni, who were both smiling, before settling on Christos, nonplussed as to what this would mean for him. 'I know how much Cyprus means to you and how much you love it there so I'm very pleased for you both.'

'Thanks, Rhys. Obviously, that means we're going to have to sell the business, as this is the money we're relying on when we're there.'

Rhys looked down once more. Christos was getting to the crux of the matter. He's clearly got someone in mind and they don't have any need for me, Rhys thought despondently. 'I fully understand.'

'Eleni and I love this business, Rhys. It's been our lives for over twenty years,' Christos resumed, holding his wife's hand, and we think you've contributed a lot to its success lately. You know it well and your work is excellent. We would love this business to be in the hands of someone we know and appreciate and that's why, if you're interested, we'd like to sell it to you.'

Rhys did not react. He couldn't believe what he had just heard. After a few seconds of silence, all he could muster was, 'Sorry, but could you say that again?'

'Sure. We would like to sell you the business. In fact, what we have to sell is the freehold of this building which includes our flat above.'

Rhys was dumbfounded and his only reaction was to stare wide-eyed and open-mouthed firstly at Christos, then at Eleni, and then finally back at Christos. As neither of them spoke, Rhys thought he had better say something. 'Just so I get this right. You want to sell me your business and your flat?'

'Yep, that's right, obviously only if you're interested?' Christos replied matter-of-factly.

Another tangible pause followed before Rhys answered uncertainly, 'Well, yeah, I suppose I am, but how much are you looking for?'

Without hesitation and with a cheeky smile, Christos advised, 'Twenty-five thousand.' He waited a split second, having observed Rhys's startled look, before adding, 'It's a fair price.'

'Twenty-five thousand! I don't even have twenty-five pounds to my name.' Rhys hesitated, leaning back in his chair, before continuing calmly. 'Thanks for thinking of me, Christos, but I'll never have that sort of money.' Rhys lowered his gaze, his face a picture of resignation, knowing that such business matters were way out of his league. But when he looked back up, he saw that Christos and Eleni were smiling, as if they knew something he didn't. He was intrigued, but all he could say was, 'What?'

'Leaving aside the money for a moment, could you imagine yourself running this place in the future and living in the flat above? I'm only asking this because we don't want to push you into something you don't want to do.'

Rhys thought for a second, wondering how it was possible to leave aside the matter of the money, and then replied, his eyes flicking from one to the other, 'Christos, Eleni, it would be a dream come true to own the Supreme. And as for your flat, well, it's absolutely beautiful. I could never hope to live in such a place. But, you know, the money? It's ...'

Before he could carry on, Christos cut in. 'Rhys, we thought you might be interested but we needed to hear it from the horse's mouth first as they say. The reason why, and I hope you don't think we've taken any liberties, is that we've discussed the matter with Mr Partridge and floated the possibility that you might be a keen buyer.'

'Mr Partridge, the manager of Midland Bank down the road?' Rhys enquired, his ears pricked like a dog hearing a whistle, though he knew the answer.

'Yeah.'

'I like him. He's a real gentleman whenever I serve him. Never any bother, he is.'

'Well, he likes you, too, Rhys. He's been our bank manager and coming here for years and told me you were the best member of staff we'd ever had. He can see that you're committed and want to do well.'

Rhys looked down and blushed. 'I try my best.' He said this in such a heartfelt way that Eleni stretched out her hand and stroked his forearm lightly.

'We asked him whether the bank might be willing to lend you the money to buy the place. I apologise again if you think we might have taken liberties?'

'Not at all, Christos.'

'That's good, because, in principle, Mr Partridge said the bank would.'

'They would!' Rhys was so shocked he almost fell off his chair.

'Yeah. He'd like to meet you properly, of course, but he said the bank would lend ninety per cent of the value, that is, twenty-two thousand five hundred pounds which they would secure against the freehold of the property.'

Rhys looked blankly at Christos and then at Eleni. All he had understood of Christos's last statement was that he would be two thousand five hundred pounds short. He had no idea what securing against the freehold of the property meant. Christos and Eleni picked up on his uncertainty and it was the latter who answered his doubts. This came as no surprise to Rhys as he knew Eleni to be a sharp businesswoman.

'What we would do, Rhys, is keep a ten per cent stake in the business. In other words, you'd have to hand over the twenty-two thousand five hundred now for ninety per cent. All we would ask you to do is pay the two thousand five hundred you owe us as soon as you can and, when Christos shows you the books in a minute, you'll see that won't take very long. You'll own the place outright then.' On cue, Christos left the table to fetch the accounts. 'Securing against the freehold means that if for some reason down the road you don't keep up with your payments, the bank can repossess the property.'

'The property is collateral then?' Rhys asked a little unsurely. He had heard the word used in a number of films he had seen.

'Collateral? That's right, you've got it,' Eleni replied with a watermelon-slice of a smile as Christos returned with a blue and white hardback accounts book.

'I'll have to pay interest, though, won't I?' Rhys asked a little worriedly.

'Yeah, you can't avoid that. That's how the bank makes its money. It'll be about five per cent above the Minimum Lending Rate,' Eleni replied.

'Sorry. I don't understand any of that.'

'The Minimum Lending Rate is set by the Bank of England. It's eleven and a half per cent today but it can vary. The Midland will charge you about five per cent on top, sixteen and a half per cent in total.'

'That sounds a lot to me.'

'Yeah, but Rhys, inflation is seventeen per cent today,' Christos interjected, 'so, in reality, you're not paying anything.'

Rhys did not understand this last point in the slightest but said nothing. He trusted Christos and Eleni to know what they were talking about.

'Pull your chair round here, Rhys,' Christos requested so that he would be sitting next to him. 'I want to show you the accounts. Other than me, only Eleni, Mr Partridge and our accountant have seen these.' Looking directly and seriously into Rhys's eyes, he added, 'Should you decide not to go ahead with the purchase, I would ask you never to reveal this information to anyone. I'm trusting you, Rhys.'

'You can trust me, Christos,' Rhys replied, proud to have been taken into his confidence.

'This is 1973, '74, '75 and year-to-date, '76. See the top lines? That's our income, our turnover. You can see how it's grown and, although we're only in August, we've nearly taken as much this year as last.'

Rhys fixed his eyes on the accounts as hard as a cat might on a bird in a garden. The numbers were healthy and showing an upward trajectory. It shocked him to know how much the business was taking. 'Phew, that's pretty impressive, Christos.'

'All these numbers here are our outgoings; you know, payments to suppliers, gas, electricity, wages, etcetera. It includes the money Eleni and I take for ourselves,' Christos went on, running his finger across the page. 'Now look at the most important line of all, Rhys, profit. This line here,' Christos pointed out. 'As you can see, the figures are pretty good and growing, even when you take into account the tax we pay, the numbers underneath. In fact, if you study them carefully, there's enough profit in this business to pay Eleni and me the two and a half thousand and the bank its loan comfortably. If things continue as they are, and there's no reason why they shouldn't, you can be debt free in a handful of years even allowing for some investment in the business.'

Rhys's eyes nearly popped out of his head. Despite failing his maths CSE at school, even he could see that Christos was correct. 'You've done so well, Christos, Eleni. You should be proud of yourselves.'

Eleni and Christos broke out into smiles so radiant they would have lit up Piccadilly Circus. This was just another example of Rhys's charm and generosity of spirit that so endeared him to them and, most importantly, to their customers.

'And one last thing to consider, Rhys,' Eleni broke in. 'Inflation is very high at the moment and property prices are forecast to go through the roof, particularly here in London. This building will be worth a lot more in the next few years, I'm sure of it, while your loan won't increase at all. What do they say? "Inflation is great for borrowers".'

Once again, Rhys did not fully understand this but it sounded good whatever. His eyes were still fixed rigidly on the profit figures as if they were nude photographs of Olivia Newton-John mud-wrestling with Britt Ekland.

'These are the figures, Rhys, but, at the end of the day, you work here, and I think you can see how busy the place gets on a consistent basis. If managed well, there's no reason why that shouldn't continue.'

Rhys finally took his eyes off the naked wrestlers and looked at Christos, finding it difficult to disagree with his last statement. 'There's no doubt about that. It's always busy here.'

'Well, Rhys, I know this must have come as a bit of a surprise, a pleasant one, I hope, and that you'll need time to think about it. Go away and do that. If you've got any questions, let us know. Mr Partridge will see us any time to get the finance sorted. Ideally, Eleni and I would like to be back in Cyprus by the end of the year. I'm not sure we could stand another English winter, though the way the weather is at the moment I wouldn't mind a bit of cold. We don't want to put too much pressure on you but we would appreciate an answer within a week or two 'cos, if you're not interested, we'd have to put it on the market.'

Rhys looked intently at them both and acknowledged how interesting their proposal was. 'There's a lot to think about, that's for certain, but I'm definitely keen. I won't keep you waiting, I promise.' After a short pause, he added in a soft voice, 'Thanks for thinking of me. I'll never forget it.' Christos and Eleni smiled once more, the latter's heart almost melting at Rhys's kind words.

The meeting seemed at an end and Rhys stood up from his chair, his head awash with numbers and ideas. He was on the point of leaving when Christos asked him to sit down for just one more minute as he had something else to say. Rhys obliged, a little puzzled, particularly as Christos's expression was quite serious.

'Rhys, I know it's none of our business,' Christos began, his voice trembling slightly, 'but it hasn't escaped our attention how much you've been hurting from pretty much the first day you joined us. I remember you telling us about your ex-girlfriend and we suspect this is the reason why.' Rhys lowered his eyes as Vicki's image flashed through his head. 'She obviously means a lot to you, but, and I'm speaking to you as a friend now, there comes a time when you've got to let her go and move on. She's married to Tommy Slater and there can be no future for you together. I don't want to be brutal but sometimes you have to be cruel to be kind. If you don't move on, she'll drive you mad. It's not easy, I know, but it's for the better.'

Rhys continued to stare down at the table, not reacting in the slightest to the words he knew to be right. Having spoken harshly but truthfully from the heart, Christos lightened the mood, his tone more jocular. 'Think of all those lovely shop assistants in Arding & Hobbs who come in here. They can hardly take their eyes off you. If I were your age again, I wouldn't be able to stop myself from flirting and seeing what I could get.'

Eleni turned her head round sharply to face her husband and looked playful daggers at him. Christos grinned and stroked her hand, winking. Rhys smiled and thought the only person who could possibly be more in love with someone than he was with Vicki was Christos with Eleni. Their relationship was everything he had wanted his to be with Vicki. But Christos turned serious once more. 'Don't take this the wrong way, Rhys, and remember I'm only saying it for your own good, but it hasn't escaped our notice that your appearance has gone down a lot these past few months. Your work is still excellent, don't get me wrong, but you look rougher and your breath often stinks of booze.' Rhys looked back down at the table top and his cheeks rouged with embarrassment. 'What we were talking about earlier is a great opportunity for you, Rhys; your own business; your own flat; a real future. But you've got to be professional. You're in charge, remember. You've got to look the part and be on top of things all the time. Drink is a mug's game. If you don't control it, it'll control you, and as night follows day, things will slip and customers will go elsewhere. Don't ever give them the reasons to do so.'

Rhys nodded but couldn't look either of them in the eye. It was no wonder Christos and Eleni were successful because they spoke sense and knew how to go about their business the correct way. He had to take inspiration from them for they were right.

'Anyway,' Christos resumed, standing up, 'we've taken up far too much of your time. Think about what we said. This could be the making of you, Rhys.'

'Thanks.'

Twenty minutes later, Rhys was lying on his bed, wearing only his underpants. His window was wide open but not a breath of air wanted to enter. With his hands behind his head, he could whiff the perspiration under his armpits but it didn't concern him. His eyes were fixed on a small piece of cracked plaster near the grubby plastic lampshade in the centre of the ceiling and he wondered how long it would take before it fell down like so many other pieces before it. In the background, Bob Marley was wailing away and the aroma of ganja was so prevalent he tried to breathe it in himself. Rhys didn't need to be a rocket scientist at NASA to know from which room it came as the ecstatic Rastafarian celebrated the West Indies' demolition of England at the Oval.

As Rhys contemplated the race between two daddy longlegs across the ceiling, he wondered whether he had just taken part in a life-changing conversation or whether the heat had made him delirious with wild and weird dreams. No, he was not dreaming. He was so grateful to Christos and Eleni that he wanted to accept their offer there and then solely to help them fulfil their ambition of returning to Cyprus before winter gripped rather than because of any benefits it would bring to him. But, unquestionably, this was a life-changing moment. He would be mad not to accept. The figures made sense and he was sure he could ask Mr Partridge for whatever financial help and advice he might need going forward. Not only that but he had never had the confidence before to suggest to Christos and Eleni that they were being far too generous in the amount of space they were giving their customers in the dining area. After all, he didn't think it his place. But on numerous occasions they had had to turn customers away and Rhys was certain he could fit in two more tables and eight more chairs without inconveniencing anyone sitting at the other tables. He also felt the Supreme could attract more customers by adding to the menu. Italian food was always popular and simple but hearty lasagne and spaghetti bolognese dishes would surely be welcomed.

With his mind working overtime, Rhys realised that he would have to find two new members of staff to replace Christos and Eleni and, momentarily, he became worried at the cost. But just as quickly the worry dissipated, for he was certain he would have to pay them less than what Christos and Eleni were currently taking out of the business for themselves. His confidence growing, Rhys smiled at the knowledge that, within half an hour of their conversation, he had already managed to increase the takings and reduce the outgoings. Yes, he would be mad not to accept and the thought sent shivers of excitement down his spine.

But what clinched it for him was the incredible prospect of living in a beautiful, spacious flat, which he would own, rather than the dump he now rented. He would be a property owner with his own business.

He couldn't believe it! His parents would be proud of him beyond belief ... as would Vicki. The flat above the Supreme was made up of three large double bedrooms, a long rectangular lounge and similar size and shape kitchen. The bathroom was square and spacious enough to include a bath tub and separate shower unit. Not only that but the flat was immaculate and newly decorated. In fact, Rhys had helped Christos paint the walls. On no occasion had he witnessed any of the familiar black patches of damp that seemed to follow him around and all the kitchen units were new. It even possessed a washing machine. What luxury! Rhys shivered once more at the prospect of owning his own place and marvelled in the knowledge that, for the first time since leaving Wales six years ago, the kitchen was not a part of the living room.

Yes, he had to accept, this was the moment his life would change. After all, he knew he could not go on as it was. Christos was right; he had deteriorated both physically and mentally in recent times. As Rhys recalled Christos's words of warning, he looked across at Vicki's photograph on the table beside him. His stomach knotted as he contemplated her moonlight smile and in an effort to prevent the depths of depression he knew would soon befall him coming on, he jumped up from the bed and walked over to the fridge. He grabbed the half-full bottle of Johnny Walker from its top and poured himself a measure that nearly filled a tumbler. He returned to the bed and sat down on its edge, cradling and looking down at the brown liquid which he then swilled around in the glass. He considered it for a few seconds before placing it on the table next to Vicki's picture.

Hearing the news from Karen that Vicki was getting married was devastating enough but when he had read the pre-wedding feature in the *Daily Mail,* it was as if a JCB digger had ripped out his guts. Their relationship had meant nothing to her. He was a waste of space with nothing to offer, a nightmare. He had read this last word at least a thousand times. All the feelings he thought she had once had for him were a mirage, a lie. He felt worthless and seriously wondered what the point was of going on, drinking three-quarters of a bottle of whisky in an hour, as if it was water, before passing out. In many respects he was lucky, for if he hadn't passed out and carried on guzzling the whisky the way he had been, then he might not have survived. When he came round, his face was lying in a pile of puke. Though disgusting, he realised he had been fortunate not to have choked on his own vomit and died like so many rock stars had done and that the emptying of his stomach had reduced the chances of alcohol poisoning. After this episode, he had stayed in bed for two days, the picture of depression and desolation. Many times afterwards he had considered other means of suicide, but, in truth, he never came close to carrying them out. He still harboured the belief that Vicki possessed a real love for him, however deluded he often considered himself. But it was enough to keep him alive.

It did not stop him from drinking, however, and from spending evening after evening alone in his hovel. He had stopped meeting his only friend in London from his previous job at the timber merchant's for the odd pint in The Falcon and even lost touch with his friends back home in Pontypridd. On two occasions, Don, Ian and Dai had reason to come to London, the first time to see the supposedly future of rock 'n' roll at the Hammersmith Odeon called Bruce Springtime, or something like that, and the other to see some new band that was all the rage called the Sex Pistols. They had tried to get in touch with Rhys in the hope of crashing out on his floor, but Rhys had never got back to them. And now, he had not heard from them in months. And why should he? If he couldn't be bothered with them, why should they be bothered with him? As Rhys recalled this from the edge of his bed, he squirmed and shut his eyes in shame.

Christos and Eleni were right. He had to pull himself together. It was time to move on. Vicki was gone. He had to accept it. As he thought once more about their proposal, Rhys understood clearly that this was the day a line had to be drawn in the sand to separate his past from his future. Christos and Eleni, God bless them. Outside of his parents and, for a time, Vicki, they were the only two people he had ever met who believed in him, who thought he had some value, something to offer in life. This knowledge moistened his eyes and he wiped them with the back of his hand. He was not useless after all and recognising this brought greater waves of emotion crashing over him. The dams in his ducts having been breached, the tears began to flow freely, forming a tiny pool of water on the floor, and he could not stop himself from blubbing like a toddler who had lost his favourite toy. Christos and Eleni, God bless them. Yes, he would accept their offer.

A few minutes later, Rhys regained his composure, blew his nose and sighed deeply. Instinctively, he stretched out his hand and grabbed the tumbler of whisky. He contemplated it for what seemed forever before, taking two paces to the sink, he poured it down the plughole.

'Well, Rhys, Christos, everything seems to be in order, so once the legal side is all tied up, we'll release the money.' A smiling Mr Partridge peered over his half-moon spectacles at his two clients who, in turn, smiled back.

Rhys, wearing his C&A suit for the first time in years, mouthed, 'Thank you.' His throat was so dry he could barely make himself heard.

'Christos, you'll soon be lying under that wonderful Mediterranean sun, and Rhys, you'll shortly be the proud owner of an excellent business. The bank is glad to have been of service.'

'Thank you,' Rhys repeated, fidgeting in his chair, for his waistline and behind were straining the fabric in his trousers. 'Rest assured, Mr Partridge, you'll receive the same quality of food and service you were used to under Christos.'

'That's good to hear. I look forward to being one of your first customers then,' the bank manager replied in a happy tone.

'And if either of you are ever in Cyprus, there's always a bed waiting for you at our home,' Christos cut in generously.

'That's a very kind offer. Thank you, Christos,' Mr Partridge replied. Rhys nodded at the same time. 'Well, I think that concludes our business unless you have any other questions?' Mr Partridge declared, closing the file in front of him.

Rhys threw his head back and slapped his brow with his hand. 'Oh, I forgot, sorry. I should have mentioned it earlier.' As Mr Partridge and Christos looked at him expectantly, Rhys dipped his hand into the inside pocket of his jacket and retrieved an oblong piece of paper, folded in two. He opened it out. 'I've got a cheque for you here, Mr Partridge, for three hundred pounds.' Rhys choked and found it difficult to continue and the bank manager and Christos noticed his eyes moisten. When Rhys had discussed Christos's proposal with his parents over the phone, they had been thrilled for him. What Rhys had not expected a few days later, however, was a cheque for three hundred pounds which he knew was everything his parents had to their name. An accompanying note explained that it was a little something to reduce the loan and help him on his way. Then, as now, Rhys had been overwhelmed by his parents' support and vowed that he would return their generosity with interest one day so that they would have a comfortable old age.

Rhys coughed and wiped his eyes before he resumed. 'I know it's not much in the scheme of things, but it's a little something to show my commitment.' Mr Partridge and Christos smiled. They did not know where the money came from but were correct in their suspicions.

'That's good, Rhys,' Mr Partridge replied with a nod, opening the file. Like all bank managers, he liked nothing better than to see some financial commitment from his clients. 'I'll make the adjustment to the loan,' he went on, taking the cheque and scribbling a few figures on a piece of paper. 'Well, unless there's anything else, I think that's it.'

Christos and Rhys looked at each other to signal their agreement and the three of them all stood up simultaneously, shaking each other's hands in turn. As Christos made to leave the office, Rhys put a hand on his shoulder to stop him. Christos turned around and, to his surprise, Rhys hugged him tightly, tears glistening in his eyes which he fingered away. Christos's eyes watered, too, and he patted Rhys lightly on the back as if he was the son he had never had.

June 1977

CHAPTER 15

'What the heck, look at you!' Rhys regretted it the second he said it. He hoped his exclamation had not appeared rude, but he couldn't believe his eyes at Karen's appearance when she approached his table in the Wimpy in Cardiff city centre. Picking up on his tone and look of shock, as if a streaker had just run in, Karen felt extremely self-conscious as she gave him a hug and peck on the cheek. 'You are Karen, now, aren't you?'

'Very funny,' she replied, her cheeks turning crimson.

'I think you look great. Really, I do.'

The fact that Rhys had had to reconfirm his point only convinced Karen that she didn't and her confidence waned. As they sat down on the tangerine-coloured plastic seats, Rhys looked her up and down playfully and there was certainly a lot to take in. Karen was wearing a coal-black leather biker's jacket with silver studs dotted all around like those in the dog-collar around her neck. Underneath, she was wearing a grubby-grey string vest over another vest with a picture of the perennially angry-looking Johnny Rotten on its front. This bottom vest was ripped in parts and on more than one occasion Rhys caught sight of a nipple as the vest moved when Karen shifted her position. In addition to the dog-collar, a heavy-link chain was hanging around her neck, similar to the one he pulled in his parents' toilet, Rhys thought, only this one held a razor blade that rested in her cleavage. The skirt she was wearing matched the jacket but was so short it was impossible to miss her black panties beneath it. Over these she wore fishnet tights which had so many tears in them Rhys wondered how they were still in place and, on her feet, Karen wore burgundy Doc Martens boots fastened with silver laces. Her hair, striped black and white like a zebra, was much longer than he remembered and pushed up high in a bundle. It was held in place by vicious-looking hooks and clasps and was as sticky as molasses. But it was her face that took his breath away. Her spikily-lashed eyes, swastika in the centre of her forehead and Morticia Addams-like lips were a sight to behold in themselves, but Rhys was transfixed by the three safety-pins, one of which was fastened to the middle of her bottom lip, the other two to the side of each eyebrow, the pierced skin looking red and sore.

'When the change?' Rhys asked as he picked up the two menus on the table, handing one to Karen.

'A couple of weeks back. I love the music and a friend of mind in hospital kept badgering me. I saw her out one day and she looked fantastic so I took the plunge.'

'Your patients must have died of shock,' Rhys commented mischievously with a glint in his eye.

'Ha ha, very funny. We're not allowed to wear this in there.'

'I think you look great, seriously. I love this whole punk thing. The energy of the music is amazing, much better than all this recent glam crud. The Stranglers are my favourites, especially *Peaches*,' and with that, Rhys sang a quick line from the song. '*Sitting on the beaches, looking at the peaches, durr durruh, they've got me going up and dowwwnnn ...*'

Karen laughed. 'I wouldn't give up your day job if I were you. Yeah, that's a great song but nothing beats *Anarchy In The U.K.*. The Pistols are awesome and this new guitarist of theirs, Sid Vicious, is just sex on legs, real eye candy.' The expression made Rhys think instantly of Vicki but the moment was fleeting.

'You gobbed on anyone yet then?'

'Definitely not!' Karen exclaimed, scrunching up her face. 'I couldn't do that.'

Rhys chuckled. 'So what do you call yourself these days? No, lemme guess. Karen Killer? Or Karen Cretin, perhaps?'

'Very funny. Just Karen will do, thanks.'

With them both smiling, Rhys and Karen put down their menus simultaneously, indicating that they were ready to order. A sharp-eyed waitress was with them at warp speed, pad in hand.

'Karen?'

'I'll have the quarter-pounder with cheese, please, and a strawberry milkshake.'

'I'll have the frankfurter and chips and grilled tomato, please, and a chocolate milkshake. Thanks.'

The pretty blonde waitress flashed Rhys a smile, which he reciprocated, before turning away. He shifted his feet and accidentally kicked his holdall. He had taken advantage of the bank holiday for the Queen's Silver Jubilee to make a flying visit home to see his parents and friends. His train to London was leaving in a couple of hours so he had arranged to meet Karen for a catch-up. Rhys was so busy with his business back in London that it was rare for him to find the time to return to Wales.

Rhys might have been shocked at Karen's appearance but in many respects she was even more shocked at his. He looked completely different to the mess she had encountered in The Falcon pub a couple of years back. His hair was shorter, with a healthy bounce, and brushed back off his forehead and behind his ears to reveal a bright-eyed and glowing complexion. Even the flecks of grey had disappeared. His light blue Double Two shirt and dark navy cords were free of wrinkles and creases and his black brogues shone so brightly Karen wondered if he had worn the brush out cleaning them. Draped over the back of his chair was a dove-grey soft-leather bomber jacket. Karen's jacket was second-hand and cheap while Rhys's looked new and expensive. But even more impressive than his physical appearance was the air of confidence Rhys carried which was so lacking the last time they had met. Karen had been intrigued to see Rhys again because the word from Jen, who was back with Don, much to Karen's dismay, was that he was doing well and now the owner of the Supreme Café. She had not believed Jen at first, thinking she must have got it all wrong, but without even asking him, Karen could tell from Rhys's demeanour that Jen was indeed correct.

'I'd be interested to know what you think about your burger,' Rhys enquired, picking up the conversation. 'I've got a Wimpy down the road from me and I'm keen to know what the competition is like. I haven't had the chance to go in there myself yet.'

'Yeah, I was going to ask. I heard through the grapevine you'd bought the Supreme?'

'You're right. The previous owners wanted to go back to Cyprus and gave me first refusal. They helped me with the bank manager to sort out the finance and everything and were just brilliant to me. I owe them everything.' Rhys looked down momentarily with an expression of longing. He missed Christos and Eleni.

'That's great, Rhys. I'm really pleased for you.'

'Thanks. It's hard work but I love it. I've got an Italian chef now, Mario, and he's added some new dishes. The waitress I've got is really good as well and is as keen as mustard. The customers love her; it's a nice little team. I've made one or two changes but not too many. Fortunately, business is really good. I owed the previous owners some money but I've paid them off already and I've managed to reduce my bank loan, too. Yeah, touch wood, well Formica anyway, things are going great,' Rhys added with a contented smile, touching the table top.

'I've got to say that's quite a change from the last time I saw you.' Before Karen could carry on, she was interrupted by three youths stumbling into the Wimpy. The two boys were obviously vying for the attention of their pretty companion like alpha males fighting over the prettiest lioness in the pack and their voices were loud. Rhys grinned for he could see she was playing one off against the other. They had been drinking and one of the boys had a string of Welsh Dragon bunting hanging from his neck while the other wore a plastic Union Jack hat. The Wimpy was filling up. After a day's partying, everyone was feeling famished.

'The whole town's drunk from what I can gather,' Rhys commented and, on cue, a group of boys staggered past the Wimpy throwing streamers and blowing plastic horns.

'The whole country more like. It's quite a day. Some of the pubs are charging 1952 prices for beer, you know, tuppence a pint or something ridiculous like that, so it's no wonder everyone's pissed,' Karen replied with a nod.

Rhys laughed. 'Yeah, I had a couple of pints with the boys myself last night in Ponty but I'm so used to not drinking now, it went straight to my head.'

'Yeah! You given up or something?'

'No. I've not given up but I've really cut back. I only drink beer now; I don't touch the hard stuff anymore. I feel so much better for it and with my responsibilities now, I've got to keep a clear head.'

'Wow! I never thought I'd hear you say that.'

The pretty waitress returned, two plates in hand, and placed them in front of Rhys and Karen. A moment later, she returned with the two milkshakes. As they tucked in, Rhys looked around the Wimpy. He disliked the orange and white corporate imagery but acknowledged it looked fresh and modern and made a mental note to ensure the Supreme kept up its appearance as well. He took a slurp of his milkshake. It was delicious, tastier than the one he offered if he was honest. He promised himself to explore a different syrup or quality of milk when back in London.

'Did you ever move out of that bedsit of yours, you know, the one you hated so much?' Karen asked, changing the subject and wiping her mouth.

'God yeah,' Rhys answered with an air of relief. Looking at Karen, he half-smiled, for, without her knowing, she had wiped away most of the black lipstick or whatever it was she had on her lips. 'When I bought the Supreme, it came with the flat above, where the previous owners lived.'

'So you own that as well?' Karen shrieked, her goth eyes open wide and mouth agape.

'Yeah, I do. It's lovely. It's got three bedrooms and masses of space and for the first time I can remember, everything actually works. I was lucky in that it was freshly decorated just before I moved in. What's more, all the kitchen and bathroom units are brand new and

I've just finished buying some furniture and furnishings from Habitat. I'm really chuffed with the place; it's everything I've always wanted, just fantastic. I still can't believe it's mine.'

'God, Rhys, you really have done well.'

'Thanks.' After a short pause, Rhys resumed on a matter close to his heart. 'How's the burger, Karen? And the chips?'

'Not bad. The burger's a bit overdone but the chips are nice.'

'The chips are pretty good, I'll give them that, but my frankfurter's a bit tasteless. I think I'll stick to good old-fashioned British bangers.' Karen didn't reply and chewed on a chip but she could see how Rhys's mind was working overtime and how committed he was to his business. It was impressive. Rhys quickly changed the subject, not wanting to sound boring or appear rude by always talking about himself. 'Anyway, enough about me. How are things with you? Ian was asking last night.'

Karen knew Rhys was fishing on his friend's behalf for they had gone out together occasionally. Deep down, Karen was in two minds about Ian and, if truth be told, he didn't help himself. 'Oh, I'm fine, you know, fighting off all my admirers,' she lied with a laugh. 'Ian's very nice but he always gets so drunk when we go out that I can't understand what he's on about by the end of the evening. Because he likes to drink and I don't drive and we live twelve miles apart, we don't get to see each other very much. Not sure what he'd think of me now if he saw me like this?'

'Oh, Ian's into punk as well so I don't think you'd have any trouble there. I know he's keen and so he should be. You're a very good-looking girl.'

Karen sliced off another piece of burger and placed it into her mouth. She appeared nonchalant but her cheeks flushed on hearing the compliment. It was the first time anyone had ever told her that and she didn't know how to react but she certainly understood what Vicki meant when she talked about Rhys making her feel like a million dollars.

Rhys took her silence as a sign that she did not want to discuss Ian any further so he let the matter drop. He had said what Ian had asked him to say so it was up to them now. He dug his fork into a few chips and put them into his mouth. Yes, they were tasty, he had to admit, but he preferred the chunky ones he offered to the thin ones on his plate and decided not to make any change to his versions.

Another decision Rhys had taken before meeting Karen was not to bang on about Vicki all the time. He would ask after her out of politeness, of course, but he knew where he stood and, so immersed was he in his business that, bit by bit, her memory had stopped consuming his mind. Even the desperate night-time hours passed by comfortably enough now. He had even taken up Christos's suggestion to see what he could get from some of the girls working at Arding & Hobbs and, on more than one occasion, pleasingly, he had got exactly what he had hoped for. Vicki consumed his life to a far lesser extent. He only thought about her every hour of the day now rather than every five minutes.

As Rhys finished his meal by wiping his plate with a piece of bread, he caught sight of Karen adjusting the safety pin in her lip. He grinned. 'It can't be easy eating with that thing there?'

'It's awful, if I'm honest,' Karen replied with a pained expression. 'All I can taste is blood.'

Rhys screwed up his face. 'The things we do for fashion.'

'You can say that again,' Karen agreed with feeling. 'At least platforms are on their way out at last.' Rhys smiled and looked up at the clock on the wall. His train would be leaving in half an hour. He was about to ask Karen how Vicki was when she got onto the subject herself in an indirect manner. 'England seem to be struggling to qualify for the World Cup next year, don't they?'

'Yeah,' Rhys replied with a nod. 'That would be two World Cups running they would miss out on. That's unbelievable for a side like them.'

'And Tommy Slater's been dropped from the team as well.'

The mention of the name induced a dull ache in Rhys's stomach though, outwardly, Karen witnessed no obvious physical reaction from him. 'Yeah, I saw that. Well, he is getting on a bit and that new kid from Liverpool who's taken his place is pretty shit hot.'

'He's not very happy. In fact, he's gone mental about it.'

Rhys had not read this in the newspapers or heard it on the news so he knew Karen must have got it from Vicki. 'Well, it's to be expected, I suppose.' Karen was about to interrupt but Rhys carried on. 'What's interesting is all this speculation he might be transferred to Leeds United this summer. I can't imagine Vicki living up there.' There it was, the first time her name had been mentioned all afternoon and, in recognition, they both sank their eyes and averted each other's gazes, slightly uneasily.

'No, nor me,' Karen answered with little doubt.

'She'd have to give up her job if she did and Vicki would hate that. By the way, is she President Mitchell yet? It wouldn't surprise me if she was,' Rhys added with a chuckle.

Karen sank her eyes once more but this time her expression changed to one of utter gloom. She didn't reply immediately and only shook her head, pursing her lips. Rhys was puzzled by this reaction but waited for Karen to say something first before opening his mouth. He was all ears and took a slurp of his milkshake, his eyes never leaving Karen for a second as he peered over the rim of the tall glass.

'Actually, she left her job a couple of years back, right after she got married.' Karen left the sentence floating in the air, not expanding on it or explaining the reasons why.

'Oh,' was all Rhys could say, leaving the milkshake alone. He looked baffled.

'Yeah, Tommy wanted her to leave straight away.'

'Why's th ...'

But before Rhys could even finish, Karen cut in with an angry rasp. 'Because he's a shyster, that's why?' Rhys was taken aback at Karen's vehemence and wondered whether she was reflecting Vicki's views or just her own. He didn't have long to wonder, however, for Karen was soon off on a tirade. 'Yeah, he's just a selfish, chauvinist shyster. He doesn't care about Vicki, only himself. All he wants is for her to stay at home and play the dutiful housewife. She loved that job and now all she does is twiddle her thumbs. He's so insecure, you'd never believe it. He won't let Vicki do anything. She's just a possession to him, someone who looks nice on his arm, a trophy. The last couple of years have been hell for her. It's a real shame.'

When Karen finally stopped, Rhys remained quiet. This was a turn-up for the books. Whenever he saw pictures of Vicki in newspapers and magazines, she always had a smile on her face, arm in arm with her famous husband. Perhaps the camera does lie after all. He was at a loss what to say and just stared at Karen who looked to be on the point of exploding. She lowered her head and took a final loud slurp of her milkshake which helped calm her down a little. Rhys was still dumbfounded, but, looking back up at the wall clock, knew he would have to make a move in a minute if he was to catch his train.

He called the waitress over and asked for the bill. As they waited for her to bring it to their table, they remained silent. Karen could see that Rhys's mind was in a whirl, his eyes distracted as he tried to evaluate what any of this might mean for him. Puffing out his cheeks, he concluded it meant nothing. If Vicki had issues with Tommy, that was for her to sort out. After all, wasn't he just her nightmare boyfriend from the past in her eyes? He didn't get too upset at this recollection these days for he had become accustomed to knowing where he stood with Vicki and had moved on ... of sorts.

The waitress returned and Rhys insisted on paying despite Karen's protest. He left a generous tip of seventy-five pence which lit up the waitress's eyes in delight. Getting to his feet, Rhys put on his jacket, picked up his holdall and, observing that the floor of the Supreme was always cleaner than that of this Wimpy, he escorted Karen outside and walked her the short distance to her bus stop. The weather was so mild they both left their jackets unzipped. As they arrived, two young girl revellers skipped past them arm in arm, one waving a Union Jack, the other a Welsh flag.

'Well, Karen, it's been great seeing you again and next time I'm down I'll give you a buzz, definitely. It's none of my business, I know, but when I speak to Ian next I'm going to tell him he needs to shape up and cut back on his drinking should you want to see each other again. I did say I'd report back but I'm leaving it at that.'

'We'll see. Yeah, you must give me a buzz when you're down next. It's always nice to meet up and if I'm ever in London I'll give you a call, too.'

'Yeah, do that, promise me.' And with that, Rhys gave Karen a hug.

A typical bloke, Karen thought with a smile, as she extricated herself from his arms. He's about as subtle as a brick, she reflected further, as she recalled how he would *report* back to Ian as if he were a soldier on a scouting mission. Karen was concerned, however, whether, for her part, she had been too subtle with him because, only a few days earlier, she'd had a long conversation with Vicki who was eager to know where the land lay with Rhys, with a view, no doubt, of making contact should things sound promising. But Karen feared she had not explored enough, indeed, at all, what Rhys now felt for Vicki and, with him about to leave, she had nothing much to *report* back to Vicki herself. She was terrible at playing these games and felt very ill-at-ease. But Rhys's next comment made her believe, helpfully, that perhaps she had touched a nerve in him after all.

'I was just wondering, Karen, what you were saying about Vicki. She can't be very happy, can she?'

'You're right there. She's really miserable, actually.' Karen was going to leave it at that but instead developed the statement, looking Rhys in the eye to make it obvious that he should take her seriously. 'In fact, it wouldn't surprise me if she left him. But, you know, we girls hate to be alone, don't we?'

Rhys was stunned by this comment. He became disorientated, not knowing what to do or what to say. He picked up his holdall but then put it back down again. A few seconds later, he repeated the action. Eventually, clasping Karen lightly by the arm, he proffered a weak and nervous, 'She wouldn't do that, would she?' His throat was so dry, the words sounded as if they had been scraped from his larynx.

Without hesitation and in a confident tone, Karen replied, 'You watch this space.'

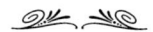

The journey back to his flat in London took four hours. To Rhys, it flew by in five minutes.

Chapter 16

'Oh, what a surprise!' A sarcastic-sounding and furious-looking Tommy Slater stared sternly at his wife, hands on hips, and shook his head in dismay. He emitted an almighty sigh before stomping off in the direction of the bedroom to retrieve a tie. He was running late and this predictable piece of news only added to his flustered state.

'I'm sorry, Tommy, but what can I do? There's no point asking me every day, it's not gonna change anything,' Vicki bellowed as she cradled a mug of coffee in her hands while sitting at the dining room table.

Unlike Tommy, who was immaculately attired in a lightweight, pale grey, linen and wool mix single-breasted suit, Vicki was still wearing her nightdress under a tightly-belted cream-coloured dressing gown. Tommy returned in a rush, fixing his tie, before rummaging in a drawer for his wallet. A taxi was waiting for him outside, ready to whisk him away to Wimbledon to watch the Ladies Final between Virginia Wade and Betty Stöve in the presence of the Queen, the two of them having received special invitations from none other than the chairman of the All England Lawn Tennis & Croquet Club himself. Tommy had accepted on his own behalf but declined on that of his wife. Vicki was not keen on tennis and, anyway, they had stopped doing things together a long time ago, so much so that there were even the first stirrings in the press at the poor state of their marriage. However, as often the case, the stories were inaccurate. Their marriage was not in a poor state; it was in a terrible state.

Tucking the wallet into an inside jacket pocket, Tommy looked at himself in the hallway mirror, ran a finger along the inside of his shirt collar, fastened one jacket button and left the apartment, slamming the door behind him without even a goodbye.

'Bye, Tommy,' Vicki spat under her breath venomously. She was fed up of the daily inquisition as if a miracle had taken place overnight. Tommy's question was even more regular than her periods and it was this that was the reason for his fury for Vicki had failed to fall pregnant and the frustration he and his parents felt at the lack of a child and new grandchild was reaching boiling point. What's wrong with her? Tommy's family would ask him, never for once believing that the problem might be with their Golden Boy. There was never a suggestion he might want to get himself checked out at a doctor's. East End boys didn't do things like that. Tommy had been encouraging Vicki to go to the doctor's herself but she had flatly refused and urged him to be patient. But his patience was wearing thin. After all, hadn't he married Vicki to have a child and, preferably, a son? Wasn't that her duty? he often said to himself and to his parents as if he was the King of England.

Vicki was glad Tommy had gone. She'd have some peace and quiet to think hard about what she should do. This would not be for the first time, and she was ninety-nine per cent there. She was going to ask him for a divorce. She would have done it earlier, much earlier, but Vicki took her marriage vows seriously and didn't want to turn her back on them at the first sign of trouble.

She had hoped Tommy might change and revert back to how he had been at the beginning of their relationship. But her hopes had proven futile.

As Vicki went over the arguments in her head, knowing that all she was really searching for was courage, she stood up and went back into the kitchen to make herself another coffee. Deeply pensive, she leaned against the fridge, the kettle hissing and rumbling in the background. She gave a slight nod to acknowledge that she had genuinely tried her best to make the marriage work.

Vicki had been devastated to give up her job but Tommy had persuaded her that were she to fall pregnant, she would have to leave it eventually, and perhaps in only a few months time. He had reminded her that as they planned to have four children, one right after the other, it was conceivable she might not return to work for years, if at all. There was some merit in Tommy's argument, she had concluded reluctantly at the time, knowing that with four children she would probably stay at home full-time, though she would have liked to have continued working right through her first pregnancy until it became impossible. But here she was, two years down the road, with no children in sight, and two possible years in a job she had loved wasted.

Yes, two wasted years of boredom, hanging around the apartment doing nothing. Sure, there had been some enjoyable dinners and functions, and Tommy never failed to shower her with expensive baubles, however grotesque. But she was afraid to breathe in his presence or talk to any other man without receiving ugly and jealous looks which put him in a wretched mood for days on end. She had given up long ago choosing an outfit for herself to wear so often did he tell her to take it off. It had come to the point where she would ask him first; at least she saved time that way. And heaven forbid should she argue back. Tommy could get so angry, his eyes almost demonic, that on more than one occasion Vicki thought he would do her some physical harm. It had not come to that yet and Vicki was always careful to back down before his mouth started foaming with rage like a rabid dog. But she hated herself for doing so, for feeling so weak, pathetic even, but she had to admit he did put the fear of God into her sometimes. Tommy Slater had to have it all his own way.

The click of the kettle nudged Vicki out of her reverie and she poured the boiling water into her mug. She added a splash of milk and sweetener and gave it a quick stir. Leaving the spoon in the sink, she walked back into the dining room and sat back down on the chair she had vacated a few minutes earlier. Tommy will be in a right mood when he comes home later, she thought, and no doubt he will have had a few drinks as well, which will only make him more boisterous and aggressive than usual. Vicki shut her eyes and shuddered at the image. He didn't drink much but only one or two were enough to darken his mood. In recent months, he had been drinking more.

Not only would Vicki not bear him a child but West Ham were struggling and he had lost his place in the England team and with it the captaincy. He was devastated and could not believe that some pimply-faced Scouse git, as he liked to refer to him, Alf Garnett-like, had taken his place. When the *Liver Birds* had come on the television one evening, he had even thrown a glass at it, smashing it against the wall, for fortunately he had missed the set altogether. He had insisted that Vicki change channels, even though it was one of her favourite programmes, before storming off to the bedroom.

There had been much speculation that Leeds United were interested in signing him and, being one of the best teams in the country, Tommy had initially been eager to join. Vicki had been horrified, however, at the prospect of living in the grim North, as she saw it. It had led to a blazing row, with voices raised so high that Solly had knocked on the door to see if everything was alright. What had particularly driven Tommy's Krakatoa-like fury was Vicki's suggestion that he live in Leeds while she stayed in London. Despite her saying that she would join him frequently, Tommy had seen this as her attempt to gain some freedom and live the life of Riley in London. Vicki was certain this was the reason he eventually turned down the move though it would have rekindled his career.

The hard dining room chair made her bum ache so she picked up the coffee and moved over to an armchair in the living room. The sunshine streamed through the window and across the foot stool where she rested her feet, providing a comforting warmth. Her toes protruded through the ends of her slippers and, observing them, she gave them a wiggle. Yes, she was ninety-nine per cent there. She would ask him for a divorce, if not tonight, then soon, very soon. She couldn't go on like this. Her life was wasting away, just awful.

A few percentage points had been added when Sophie stunned her a few weeks earlier by revealing that she was leaving Giles and getting divorced herself. It had helped Vicki in her anguish to know that a close friend had taken the plunge. Giles was in a dreadful state, despite his wealth. The drugs had taken hold and Sophie's life was a living hell. Vicki admired Sophie for her decision and strength of character, particularly after being so critical of her subservience to him in the past. Sophie had acted while she just dithered. After only a couple of weeks, Sophie had entered into a new relationship with a man Vicki had met and liked and believed to be good for her. Sophie claimed to be in love but Vicki knew this to be nonsense. Perhaps in time, but not now, she thought, though she wished her friend every happiness.

Fiona, too, had left Jeremy. They had never married but Vicki's sister had come to her senses when discovering condoms in his trouser pocket one day. Fiona was on the Pill. She had torn the trousers to shreds, together with three of his best suits, before packing her bags and returning home to her parents. Vicki was relieved because Jeremy's shenanigans were driving her sister mad, 'doing my head in' as Fiona repeatedly said, and making her sick with worry. He was bad for her. Good riddance. Mind you, it had not stopped Fiona from enjoying herself. She claimed not to be in a relationship, and this was true, but she seemed to be keeping a number of male colleagues at her estate agency very satisfied indeed. Vicki shook her head at the knowledge and despaired of her parents ever discovering the true nature of their sweet younger daughter.

Yes, they'd had the courage to leave their partners and change their lives. She would do the same. Tommy would go crazy, she was certain, and the media would be in a frenzy and on her back for a while. She shuddered at the thought and cupped the coffee more tightly as if it possessed the magic powers necessary to help her face them down. It would blow over quickly enough, she reasoned. She hoped so, anyway. In practical terms, she would have to move back in with her parents for she had little money to her name. Fleetingly, it crossed her mind to push for a financial settlement with Tommy. But, just as fleetingly, the thought passed away. She just wanted to be out of the marriage with no complications. She'd get a job and start again.

She sighed deeply and puffed out her cheeks for a mountain seemingly the size of Everest loomed large in front of her and she was only in its foothills, with no husband, no work and no property of her own. In her anxiety, the mountain looked intimidating and she sighed once more, wondering whether she would ever scale it. She had no option and steeled herself to the challenge.

Looking directly ahead, Vicki gazed at the burgundy flock wallpaper, patterned with every type of exotic creature imaginable, and shook her head at the memory of Tommy bawling her out with the rage of the damned when she had objected to it. He thought it added style and class to the living room; she thought it made it look like a cheap Indian restaurant. Talking of which, her old friend from work, Brenda, had a penchant for Indian food, which was increasingly popular, and they had met up in one such restaurant off Piccadilly Circus not so long ago.

Vicki liked Brenda and had kept in touch with her after leaving work. She now wore an engagement ring, no doubt having battered Trevor into submission, Vicki thought ungraciously, but, worryingly for her friend, no wedding date had been set. Her old job had been filled but Brenda confided in her that she was so highly thought of by the senior management that there was every likelihood a position would be found for her should she ever want to return. There were no guarantees and, initially, such a position might not be at the level she had attained before resigning, but the signs were promising and, when she left Tommy, Vicki resolved to make a formal approach. With a good job, she would soon be earning enough to afford a flat for herself.

Perhaps the slopes of the mountain were not so steep after all, Vicki pondered, recalling the conversation with Brenda. She would need to be patient but the summit was not insurmountable. A good job and flat were not out of the realms of possibility. This only left her to find a nice boyfriend for, deep down, she did not want to be alone. She was not getting any younger and still craved starting a family of her own.

She was not unattractive, she thought, though she did not feel it at the moment. Some men might even think there was some kudos in going out with the ex-wife of Tommy Slater, Vicki tried to convince herself. More glumly, she believed the opposite might also be true with other men being intimidated. The idea of going through the ritual of dating again depressed her and she despaired whether she would ever find love again, for she had been in love once, and still was ... with Rhys. She thought she had been in love with Tommy but now acknowledged it was never the case. Tommy loved her to the ends of the earth and she squirmed at the belief that, inadvertently, she had deceived him. It had not been her intention, though he would never see it that way. Looking back objectively, Tommy had been in the right place at the right time to take advantage of the depressed state she had been in over her relationship with Rhys. She had been vulnerable and looking for a way out and Tommy had been the route.

'Why would anyone ever want to go out with me? I'm all over the place, a confused old cow who doesn't know what the hell she's doing.'

It helped Vicki to holler it out rather than think it and she shook her head, tears forming in her eyes. She had made mistakes and had hurt and would hurt the only two men who had ever loved her. Despite the way Tommy was, he had deserved better than to be led on by someone who didn't love him. Many girls would put up with the way he was, and share his tastes, and he deserved to be with someone like them, not a deceitful mess like her, for that is how she saw herself.

Placing the coffee mug on a small table next to the armchair, she wiped her eyes with the sleeve of her dressing gown. But this only induced further tears and she had to tilt her head back and look upwards to stop the fine lines running down her cheeks turning into torrents. Vicki licked at the salty taste on her lips as the tears found the valleys in her skin that led to the corners of her mouth. The tears were for Rhys. She couldn't get him out of her mind, yet another deceit she had hidden from Tommy, particularly during their love-making. Deep inside her, she was convinced Tommy knew she really loved Rhys, though he could never bring himself to say it. Probably the way he controlled her life was an admission of sorts, ensuring that she was never free to seek out the true love of her life.

It had been such a long time since she had seen Rhys last that she wondered whether he would even find her attractive anymore, so ugly and disgusted did she feel about herself at that specific moment. She really needed someone to boost her confidence. Only Rhys could do that and she shivered when recalling the way he had made her feel like Miss World on so many occasions. How she craved for him to do so again. But would he? Or more upsettingly, would he want to? Karen had told her only the other day how he had transformed his life; he had his own business, a beautiful flat, money in his pocket and, though Karen did not say it, probably a harem of gorgeous women in his bedroom.

When Karen had described his appearance, Vicki had even detected a longing in her voice that made her jealous. Karen claimed not to know if there was anyone special in his life and that she had not broached the subject with him. In her sensitive state, Vicki wondered whether Karen was holding back, not wishing to hurt, or devastate, more like, her friend or whether Karen had her own beady eye on him for herself. And anyway, why would Rhys be interested in her now, the person who had ripped out his heart and guts without a care in the world? She didn't deserve Rhys or Tommy or anyone else, if truth be told. Yes, she was a stupid old cow worthy of nothing more than a role in a Jackie Collins novel, she mused, disgusted with herself.

With these thoughts ringing around her head, Vicki stood up abruptly, as if the sudden movement would dislodge all this negativity. She sighed deeply and wiped her eyes and nose once again. Feeling a little better, she dragged herself into the bedroom and opened her side of the wall-to-wall wardrobe. She sank to her knees, as she had done for virtually every day of her two years of marriage, and cast her eyes over the racks of shoes below her. Behind the racks were more shoes, but this time still in their original boxes. She reached over the racks and removed two of them, placing them beside her. Beneath them was a third box which she also removed. Still on her knees, Vicki placed this one in front of her, lifted the lid and folded back the cream-coloured tissue paper. Inside were a pair of dark navy shoes that she used to wear to work. She took them out and placed them to her side. She then opened out the tissue paper at the bottom of the box to reveal a number of small rectangular packets. Vicki picked up the one which was already open and slid out its contents. This was her final and most devastating deceit of all, the most tangible proof that she had never loved Tommy in the first place. Pinching at the silver foil, she removed the last contraceptive pill, knowing that they had already done their job for the month, and placed it into her mouth.

August 1977

Chapter 17

'Phew, another busy day over,' Rhys said to himself as he locked the door of the Supreme, the low sun casting broad shadows behind him. He walked around the side of the building to the back where a set of stone steps led up to the front door of his flat. He was perspiring and looking forward to the hot shower that would freshen him up and take away the smells of grilled and fried food.

After entering the flat, he went straight into his bedroom and stripped off his clothes, leaving them in a heap at the foot of the bed. He walked over to the fitted wardrobe and slid open the slatted pine doors where he removed and slipped on a stripy green and white dressing gown, knotting the cord tightly around his belly. He ignored his slippers to allow his sweaty feet to breathe a little and shuffled into the kitchen. Once there, he poured some orange cordial into a pint glass and added water from the tap. After dropping in a couple of ice cubes, he sunk half the drink in one go. Finally relaxing for the first time that day, he sat down on a cushioned pine chair and placed the glass on the matching kitchen table, in the centre of which the leaves of a rather tired-looking spider plant were flopping languidly over the rim of its pot.

'I might have to get another waitress at this rate. We're so busy and Mandy's run off her feet, poor girl. I'll give her and Mario a few extra quid in their pay packets on Friday. They deserve it.'

Picking up the glass, Rhys drank more of his squash. He had got into the habit of talking to himself for it helped him to concentrate his mind. Placing the glass back down, he exhaled a long sigh. Thankfully, he could feel himself cooling down. Looking up, he gazed around the kitchen. He loved the flat and only now, nearly one year on, did he finally accept that it was his, believing irrationally that Christos and Eleni would waltz in one day and take it back off him. The cupboard doors were painted blue-white, with a fine and attractive light grey grain showing underneath. The Formica work surfaces were a mottled black and white and the lino on the floor patterned in bold black and white squares like a chessboard. The walls and ceiling were painted in a cool-inducing oyster-white shade and, over the window, metal white Venetian blinds were pulled halfway up. The overriding effect was a kitchen that felt bright, light and spacious and with the small colour television in one corner and portable radio sitting on the Welsh dresser opposite, Rhys found that he spent a lot of his time in the room.

Business was booming and flourishing beyond Rhys's wildest dreams. Today had been exceptional, like a fruitful day at the Klondike. Indeed, Rhys anticipated being able to pay off another fifteen hundred or even two thousand pounds of his bank loan at the end of the month. He was even mulling over buying a car. London was a nightmare to drive around and parking was impossible, and he rarely ventured far. Yet whenever he saw an Alfa Romeo GTV pass by, his knees would weaken at the car's beautiful curves. Not even Agnetha from Abba had that effect on him. And he could afford it. But was it sensible? And so, yet again, he put off the decision.

Yes, Rhys's life had turned around and the only problems he had were enviable ones. Should he take on more staff? Should he buy a car? How much should he pay back the bank? And yet, today, his mood was one of despondency, his Technicolor world resorting to black and white. To reflect it, he sang croakily and in a low voice the words to one of the songs that had been playing constantly on the radio in the café all day.

'I just can't help believin', when she smiles up soft and gentle, with a trace of misty morning, and the promise of tomorrow in her eyes ...'

For the king of rock 'n' roll, Elvis Presley, was dead and the world was in mourning. Whether it was Tony Blackburn, Dave Lee Travis or Simon Bates, all the DJs throughout the land appeared to be on the brink of tears. Rhys liked Elvis and it was impossible not to get caught up in the mood of the day. The knowledge that Elvis had been found slumped over in his own vomit, having fallen off the toilet, only added to Rhys's sorrow. What a tragic and pitiful way for such an iconic figure to be discovered. The king is dead, long live the king, Rhys suddenly thought. But who would take over his mantle? No one came to mind who could compare. Tom Jones, perhaps, from his own home town of Pontypridd? Not if he kept hiding himself away making easy money in Las Vegas, Rhys concluded.

Finishing his squash, Rhys stood up and rinsed out the glass, leaving it to dry on the draining board. He switched on the television where a reporter was providing further details of Elvis's death from outside Graceland. After only a brief listen, Rhys switched it off. He shuffled over to the radio and pressed down on the button.

"You ain't nothin' but a hound dog, crying all the time ..."

Rhys switched that off, too. It was impossible to escape Elvis today. He looked up at the clock on the wall. One minute to seven. Without fail, his mother called him at seven o'clock every day to see how he was doing. She was a big Elvis fan and Rhys was certain she would be miserable when she came on the line. He smiled at the recollection of his parents attending a fancy dress party wearing Elvis costumes only the New Year just gone. His mother had dressed in a white jumpsuit and white studded cowboy boots, worn over-large sunglasses and greased back her hair. That was funny enough, but his father thought he still possessed the waistline of Mark Spitz and chose a black leather trousers and jacket combination from Elvis's slimmer days. Unfortunately for him, however, he more closely resembled an overweight Hell's Angel and nearly sweated to death. Rhys had not laughed so much in years when he saw the photographs afterwards.

He needed that shower and moved into the living room, unable to avoid the body odour following him around. He'd try and keep it short with his mother, though he had to be sensitive to her Elvis mood. He sunk down into the deep, soft cushion of his maroon sofa next to the telephone table. The sofa was so long and comfortable that he had fallen asleep on it on numerous occasions whilst watching television and never bothered dragging himself away from it to his bedroom when the crackling sound of static and bright, jumping black and white dots eventually woke him up. The low, early evening sun blazed into the room through the sash window opposite, blinding and discomfiting him so much he got up and drew closed the chocolate-brown and amber curtains. He switched on his newly acquired lava lamp on a table nearby. Thick globules of red and black slowly rose and fell inside as it lit up the room. Almost immediately, the phone rang. Rhys strode purposefully across his pale green shag pile carpet and picked up the receiver.

'Hi, Mum.'

There was a tangible silence on the other end of the line before a low voice responded weakly. 'Hello, Rhys.'

Rhys's stomach went hollow and his knees buckled. Without saying a word, he sat down, his mouth agape, perspiration forming on his brow and upper lip. He remained mute for what seemed an eternity. It was Vicki. He felt disorientated and his brain waves flew in every conceivable direction except towards his tongue.

Sitting on the finely embroidered silk eiderdown which adorned the bed in her parents' bedroom in Godalming, Vicki began to shake uncontrollably as the silence tormented her for she was unable to gauge Rhys's reaction. Was he pleased to hear from her? Was he angry? Was he shocked? Was he upset? All of these things, perhaps? She just couldn't tell and tears welled up in her eyes. They had spoken only two words to each other in three and a half years and their effect was killing them.

Rhys finally got a grip of himself and managed a barely perceptible 'Vicki?' into the receiver. It came out as a question though he already knew the answer.

Vicki ran the back of her hand across her eyes and stifled a sniffle, feeling a sense of relief that Rhys had not come over all angry or slammed down the phone on her. Deep down, she knew he wouldn't. He wasn't the type.

'I hope you don't mind me calling you. It's been, well, such a long time and, well, it's just nice to hear your voice again.'

Vicki had not rehearsed what she would say. She decided to go with the flow and make it feel as natural as possible. Despite their problems when they were together, they had never failed to converse easily with each other, unlike Vicki with Tommy or with previous boyfriends, where evenings out often resulted in stilted chat and long periods of tortuous silence. She put her trust in the belief that talking to Rhys would be just like the old days. She hoped so anyway ... desperately.

'I'm just, well, in shock you've called. I never imagined in a million years you would,' Rhys replied, his tone underlining his surprise. 'I, uh, don't know what to say if I'm honest. I'm speechless.' He hesitated, still unable to take in that it was Vicki on the line. But just as Vicki was about to say something, he resumed in that calm, concerned way of his that was so familiar to her. 'I'm so glad you did. It's wonderful to hear your voice again.'

Vicki's whole body shivered. No one would ever make her feel as special as Rhys did. 'The same with you,' Vicki concurred, wiping more tears from her eyes and blowing her nose. Her emotions were running high and wild. Just knowing that Rhys was so clearly delighted to hear from her made her want to break down in sheer happiness.

Rhys could not fail to pick up the obvious tremor in her voice and the blowing of the nose only served to confirm that Vicki was crying. He was much calmer now, coming to terms with the knowledge that Vicki was actually on the other end of the phone. His composure had returned and he felt in control of himself. The blockage between his brain and his tongue had been smashed into oblivion. Vicki, however, was struggling and Rhys's innate goodness only wished her to feel comfortable and at ease.

'Hey, Vick, there's no need to cry. What's there to cry about? Come on, you're a big girl now, everything'll be alright. It's only me, not some nutcase like Idi Amin.' Rhys felt so much love for her that all he wanted to do was envelope her in his arms and give her the reassurance she needed. He heard a sniffly chuckle on the other end of the line and smiled. 'That's better.'

'Yeah, it's just, you know, well, so long that, I dunno, it's just got to me a bit. I promised myself I wouldn't cry but what do I know?'

Rhys smiled. 'Well, there's a lot of crying going round at the moment what with the news about Elvis. You've probably caught some of it.'

Vicki chuckled and sniffled once more but she, too, was regaining her composure and in fact experiencing a warm glow inside at the knowledge that Rhys was friendly and concerned ... loving even. Any nerves she had were gone for the moment. The mention of Elvis shook her out of her emotional state as her thoughts turned to the King.

'Isn't it terrible news? I can't believe he's dead. Just awful, it is. Even Mum's walking round in a trance.'

Rhys noted the last comment. Was Vicki calling from her parents' home? He let it pass for the moment. 'Yeah, just shocking. It's one of those occasions when you'll always remember where you were when you heard the news.'

'Unless it's you and JFK, of course,' Vicki interrupted playfully.

Rhys sniggered, feeling pleased that Vicki had remembered his comment all those years ago during their stroll around the park in Pontypridd. 'Yeah, you're right. Hopefully my brain cells will be in better working order in future.'

Vicki smiled. 'Well, I was sitting at the kitchen table in Godalming when I heard. My mum burst through the door with the news. Dad and Fiona just sat there open-mouthed, not knowing what to say. Same as me, actually. Just terrible, it was.'

Vicki had answered Rhys's curiosity. She was at her parents' then.

'I hope your mum and dad are well, by the way?'

'Yes, they are, thanks. Yours?'

'The same, thanks. They still smoke like chimneys; I guess some things will never change. How's Fiona? She still with Jeremy? She married yet?'

'Ah, don't go there! I'll be here all week if you want to know about Fiona's love life. But no, she's not with *him* anymore, thank God.' After a slight pause and in a manner that made Rhys jump, Vicki hollered, 'ARE YOU LISTENING, FIONA?'

There was no response other than the click of a line being cut.

'What was all that about? I nearly fell off my sofa?' Rhys asked in puzzlement.

'Well, it's just I'm in my parents' bedroom and I'm sure the nosey parker's listening in on the phone downstairs. She's the only one in at the moment.' Rhys was about to speak when Vicki carried on, deliberately leaving the implication that not everything was going well between her and Tommy. 'Yeah, I don't think my parents ever thought their two girls would be back home at our ages.'

Vicki waited for Rhys's reaction, scrunching up her face. Even he would pick up on this revelation, surely? There was no response. All Vicki could hear was silence. Rhys's brain whirred wildly, trying to make sense of her comment. The delay was beginning to unsettle her so she thought she'd give him another nudge. But before she could, Rhys broke in tentatively. 'Umm, did I hear you right that you're back living at home?'

'Yeah, I am. I'm not with Tommy anymore. We're getting divorced.' Vicki waited for Rhys's reply but once again there was silence. She added for accuracy, more than anything, 'Well, I've asked him for a divorce, let's put it that way.'

Rhys was stunned. The receiver trembled in his hand and rigor mortis seemed to have set in around his mouth. The silence on the line was deafening. Vicki swallowed twice, her throat suddenly dry, and she licked her lips. She was in trepidation as to how Rhys would react, that's if he was still on the line, for the silence appeared to last forever.

'Rhys?' There was no answer. 'Rhys? Are you still there?'

After another short delay, Rhys finally responded, unable to disguise his shock and surprise. 'Yeah, sorry, I'm just, you know, umm, taken aback, I suppose. I could never have imagined anything like that.' There was a further delay before he added genuinely, 'I'm sorry, Vicki, it didn't work out. It must be really tough and I feel for you. I hate to think of you going through a bad time.'

It was a lovely, kind thing to say, full of concern for her, so typical of Rhys, Vicki thought, and a lump formed in her throat. He was also treading warily. Rhys understood immediately the implications of this news, only underlined by the fact that Vicki had called him up. She was trying to rekindle their relationship, he was certain, and he knew he would find it nigh on impossible to resist her. It was his ultimate desire to be with Vicki again, a seemingly impossible desire that now, incredibly, appeared possible once more. But instead of elation, he felt nervous, ill-at-ease and full of doubts. Was Vicki just vulnerable coming off her failed marriage? What did she really feel for him? Could he go through the sheer gut-wrenching agony of rejection again? And, at the end of the day, wasn't he just a nightmare to her?

'That's really kind of you to say, Rhys,' Vicki replied, a tear in her eye.

'I had an inkling things might not be right when I met up with Karen the other day. She implied it wasn't going too well between the two of you but I never thought it would come to this. There's been nothing in the newspapers, has there?'

'No, not yet, but I'm sure there will be soon. I only told Tommy two nights ago. I'm bracing myself for when the press comes knocking but it'll all blow over quickly enough.'

'How did he take it?' Before Vicki could respond, Rhys added frantically, 'Sorry, I shouldn't be asking personal questions like that.'

'No, that's okay. Badly, if you want to know, very badly,' Vicki replied, running her fingers lightly across her right eye which made her flinch. She wanted to reveal more but thought the better of it.

Another brief silence ensued as Rhys considered delving more deeply. It was none of his business, he decided, however, so he let it pass. Instead, he changed the subject. 'I've got to say I had a hell of a shock when

I saw Karen in Cardiff. I was worried she was going to gob on me.' Rhys heard Vicki laugh, which triggered the same from him.

'You're right there. She's really into punk. I couldn't believe it myself when I saw her. When she came up to London the other day, she dragged me down to that punk shop on the King's Road. Sex, it's called. Pretty subtle, uh? It was chaos in there. I felt right out of place in my boring old clothes. Karen wanted me to buy some ripped fishnets and T-shirts. I couldn't get out of there quickly enough.'

'So you're not a punk rocker then?' Rhys asked in a happy voice.

'No chance! When you see me next, you won't notice much difference.'

Inadvertently, Vicki had raised the issue of meeting up again. She had wanted to build up to it carefully but it suddenly came out and she scolded herself, screwing up her face and going quiet. Rhys picked up on her silence and went quiet himself. It was not lost on him once more that Vicki clearly wished to see him again.

'Well, I hope not,' he finally replied in a calm voice. After another momentary delay and plucking up courage, he ventured, 'You're pretty damn gorgeous as you are.'

Vicki swelled with ecstasy, her mouth stretched from ear to ear in utter joy, feeling as beautiful as the three *Charlie's Angels* all rolled into one.

'Well, thanks. That's really nice of you to say so. Karen tells me you're not looking so bad yourself.'

'I try' was the best Rhys could reply, modestly.

'She tells me you're doing really well now, what with you owning the Supreme and your own flat. It's wonderful, I'm so pleased for you.' Just as Rhys was about to respond, Vicki threw in, 'Oh, and I hope you don't mind my asking her for your number by the way.'

'No, not at all, of course not.' After a pause, Rhys carried on, but his tone was more measured. He was feeling sensitive and the thought occurred to him that Vicki might only be interested in rekindling their relationship because he had attained a degree of success rather than because of him as a person. This possibility worried him. 'Yeah, I've been really lucky. You remember Christos and Eleni? Well, they sold me the place but more importantly gave me the confidence and belief that I could run it properly and make a living out of it. They helped with the bank and everything. I owe them a lot.'

'Yeah, Karen told me,' Vicki replied, her pride in Rhys coming through in spades.

'There's so much to do, though. Mandy's run off her feet, the chef, Mario, too, but I love it.'

Without warning, Vicki's stomach lurched and she did not immediately reply. It was the first time another girl had been mentioned and the jealousy struck hard. Who's Mandy? She's clearly someone who works for him but was there anything else in their relationship? Things had been going well and Vicki did not want to ruin the phone call or become upset by discovering that Rhys was seeing another girl. Consequently, she did not delve more deeply. She would have to know at some stage, there was no doubt about that, but not now.

'Yeah, I can hear it in your voice,' Vicki answered admiringly though her tone was rather flat.

'What about yourself, Vicki? Karen did tell me you'd stopped working.'

'Ah, that's another story, but I've got high hopes they'll take me back in some position or other. You remember

Brenda? Well, I'm still in touch with her and she's trying to pull a string or two for me. Fingers crossed.'

'Yeah, fingers and toes crossed here as well. It was a shame you left 'cos I know how much you loved that job. Hopefully they'll offer you something, they'd be mad not to. You watch, you'll be President Mitchell before you know it, I'm sure, though you might be a bit older than I originally thought before you make it. None of us are getting any younger, you know!'

Vicki smiled and swelled with confidence once more. Rhys knew how to touch all the right spots to make her feel fantastic. How she missed his encouragement and belief in her abilities.

'Thanks, Rhys, I hope so, though I wish you hadn't reminded me how old we're all getting.'

'Time's just flying by,' Rhys clichéd with an air of exasperation. He hesitated before adding forlornly in a low voice, 'Though the past three and a half years have been never-ending.'

Vicki waited a few seconds before replying in a voice as soft and warm as the faintest of breezes on a Caribbean evening, 'I know.'

Another brief period of silence ensued as they thought about the lost years they could have had together. They did not need to say anything, the silence said it all, and they longed more than anything to hold each other in their arms.

Rhys recognised how difficult it must have been for Vicki to pick up the phone. She could have fallen flat on her face and he admired her for her courage. Accordingly, he realised that it was now only right that he took up the initiative. 'God, Vick, there's so much to catch up on. I still can't believe I'm talking to you, it's like I'm in a dream world.'

'Yeah, same here. Just to hear your voice again is wonderful.'

Rhys smiled. 'It would be great to meet up, you know. I'd love to see you again,' he suggested calmly. He had not the slightest flicker of doubt that she would agree.

Vicki's heart skipped a beat and instinctively she raised a hand to cover her mouth as an inadvertent yelp found its way between her lips. She had hoped so much he would ask. 'I'd love to.'

'I'm thinking about your dad's phone bill as well,' Rhys joked and Vicki laughed. 'I'm only really free on Sundays now. The evenings are okay for me as well but why don't we get together this Sunday coming if you're around?'

'Sunday'd be great. What shall we do then? I don't mind coming up your way.'

'Thanks. You still got the MG then?'

'Yeah. She's been gathering dust in the garage here but started first time this morning.'

'You're not going to swap it for a Marina then?'

'Christ, no! They're always breaking down, I hear.'

'Well, at least they go,' Rhys threw in with a chuckle. 'The Allegro doesn't even start, stupid square steering wheel or not!' They both laughed. 'I tell you what, why don't you drive up here for say eleven o'clock? The forecast is for warm and sunny weather so maybe we can go for a walk on Clapham Common and get a drink and some lunch at The Windmill?'

'That sounds perfect, Rhys.'

'When you arrive at the Supreme, just go round the back and you'll find the steps up to my flat. It should be easy enough parking as it's Sunday.'

'Great. I look forward to it.'

'Same here,' Rhys replied before adding, 'a lot.'

Vicki smiled. 'Me, too.'

They said their goodbyes and replaced the receivers. Vicki flung herself back on the bed and grabbed a pillow which she hugged tightly to her chest. She had the widest of smiles etched across her face and rolled left, then right, and then left again in her excitement, squeezing the life out of the pillow.

By contrast, Rhys sat as still as a waxwork on the sofa. He, too, was excited, ecstatic even, but he remained wary. There was so much he needed to know first before he could contemplate another relationship with Vicki, but he knew deep down he would not be able to resist her. Sunday would be a momentous day, he thought. After three and a half desperate years, he would be seeing the love of his life again. He wished it was tomorrow. The next three days would be torture, though paradoxically, a delicious one.

A couple of minutes passed by and the whiff under his armpits reminded him of the shower he had been meaning to take. He blew out his cheeks and stood up, but, almost immediately, the phone rang again. He fixed a curious gaze on it as if he were Jimmy Carter receiving a call on the hot line from Brezhnev. Had Vicki forgotten to mention something? Had she remembered she had something else lined up on Sunday? Gingerly, Rhys picked up the receiver. 'Hello?'

'Thank God for that! You're off the line, finally!'

Rhys relaxed. 'Oh, hi Mum. Sorry about that.'

'You've been on the phone for ages. Anything interesting?'

Rhys broke out into a smile as wide as the Grand Canyon. 'You can say that again!'

Chapter 18

'Right, who's up for one across the road then?' a voice rang out from the back of the home dressing room at Upton Park, the home of West Ham United FC. All the players changing back into their civvies knew 'across the road' meant the Boleyn pub, a citadel to West Ham players and fans alike.

'I'm in, Billy.'

'Me too.'

'Yeah, and me.'

'I'd love to, but gotta meet the missus, sorry.'

'Same here. Gotta meet Sharon. Promised her an afternoon up West.'

'Under the thumb, you two are,' Billy replied playfully, bringing smiles to the faces of his teammates.

Tommy Slater, however, said nothing. He remained seated, his eyes fixed directly ahead as if in a trance. He was still wearing his training kit, arms folded, legs outstretched, his socks rolled down to his ankles.

'I don't envy you, Tommy, all the hot water's gone.'

Tommy did not even raise an eyebrow in the direction of the comment. His mood was foul, his rigid look turning into a scowl. The first match of the season against Norwich City was only two days away on Saturday and the West Ham United First Team squad had assembled for their pre-season photograph in front of the main stand. Tommy's beaming smile as he sat in the middle of the front row, hands on knees and ball between his feet, hid the anger and despair that was ripping his guts to shreds. When looking at that photograph in years to come, no one would ever guess the anguish he was feeling.

As all the players were in attendance at the ground, the manager had decided on a light training session afterwards, not that anyone had told Tommy. He flew into tackles as if it was the FA Cup Final and, on one occasion, a teammate squared up to him when Tommy caught him painfully on the achilles. Tommy responded by throwing punches at him as if he were John H Stracey, the local boy and former recent World Welterweight Champion, who was a lifelong Hammers' fan. He had to be pulled off his cowering teammate, compelling his manager to intervene and end the training session there and then in order to let tempers cool.

Everyone could sense that something was up with Tommy the second he arrived at the ground that morning but he refused to reply to any questions why. It was just one of those things, his teammates concluded, and they let him stew in peace. As long as he was alright for Saturday, that was all that mattered. When they had all traipsed off to the dressing room, Tommy had stayed out on the pitch and changed from his football boots into training shoes. He then proceeded to run up and down one of the terraces twenty times as hard as he could. Bent over double and panting like a knackered dog, he almost threw up afterwards, his kit drenched in sweat, but even this failed to rid his body of the agony of losing Vicki. And now, as all his teammates finished changing around him, he knew that he would never get her back.

Monday night had been the worst night of his life, he reflected, as he kicked violently at the discarded trainers lying by his feet. He crossed his left leg over his right, his heel beginning to ache as it took the weight and pressed firmly into the harsh concrete floor. He adjusted it slightly to ease the dull pain before thinking back yet again to that wretched evening.

Tommy had been stunned and in need of a chair, for his legs had turned into the most wobbly of jellies, when Vicki, all nerves and tension, had asked him for a divorce. He had not seen it coming. She had seemed happy enough, he thought, as he refolded his arms and shook his head. He just couldn't understand it. Didn't most women like to stay at home and potch around the house all day? It was better than work, surely? And didn't most women like to dote on their man and accept the way the man wanted it to be? It had always seemed that way to him when growing up in the East End. And look at all the clothes and jewellery he had bought her, the luxury she lived in, the functions and dinners she had attended. How could the ungrateful cow not appreciate any of that? His mind wandered to numerous girls he knew who would die for such a life. What a bitch, Tommy thought, not for the first time, though he had taken umbrage at his brother who had called her a stuck-up slag when he called him to convey the news. He had slammed the phone down on him for the insult, reminding him first that it was his wife who more closely fitted the description.

Perhaps he was better off without her, Tommy mulled, trying to look on the bright side, as Billy touched him on the shoulder before exiting the dressing room. After all, Vicki was probably infertile. Must be something to do with the air those posh tarts breathe down in Surrey, he considered nastily. You only had to look at East End birds to get them up the duff, he mused. Yeah, having a kid with Vicki was looking right dodgy. I'm better off without her, he decided, though the ache in his stomach and trembling of his body told him otherwise. He sighed deeply and looked up and around him. Only a handful of teammates remained, either fixing their ties, combing their hair or zipping up their kit bags. Their cheeks were still pink through exertion and their hair damp and shiny. One of them lit a cigarette which he had been gasping for and offered a teammate another. Dry mud and twisted pieces of dirty-white tape were strewn all over the floor and the aroma of soap, shampoo and deodorant swirled around the air, though the rasping fart of the team's centre-forward soon added a less-appealing smell to the mix.

'Sorry about that, Tommy, still got last night's ruby in the system.'

'You might want to crack one on Saturday, Al. The Norwich centre-half won't want to get near you,' Tommy replied, accompanied by his first smile of the day. He loved the banter of the dressing room and it helped him to forget Vicki for a second or two. But it was short-lived. He just couldn't get Monday night out of his head.

Al laughed. 'Not a bad idea that, Tommy,' he answered before picking up his kit bag. 'See you Saturday, big man,' and noticing a teammate outside the door dragging hard on his fag, he rushed out to join him. Tommy remained alone and the chatter tailed off to nothing as his teammates strolled down the corridor away from the dressing room.

The ensuing silence led to a greater clarity of thought and he wondered whether he could have kept his temper better in check when confronting Vicki, cringing and shaking his head at the images of the two broken glasses, broken kitchen stool and upturned armchair. But hindsight is a wonderful thing, and he was in such a rage on Monday that all reason flew out of the window.

'Who the hell does she think she is, the bitch? No one does that to Tommy Slater,' he blurted out defiantly.

She had deserved the slap as well. His brother and friends all thought it acceptable to give their women a smack every now and again to keep them in their place and even conjectured that women actually liked it, but Tommy had never bought into this. On many occasions he had been angry enough to hit Vicki, but he had always resisted it ... until Monday. He could not help himself for it was clear she would not relent to his wishes and back down. That incident had been the end, with Vicki rushing out of the apartment, an already packed suitcase in one hand, the other covering her eye. 'Fuck off' were the last words he spat at her, feeling better for the slap. Perhaps his brother and friends were right after all, though it had not had the desired effect of forcing Vicki into submission.

'Fucking cow! Fuck off then. What do I care?' Tommy yelled out to let off steam. The startled dressing room attendant loitered outside and walked away, thinking it the wisest course of action. 'Who the fuck do you think you are? No one walks out on Tommy Slater like that. I can have any fucking woman I want.' He recalled the smile Sylvia Kristel had given him at a function at the Café Royal in Piccadilly a few weeks back. 'Yeah, I could even fuck Emmanuelle herself if I wanted to, you fucking whore!'

Tommy's face was puce with rage but releasing the pressure had the desired effect for, a few minutes later, he was relatively calm again. He was also realistic. There was no way Vicki was ever going to come back to him.

'Fuck her,' he said quietly under his breath. 'If she wants a divorce she can have one, but she's gonna have to wait. I'm not gonna let her fuck off and marry any old Tom, Dick or Harry whenever she likes. Yeah, she can fucking well wait, the cow,' Tommy added, his voice overflowing with bitterness. 'Let some other wanker find out she can't drop sprogs. Teach 'em right.' And particularly if that wanker happens to be that ex-sheep-shagger of a boyfriend of hers, Tommy thought with venom. Vicki had not mentioned Rhys's name once on Monday night, nor ever, but Tommy always suspected she carried a bright light for him. Well, he'll make sure they never have a nice life together.

'Yeah, Vicki's picked the wrong person to mess about with here. I'll show her. If she thinks she can just run off with someone else, she's got another think coming.'

This statement of defiance emboldened him though his immediate concern was whether anyone outside the dressing room had heard him. He stood up and took a few strides to the door. He looked left and right but saw no one. Coming back in, he decided to make a move. He was dry now and decided to shower back home. If fact, he wouldn't even change; he'd drive home as he was. Sitting back down, he put on his training shoes, his mind still spinning like a top, full of swirling unstructured thoughts. There was no way he could hide the break-up of his marriage from the press so he tossed around which journalist he would give the story to. As ever, Tommy wanted to be in control. The break-up would be portrayed as sad but amicable with no hard feelings and the public would get to know that they still loved and respected each other. He would come out of this unfortunate episode as someone who had tried his best to make the marriage work. Above all else, he would maintain his positive public persona. Later on, he would drip-feed snippets to his favourite journalists to show up Vicki in a more unfavourable light. Maybe she would crack up like Cheryl had, he hoped. As Tommy stuffed his civvies into his kit bag, he repeated his last statement.

'Yeah, Vicki's picked the wrong person to mess about with here. I'll show her.' Ominously, as he strode out of the dressing room with a cruel grin on his face, he added, 'And the press will be the least of her worries, I promise.'

Chapter 19

The doorbell rang and Rhys thought he was going to have a heart attack. His legs felt so rubbery he could barely leave the kitchen chair. The clock on the wall showed five past eleven. For the hundredth time that morning he checked his wristwatch, which also showed five past eleven, as if he were a commando synchronising time for an assault on an enemy position. So badly had he slept the night before that he had risen at the crack of dawn and been dressed and ready to go out hours earlier. Time had never elapsed so slowly in his life. The last five minutes, in particular, had been agony, out of worry that Vicki would not be turning up. Surely the clock was running fast, he had thought, only for his wristwatch to confirm it was not. Rhys steadied himself, took a deep breath, and strode purposefully to the front door, wiping imaginary crumbs off his cobalt-blue Fred Perry polo shirt on the way. This was it and, with a final sigh, he opened the door.

'Oh my God, it's Purdey!'

The first thing that struck him about Vicki was the difference in hairstyle from her more familiar honey-blonde corkscrew and, in his nervousness, the words tumbled out of his mouth in a manner that seemed less complimentary than he had wished them to be. An equally nervous Vicki looked down before looking back up again, her eyes flicking furtively left and right as if she had no control over them. Finally, they settled on Rhys. She thought he looked fantastic as did Rhys of her.

Like him, Vicki had been on edge all morning and had arrived on Lavender Hill twenty minutes early. She had parked in a side road opposite a laundrette and only stopped looking at her watch in the meantime when considering her appearance in the rear-view mirror. Did she really like the new hairstyle? Had she overdone the make-up? Why had she changed from her usual safe pink lipstick to one much rosier? Her confidence had drained as she wondered what Rhys would think of her and so often had she run her fingers through her hair that she had spent five minutes removing loose strands from her pale yellow shirt. Undoing one more button at the front for luck, she had finally left the car. She may not have been totally satisfied with her appearance but at least she had made a big effort.

'Hello, Rhys, Joanna Lumley here,' Vicki joked and she shaped her hands to form a karate chop pose like the beautiful and alluring New Avenger.

'Joanna Lumley! Give me Victoria Mitchell any day of the week,' Rhys replied full of charm, stepping out of his doorway to greet her and enveloping her in his arms. Vicki placed hers around him and they held each other tightly, not saying a word. Vicki's head rested on his shoulder and they breathed in the familiar body smells they thought they would never experience again.

After planting the lightest of kisses on the top of Vicki's head, Rhys took a step back, holding her upper arms and stroking them with the gentlest of touches. He was on the point of speaking when he noticed some faint yellow and purple colouring around Vicki's right eye. His smile vanished for he could see instantly that her eye was bruised. Vicki noticed his expression and lowered her gaze. Before Rhys could ask the question, Vicki volunteered the answer. 'I thought it might have faded away by now but it's like I said on the phone, Tommy didn't take my asking for a divorce too kindly and unfortunately he'd been to see *Rocky* a few too many times.'

Rhys placed his index finger under her chin and Vicki raised her head, looking Rhys straight in the eye. He could see the bruise more clearly now and felt his blood boil. 'He should be ashamed of himself. That's the most disgusting thing a man can do to a woman.'

'Yeah, you're right. My dad said the same and was as mad as hell. He wanted to go round and sort him out.'

'Don't blame him. If he's still up for it, I'll join him.'

Vicki grinned. 'I'm sure he is but let's just leave it. I want nothing more to do with Tommy. It's over.' Rhys said nothing but Vicki could see he was seething. 'Anyway, are you going to invite me in or are we going to stand outside your front door all day?'

'Yeah, sorry,' Rhys replied with a shake of the head and embarrassed smile. He stood aside and beckoned Vicki to cross the threshold. He followed her inside and closed the door behind them.

'Wow, what a lovely place you've got,' Vicki blurted out as she walked along the hallway. 'It's so big.'

'I'll give you a quick tour.' Opening a door, Rhys invited Vicki to peer inside as if he were an estate agent showing a prospective buyer around. 'This here is the bathroom.'

Vicki looked around, her eyes open wide. 'It's fabulous,' she commented, trying surreptitiously to fathom whether any feminine products were lying about.

'And these are the two spare bedrooms,' Rhys carried on as he walked further along the hallway, pointing left and right. 'I just keep odds and ends in them for now so mind the mess.' Vicki did not say a word as she surveyed them both. 'And over here is my bedroom.' He stepped aside to let Vicki past. She lingered longer, again trying to uncover any evidence of a female's presence. She saw none. 'Along here are the kitchen and the living room.' Vicki left Rhys's bedroom, took a few paces to the kitchen, stepped inside and looked around. She then brushed past Rhys and entered the living room, her head swivelling round as if a radar picking up transmissions.

'My compliments, Rhys, it's fantastic,' Vicki finally replied, her eyes as large as saucers.

'Thanks, Vicki. I love it here and it helps that I'm at the office in thirty seconds flat,' Rhys joked. 'Would you like something to drink; tea, coffee?' he added, returning to the kitchen.

Vicki followed him in. 'A soft drink would be nice. I feel really thirsty.'

Opening the top compartment of the fridge and peering inside, Rhys advised, 'I've got coke, orange juice or your favourite dandelion and burdock Corona pop if you prefer? I bought it specially as I thought we might go and have a picnic on the Common.'

'I was wondering what the basket and blanket were doing on the floor. Dandelion and burdock would be great, thanks. I haven't had that in ages.' After a slight pause, she added, 'That's very thoughtful of you, Rhys.'

'No problem,' Rhys answered nonchalantly, grabbing the bottle and pouring the pop into a tall glass. 'We can still go for a drink in The Windmill afterwards, but it's such a beautiful day I thought a picnic would be fun.'

'It's a great idea. I wish you'd told me earlier, I could have prepared something.'

'Oh, there's no need. I rustled up some stuff myself. If you look in the basket, I made some tuna and sweetcorn and Cheddar and Branston sarnies; brown bread before you ask 'cos I know how fussy you are.'

'I'm not fussy!' Vicki replied, thumping Rhys playfully on the shoulder.

Rhys sniggered Muttley-like. 'Only kidding. There's a couple of pork pies in there as well, some fruit, some Stilton and a nice Bakewell tart.'

Vicki looked inside. 'Gosh, you shouldn't have. It looks wonderful.'

Rhys poured himself a glass of pop as well. 'There should be a couple of baguettes in there, too.'

'Yeah, there are. Two sticks of French bread and some cream for the tart wrapped in silver foil.'

'French bread? I thought I bought baguettes?'

'Very funny,' and the two of them smiled at each other. Vicki took her pop from Rhys, deliberately brushing her fingers lightly against his, and they clinked glasses before taking their first sips. 'Thanks, Rhys. You must have spent ages putting this together?'

'Not really. It's easy when you live above the shop. Most of the stuff's downstairs. I love the hair, by the way. It suits you.'

'Thanks. I'd been thinking about it for ages and took the plunge last week. Tommy expressly forbid me before, can you believe it? I'm glad I did it 'cos I do like the style and the colour worked out well, I think. I got fed up of being blonde all the time so went for this chestnut tint.'

'You chose well, though it does seem odd not seeing you in your corkscrew.' The comment reminded Rhys of something and he changed the subject. 'Wasn't it terrible what happened to Marc Bolan, dying so young like that?'

Vicki's face turned sad. 'Oh, it was just awful that crash he had in Barnes. He was so talented, such a waste of life. There's a shrine by the tree he hit, I hear; I intend going one day. Just terrible it was.'

'Yeah, a terrible year all round for pop stars if you include Elvis,' Rhys agreed. 'You were right about Marc Bolan, he really did make it big. I remember you telling me about him all those years ago before he was famous, though it wasn't just his music you liked if I recall,' Rhys responded with a mischievous grin.

Vicki smiled. 'Yeah, sex on legs, he was. You know all about that, don't you?'

Rhys took a large swig from his glass, feeling a slight erection coming on. 'Yes, I do!' They both laughed. 'Anyway, Vick, finish that. It's too nice to stay indoors.'

Vicki gulped down her pop and rinsed out the glass, doing the same to his. Rhys placed the bottle in the picnic basket, picked it and the blanket up, and left the kitchen, Vicki following close behind. He grabbed his wallet and Emerson Fittipaldi sunglasses from a narrow table in the hallway, opened the front door, and they both exited into the bright sunlight.

'I must get my sunglasses from the car,' Vicki stated and they strode the short distance to where she had parked it. Once there, Rhys patted its bonnet lightly as Vicki rummaged in the glove compartment.

'Long time no see,' Rhys declared. 'She's still a real beauty.'

'Yeah, I love her. It was a shame she was locked up for so long at home. I never drove her in London; it's a waste of time.'

'You don't have to tell me. I've been thinking about getting a car myself but I'm not convinced.'

Putting on her sunglasses, which were modelled on those worn by Audrey Hepburn in *Breakfast at Tiffany's* and covered almost half her face, Vicki locked her car and they crossed over Lavender Hill to take the short walk up to Clapham Common. The temperature was rising rapidly and when they reached the Common, where the sun stretched its golden swathes across the grass from a crystal-clear azure sky, blemished only by a couple of whispery-white vapour trails from jets arrowing off to distant lands, they were both perspiring.

'Phew, it's a real scorcher today,' Rhys commented. 'Wish I'd put my shorts on now.'

'You're right there. It's definitely shorts weather, though I do like your trousers, by the way. I think I only ever saw you in jeans.'

'Thanks. They're nice and light and cool, though I'm a bit sceptical whether they're wrinkle-free as they claim to be,' Rhys replied, wiping a sweaty palm along the side of his khakis to flatten a crease. 'There's a nice spot over there under the tree.'

They followed a narrow concrete path that ran across the Common until they reached a giant oak tree on the south edge. Walking and chatting side by side, they occasionally brushed into each other and smiled broadly when Rhys pointed out an excitable spaniel hurtling across the grass in pursuit of an imaginary tennis ball which its owner had feigned to throw. It crossed Rhys's mind whether he should hold Vicki's hand as he had always done in the past but he resisted the temptation. Though they were getting on easily, as if they had never been apart in fact, it felt premature. Vicki, for her part, longed for him to do so.

Entering the shade under the overhanging branches, Rhys put down the basket and laid out the blue-, red- and white-checked blanket on the firm terrain. Vicki unstrapped the straw-coloured ties of her espadrille wedge sandals and slipped them off before opening the basket and removing two paper plates and some white plastic cutlery. Rhys helped her take out the sandwiches and baguettes and placed them on some other plates. Vicki grabbed the bottle of pop and poured out two beakers. She put them down for a moment so that she could sit down comfortably, hitching up her white linen trousers in the process. Picking the beakers back up, she handed one over to Rhys who sat down beside her. His legs were folded under him while Vicki's were stretched out in front.

'Your good health,' Rhys toasted in his best Eton accent.

'Yeah, cheers, mate,' Vicki replied in her best Cockney.

They both smiled, touched glasses and took a gulp.

'This is so nice,' Rhys resumed, holding his face up to receive the rays of the sun that streamed through a gap in the branches. 'Reminds me of the park in Pontypridd. Remember that, New Year's Day, 1970. First day of the decade. That was a lovely sunny day as well.'

'Yeah, I remember it well. I'll never forget it. It was a bit colder than this, though.'

'Too right. Freezing it was, but still a beautiful day.'

Looking away from the sun, Rhys grabbed a pork pie and rummaged in the basket for the mustard. Vicki took a bite from a tuna and sweetcorn sandwich and gazed at two handsome, bare-chested teenage boys in shorts kicking a light brown, leather rugby ball to each other, their T-shirts lying next to a plastic orange football and two cans of Coca-Cola.

'Who was that rugby player you always went on about at the time? John Barry?' she asked teasingly.

'Ha ha, very funny. He's the one who writes the James Bond music, isn't he? Barry John, it is. Please get it right. He's only the best rugby player there's ever been.'

'Didn't he retire early or something?'

'Yeah, he did. Shame that. His replacements haven't been bad but no one will ever be as good as the King.'

'What, did Elvis play rugby as well?'

'Ha ha, you're in a witty mood today, aren't you? Barry John was known as the King, too.'

Vicki grinned and took another bite of her sandwich. Looking to her right, she saw two teenage girls throwing a frisbee to each other and moving nearer to the two boys. She smiled and wished them luck for the boys were real hunks.

'God, this mustard's hot!' Rhys fanned his mouth and emitted some short, sharp pants.

'I prefer Dijon to English, it's not so fiery.'

'We've got both in the caff and I must have grabbed this one by mistake 'cos I prefer Dijon too.'

'You must be so chuffed, Rhys, about the Supreme?'

'Yeah, I am. It's doing really well, touch wood, and the customers seem pretty happy. I know it's early days but I can see myself opening another one some time soon.'

'Yeah, that would be amazing.'

'What's important is to have good staff. I'm very lucky to have Mario and Mandy.'

'Mandy been with you long then?' Vicki asked nonchalantly, probing.

'Since I became owner, pretty much. The customers love her.'

Vicki finished her sandwich and broke off a piece of baguette, saying nothing. She unwrapped the Stilton and cut off a piece. There was a brief period of silence as they munched on their food and gazed straight ahead, observing two boys racing each other on their Chopper bicycles. It dawned on Rhys that buying a bicycle might be a good way of getting around London and keeping in shape at the same time. He locked the thought away for further consideration later.

Noticing how quiet Vicki had gone, Rhys suspected she was musing about Mandy, that suspicion being reinforced when Vicki asked, seemingly without a care in the world, 'Why do they love her?' Vicki took a sip of her pop, inwardly cringing, for she had not been able to hide a hint of jealousy.

Rhys took a sip of his pop, too. He could read Vicki like a book and thought he would play along with her a little. 'Well, she's really efficient and always serves them with a lovely smile. I suppose it helps that she's got legs up to her armpits and tits like Dolly Parton. I think the male customers come in to lust over her rather than to actually eat anything.' He giggled.

Vicki wasn't giggling, though. She took another sip of her drink, and then another, her expression po-faced. She brushed an imaginary fleck of dust off her trousers.

'Yeah, Mandy's really good,' Rhys continued, pausing a few seconds for effect before finally revealing, 'but her fiancé's keen for them to go travelling before they get married so I don't know how long I'll be able to keep hold of her.'

Vicki turned sharply towards him, her body relaxing. Trying to show maturity, Vicki expressed, 'That's a shame if she's so good.'

Rhys turned to face her and replied with a grin, 'Yeah, it is, but that's life, I suppose.'

Vicki grinned back and they read each other's minds. 'Piss off,' she responded, thumping him playfully on the arm, unable to stop herself from breaking into an embarrassed smile. Rhys burst out laughing. Vicki broke off another piece of baguette and sliced into the Stilton, knowing her cheeks were flushed and knowing Rhys knew, too. 'Fancy a bit? The Stilton's delicious.' She was tempted to stab the sod just to wipe the smile off his face.

'Yeah, wouldn't mind. It looks it.'

Cutting off a piece and handing it to Rhys, Vicki took a bite of hers and closed her eyes as the sunshine now beamed through a gap in the branches that led directly to her face. 'Mmm, this is so nice,' she remarked, happily closing the episode of Mandy and her long legs and big tits. But, mischievously, Rhys had one final question to ask.

'So, you interested to know about Mario as well then?'

Vicki looked across and thumped him again, this time almost carrying out her threat to stab him with the plastic knife, before they both began to laugh. In truth, Rhys hated playing these games; he always believed it better to air matters in the open. How people reacted afterwards was their concern; at least they would know his position. 'No, Mandy's nice but I'm not seeing anyone.'

The statement was short and, in itself, mundane but it electrified Vicki. She looked at him and placed her hand over his. He did not retract it. A few seconds later, she took hers away, but they had made their points and relaxed as a consequence.

The strong sunshine was now filtering through a number of gaps in the branches and they both raised their faces to experience the delectable warmth. This, combined with a full stomach, made Rhys feel a little sleepy but the shout of 'Howzat' shook him from his slumber. For her part, the warmth of the sun reflected what Vicki felt inside. Without their realising, a group of boys had set up some stumps and started a game of cricket on the open expanse in front of them. Rhys observed the disgruntled expression of the batsman, in reaction to the umpire's raised finger, and handing of the bat to the incoming boy. The first three balls he faced he played with perfectly correct forward defensive strokes. He's been watching too much of Geoff Boycott, Rhys thought with a smirk. The sun was now discomfiting Vicki and she shifted her position to escape it, her cheeks and forehead glowing.

'Phew, that was hot,' she commented, observing the cricketers herself. She poured herself another beaker of dandelion and burdock pop and drank half of it in one go. 'Any good?'

'He's a bit slow, this one.'

'Cricket's really popular these days.'

'Well, England just beat Australia for the Ashes, so everyone's happy.'

'Yeah, my dad's been following it. He sits in front of the telly all day apparently, so my mum says, much to her annoyance. He got invited to Lord's for the Test Match. He absolutely loved it.'

'I can believe it. Lord's is superb.'

'Fancy some Bakewell tart? If you want cream, we'd better eat it now, as the heat's gonna make it go off in a minute.'

'Yeah, you can't beat a nice tart,' Rhys rasped lecherously.

'Men!' Vicki replied, shaking her head with a frown as she cut off a triangle and placed it on a plate. She sliced another triangle for herself and Rhys poured some cream over both. 'Mmm, this is heaven,' Vicki enthused as she tasted her first mouthful.

'Mmm, I agree. Delicious.'

As they savoured the tart and cream, they continued to gaze at the cricket match. A new batsman was entertaining them with thrilling bludgeons, one of which sent the ball flying high over their heads into the tree.

'He's some batsman, this boy, a bit like this new England player, Ian Botham. My dad says he smacks the ball around all over the place.'

'He's a great bowler, too,' Rhys replied admiringly. 'Let's hope he's not a flash in the pan 'cos I reckon he could have a big future.'

Vicki didn't reply and savoured another mouthful of tart, wishing with all her heart that they could have a big future as well.

It was as if they had never been apart. The whole idyllic afternoon passed off like a scene from Dante's *Paradiso,* a journey through Heaven. Neither of them thought it could have gone any better as they conversed about everything and anything, recalled old times, family and friends, joked, laughed and teased each other mercilessly. They also argued good-naturedly, particularly when

Vicki opined that Margaret Thatcher had a good chance of becoming Prime Minister now that she was the leader of the Conservative Party. Rhys thought the sun had gone to her head at such a preposterous opinion. Though his beloved Harold Wilson had surprisingly retired mid-term, the country remained in the equally good socialist hands of Jim Callaghan, Rhys argued back with conviction.

After their picnic, they had strolled over to The Windmill pub for a couple of shandies, lying on the grass and enjoying the sun with other thirsty drinkers. After that, they had wandered back across the Common in the direction they had come from. Vicki remained barefoot throughout, loving the feel of the grass beneath her toes. They had stopped for a while at the Long Pond to observe the youngsters playing with their model boats under the watchful eyes of their parents. The sight of these young families, the parents the same age as them, enjoying the day out together, their children so excited and full of enthusiasm, was a delight. As they left the pond and strolled slowly towards the bandstand, Vicki carrying the blanket under her armpit and espadrilles in her right hand and Rhys carrying the basket in his left, a toddler bumped into them from behind on his orange Space Hopper. His parents apologised profusely, though there was no need to as there was no damage done, and Vicki and Rhys just smiled back warmly. The toddler quickly bounced off, shouting boisterously, followed by his mother and father who so obviously loved him as much as they loved each other. The young couple walked hand in hand ahead of Rhys and Vicki, the mother's head on her husband's shoulder, keeping an eye on their little terror. It was while observing this that Rhys slipped his free hand into Vicki's which she accepted as if it was the most natural thing in the world.

At the bandstand, Vicki sat in the shade, waiting for Rhys to return from the ice cream van with a Ninety-Nine for him and a Mivvi for her. She saw in the distance the two rugby-playing boys and the two frisbee-throwing girls sitting together in their tight little group of four. Lucky them, she thought, breaking out into a knowing smile.

The sun was getting lower, reflecting the time of day and, after finishing their ice creams and chatting for a while longer, they gathered their belongings and wandered back towards Lavender Hill. Rhys took a slight diversion towards the north side of the Common to observe the magnificent, five-story Victorian town houses that ran alongside and which overlooked them.

'Aren't they fabulous, Vick? Look at the views they've got over the Common, just wonderful,' Rhys sighed.

'You can say that again. God knows how much they cost, though? Property prices are going through the roof here, I gather.'

Looking away in a resigned fashion, Rhys nodded.

Turning to their left, they headed back along the Common until the grass came to an end and met up with the main road. Vicki sat on a rusty railing and put on her espadrilles. They crossed the road and ambled down Lavender Sweep, a pleasant curve of a road which led to Lavender Hill. Vicki was noticeably quiet and pensive which Rhys picked up on. 'Penny for your thoughts?'

Halfway down the Sweep, Vicki stopped and turned to face Rhys. They were still holding hands. 'I just wanted to say how sorry I am for what happened, Rhys. I know how hard it must have been for you.'

It was the elephant in the room, the subject they had avoided. Rhys looked down evasively at the pavement and hesitated, stretching for the appropriate words. 'It was a tough time but there's no need to apologise. I know I made mistakes and I don't blame you for what happened.'

They smiled and hugged each other, blocking the pavement and necessitating a family of four, with grins on their faces, to walk on the road to get past them. They released each other and resumed their slow walk towards Lavender Hill. Now that Vicki had mentioned it, Rhys chose this moment to bring his inner feelings out into the open. 'You know me, Vick, I don't like to hide anything. I think it's important you know what's going on in my head. You're everything to me, you always have been.' It was his turn to stop now and look her in the eye. 'But I can't go through again what I've been through. The pain is too much. Today has been one of the best days of my life and nothing would make me happier than to have so many more of them with you. But only if you truly wanted to be with me. I couldn't face it if we started up something again only for you to break it off quickly afterwards. I can't predict the future, so it's unfair of me to expect you to, either, but all I do ask is that if you want to give it a go again, be true to yourself and fair to me that it's what you really want.'

Before Vicki could reply, Rhys turned and resumed walking towards Lavender Hill, leading her by the hand. She stared down at the pavement, wracking her brain for an appropriate response. She decided to be led by her heart. 'I can honestly say that I haven't stopped thinking about you since the day we split up. I dunno, looking back, I think I was all messed up in the head, not knowing what the hell I wanted.'

Rhys interrupted her. 'Maybe, but I know I didn't make it easy for you. Being out of work, with no money, no prospects, I just lost confidence in myself and shrivelled up. I couldn't face your friends or family or anyone, to be honest, 'cos I felt so ashamed about my situation. I should have realised how unhappy you were. It's like I said, I don't blame you for what you did.'

'Let's just say we were both at fault,' Vicki replied as they arrived on Lavender Hill, the Supreme just to their right across the road. They stopped for a moment outside a newsagent, with full metal shutters daubed in graffiti barring anyone's entrance. 'It was a bad time,' Vicki resumed. 'Let's just put it behind us and move on. We're better, more mature people now, I know. I appreciate what you said back there and I want you to know, Rhys, that I'll never mess you around again. You've got my word on that. I love you, Rhys, I always have done.'

On hearing this, a lump suddenly rose in Rhys's throat and he had to turn his face away to prevent her from seeing tears forming in his eyes, though he could not hide the trembling of his body. After all the years of searing pain, anguish and depression, he could never have dreamt he would hear Vicki say such words again and the moment overwhelmed him. Witnessing Rhys's gamut of emotions triggered the same in Vicki and her eyes moistened. They held and hugged each other without saying a word as if the world would end in any minute and it was fully ten of them before they let go.

'Tell you what, let's see whether some poor sod is living in our old flat,' Rhys suddenly declared in a bright tone, wiping his eyes with the corner of the blanket.

They crossed the road, walked a short distance along Lavender Hill past the Supreme, and then turned left into

Latchmere Road. A few yards further along, they stood outside the entrance to the building of their flat. They looked up at the top window and saw a Jamaican flag serving as a symbol of pride as well as the occupants' curtain, not that it was strictly necessary for the window was grimier than ever.

'Well, I know I never liked the place, but good luck to you, whoever you are,' Vicki said, staring upwards.

'I wonder if all the ganja they're smoking will finally dry it out,' Rhys commented with a smile. Vicki turned to look at Rhys and they laughed.

They left the building and strolled over to where Vicki had parked her car with Rhys trying to convince her that the bedsit he had moved to afterwards was even worse than their old flat. Vicki didn't believe him for she thought it impossible. They finally arrived beside the MG. It had crossed both of their minds whether they should spend the night together, but, with neither of them having to say it, they knew that the day had been so immense that it would be better if they just went away separately at this stage to let it all sink in and see what it meant.

'I couldn't have asked for a more wonderful day, Rhys. It's been fabulous. Thanks for the picnic and everything.'

'My pleasure, and same here. I'm going to pinch myself when I get in to see if this is all for real. We could do something similar next Sunday if you're around? Perhaps we could go into the West End or take a walk in Richmond Park?'

'I'd love to,' Vicki replied, the picture of happiness.

'Thing is, I don't know if I can wait till then. How about we go to the pictures one evening? I've been meaning to see *Annie Hall* for ages. Everyone's raving about it.'

'Yes! That's a great idea. I love Woody Allen.'

'Good. I'll check it out and give you a buzz at home to arrange it.'

Just as Vicki went to unlock the driver's door, Rhys eased her gently round to face him and nestled her lovingly in his arms. He kissed her cheek and then twice on the lips before letting go of her. With the reluctance of a young girl being dragged away from Disneyland, Vicki finally got into the car. She started the engine and, with a radiant smile, drove away.

Rhys stood rooted to the spot. For some strange reason, an old primary school teacher's image appeared in his head, solely because he remembered her requesting her pupils to write an essay on their perfect day. Rhys smiled. Whatever he had written all those years ago would never have compared to the day he had just experienced, for today had truly been his perfect day.

A couple of miles away, haring home down the A3 with her smile having never left her face, Vicki thought exactly the same.

December 1978

Chapter 20

'Hey, Vick, you're gonna be popular taking that into the theatre,' Rhys commented, locking his gaze on the large, stiff-sided Selfridges bag she was carrying. 'There'll hardly be any leg room in there and the play's always a sell-out.' He gave her a quick kiss on the lips and stroked her arm with affection.

'I know,' Vicki replied sheepishly, her breath misting in the freezing air, 'but the coat is so beautiful I just had to have it. It's so cold this winter, I need one,' she continued, trying to justify her purchase.

Rhys peered into the bag and cast his eye over the long suede coat with cream fur collar. 'You're right, it is lovely, but what's wrong with the one you've got on and the two back at the flat?'

'But there was twenty per cent off this one. It's a bargain! The sales have started early.'

'Mmm, if you say so.'

'Oh, you men never understand anything,' Vicki retorted with a playful thump on the arm. Rhys didn't say a word. It was true. There were some things about women and shopping he would never understand.

Pulling up his coat collar, Rhys hooked one arm around Vicki's and, taking the bag from her, carried it in his free hand. It was late afternoon, the Saturday before Christmas, and the West End was heaving, the bustle of the crowds intense. Rhys had left the Supreme early for once to meet Vicki outside the famous department store, with its imposing stone columns standing guard imperiously over Oxford Street, for they were meeting up with Karen and Ian for an early dinner before they all moved on to St Martin's Theatre to watch *The Mousetrap*.

Their walk along Oxford Street was painfully slow as the pavements were so full of shoppers and festive season revellers that it was impossible to take two strides without someone blocking their path. It did not help matters that Vicki stopped outside virtually every shop to peer in the window to see whether there were any other goodies she could buy. It frustrated Rhys a little for they were running late but he loved seeing Vicki so happy. Despite the cold, the whole scene before their eyes gladdened their hearts. Lights of every colour imaginable shimmered against a background wall of darkness and light flurries of snow only added to the Christmas ambiance. Finally arriving at Oxford Circus, they stopped for a moment to observe with immense curiosity some Hare Krishna, with their shaved, painted heads and pink robes, chanting their mantra. Wondering how they had not frozen to death in their thin garb and open sandals, Vicki and Rhys eventually turned right down Regent Street where they were able to make quicker progress, the Christmas decorations even more impressive across the much wider road.

'It's great how Karen and Ian are getting on so well. I do hope something comes of it,' Vicki stated, stopping briefly to marvel at the enormous, multi-coloured Lego castle in the window of Hamleys.

Rhys was equally impressed with the long, intricate lay-out of the Scalextric track with new racing cars and pit complex on and beside it. 'Yeah. I hope so, too. Ian's pretty keen, I know.'

'Yeah, Karen, too.'

'Do you think the theatre lets punk rockers in?' Rhys asked semi-seriously.

Vicki laughed. 'I'm sure they do. Well, if they don't, she'll just have to wait outside.'

'Maybe she could go off for a pogo somewhere and find someone to flob on?'

Vicki thumped his arm. 'That's disgusting.' They left Hamleys, still arm in arm, and carried on down Regent Street. 'I still can't get over Ian booking The Savoy this evening, though,' Vicki continued. 'He must be keen, rooms cost a bomb there. I know Karen is really excited. I never took him to be such a charmer, Ian. They could easily have stayed with us at the flat like before.'

'Yeah, I suppose so, but it is Christmas after all. He just wanted to do something special.'

'I wonder if they let punk rockers in there?' Vicki surmised, looking at Rhys.

He looked more worried. 'There's a point. It is quite posh.'

'Perhaps we should have made up a spare room after all.' They burst out laughing.

They continued their progress down Regent Street, Vicki glancing quickly through the entrance of the Café Royal to see if there was anyone she knew inside, before following the sweep into Piccadilly Circus, where the lights were the brightest of all. The snow was falling more steadily now and if it had not been for all the pedestrians, a fine carpet would have formed quickly on the pavements. They pulled up their coat collars even higher as a sharp cold wind whistled up Lower Regent Street, the other side of the Circus, to greet them.

'How was the Supreme today, by the way? Busy?'

'Yeah, like mad. The two girls never stopped. I left Mario in charge and to close up.'

'He's a good person, Mario. I like him a lot.'

'Yeah. He's my right-hand man and a great chef. I trust him implicitly. He brought his young son in today to help Beryl with the washing up and didn't even ask me for any money. I will slip him a few quid though when I see him next.' Vicki pulled Rhys closer and leaned her head into his shoulder in recognition of his generosity and kindness. But then, as they wandered past Eros in the direction of Leicester Square, Vicki stopped and looked over her shoulder. 'You still think someone's following you?' Rhys asked in a concerned, deadpan tone, turning round himself and looking, for what, he did not know.

Vicki scanned the area but observed nothing untoward. If she was being followed, he or she had hidden back in the crowd. 'I dunno, it just feels like it sometimes. But something funny's going on, I can sense it.'

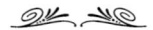

༺ ༻

'Hi Karen, hi Ian,' Vicki shouted from afar, waving at her two friends who were standing outside the Angus Steak House near Leicester Square. They looked frozen, particularly Karen, who, despite the temperature, was wearing ripped fishnets under her leather miniskirt. At least her heavy leather jacket provided some warmth, aided by her only other concession to the weather, a long, thick woollen scarf.

Vicki approached them first, open-armed, her slave, Rhys, still carrying her Selfridges bag two steps behind her. She hugged and kissed them both before Rhys did the same with Karen, though his greeting of Ian was more perfunctory.

'You been waiting long? Sorry we're late,' Rhys asked apologetically.

'Not that long, only a few minutes,' Ian lied.

Karen turned her head sharply towards him, droplets of water flicking off her close-cropped bright ginger hair, her face cross. They had been waiting twenty minutes. 'We were wondering where you'd got to?' Karen butted in more sternly.

'Only looking in every shop window between Marble Arch and Piccadilly Circus, that's all,' Rhys exaggerated, nudging Vicki lightly with his elbow. Vicki's elbow back was considerably firmer. Karen and Ian looked at each other slightly bemused. They did not know London well so were ignorant whether the distance was a great one or not. They assumed the former.

'I bet you one day we'll all be carrying mobile telephones, you know, like walkie-talkies, so that everyone can keep in touch more easily,' Ian threw in as if he would be the inventor of such an incredible device.

'Don't be so ridiculous,' Rhys scoffed, the two girls nodding in agreement, thinking Ian had gone mad.

'Come on, let's go in before my lips turn blue,' Karen implored, shivering.

'But your lips are blue!' Vicki retorted and they all burst out laughing.

Inside the restaurant, a waitress showed them to a table for four by a window. The two couples sat opposite each other on pillar-box red, crushed velvet banquettes.

It was clearly a corporate colour for the sign outside, carpet, staff shirts and menus were all in the same shade.

'Right, what are we having?' Rhys began, contemplating hard the menu he was holding. They were so large, Karen and Ian opposite him were hidden from view. 'Time's pressing so I think we should skip the starters or we'll miss the play. If there's time, we could have a dessert instead. Everyone agree?'

'Yep.'

'Sounds good.'

'Alright with me, though the prawn cocktail looks good,' Ian advised with the look of a child arriving outside Willy Wonka's Chocolate Factory only to find the gates locked.

'Sorry, mate, no time.' Rhys glanced sideways at Vicki with a playfully stern look. He received yet another elbow in the ribs for his trouble.

'Mate! You really have been living in London too long!' Ian exclaimed, putting down his menu.

Rhys laughed. 'You're right there. Sorry, butt.'

'That's more like it,' Ian returned, both he and Karen nodding their approval. Vicki smiled, feeling decidedly like the English runt of this particularly Welsh litter.

The waitress arrived, pencil and pad at the ready.

'We all decided?' Rhys asked. His friends all nodded. 'Karen, you go first.'

'I'm going to have the quarter chicken with chips and peas, thanks.'

The waitress scribbled away.

'Vicki?'

'I'll have the gammon and pineapple, please, with chips and peas.'

'I was tempted by that, myself,' Rhys commented. 'Ian?'

'I'll have the plaice, chips and peas, thanks.'

'Tartar sauce?' the waitress asked in a broken accent, still scribbling.

'Yes, please.'

'And I'll have half a roast chicken with chips and peas, thanks. Oh, and some onion rings as well, please.'

'Any drinks with your meals?' the waitress continued.

Rhys motioned to Karen.

'Half a lager for me.'

'Vicki?'

'A glass of dry white wine, please.'

'I'll have a pint of lager,' Ian followed.

'I'll have the same,' Rhys finally concluded.

The waitress struck her pad sharply once with a final full stop and gathered up the menus before walking away. Ian and Rhys followed her tread automatically, without being conscious of doing so, for she did have a lovely behind.

As they began to chat away, Rhys made a quick scan of the restaurant. It was so busy he knew it had to be making a small fortune. At the entrance, a queue of at least twelve people, he estimated, had formed, waiting for tables to become free. He breathed in the aromas of grilled meat and fried potatoes, ketchup and mustard. The whole mix was intoxicating and he loved it. Why can't I own a place like this one day? he thought, knowing that there was no reason at all why not.

'Hey, Rhys, you not checking out the competition again, are you?' Karen wondered, seeing how his attention was momentarily elsewhere.

'If only! Be hard pressed for the Supreme to compete with this,' Rhys replied, but, after a brief pause, he added, 'One day, perhaps.' The look in his eye was so steely that his three friends knew that that day would not be too far away. Vicki stroked his thigh with pride beneath the table.

'It's certainly a lovely place, this,' Karen replied, looking around. 'You can't beat a good steak house for proper food.'

'You're right there,' Vicki agreed, 'but the irony is that none of us is actually eating steak!'

The whole table broke out into laughter.

'Oh, congratulations, by the way, on the promotion, Vicki. Rhys told us all about it,' Ian cut in, changing the subject.

'Thanks, Ian. It's strange having my old job back but at least I know what to expect.'

'I've never known you to work so hard, what with you being the sales and marketing director again. God knows what it'll be like when they make you president?' Rhys threw in, breaking open a bread roll and unwrapping a tiny oblong of butter.

'That's a long way off, if at all! That's a massive step. They'll probably ship someone in from their parent company in the States should the position become vacant.'

'Nonsense. You'll get it next.'

'I wish I had your confidence, Rhys,' though once more Vicki felt emboldened at his support for her abilities.

'Though if you come in drunk like you did last night, they might wonder whether they want a pisshead for the top job!'

'Oh, don't remind me. I've only just about got over my hangover.'

'Why so drunk?' Karen asked, all ears, just as the waitress returned carrying a tray with their drinks.

'It was our Christmas party, in a wine bar not so far from here down the road. We booked the whole place and everyone got pretty merry, as you can imagine. Our president, Brad, was the worst of the lot and the word is he left with one of the accounts girls. Can't wait to find out what happened on Monday.'

'Looks like you might be president by Tuesday then at this rate,' Rhys interrupted and everyone laughed.

'Nah. He's really good is Brad. He likes a drink and a good time.'

'Any jobs going? Sounds like the sort of place I might enjoy,' Ian threw in to further laughter. 'By the way, we've got a wine bar now in Ponty. Going all posh, we are. But, thing is, it's a bit like us and steak houses. Everyone goes there to drink beer!'

Their laughter was now loud enough to turn the heads of those dining close by to wonder what was going on.

'Cheers, everyone,' Rhys said when the laughter subsided and they clinked each other's glasses before taking a sip.

'You two had a nice day then?' Vicki asked, picking up the conversation, directing her remarks at Ian and Karen opposite.

'Yeah, really nice,' Karen answered. 'We were up at the crack of dawn and caught the early train in Cardiff. We managed a few sights, you know, Big Ben, the Houses of Parliament, Trafalgar Square. We'll do a few more tomorrow before going back. I fancy Harrods but he wants to go to Soho,' she went on, looking daggers at Ian.

'I wonder why! You men are so obvious!' Vicki broke in with a loud sigh.

'I think it's important to experience all the cultural delights of London when you're here,' Ian replied with mock pomposity.

'Yeah, yeah! Especially if they've got big tits, no doubt,' Vicki replied to hearty chuckling.

'Hey, Ian, I think you're in luck,' Rhys interrupted with a glint in his eye.

'Why's that then?'

''Cos Harrods is closed on Sundays!'

Vicki and Karen just stared at each other, shaking their heads, as Rhys and Ian laughed.

'Talking of Harrods, a funny thing happened there the other day,' Vicki declared, her expression serious. She was on the point of developing her statement when the waitress returned, somehow balancing all four of their meals in her hands and on her arms. The smells were enticing and portions immense. They were so famished they could not wait to get stuck in. Skilfully, the waitress set the plates down in their correct positions and brought over some ketchup, vinegar and mustard from a nearby table.

'This looks fantastic. Look at the size of your plaice, Ian, it's overhanging your plate both sides,' Karen commented, briefly forgetting Vicki. No one disagreed as they contemplated their meals, Ian shaking some vinegar over his chips before passing the bottle to Rhys.

'Sorry, Vick, you were saying,' Rhys resumed, cutting a wing off his chicken.

Vicki swallowed a slice of gammon before carrying on. 'Yeah, a work colleague of mine, Brenda, was having something to eat with a girlfriend of hers in one of the food halls when this bloke came up and joined them.'

'What's wrong with that?' Ian wondered, plunging his fork into some chips. 'Are they a couple of lookers then?'

Karen admonished him with an unhappy expression. 'Ian! Don't be so crass.'

Ian placed the chips in his mouth, not knowing what crass meant but realising it was probably not very complimentary.

'Well, he made out he owned a clothing factory near Manchester,' Vicki resumed, 'and that he had met Brenda at a trade show, though she couldn't remember him. He had all the chat and that and got onto the subject of me. Somehow, he knew I was working with her and, because of my relationship with Tommy, was just gossiping about what I was up to and stuff like that.'

'I remember you telling me this,' Rhys interrupted without concern, slicing off a piece of chicken breast.

'After a bit, Brenda got suspicious 'cos he seemed to go on about me a lot and she admitted she might have opened up a bit too much about, you know, me living with Rhys again and what I thought about Tommy. She was angry with herself afterwards, particularly as this bloke had a southern accent and didn't seem to have the slightest clue about the industry. She thought she should have seen through him earlier. He was just a shitty journalist digging for a story. I don't blame Brenda, it's easy to be taken in by scumbags.'

'You don't think he was working for Tommy then, do you? You know, dredging up stuff to help him should you go after his money in the divorce,' Karen opined, looking worried.

'But I don't want his money, and he knows it! He can keep it for all I care. But I can't help feeling he's up to something. It wouldn't surprise me in the slightest if that journalist was working for him, you know. He's got so many of them dangling on strings, dancing to his tune, you'd never believe it. He's like a puppeteer.'

'So the divorce is dragging?' Ian asked, spearing a piece of fish with his fork.

Vicki threw her head back in despair. 'You can say that again. He's always coming up with some excuse or other. He just won't accept reality and get on with it. I'm sure he thinks I'm going to go back to him.'

'You just need to stay calm, Vicki. I know you're impatient but next summer will be two years since you left him and he won't be able to stop it then.' Rhys followed up his reassuring words with a touch of her leg and a more relaxed Vicki smiled back at him.

'He's such a pig is Tommy. I always told you he was a shyster, Vick,' Karen threw in. Vicki looked at her sternly but said nothing. That had not always been Karen's opinion.

'He's losing it as a player as well,' Ian broke in. He finished chewing some peas before adding, 'He's not even in the West Ham team now and is on the transfer list.'

'Perhaps the New York Cosmos might come in for him with a bit of luck,' Karen cut in. 'That'll keep him out of your hair for a while, Vicki, if he goes over there.'

They all chuckled but Vicki still had her worries. 'It's not just this Harrods business that's odd. I'm sure I'm being followed as well.'

Rhys sighed with strained patience, but discreetly, so that no one would know, for he had heard Vicki mention this a few times before and thought she was being paranoid as she had never been able to come up with any sighting or evidence. For the benefit of his friends, he repeated what he had said to her on those other occasions. 'Try not to let it bother you, Vicki. It's probably nothing, but if you do come up with something, let me know and we'll go to the police.' Vicki and the others nodded. It was all they could do in the circumstances but agree with him.

Placing her knife and fork down onto an empty plate, Vicki suddenly blurted out, 'Anyway, enough of Tommy Slater. We're here to have a good time, after all.'

'Well said, Vick,' Karen replied, eating the last of her chips.

'You enjoyed that, Kar?' Rhys asked politely.

'Yeah, delicious. Better than tasting blood all the time.' They laughed. It had not taken long for Karen to remove the safety pin from her bottom lip.

'You didn't fancy sticking it somewhere else then?' Rhys continued in all innocence.

Simultaneously, Karen and Ian blushed as bright red as the waitress's shirt and lowered their eyes. Instinctively, Rhys and Vicki looked at each other, mouths agape, their minds working overtime, surmising where she might have pinned it. Correctly, as it turned out, they concluded that it was now more than likely attached to one of Karen's lips that was strictly not for public view.

'I really enjoyed that,' Vicki pronounced with a happy face as she buttoned up her coat in the foyer of St Martin's Theatre. Rhys and Ian were doing likewise though all Karen did was rearrange the scarf around her neck. She had yet to take off her leather jacket all evening. It had been cloyingly warm inside the theatre and she had been tempted to do so but she did not feel that revealing her

T-shirt, with the slogan *Never Mind The Bollocks, Here's The Sex Pistols* written large on its front was quite appropriate for such an occasion. Rhys had purchased plumb seats only five rows back from the stage in the stalls, so close to the characters in fact that Karen feared that even Detective Sergeant Trotter might throw her disapproving looks.

'Yeah, same here,' Karen agreed. 'The set was gorgeous. Wouldn't it be wonderful to live in a place as beautiful and olde-worlde as Monkswell Manor?' she carried on, sounding like the ultra-conservative Margo Leadbetter in *The Good Life*.

Her friends all looked at Karen incredulously. They were certain that her punk idols, Rat Scabies, Siouxie Sioux and Ari Up would not have come out with such a comment, and this from someone who loved bands with names such as The Nipple Erectors and The Vibrators. They all began to laugh.

'What's so funny?' was all a bemused Karen could say.

'Never mind, Karen, never mind,' Ian replied, patting her gently on the shoulder.

Yes, Karen certainly had the look but not yet the attitude of a punk rocker.

'Now, remember what they said. We mustn't reveal the ending to anyone, alright!' Rhys reminded everyone.

'Not much chance of Ian doing that,' Karen replied, looking at her boyfriend. 'You slept right through the last act. I had to nudge you a couple of times when you started to snore.'

'Gerroff. You're having me on.'

'You were getting a bit loud, Ian,' Vicki cut in to his embarrassment.

'Well, it has been a long day,' he replied unconvincingly.

Exiting the theatre, they were met by a rush of sharp, freezing wind that made them dip their faces behind their coat collars and scarves.

'Jesus, it's cold,' Rhys blurted out as Vicki hooked her arm around his so tightly he nearly toppled over. Karen's cheeks turned almost as blue as her lips as she linked arms with Ian. 'We'll walk you to The Savoy,' Rhys followed up. 'It's not far.'

'You're so lucky, you two, staying there. I'm so envious,' Vicki commented as they proceeded down Garrick Street in the direction of the Strand where the hotel was positioned on the banks of the Thames. Ian and Karen looked at each other excitedly and grinned, saying nothing.

'How long's *The Mousetrap* been going?' Ian threw into the conversation as they picked their way through other theatre-goers who had just exited their shows. He answered his own question with another question. 'Twenty-six years, isn't it?'

'Yeah, that's right,' Vicki replied. 'Just amazing.'

'Can't believe how, if I'm honest, because I thought it was a bit slow and complicated at the end.'

'How would you know? You were sleeping!' Karen interjected and Vicki and Rhys laughed.

'Yeah, well,' Ian blustered. He went quiet for a moment as they continued down Bedford Street. Arriving on the Strand, he piped up confidently, 'I'll tell you one thing, though, there's no way it'll last another twenty-six years, that's for sure!'

Crossing over the road, they turned left and proceeded up the Strand until, turning right, they arrived at the shimmering, art deco, silver Savoy sign, with the gold statue of Count Peter of Savoy standing imperiously on top. They ambled underneath right up to the dark-wooded entrance doors and stood outside. Vicki noticed a few black cabs in line with yellow lights on, showing they were available, and thought she would suggest one to Rhys when they left their friends. She was so cold, the prospect of traipsing home on the draughty tube and train was deflating.

'Well, Rhys, Vicki, we'll grab a taxi and be on our way. It's been a great evening.'

Vicki was perplexed, wondering whether she had heard Ian correctly. She also wondered why everyone was smiling and staring at her. Karen, in particular, could barely contain herself and her face radiated happiness.

'Sorry, have I missed something?'

No one answered.

'Here are the keys to the flat, Ian,' Rhys broke in, handing him a leather pouch. 'You know where everything is, don't you? Just make yourselves at home.'

'Ah, excuse me, but can someone explain what's going on? I thought you were staying here tonight?' Vicki interrupted, looking at Karen.

Karen shrugged her shoulders. 'I'd let Rhys explain.'

Vicki stared up at her boyfriend with the curiosity of a kitten.

'Well, it's a bit of a surprise, I know, but we're the ones staying here tonight, not Karen and Ian. I've been planning it for ages.'

Vicki raised her hand to her mouth, turning her stare away from Rhys momentarily and directing it towards Karen. 'Is this true? Are you in on this?'

'Yeah, we've known all along,' Karen replied, clasping her friend to her. 'You'll love it.'

Letting go of Karen, Vicki turned back to Rhys. It finally dawned on her what a fantastic surprise it was and, looking through the entrance doors, marvelled at the opulence inside which she would soon be enjoying. 'Rhys, I can't believe it!' she shrieked, grabbing hold of him and hugging him so hard he thought she would break his back. Her face was brighter than a full moon on the darkest of nights. 'You sods! All of you!' Everyone laughed, patting her on the back and shoulder. 'But I haven't got any of my clothes or stuff with me!' Vicki blurted out, her practical side taking over.

'Suits you, doesn't it, Rhys?' Ian joked, earning a punch on the arm from Vicki.

'You know what I mean, for tomorrow.'

'Don't worry, it's all sorted. I packed a few things you might need and checked in earlier before we met up. They're in the room,' Rhys answered. 'Karen and Ian dropped their bags off at the flat this morning when you were out.'

'Slipped in some Ann Summers, I hope, Rhys?' Ian joked once more, earning thumps not only from Vicki this time but also from Karen.

'God, I can't believe this!' Vicki exclaimed with a shake of her head. I was so jealous of you, too, you lying cow!' she added, addressing Karen.

'Well, we'd better make a move before we freeze to death,' Ian interrupted, standing next to a taxi and banging his gloved hands hard together. 'I wish I'd worn my Starskey cardigan now, it's so cold.' The dense plumes of condensation streaming from his mouth mixed with those of his friends and created a milky-white mist around them as if they were standing on a film set swirling with dry ice.

Rhys thrust a five pound note into Ian's hand to pay for the cab, despite his protest, before Ian jumped through its open door inside where Karen, having said her goodbyes to Vicki and Rhys a moment earlier, was already seated.

'Just leave the keys and pull the door behind you tomorrow. Have a good day and we'll speak soon,' Rhys shouted as the cab pulled away, the four of them all waving and mouthing their farewells.

With the taxi gone, Vicki flung her arms around Rhys's neck and kissed him repeatedly on the lips. 'You're unreal. I love you so much,' Vicki told him, her eyes raining mischief. 'Come on, let's go inside. I want to warm you up.'

'Oh my God, look at this. I can't believe it.' Vicki was awe-struck as she entered their eye-popper of a room, stopping a moment to survey the surrounds, Rhys a step behind her. It was not the most expensive room in the hotel, but it was not the cheapest, either. Rhys did not reply and appeared a little nervous, to Vicki's eye, but then again it was not a setting he was used to, she thought, nor her, truth be told. The colours of the carpet, armchair, sofa, bed cover and curtains all blended beautifully, a mix of beige, amber, cream and gold and the Edwardian yew desk and chair, so finely polished that Rhys was afraid to touch them, co-ordinated perfectly with the furnishings, as did the golden chandelier and wall lights that emitted a soft yellow glow. Also perfect was the temperature of the room, the heat rising from the boxed radiators a relieving contrast to the bitter cold outside.

Vicki strode over to the window at the far end of the bedroom, pulled back the net curtains and gazed outside at the River Thames, the water chopping black and silver in its flow. On the opposite bank of the river, Vicki viewed a checkerboard pattern of lit and unlit windows on the Royal Festival Hall while, to her left, numerous twin specks of lights eased their way in both directions across Waterloo Bridge.

'As long as I gaze on Waterloo sunset, I am in paradise ...'

Vicki may not have been gazing on a Waterloo sunset but she certainly thought she was in paradise as she sang quietly to herself, paying homage to the city she adored.

Rhys approached where she was standing, nestling her in his arms from behind and resting his hands on her belly. She stroked them with the lightest of touches. He seemed a little tense.

'What a fabulous view, Rhys. This is a great city; I love it here, almost as much as I love you,' and with that she gripped one of his hands and raised it to her mouth to plant a kiss. He reciprocated, kissing the top of her head, moving his free hand to his side.

'I'm so glad you said that because I love you, too, Vicki, with all my heart.' He kissed the top of her head once more. Still looking out of the window, Vicki squeezed his hand in recognition. Rhys saw her smile in the reflection of the glass.

Almost immediately, Rhys took a step backwards and, taking a deep breath, gently eased Vicki round to face him. They kissed passionately. Vicki still sensed his tension but thought nothing of it.

She was not mistaken, however, for Rhys was a bag of nerves. A few seconds later, his free hand having slipped unnoticed into his pocket, he pulled out a tiny Kingfisher-blue box and raised it in front of him. Vicki saw it and placed her hand over her mouth to stifle a gasp and when Rhys opened it to reveal a white gold sapphire ring set in a cluster of diamonds, she almost buckled at the knees. Her wide eyes of wonderment misted over and she began crying the happiest tears of her life even before Rhys had the opportunity to say the words she had so wanted him to say.

'Vicki, will you marry me?'

May 1979

Chapter 21

Rhys entered the Supreme the first Friday of May in the middle of the morning wearing his new dark grey pinstripe suit. He never wore a suit to work but he had just arrived from the bank where he had been to see Mr Partridge. On leaving, he had removed his tie straight away for it was strangling him. It was not so much the tie, if truth be told, as the top button of his shirt and he grumbled at the inescapable fact that he had put on weight recently. The fact that his suit trousers were three sizes larger than those of his C&A suit was confirmation enough. Relieved to have undone the top button, he unfastened two more and stretched the collar out wide across the lapels. He liked to wear his shirt in this style under a jacket, much like John Travolta had done in *Saturday Night Fever,* though, if he did not stop eating, this would be the only way he would ever come to resemble the snake-hipped actor, he thought with a chuckle. Rhys liked wearing his new suit and contemplated buying another though he drew the line at the pristine white one worn by Tony Manero in the film.

Other than his weight, Rhys had nothing much else to grumble about. His life could not have been better. The meeting with the bank manager had gone exceptionally well, with Mr Partridge agreeing to finance the purchase of the café in Wandsworth High Street that Rhys had had his eye on for some time and which had come onto the market. He wanted to ensure that everything was in order at the Supreme first before calling the agent to put in a formal offer and, on observing Debbie and Maureen flitting efficiently between the tables which were nearly fully occupied, Rhys rested easy in the knowledge that the customers were in good hands. He surveyed the premises briefly and was content at the standard of cleanliness and décor. He moved into the kitchen after exchanging pleasantries with the two waitresses and several customers.

'Hi Mario, Beryl. Everything okay?'

Mario turned round from the cooker where he was grilling some sausages. 'Oh, hi Rhys. Everything's fine, no problems. We might be running a bit short of butter but I think we can manage. Beryl can always pop down the supermarket to get some if we need to.'

Rhys smiled and left the kitchen. In fact, he left the Supreme altogether to go upstairs to change, happy in the knowledge he had staff he could trust. The café was doing well and making enough money for Rhys to consider expansion. Before changing, he went into the living room to telephone the agent. While waiting on the line, he looked around him with pride, not so much at room itself, but at Vicki, who had added tasteful little touches here and there as she had done elsewhere in the flat.

After making his offer, which the agent believed would be accepted, Rhys replaced the receiver and sat down for a moment. He was feeling tired, having stayed up until three o'clock in the morning with Vicki. He was so looking forward to their wedding at St Peter & St Paul's in Godalming, though there was no definite date set yet as it depended on when Vicki's decree absolute would come through and that might even mean the following year. Not that you would think it? Rhys chuckled, shaking his head, for the way Vicki and her mother were talking, anyone would think the wedding was imminent. They were already making arrangements, which he tried desperately to keep out of, for, if he didn't, he would never find time to do anything else. Ian would be the best man but there was currently a stand-off between Vicki and Karen about the latter being a bridesmaid as the two girls disagreed passionately about Karen's desire to retain her punk rocker look. She would wear the correct dress and shoes, of course, but Karen refused to alter her make-up or remove any safety-pins. Accordingly, they were not speaking at present, but Rhys knew it would all blow over soon enough though Vicki was not so certain. 'Women!'

As Rhys smiled to himself, he tilted his head right back onto the top of the back of the sofa and looked directly up at the ceiling before shutting his eyes. He was so tired, he wished he could stay in this position all day. He would allow himself ten minutes, he decided, though it did concern him he might fall asleep. He recalled the easy conversation he'd had with Vicki's mother the previous evening on the telephone as they threw around ideas for the style of suits and flowers for buttonholes the gentlemen would wear. It gave him the greatest pleasure to know how well liked he was now by Vicki's parents. They had seen how committed he was to their daughter and how much he loved her and, after the disaster of Vicki's marriage to Tommy Slater, they were desperate for her to find happiness and fulfilment with someone else. They also knew how deep-rooted Vicki's love was for Rhys and, ultimately, that was the most important thing to them. It helped, of course, that their prospective son-in-law was making a success of his life and they were pleasantly surprised at how much Rhys had matured and changed beyond recognition over the years. They never doubted for one second that he would care and look after their daughter for the rest of her life and that comforting knowledge created a warm feeling inside them.

In fact, their main worry now was Fiona, who seemed to have a different boyfriend every week. When Rhys had been with Vicki and her family one evening in Godalming, her mother had argued with Fiona about her settling down like her sister 'with a nice young man like Rhys'. When Rhys heard these words it finally dawned on him conclusively that he had been accepted by Vicki's family. With a lump in his throat, he turned his head and looked at Vicki who, stroking his hand, smiled back.

Even Tommy Slater's intransigence over the divorce would soon be a thing of the past for, in August, he and Vicki would have been living apart for two years. Her father's excellent solicitor would push for the decree nisi and decree absolute to come through as quickly as possible but he warned everyone to be patient for there was no knowing exactly how long it would take. Not that Vicki and her mother were listening!

With his eyes shut tight and head still resting on the back of the sofa, Rhys's demeanour turned more severe as the image of Tommy Slater suddenly appeared in his head. If he possessed just one ounce of decency in his bones, rather than a body full of spite, he might well be married to Vicki by now, he mused. Slater had made life very difficult for her and Rhys's eyes burned with anger when remembering the article in *The Sun* newspaper which implied that Vicki had been seeing a number of men behind Slater's back during their marriage and making her out to be some cheap tart. Rhys's usual mild manner had exploded like a firecracker when reading this and he had ranted and raved about wanting to do something about it, not that he had the slightest idea what. Vicki had managed to calm him down and implored him to ignore it, which, in her view, was the best way of dealing with these things. Rhys knew she was right but he had found it very difficult to do so.

On another occasion, Slater had managed to get through to Vicki by phone in work on the premise of discussing the divorce, but, instead, he ended up bawling her out and calling her every disgusting name under the sun, or, as Vicki put it to Rhys later, singing along to Simon & Garfunkel, *"With words you never read in the Bible"*. Rhys grinned and admired the calm way Vicki was handling everything but he despised Slater for his disgraceful attitude.

The ten minutes' rest quickly turned into half an hour. He was just so tired. Despite this, his mind remained active as all these memories, good and bad, flooded back. Anyway, Mario and the girls were more than capable of running the café by themselves. Yes, Tommy Slater, he was a right piece of shit, Rhys concluded, but, thankfully, he would soon be out of their lives for good. He suddenly woke with a start. Rhys had dozed off, but, looking at the clock next to the telephone, it had only been for five minutes. He finally stirred himself and stood up, his limbs feeling stiff.

'God, I'm turning into an old man. I've got to find time to do some exercise and lose some weight and I must buy that bike I keep going on about. After all, I am the wrong side of thirty now.' Saying it made him feel better not that he was convinced he would live up to his words.

After stretching his arms high above his head, he strolled into the kitchen and switched on the radio. Rod Stewart was singing *Maggie Mae*. Rhys groaned. Life was wonderful; he had his own business and a second one on the way; he owned his flat; he had a gorgeous girlfriend he loved beyond words and whom he would soon marry; he had kind, loving parents he adored; he had money in the bank and a group of close friends. And yet, today, deep down, he felt miserable and the song reminded him exactly why, for Margaret Thatcher had led the Tories to victory in the General Election the previous day and his beloved Labour were out of government. Despite Mr Partridge believing this would be good for businessmen, Rhys was not so sure. He seemed to have done pretty well under Labour, he argued back.

No, he thought Thatcher would be divisive and that working class communities like Pontypridd would suffer badly. Hopefully, she'd only last the one term, if that. The policies she was proposing would get her kicked out next time, he was certain, once everyone could see what a terrible effect they were having on the country. Let's hope she doesn't get involved in an easy war somewhere for victory was always good for sitting governments, Rhys mulled. He chuckled at the crazy thought for it was hardly likely. Vicki did not care for Thatcher, either, but she gave her great credit for having the strength of character to become the first female Prime Minister of the country, and, as they snuggled up on the sofa the previous night watching the election results, even Rhys had conceded her that ... but only just!

Switching off the radio, Rhys left the kitchen. Just as he was about to go into the bedroom, he stopped to observe himself in the hallway mirror. The beginning of a double chin was clearly in evidence, which made him puff out his cheeks in disappointment, and he was not so sure about his Bee Gee look either, with long hair swept back and neatly trimmed beard, flecked with grey. Vicki liked it, though, comparing him to the handsome Barry Gibb. Rhys thought he looked more like Jesus Christ.

'Well, could be worse, I suppose,' he muttered, smiling to himself, before entering the bedroom. He kicked off his shoes, took off his jacket, which he placed over the back of a chair, and unbuttoned his shirt, which he flung onto the floor ready for the laundry basket. After unbuckling his belt and tossing it onto the bed, he began to slip off his trousers. It was while doing this that he heard the noise of a key turning in the front door lock. This startled him and he looked instinctively in the direction of the sound though he could not see the front door itself. Only Vicki possessed another key and she was at work. Decidedly perplexed, he took a few paces to the bedroom door before exiting. At once, he saw Vicki approach him.

'Hey, Vicki, you gave me a surprise. How come you're home?'

She did not answer the question. 'I popped in downstairs to see if you were there but they said you'd gone up.' The tone of her voice was nervy and her face carried an expression that was part smile, part serious.

'Yeah. I was just changing,' Rhys replied as they met in the hallway, exchanging a kiss. 'It went really well at the bank. Mr Partridge will lend me the money and I've put an offer in. Fingers crossed!'

'That's great!'

'But how come you're home?'

'Oh, I just had a doctor's appointment, that's all. I'll be going back to the office in a minute.'

'Doctor's appointment? Anything wrong? They going to amputate something?' Rhys replied half in jest, half in concern.

Looking down at the carpet but then straight back up again into his eyes and holding his forearm lightly, Vicki hit Rhys with it. 'No, nothing like that. I'm pregnant.'

Rhys went as rigid as a statue, his mouth half open, his brain trying to come to terms with this unexpected piece of news. He would never forget this moment nor, with a smile, how he was dressed for such a momentous occasion as he stood in his short, faded grey socks, a small hole starting over the big toe of one of them, and his amber and black y-fronts, his belly and fleshy handlebars all floppy and squidgy around his middle. But it only took a brief second for the news to strike home and his face, initially so full of shock, soon changed to one of beaming delight. Seeing his face light up so much triggered the same reaction in Vicki and they hugged each other more tightly than a boa constrictor would its prey, as if they were trying to merge their bodies into one. Rhys didn't say a word. He didn't need to. Feeling his tear on her cheek told Vicki everything.

October 1979

Chapter 22

'Cheers, Tommy.' Bill Smith took a swig of his lager and the ex-captain of West Ham and England did the same opposite him. They were sitting at a heavily stained table in a corner of the Pontefract Castle pub in Wigmore Street in the West End of London, the flickering lights of the fruit machine nearby standing out brightly against the more sombre dark-wooded surrounds.

The chief football correspondent of *The Sun* newspaper had arrived early and the battered and scratched ashtray in the centre of the table already contained four of his cigarette butts, their fleshy colour protruding from a small mountain of grey-white ash. An open red, white and gold packet of Embassy and green and white Holiday Inn book of matches lay alongside. Tommy glimpsed disapprovingly over the rim of his pint at the cigarettes, for he hated smoking, but he was in no position to upset Smith as he sought the information only the football hack could provide.

It was late morning and the pub was still relatively empty, in a lull before the storm of lunchtime drinkers thronged in from the offices around. They had met up at the same time and at the same table several times before and were relaxed that no one would be able to overhear them. It helped that the music in the background was louder than usual today with Kate Bush, as Cathy, imploring at that particular moment for Heathcliff to come home now.

'Ah, that's better,' Smith sighed, wiping his mouth uncouthly with the back of his sleeve. 'So, how you doing, Tommy? Still mulling over that move to Southend?'

'Yeah, I am. No one else has come in for me yet, so, at the moment, it's my only option. I'll leave it a bit, though. You never know, there's still a chance I might get a call from United or Cloughie, with a bit of luck?' They both sniggered but Smith's was full of irony. Even if Tommy could not bring himself to accept it, Smith knew that he was finished as a top-class footballer and that he was lucky that even a lower league club like Southend United was interested in him. 'Don't worry, Smithy, you'll be the first to know what happens.'

'Cheers, Tommy. Appreciate it.'

As the conversation died, they grabbed their pints simultaneously and took further swigs of their lagers, Smith following up with a loud belch and a long, slow drag on his cigarette.

'So, Bill, anything new happening?' Tommy finally asked impatiently.

Smith knew precisely what Tommy was referring to. For the best part of two years, on and off, he had been keeping tabs on Vicki for him, well not actually Smith himself, but a young reporter he had taken under his wing. Tommy had been careful to explain the reasons why at the beginning. He had lied to Smith by telling him that Vicki was planning to grab every penny she could get her hands on in the divorce and asked him to dig up anything which might help him in a likely court case. He had given Smith the story about Vicki being promiscuous during their marriage, which *The Sun* had run without question, and Smith had ordered his reporter to find out if she was still putting it about a bit, as he so eloquently put it. Smith could see how highlighting Vicki's penchant for the opposite sex during and after her marriage could be construed in court as her never having been fully committed to Tommy and that, in essence, she was a slut and a money-grabber.

Initially, Smith thought he had struck gold when Tim, his reporter, discovered that Vicki had returned to her previous long-term boyfriend and had subsequently moved into a flat with him in Battersea only a few weeks after leaving Tommy. He believed Tommy would be pleased to hear this for a case could be made in court that Vicki had never been in love with him in the first place and had only married him for his money all along which she planned to share with her true love afterwards. How could a judge not be sympathetic to Tommy in these circumstances? But, to Smith's surprise, Tommy had been furious when he relayed this news, slamming his fist into the table, his face turning puce. It was clear to Smith that Tommy still had feelings for Vicki even if he did keep calling her by disgusting names. What was equally surprising to Smith was Tommy's incandescent reaction to information Smith did not believe to be important like Vicki restarting her old job and subsequent promotion.

'Fucking old bag. She should be at home like normal tarts, looking after their blokes and dropping sprogs, rather than thinking she's so high and mighty. Who the fuck does she think she is, slag?' Being from the old school, Smith had some sympathy with Tommy's views, though he would not have expressed them in quite the same way.

As Tommy waited for Smith's reply, the latter scrunched his cigarette in the ashtray and slowly drew another from its packet, making Tommy roll his eyes in annoyance and further impatience. Smith was delaying his response because, after much consideration, he had decided to tell Tommy that he was pulling Tim off the case for he had nearly been found out on a couple of occasions and, worse still, had been shouted down by a female colleague of Vicki's recently in a pub across the road from their work who recognised him chatting up one of the young secretaries, digging for information. It was the same female colleague who had rumbled him in Harrods and Tim had been forced to shift himself smartly from the pub for there was no messing with Brenda, the veritable iron fist clad in cashmere, when she got angry.

But this was not the only reason Smith was pulling Tim off the job. He had begun to suspect that Tommy possessed some other sinister motive for wanting information on Vicki. Smith had not thought anything of it, at first, but Tommy was obsessed in knowing any regular, routine patterns of movement Vicki observed, like timings to and from work, to and from her local supermarket or anything similar. Tim had provided as much information as he could. However, Smith had become increasingly puzzled how any of it could be significant or relevant in a divorce case. He never asked Tommy why he needed it ... he did not want to know the answer.

'I've got a bit more news, Tommy, but I think we're coming to the end now,' Smith finally replied. 'We're scraping the barrel, to be honest. Her movements haven't changed much, if at all, since the last time and Tim's getting fed up traipsing around after Vicki as if he were her shadow. Her work's got wind of him as well so I think he's done.'

Decade

Tommy took a sip of his lager and looked sternly at Smith. He was probably right, he concluded. He had all the information he needed, truth be told. Now, he could just calmly go away and ponder what to do.

'Yeah, suppose you're right, Bill. Tim's done a great job. Tell him I appreciate it and here's another monkey for the two of you.' Tommy handed Smith an envelope full of fivers and tenners and took another swig of his drink. 'You said you had a bit more info, though?'

'Cheers for that, Tommy,' Smith replied, stuffing the envelope into his coat pocket. 'That's right. When Tim was chatting up one of the birds from Vicki's work in the pub the other day ...'

'Did he pull her, Bill?' Tommy cut in with a smirk.

'No chance! I'm sure he would've done 'cos Tim'll shag anything but he got rumbled and had to scarper. Before then, though, he learnt a couple of nuggets you might find interesting.'

'So, what's that?' Tommy was all ears, holding his pint glass close to his lips but waiting for an answer before taking a drink.

Smith dragged long and hard on his cigarette and looked Tommy directly in the eye. He knew he was not going to like it. Nevertheless, he decided not to beat about the bush and so hit him with it straight. 'Vicki's expecting a baby in the New Year and they're planning on getting married shortly afterwards.' Quickly taking a swig to finish his lager but this time finding himself unable to keep looking Tommy in the eye, Smith waited for his reaction. The initial one surprised him for Tommy did not move a muscle and appeared relatively calm. But then, Smith looked up and saw a trickle of perspiration run down one of his temples. At the same time, Tommy's stomach and chest began to heave. All of a sudden, Tommy exploded from his seat like a stick of dynamite and pushed over the table they were sitting at violently, prompting Smith to take evasive action. His packet of cigarettes and book of matches shot away and his pint glass smashed on the floor where the ashtray ran round on its rim a short distance, strewing its contents everywhere.

Now up on his feet, his face red with rage and glistening with sweat, the veins in his head pulsing furiously, Tommy flung his glass against the overturned table and a multitude of icy shards flew away in every direction. The bar staff and other customers in the pub were all transfixed, not just at the violence of the action, but also at who had perpetrated it. Tommy couldn't care less. Snorting like a bull entering the ring to face a matador, he grabbed his jacket and stormed out of the pub faster and more aggressively than a soldier in the SAS, slamming the door behind him so hard its glass panes reverberated in their mouldings. His mind was made up. He knew what to do now.

December 1979

CHAPTER 23

'She'd better fucking be there this time,' he muttered under his breath, glancing at his watch, as he stood outside the Stargreen Box Office in Argyll Street for the third night in a row, pretending to study the multi-coloured squares of cards in the window, each one advertising in bold, black felt-tip pen which theatre show or concert they held tickets for. To his right, a seemingly never-ending line of heavily coated and hatted people was entering the Argyll pub whilst, behind him, he sensed a similar, never-ending line of people, laden with Christmas shopping, bustle past him, invariably heading for the tube station on Oxford Circus or in the opposite direction towards Liberty's department store at the bottom of the street.

He had chosen his time and position deliberately in order to take advantage of the environment around him. In addition to the busy street, it was cold enough to justify wearing his green Parka coat with its faux-fur rimmed hood pulled over to cover his head. Underneath, a mottled-grey, woollen beanie hat was pulled far down over his eyebrows while a thick, cable-knit black scarf was wrapped around his neck and chin right up to his nostrils. He was uncomfortably hot but that was the least of his concerns, the main one being the cause of his anxiety now.

Two days earlier, standing in the same spot, at the same time, though wearing different clothing, namely a brown duffel coat and shamrock-green beanie and scarf, he was all keyed up as he waited for Vicki to exit her office in Regent Arcade House to his left at precisely six o'clock. This was her normal routine. She would then pass in front of Stargreen on her way to the tube station. A rush of adrenalin coursed through his body when he saw her leave the building, but, to his dismay, she turned in the opposite direction instead and slowly crossed the road as if heading for the London Palladium where the posters outside were advertising Yul Brynner starring in *The King and I*. Before reaching the famous theatre, however, she dived into the pub next door, no doubt joining some work colleagues for a drink.

It had been the same the day before when waiting in yet another different colour combination of clothing. This time she had not appeared at all and, feeling very conspicuous, he had left when his watch showed six-thirty. He knew she sometimes travelled in her job and wondered whether this was such an occasion or whether she had broken up early for the Christmas holiday. Or, had she finally left work for good until the birth of her baby, for Vicki was now heavily pregnant, and so delaying his plan until well into the New Year on her return? He had considered leaving it until then for he was starting to feel very ill-at-ease loitering around Argyll Street, however heavily disguised, day after day, waiting for Vicki to make an appearance. But the adrenalin was pumping so much, he knew he had to get it over with as quickly as possible. What if she had decided to give up work altogether? The moment was now for, if not now, it might be never. Furthermore, the prospect of a Christmas full of angst, knowing he might have missed his opportunity, was an unappealing one so he decided to give it one more try. If she did not appear tonight, he would leave it and reassess the situation in the New Year.

He glanced at his watch again, never taking his eye off the entrance to Regent Arcade House which was not even ten yards away. Two minutes to six. It was getting close, very close, and he steeled himself, gritting his teeth under his scarf. His clenched right hand was deep in the Parka's pocket. The slag's had it coming for a long time, he reflected. She deserves it, the bitch. Be alert, he urged himself, for she could appear at any moment and he knew he only had a fraction of a second to react. Then walk away, nice and easy, round the corner towards the crowds of Regent Street and down the tube. Yes, nice and easy. He would be gone before anyone could work out what had happened. He smiled, proud of the plan he had settled on, which, with a little bit of luck thrown in, he was confident of carrying out successfully. Be alert, be alert, be alert.

There she was. He stiffened when he saw her, ready to pounce. But Vicki stopped outside the entrance, conversing with a man she had exited the building with. His heart began to pound even harder and his lips went suddenly dry. He hoped desperately she would pass his way as normal and not head off in another direction. The wait was killing him, giving him too much time to think about what he was going to do and it unnerved him terribly. He had planned to put his trust in the adrenalin rush and spontaneity of the moment, but, now, he had to wait. What are they talking about? Come on! At least the flow of people in the street was incessant. He could get away easily enough. As he waited, he could not fail to notice the huge bump in her belly and it dawned on him that in a second or two, not only one but two lives would come to an end. He couldn't give a fuck.

She's coming my way! He turned to face her and, as they met, he took his hand out of his pocket and slammed it into her chest. Vicki gasped, the force of the blow knocking the breath out of her. As a reflex, her hands shot up in the air, forcibly knocking the arm of her assailant. 'Shit!' he cursed, stopping momentarily to look in the gutter. He had wanted to take it away with him and dispose of it later. He strode past Vicki who, holding her chest, suddenly felt faint. She moved her hands away and observed the red palms before collapsing to the ground, unconscious. He strode on and turned right into Little Argyll Street, in the direction of Regent Street, but his progress was slower than he had hoped. The crowds he had believed would be his friend were now his enemy as he was forced to continually stop-start his step. He was impatient to run and scatter everyone in his way like a raging mammal, but he kept calm, not wishing to bring attention on himself.

But he didn't get that little bit of luck thrown in. Two suited young men, wearing dark overcoats and enjoying a cigarette outside the Argyll pub next to the Stargreen Box Office, pints in hand, and eyeing up any attractive young woman who passed their way, had witnessed everything. One of them had been looking down Argyll Street and caught sight of Vicki's lovely face coming towards him. He nudged his friend who followed his gaze. All of a sudden, someone in a green Parka, with his back to them, appeared to punch the beautiful young woman in the chest and walk on past her. They were startled and remained rooted to the spot, not believing their eyes, but when Vicki collapsed to the ground, a maelstrom of rage swelled up inside them as their brains finally made sense of what had happened. Flinging their cigarettes away and placing their pints down on the pavement, they rushed over to Vicki and saw the blood on her hands and on the front of her coat. They shouted at those pedestrians who had stopped to observe the scene to tend to Vicki and to call an ambulance for they only had one thing on their mind.

The young men were keen sportsmen, fit and strong. They jumped up from Vicki determined to catch the perpetrator in the green Parka. Neither of them cared about shoving people out of their way as they reached the junction of Argyll Street and Little Argyll Street where they stopped opposite the entrance to the Dickens & Jones department store, one of them looking in the direction of Liberty's, the other in the direction of Regent Street.

'There he is!' the latter yelled, tugging at the sleeve of his friend. 'Stop! Stop that man in the green coat!' he screamed before they set off aggressively in his direction, as if on the rugby field, barging everyone out of their way.

'Shit! The perpetrator knew he had been rumbled and, panicking, began to run. He jumped off the pavement and onto the road where there was less hindrance. But the game was up and, just as he reached Regent Street, one of his pursuers dived onto his back as if making a match-saving tackle and they tumbled to the Tarmac in a heap, his friend immediately by their side. They turned the perpetrator round onto his back and pinned him down.

'You're fucked, mate. We saw what you did,' one of his assailants shouted angrily. 'You're going inside for that.'

The perpetrator had no fight in him and was resigned to his fate as one of the young men straddled his chest while the other went off to find a policeman. A small crowd gathered round, intrigued and bemused at what had happened, peering down at the man on his back as best they could.

A similar crowd had gathered around Vicki, including Brad, her boss, and whom she had been talking to at the entrance to Regent Arcade House. He had crossed the road, but when he heard the commotion behind him, he turned round and saw Vicki slumped on the pavement. He was at her side in an instant and reassured to hear that a member of staff in Stargreen was calling for an ambulance.

Brad observed the blood on Vicki's chest, which was spreading alarmingly, unwound his scarf, and pressed it as firmly as he could onto the wound. A concerned young woman knelt down and cradled Vicki's head but there was no sign of any movement.

'Come on, Vicki, hold on, there'll be an ambulance here in a second,' her boss encouraged her, but she looked pale and listless. Brad felt her pulse. It was very weak. 'Hold on, Vicki, hold on!' he yelled, the only time he had ever had reason to raise his voice at her.

A policeman soon arrived beside Vicki and spoke into his radio for support before pushing back the crowd. It was then that he noticed something in the gutter, smeared in blood.

Back where the perpetrator had been caught, the young man straddling him was seething and wished no more than to punch him as hard as he could in the face. He settled instead for pulling down his hood, ripping away his scarf and tearing off his beanie. The crowd moved closer to get a good look at the man. They did not recognise him. It was Freddie Butcher.

The policeman next to Vicki lowered himself down on his haunches to get a closer look in the gutter. He already knew what it was; a flick-knife.

New Year's Day 1980

Chapter 24

It was still dark outside as Rhys shuffled listlessly into his living room, for the morning had not yet broken. Occasionally, he heard one or two distant voices as revellers made their way home after a very late night of festivities. The flat was chilly as the central heating had not yet kicked in but Rhys was oblivious to it. He was oblivious to everything, in fact, his mind unable to rid itself of the image of Vicki lying in intensive care in hospital attached to lines of nutrients and drugs that were keeping her alive. He had truly believed that he would never again experience the pain he had felt when he had broken up with Vicki. But this was worse, ten times worse, no, one hundred times worse.

He sat down on the sofa, staring at the floor, numb and motionless, his parents' snoring providing some faint background sound. They had been at his side the second he had broken the news, providing comfort and helping him to bear up to the sheer unadulterated agony that inflicted his whole being. But now, sitting by himself and thinking calmly and rationally for the first time since the attack, he accepted that this would be the day he would become a father but lose his beloved Vicki. Tears welled up in his eyes. He had cried so many these past few days that he was surprised the well had not run dry.

Yesterday evening had been the defining moment. The hospital consultant, flanked by his registrar and a senior nurse, had explained precisely, professionally and with feeling to Rhys and his parents and Vicki's family that Vicki's condition was deteriorating. She had lost so much blood in the initial stages that it had been a miracle she had survived, but her condition had not improved and had now taken a turn for the worse. Of equal gravity was the concern for the unborn child. Vicki was so weak that it was improbable she would survive an operation to give birth to the baby who was now at full term. If they operated, there was every likelihood the baby would be born healthily but they had little time to lose. If they did not, the baby would almost certainly die.

Rhys had taken the news stoically, as had his and Vicki's parents, but Fiona had burst into floods of tears, burying her head into her mother's bosom. Rhys had asked just the one question, his eyes moist and voice hesitant. 'When you say Vicki would be unlikely to survive the operation, what per cent chance do you think she has?' Rhys hated the way he had expressed himself, feeling more like an accountant than the grief-stricken fiancé he was. But, at that moment, it was the only way he could assess more accurately the condition Vicki was in.

The consultant looked gravely at him and then at Vicki's family. He had been expecting the question, so often had he been in the same position before. In a firm voice, he answered, 'Less than ten per cent.'

Vicki's mother gasped and covered her mouth in shock while her father went white and gripped his wife's other hand. Fiona's floods of tears turned into torrents and were accompanied by howls of anguish while Rhys's parents looked stony-faced at each other. Rhys felt physically sick but, outwardly, remained relatively composed. 'Thank you for your honesty, Doctor,' he calmly replied.

'We'll do our very best, I promise you, to ensure the baby is born alive and to give Vicki every chance. I don't know Vicki or what her character is like but a fighting spirit counts for a lot in these situations.'

Rhys nodded but his brain was a fog. He glanced towards Vicki's father and then her mother and, without saying a word, his expression asked the question and their looks provided the answer. In reality, they had no option. The operation would have to go ahead to save the unborn child. The consultant confirmed it would take place the following morning, leaving Vicki's loved ones to spend the most desperate nights of their lives. They would never forget the last day of the decade for as long as they lived, or the first day of the new one. Never have prospective grandparents, father and auntie felt more wretched in their lives.

Now, at the start of the most momentous day of his life, Rhys wiped his eyes. He was determined to be as strong and composed as he possibly could, not just for his own sake, but for the sake of Vicki's family. Vicki was going to a better world, he tried to convince himself, and one day he would join her. He was not religious in the slightest, but, in these desperate moments, he clutched onto whatever straw he could find, however flimsy. At least the world Vicki was going to was not full of scum who attack innocent people with knives in the street. They can all burn in Hell.

The tears would not go away, however. It was one thing trying to be strong, completely another being it.

At least the hospital had not rung during the night; Vicki was still alive. Instinctively, Rhys turned to look at the telephone. It remained silent. Turning back, his gaze fell upon the Christmas tree in the corner of the room, bedecked in round and star-shaped baubles of various sizes and shimmering colour. At its base, numerous wrapped parcels and boxes were lying one on top of each other like multi-coloured rocks. Rhys looked at them sadly. They would go undelivered this year. His eyes remained fixed on them but his mind was in a different world, a world where Santa Claus, snowflakes and red-nosed reindeers played no part.

Among the presents, his eyes were suddenly drawn to the white envelope which held the card he had bought for Vicki. Alongside it was a larger burgundy-red envelope with his name scribbled on the front next to Vicki's hand-drawn heart. They both remained untouched and unopened. But staring at Vicki's handwriting compelled him to make some kind of connection with her, as if by reading her words she would be standing there in front of him, alive, animated ... beautiful.

Rhys stood up and took four steps to the tree. He picked up her envelope and returned to the sofa, carefully tearing it open and sliding out the card. The picture on the front drew another tear and a smile all in one. It showed a handsome young couple, snuggling up tightly, arm in arm, walking through a frosty but sunlit park, so obviously in love with each other. It was a glorious winter scene. Opening the card, Rhys was surprised when a folded piece of paper fluttered to the floor. Before picking it up, he read her message, receiving it as if she were saying the words herself.

"To Rhys. Thank you for the most wonderful decade of my life. We made it in the end and I cannot wait for the next one and the ones after that. I hope the card and the label remind you of our first day together. I can't wait to walk up the aisle with you and give birth to our baby. I love you more than you will ever know, Vicki xxxxxxxxxx"

Rhys broke down. His howls of despair were so loud his mother was soon beside him, her arm around his shoulders, crying herself, his father standing in the doorway.

'Why, Mum, why? It's not fair. She can't die, she's too young. I can't live without her, Mum. She can't die. Please God, help her, help her!'

Rhys's sobbing was out of control, his tears guttering down his cheeks and running off the end of his chin onto his lap and carpet. His mother held him as tightly as she could, letting Rhys rest his head against her shoulder, but there was nothing she could say. Her husband went back into the bedroom, grim-faced. He felt helpless. They all did. There was nothing they could do.

Regaining some composure, Rhys noticed the piece of paper on the carpet. He bent over, picked it up and unfolded it. He was confused for a second as he stared at the Babycham label. He turned it over. On the back was written, *The White Hart, Pontypridd, 1.1.1970.* The memories came flooding back. Exactly ten years ago to the day, they had toasted the New Year with a glass of Babycham. Unbeknown to him, she had removed the label from the bottle and kept it. Still holding the label, Rhys doubled over in agony, the tears returning in torrents. Defiantly, he turned to his mother and vowed, 'I won't let her die, Mum, I won't,' before breaking down once more. His father heard him from the bedroom, full of pride and admiration, but he knew it was useless.

'Hey, don't cry. It'll be okay,' Rhys assured Fiona as he cradled her in his arms in the family room that served the intensive care unit. Her face was planted in Rhys's chest, her eyes red raw and sodden with tears, her hand constantly dabbing at her nose with yet another paper handkerchief. Rhys stroked her back lightly, his parents looking on ashen-faced from their chairs beside him. 'She's as tough as old boots is Vicki. You watch, Fi, she'll get through this, and the two of you'll be playing with your new nephew or niece in no time.'

His tone was calm and exuded confidence but it only led to more sobbing and wails of anguish from Vicki's distraught sister. Rhys stroked her back more vigorously, and then the back of her head, but to no avail. He wondered, like him, whether Fiona would ever recover from this. He could try and put on as brave a face as possible but the game was up, and everyone knew it, even if they would never admit it. Fiona's pain was too much to bear for Rhys and his parents and succeeded only in drawing tears from their eyes also.

Without warning, the door opened and Vicki's white-faced parents walked in. Fiona immediately extricated herself from Rhys's arms and clasped her mother. Vicki's father had never failed to achieve whatever he wanted in his life, but, at this particular moment, he bore the look of a beaten man.

Fiona's grief triggered her mother and her eyes moistened. 'It'll be fine, Fiona, don't you worry,' were the only words she could muster as she patted her back. She did not believe any of them. They had just returned from spending a final few moments with Vicki before she went into theatre for the operation. In her despair, Fiona had been unable to steel herself to do the same. Rhys's spirits slumped when he observed the suffering felt by Vicki's family and his gut knotted at the knowledge that it was now his turn to spend a final few minutes with the girl he loved. A sad-faced nurse held open the door, waiting for Rhys to accompany her to Vicki's bed. His legs felt so rubbery he could barely put one foot in front of the other.

During the few brief seconds it took to reach Vicki's bedside, Rhys implored himself to stay strong and to hold himself together. He gulped down gallons of air in an effort to maintain a semblance of composure. But when he arrived at her side, he was overcome with a gut-wrenching grief so powerful he wanted no more than to climb up onto the bed and die beside her so that she would not be alone on her journey to Heaven.

Sobbing uncontrollably, Rhys held her hand and buried his head into the side of her body, gripping the blanket with his other hand so tightly the veins stood out proud. She looked dreadful and, to Rhys's eyes, had already taken on the appearance of a corpse. Her skin was loose and sallow, her hair limp and her breathing barely discernible. Her eyes were closed and there was no strength in the fingers he stroked. Rhys had rehearsed a few words he had wanted to say but his mind was a mess. He remembered, however, to take the Babycham label out of his pocket and place it into Vicki's hand.

'Hey, Vick, I opened your card,' he finally said, his voice croaking. 'I found the label. Ten years ago today, Vicki, ten years ago today, a whole decade. That was the best day of my life.' He had to stop to blow his nose and wipe his eyes with a tissue and it took fully a minute before he could resume. 'I've put it in your hand, Vicki. Hold onto it and don't let go.'

For the first time that morning, Vicki showed signs of life and her fingers tightened around it and, seeing her do so, Rhys put his hand over hers and held it in a fist. She was listening, she had strength, she was not lifeless. He had to encourage her to fight.

'Never let go of it, Vicki,' Rhys implored. 'It's to let you know I'm with you all the way in this. You've got everything to live for, Vicki, everything, but you've got to fight, Vicki, fight, and never give up. Your family needs you, I need you and our baby needs you. In a few weeks, we'll be married with a child, everything you and me have always wanted. Don't give up, Vicki, please, I beg you.'

Rhys buried his head once more in her side and placed his hand on her stomach, on their child. He remained in the same position for fully two minutes, his tears dripping onto Vicki's bare arm. He would have stayed there forever but for the gentle hand of the consultant on his shoulder indicating it was time for the operation.

'DON'T DIE ON ME, VICKI!' Rhys yelled, 'DON'T DIE ON ME! OUR BABY NEEDS YOU. FIGHT! VICKI, FIGHT!' And with that, Rhys ran from the ward and out into the reception where, leaning against a wall, he cried his heart out.

Sister McLaughlin, who had been tending to Vicki, was an experienced nurse and accustomed to grief. It came with the territory and she was hardened to it. But never had she witnessed such anguish and suffering in her life and, for the first time in her long career as a nurse, she could not prevent tears from rolling uncontrollably down her cheeks.

CHAPTER 25

The view was truly inspiring, Tommy Slater reflected, as he marvelled at the majestic cupola and spire atop St Paul's Cathedral. It was one of the reasons he had bought the apartment in the first place. Not far beyond St Paul's was the East End, his turf, and fond memories of his time growing up in Hackney flashed across his mind. They were the best days of his life, he concluded with a poignant smile, unlike the past few which had undoubtedly been the worst. It was New Year's Day and, unbeknown to him as he scanned the horizon, Vicki was being wheeled into the operating theatre at that precise moment, though he was aware that her condition was critical and that she was unlikely to recover.

Freddie Butcher was in custody and as good as his word to Tommy. He had not implicated him in the slightest, even though it was Tommy who had put him up to it. He was not a grass, Butcher reflected with pride, sitting in his cell, knowing that Tommy would take care of his family financially. He had done the crime and he would do the time, that's all there was to it. He had fucked up and got caught. No one else was to blame.

'He's a good mate is Freddie,' Tommy said softly to himself, full of respect. But despite his best friend's loyalty, Tommy knew he was in deep trouble and shook his head in a sad, resigned manner. The net was closing in, the Fat Lady warming up her tonsils.

Turning on his heel, he paced to another vantage point in profound contemplation, his eye falling on the almost complete National Westminster Tower. He could hardly miss it for it was already the tallest building in the country and a symbol of the financial might of the City of London.

The media was all over the story, full of conjecture as to why his best friend would want to murder his ex-wife. But even more worryingly, so were the police, who had called on him twice already and clearly suspicious of the part he had played in the affair. He had tried to brazen it out, knowing that if Freddie kept schtum, there was a good chance he could stay in the clear. But the telephone call he had taken just before midnight was a devastating one and Tommy knew it was only a matter of time before his involvement became obvious.

The call had been made by Bill Smith, who told Tommy that *The Mirror* would be splashing next morning on how a *Sun* employee had been following Vicki's movements for nigh on two years and reporting them to him. Tim, the stupid fucking idiot, had not been able to keep his mouth shut in the pubs around Fleet Street, though, in his defence, he could never have foreseen that his actions would have played a part in the attack on Vicki.

The bemused editor of *The Sun* had asked the young reporter for an explanation for he'd had no knowledge of what he'd been up to. Tim had admitted to Bill Smith's involvement and, in his vein-bursting fury, the editor had fired them both. There was no way he was going to allow his newspaper to be implicated in an attempted murder. The telephone call had begun in 1979 and ended in

1980. With heavy irony, they had both wished each other a happy New Year.

Tommy had not gone to bed after the call. He had sat up all night drinking whisky after whisky, thinking, and when morning had broken, he had not gone out to buy a copy of *The Mirror*. It had not been necessary. The story was all over the radio news and the ringing of his telephone and buzzing of his apartment was incessant. The heavy knock on the door of a burly Old Bill or two could not be far away.

But despite the storm that was raging around him, Tommy's main concern was not the heavy hand of the law but the terrible injury that had been inflicted on Vicki. Turning his gaze back upon St Paul's, he lowered his head in shame at what he had instigated. Her blood was on his hands right up to his elbows. He knew he was not perfect. He had his faults, terrible faults, he now accepted; jealousy, arrogance, selfishness, spite, pride, possessiveness. But he loved Vicki and ultimately could not bear what he had done to her and her unborn child. His eyes moistened at the knowledge that he had acted like a monster. She did not deserve to die and he deserved every drop of vitriol and opprobrium that was going to come his way.

'I've fucked up big time,' Tommy admitted. 'It's all over. I'll never get out of this.' They were the same sentiments he had expressed during the night. 'Look at me; a has-been footballer on the slide who murdered the love of his life. I've got no wife, no kids, no family of my own. All I've got is a few quid and some respect. But what's the point of money when you're doing twenty years inside? And respect? Well, you can kick that into touch for starters.' He shook his head, desolate.

It's a chilly start to the year, he thought, as a freezing wind whistled around his ears. He looked up instinctively, observing the monochrome sky, and felt a spot of rain on his forehead, cold, heavy, on the cusp of sleet. He had chosen well to put on his overcoat, he nodded, looking back down and across the rooftops of London once more. How St Paul's had survived the Blitz that had so devastated his family and the families of his friends in the East End during the war remained one of life's great mysteries, he pondered incongruously at that moment.

Yes, it had been a great decision to buy the apartment, he reflected, for he so loved the views ... as he did so now, but this time from the flat roof of Cromwell Tower, all forty-two floors of it, high above his home. Coolly and calmly, and with his head held high, like all the times he had walked up to the penalty spot to slot home a goal, he took a few paces to the edge of the roof with that characteristic straight-backed posture of his, jumped up onto a concrete block and looked over the side. Once there, for he knew it was the only realistic option open to him, he stepped over a metal rail and, without the slightest hesitation, threw himself off.

Two Decades Later

Chapter 26

No, the singing was not like how it used to be in the good old days, Rhys pondered, as he sat high up in the West Stand of the newly completed Millennium Stadium in Cardiff, awaiting the start of the Wales versus France rugby international. He did not care much for the stadium, either, if truth be told. Yes, it was impressive to the eye and packed with every modern facility under the sun but it lacked the heart and soul of the old Arms Park he loved so much. A bit like New Labour and Tony Blair when compared to the old Labour Party and Harold Wilson, he mused disapprovingly, as he wiped a smudge mark away from his spectacles with a handkerchief. Who could you rely on today to look after the interests of the working class? he asked himself. Ruefully, he shook his head. There was no one. The world had changed beyond recognition, and not all of it for the better.

With his father nudging him out of his reverie of remembrance, he scolded himself for turning into a grumpy old man. He had certainly aged, he conceded, with his hair thin and peppery and forehead lined, but he took immense satisfaction in his trim waistline. Buying that bicycle all those years ago had certainly paid dividends. His mother was sitting the other side of his father, both of them complaining how smoking was forbidden in the new stadium. They would have to wait another two hours for a cigarette. Other than when they were asleep, they did not think they had ever gone so long without a drag.

Sitting next to them were Vicki's mother and father, resplendent in their Burberry and Barbour coats respectively. Nothing gladdened Rhys's heart more than how close he and his parents had become to them over the years. Fiona had not been able to attend as she was living in Frankfurt with her banker husband, her third marriage. Or was it her fourth? Rhys wondered. It was hard to keep up with her anymore.

On his other side, Ian and Karen were taking swigs of lager from their floppy, plastic glasses, as was their daughter, Madonna, and her friend, Eleanor. The two girls were barely sixteen, but, as Rhys gazed in their direction, he realised that at least one thing had never changed over the years; underage drinking. He just hoped they would not get involved in drugs, which were much more prevalent among teenagers today than during his time. Rhys never asked Ian or Karen whether they regretted naming their daughter after the pop sensation of the time, and this time for that matter, but he sensed that they did. Rhys got on well with Madonna for he amused her with tales about her parents. When he had shown her photographs of her punk rocker mother, Madonna had doubled over in stitches of laughter and, borrowing them from Rhys, could not wait to show them to her friends at school.

The events around Christmas and New Year twenty years ago were never far from his mind, however. How could they not be? No human being should be made to endure the anguish of those desperate times. It was the people sitting next to him now who had helped him get through those agonising days just as he had helped them.

Since then, life had been good to Rhys. He was now the proud owner of three restaurants in London and one in Cardiff, though he loved nothing better than to go back to the Supreme for a coffee and a natter with Mario to whom he had sold it. He was also now living in a beautiful, five-storey, Victorian townhouse overlooking Clapham Common, the first day he walked through the front door being one of the happiest of his life. He also owned a beautiful villa in Cyprus next to Christos and Eleni and looked forward to every winter and summer when he would spend a few days in their company. He owed them so much. More than anyone, they had made him change his life and become the success he now was. Yes, he reflected, as he looked down at his gleaming Church brogues and pulled up the collar of his dark navy Crombie overcoat, life had been good to him these past two decades.

The atmosphere was building in the stadium and Rhys fretted when, looking at his Patek Philippe wristwatch, he realised that the players would soon be emerging for the kick-off. He glanced upwards towards the entrance to the stand, but, after a few seconds, and with a frown, he looked away. Wondering what to do, Rhys considered using the new mobile phone he had taken ownership of and which rested like a dead weight in his coat pocket. He had not managed to programme in any numbers as yet; it all seemed so terribly complicated to him. But he did have the number scribbled on a piece of paper in his wallet, lying next to the folded Babycham label. Vicki's consultant had given it to him all those years ago and it had never left his person since. When the consultant had done so, Rhys had sunk to his knees, crying Niagara-like torrents of tears ... but they were tears of overwhelming relief and happiness. It was the sign that Vicki had pulled through and was out of danger. She had held onto it for days on end and the consultant had told Rhys it had kept her alive.

'Here she comes, Dad,' an equally fretful Eleanor shouted over to Rhys as she caught sight of her mother, wearing a tightly-belted, beige Aquascutum raincoat, bounding down the steps before edging her way to the empty seat next to her husband. Vicki was as beautiful as ever, her hair, long, straight and auburn in colour, pushed back behind her ears to show off that unblemished, golden-brown skin of hers and sparkling pale blue oval eyes. She did not have a line on her face and could easily have been mistaken for Eleanor's elder sister.

'Women!' Rhys muttered sotto voce, relieved that Vicki would be in time for the start of the match. As she settled in her seat, Rhys asked her in an exasperated tone where she had been.

'Men! When will you ever understand that when we go to the toilet we have to wait for a cubicle to become free? We can't just stand up in front of a wall with our willies in our hand like you can.'

Rhys laughed and squeezed her thigh. They looked deeply into each other's eyes and kissed quickly on the lips, after which President Mitchell rested her head on his shoulder, the two of them smiling and waiting for the players to run out onto the field, the greenness of which reminded Rhys of Central Park and Washington Square Gardens in New York where he had fulfilled his ambition of walking with Vicki on several occasions. They were in love with each other as much as the first day they met.

'Here they come!' an excited Eleanor yelled.

After the French team had made its entrance, the noise in the stadium reached fever pitch before the crowd erupted at the sight of their heroes in red.

"Wales, Wales, Wales, Wales ..."

'There he is!' Eleanor yelled out once more.

And there he was, the Welsh outside-half wearing the fabled number ten shirt running out to represent his country for the very first time. In his heart of hearts, Rhys could not bring himself to believe he was as good as Barry John, for no one in his eyes ever would be, but he was pretty damn close. More importantly, however, he was their son, Christopher, who Vicki had fought against all the odds to bring into the world and, on seeing him enter the field, Rhys and Vicki were transformed into the two proudest people on earth.

THE END

Author: Roberto Rabaiotti
Email: roberto.rabaiotti@btinternet.com
Twitter: @londonrab